THE ESSENCE

Also by Dave Hutchinson:

The Push
Sleeps With Angels
Nomads

THE ESSENCE
DAVE HUTCHINSON

NEWCON
PRESS

NewCon Press
England

First edition, published in the UK December 2025
by NewCon Press
41 Wheatsheaf Road, Alconbury Weston, Cambs, PE28 4LF, UK

NCP355 (hardback)
NCP356 (softback)

10 9 8 7 6 5 4 3 2 1

ISBN: 978-1-917735-13-1 (hardback)
978-1-917735-14-8 (softback)

Cover Art by Ben Baldwin
Front cover graphics by Ben Baldwin
Editing and typesetting by Ian Whates
Back cover layout by Ian Whates

A Man Walks Into A Bar

One

The hospital was not, strictly speaking, a hospital. It was more of a rest home for fuddled gentlefolk. It occupied a big house in several acres of grounds tucked away at the end of a leafy cul-de-sac on the edge of Mill Hill, just far enough from the M1 for the double glazing to reduce the sound of the motorway to a low, reassuring rumble, but close enough to the main railway line out of St Pancras that, when the wind was in the right direction, it sounded as if intercity trains were passing through the gardens. It had been there long enough that its neighbours, a handful of similar large houses all shyly hiding their faces behind high walls, had long ceased to notice the private ambulances that came and went at odd times of the day and night.

Entering via the front gates, which presented as antique wrought iron but were actually of a far more durable alloy and controlled electronically from the security office, one was first confronted by a small landscape of neat lawns and flower beds and rockeries, about which a gravel driveway looped, sufficiently wide to accommodate a single vehicle.

Beyond that stood the house, a full-throated Mock Tudor monstrosity complete with half-timbering and herringbone brickwork, built in the 1920s for a minor dynasty of Home Counties brewers, now long extinct. To one side stood a vaguely Arts & Crafts structure known as 'The Stables', which now housed the Hydrotherapy Department – a fancy term for a swimming pool – where those residents who had demonstrated some innate talent for buoyancy could doggy-paddle for an hour at a time.

At the other side of the house a paved path curved through a short avenue of trees and out to the formal gardens at the rear, planted with more shrubberies and rockeries and lawns, all centred on a single massive oak. The oak, said to be several hundred years old, had been here before the house was built; a remnant of a far older landscape. If you walked past the tree – quite a distance, the size of the gardens was always a bit of a surprise – you came to the high brick wall which surrounded the house. There was a kind of tide mark, at a little more than head height, where the original brickwork had been built up decades ago, until the wall was almost twenty feet high. You could still see periodic marks, near the top, where brackets had once supported closed-circuit television cameras, but these days surveillance was almost too small to see.

Inside, the house smelled strongly of furniture polish, undercut by a faint, disquieting layer of disinfectant and sweat and boiled cabbage. There were noticeboards and a reception desk in the entrance hall, and worn institutional furniture. The staff all wore smart-casual clothes and identity badges clipped to their shirts, except when they ventured into the wing where the Acute residents were kept, when they suited up in full PPE as if they were entering the hot zone of a fever clinic.

Michael had spent some time in the Acute wing. Logically, he supposed, it had been his first port of call on arriving at the hospital, although he had no memory of it, no memory of being attended to by gowned and masked figures. His first memory was of sitting in the Television Room, as if he had just woken from a long, restful sleep, watching a quiz show whose name he knew but couldn't quite call to mind at that moment.

Apparently, he had subsequently taken a bit of a turn and been returned to the Acute wing for a while, and he sometimes became confused as to whether his awakening in the Television Room had come after his first stay there or his second. Sometimes, the distinction seemed to matter.

It was hard to work out how many residents – never 'patients' – there were. There seemed to be a discreet churn; new faces arrived without fanfare, became familiar, and then one day were simply not there any more. Michael thought there were perhaps a dozen or so at any one time, if one didn't include the Acutes, who nobody ever saw until they were released into the general population blinking as if they had just spent a long period underground.

"You know, I have no idea," Bob, his therapist, said one day while they were taking a walk in the garden. "I've never done a head count."

"Someone must know," Michael mused.

"Oh, no doubt." Bob thought about it. "Aggie would know; you could ask her. Is it important?"

At the time, Michael had been having difficulty separating the important from the trivial, and he had been gently warned to be aware of incipient obsessions, so he just shrugged.

Aggie was the Director's secretary, a kindly Home Counties woman of a certain age who was most often seen bustling down the corridors with a bundle of files clasped to her bosom. The Director himself was not so often seen, although Michael thought they must have met because he had a memory of a small tweedy man in late middle age with watery eyes and a spiderweb of broken capillaries on his cheeks.

Even more rarely seen was the Medical Director, a tall, slender woman named Reese, whose occasional appearances in public had the aspects of Royal visits. At the head of a little group of doctors, she would breeze into the big room where half a dozen residents were taking part in occupational therapy, always with a few words for everyone, congratulating them on their paintings or clay sculptures, and then breeze out again, not to manifest again for another week or so.

The doctors were all young – Michael didn't think any of them was over thirty – and relentlessly upbeat to a degree that he, not always inclined to be upbeat, sometimes found oppressive. They all had the same sheen of efficient anonymity, and he never learned any of their names. Similarly the nurses, who all had the stocky build and flatfooted centre of gravity of prison warders; and the security staff who amiably patrolled the grounds and kept everyone safe and had the look – to Michael's eye – of people who had taken early retirement from the Met after a period with Special Branch. They'd nod hello if you bumped into them while you were taking a bit of a constitutional, but they weren't inclined to conversation.

As to why he was there, well, that was a bit foggy. He didn't remember being unwell particularly, although he thought there had been a time when he had been very tired, and none of the doctors ever actually bothered to tell him.

"What am I doing here?" he asked one of them one day.

The doctor, who had been filling in a form on a clipboard, looked at him as if he'd enquired about her sexuality. "You're here to get better," she told him, forcing cheerfulness.

"Better from what?"

She finished the form and stood up. "You're doing very well," she said, and walked away.

Still, he supposed it was nice that he was doing very well.

Even so, he found there were days which he had edited from his memory. All the days in the hospital were roughly the same and tended to run together into a single *ur*-day and it was easy to lose track of where you were in the week, but there were blanks, days when literally nothing had happened. Either he had briefly relapsed, or the doctors were fiddling about with his meds; he didn't know, and again no one seemed inclined to tell him.

In the early days, his meds had come in the form of a bewildering variety of pills, some large, some small; round and oval, white and beige and red and blue and salmon-pink, never the same combination two days in a row. As the weeks and months passed the combination settled down, and then tablets began to disappear one by one, until he was left with a red one and a blue one every day.

"This is like *The Matrix*," he told the nurse who brought his medication.

"I wish," the nurse said, noting down the time and dosage on his iPad. "I could use a nice new leather coat."

He'd grown accustomed to the morning knock at the door which announced the arrival of his meds and, therefore, the beginning of his day. This was followed by breakfast, which seemed designed to be as forgettable as possible. Then the rest of the day was his own. Every resident was given a laminated card which detailed the various activities available to them on different days, and there was a big calendar in Reception for those who found it difficult to keep track of where they were in the week. None of the activities was mandatory, but Bob was keen that Michael should take part in at least one every day, so some days he spent time in Occupational Therapy, and others he spent swimming laps in Hydrotherapy. Mostly, though, he sat reading in a corner of the Day Room, the long double-glazed gallery which had been built onto the back of the house at some point during the country's last boom in conservatories. He was currently enjoying, in a slightly baffled way, a novel called *The Heart of the Maze*, about a private detective in 1930s Los Angeles becoming involved in some kind of satanic conspiracy. He thought he might have embarked on it more than once, his reading interrupted by one or more stays in the Acute wing, because some passages seemed familiar to him.

In between, there were daily sessions with Bob. Bob was in his forties and favoured corduroy and seemed ever so slightly unmoored from the modern world, as if he lived most of the time in a little village out in the depths of the Wiltshire countryside without broadband or reliable television reception. Their conversations mostly revolved around the weather and cricket. Michael hated cricket, but he thought it was polite to make an effort.

From what he could gather, Bob was something of a fundamentalist when it came to cricket. He poured scorn on the limited-over forms of the game, spoke darkly of something he called 'Bazball', and described the colourful uniforms worn by players in the modern game as 'clown costumes'.

"First-class cricket – three days at least," he said one day. "That's the purest expression of the game, Michael."

"Yes," Michael said. "I agree."

Bob regarded him genially. "You don't sound so sure, old son."

"I'm not really an avid follower of cricket, Bob, to be honest."

"Do you have an interest in *any* sports? I forgot to ask."

Michael thought about it. *Did* he? He had no idea. "Is it relevant?"

"No, of course not," Bob said, taking a pencil from the desk in front of him and tapping the end of his nose with the eraser end. "I'm just making conversation. Are you a rugby man? Football? Snooker?"

It occurred to Michael to say yes to one of these, just to move the conversation away from the subject, because for no reason he could put into words he sensed danger here, but he knew if he did that rugby or football or snooker would turn out to be Bob's second-favourite sport and he'd be stuck with having to talk about it, so he said, "Not really, no."

Bob put the pencil down. "That's quite unusual, you know."

"Is it?"

"Most people will pay attention to *some* sport, even if it's just now and again. Wimbledon? The Olympics? The Grand National?"

The issue of sport was a blank spot in his memory, but he wasn't about to admit it. "It's just stuff that's on television," he said. "I might watch the Wimbledon finals, if I'm not doing anything else."

"So you're a tennis fan?"

"No."

"Can you name a tennis player?"

"Bjorn Borg."

"A recent one."

"Roger Federer."

Bob shook his head. "No, a *recent* one."

Michael thought about it, but he came up blank. He shrugged. "I told you, I'm not a fan."

Bob looked at him with an expression of mild exasperation. "Did you do sport at school?"

"The usual stuff. Rugby, football. Cricket. Without any great distinction, I'm afraid."

"And none of it stuck?"

"Not really, no."

"Extraordinary." Bob shook his head. He reached out and tapped the face of his phone to wake it up and look at the clock. "Well, it's lunchtime. See you tomorrow?"

The more rehabilitated residents were allowed to take meals in their rooms, but everyone was encouraged to eat in the dining room, tucking into a menu of meat and two veg which was occasionally enlivened by a mild curry. The atmosphere in the dining room was very *English*, very quiet and polite and reserved, like a scene from *Brief Encounter*, but now and again there were distractions, like the day when one chap began to complain loudly and with much profanity that they had been served roast beef two days in a row and had to be wrestled out of the room and upstairs to Acute by three nurses. Some time afterwards, Michael couldn't be sure if that hadn't been him. Quite a lot of what he understood about the world at that point in his rehabilitation seemed to come to him with a bit of a time-lag.

As a rule, the residents tended to keep themselves to themselves, even when eating or taking part in association time. The eldest was an old Foreign Office type with an unruly fringe of white hair, who spent most of his time sitting quietly in front of the television, and the rest in Occupational Therapy creating huge apocalyptic oil paintings. The youngest, a small, birdlike girl, faced the world through a permanent, brittle smile which seemed to take all her energy to maintain. Michael tried to engage some of them in conversation, without much success, and eventually he gave up.

He presumed that all the staff of the hospital were either Service or ex-Service brought back from retirement. Certainly they would have to be vetted and cleared to a high level, as residents could occasionally, in extreme moments, be indiscreet. It occurred to him that Bob, as one of the therapists, probably had a higher clearance than he did, although they had never once discussed his work. And after that, it occurred to him to wonder what he was supposed to do if one of the other residents confided to him something that he was absolutely never meant to know. And then he started to obsess over the possibility that this had already happened during one of his blank periods and he was now, without realising it, in possession of information vital to national security. And shortly after that he started to feel tired all the time, and when he next paid attention to the calendar in Reception almost a week had passed and he had a vague memory of somebody shouting.

Still, as the weeks passed and his good days began to outnumber his bad ones, he was allowed to walk the mile or so into Mill Hill, accompanied by one of the nurses, for what was termed Acclimat-isation. This initially involved buying small items in shops, using an allowance doled out to him by Aggie and which he had to sign for and return any change. The first time he tried this, he felt an almost physical wave of apprehension as he stepped out of the gates. The cul-de-sac beyond, with its neat grass verges and plane trees, seemed a landscape full of threat, and he had to force himself to walk along it to the junction with a side-road, and then to the main road, and then into Mill Hill. Here, visiting a newsagents' to buy a tin of Coke and a bar of chocolate, he was so discomfited that he entirely forgot the function of money and had to be gently helped by the nurse. The woman behind the counter must have been used to residents coming into her shop, because she didn't bat an eyelid.

Subsequent ventures into the outside world went better, bit by bit and day by day, and eventually Michael and his minder graduated to having a coffee in a branch of Starbucks, and then to lunch, usually in an Italian restaurant on the Broadway. In the course of a monologue on the shortcomings of the Middlesex Cricket Club, Bob told him that these excursions were intended to allow residents to reengage with other people and the many small systems and rituals of society. It didn't work for everyone. The birdlike girl went out for a solo Acclimatisation one day and never came back. She was glimpsed one more time, in the form of an almost unrecognisably sulky photo, in a police appeal for information on the news. One of the nurses hurried to change the channel, but she was too late to stop everyone in the television room hearing that the girl's name was Bethany.

Michael assumed that Bethany's bid for freedom would put a crimp in the Acclimatisations, but they went on without pause. He was allowed to go into Central London several times with a nurse, and then one day Aggie was issuing him with his allowance and she said, "You know, there's nobody available to go with you today, Michael. Why don't you go alone?" and he gaped at her for so long that she had to remind him to sign for the cash and to bring back any receipts.

He walked down to Mill Hill Broadway station and sat on a bench on the platform, convinced this was some kind of trap. Other passengers arrived in ones and twos, but no one paid him any attention. A southbound train came in and they all got on, and when it left Michael was still sitting on the bench, staring across the tracks at the northbound platform.

A little behind him, on the other side of a wall, the traffic roared by on the M1. In short order, two intercity trains went by on a concussion of displaced air. More passengers arrived. Another southbound train came in. The passengers got on. Michael did not.

He reached into his pocket and took out his allowance. He'd been given an Oyster card loaded with just enough money to get into town and back again, and sufficient cash for lunch and some odds and ends, with a little left over in case of an emergency. It wouldn't get him far. He remembered that there was cash at home, but his keys were with the rest of his possessions, in safe keeping at the hospital, so he couldn't get into the house. How had Bethany got away with it? Outside help? Michael could think of a couple of people who might take him in, but not for long and they weren't in London anyway. He put the money away again and watched another train pull in and pull out.

What the hell was he thinking? He was safe in the hospital. He was warm and he was dry and there were people there who wanted to look after him. The food wasn't very good, but it was food, and he didn't have to worry about shopping or cooking. It seemed, somewhere way back in his memory, that having too much to worry about was what had started all this in the first place.

The simple fact of having a choice suddenly seemed paralysing. He could go into town, or he could just turn round and go back to the hospital. Or he could go for lunch at the Italian restaurant; there was no rule saying he had to spend his Acclimatisation wandering around the West End. The discovery of free will was agonising and exhilarating, even if it was only free will in a narrow sense – whatever he decided, he had to be back at the hospital in time for dinner. Perhaps that was the whole point of the exercise, to reintroduce him to the concept of

Choice after weeks of having none. Perhaps one day he would have the choice of not going back to the hospital at all.

If he had been given a choice, it seemed impolite not to exercise it. A southbound train came in. He chose.

After that, there were more excursions, and with each one came a gradual sense of relaxation. He still had to visit Aggie for spending money, but he was allowed to choose which day and time he wanted to go out, and eventually he was coming and going more or less as he pleased.

One afternoon, returning from lunch in Mill Hill, he bumped into Bob in the entrance hall. They nodded hello to each other, then Bob said, "Oh, by the way, you can go home when you want."

Michael blinked at him. "I beg your pardon?"

"You can go home." Bob leaned forward and clapped Michael on the shoulder. "We're all very pleased with your progress. Go and see Aggie when you're ready, and she'll make the arrangements.

Michael found himself quite unable to think of anything to say.

"It's normal to feel a little bit overwhelmed, but we're more than confident you're up to it," Bob told him. "We'll be checking in from time to time, to make sure you're settling nicely, but please don't think we're keeping tabs on you."

Michael said, "But…"

"Or you could stay here a little longer, until you feel more comfortable with the idea," Bob went on. "Entirely up to you, old son."

"You mean I'm all right again?" The concept seemed absurd.

Bob chuckled. "Well, *nobody's* exactly *all right*," he said. "That was a psychiatrist joke, by the way," he added. He clapped Michael on the shoulder again. "Really, you've made fantastic progress since we first met; you should be very proud of yourself." He checked the time on his phone. "Got to go, but I'll see you later. And don't leave without saying goodbye, yes?" And with that, he walked away.

Michael found himself completely flatfooted by the news. Upstairs, he stood in the middle of his room, his mind a blank. This little room, with its en suite shower and toilet, its little shelf of books, its rickety old wardrobe and chest of drawers, and its view out on the gardens at the back of the house, had been his home for… well, how long *had* it been? He couldn't even remember his own home very clearly; it seemed ridiculous that he actually owned a house, when he had everything he needed right here in this one room. He sat down in the armchair by the window and looked out at fluffy white clouds ambling across the sky.

Did he feel well? He couldn't really remember what he had felt like before, so he had nothing to compare it to. Physically, he felt fine; he went for a long walk every day, and if the weather wasn't very good he spent an hour or so on one of the exercise bikes in the basement Physical Therapy department. Mentally and emotionally? He had no idea. He seemed to be coping with the very simple demands his life here made of him, but that didn't mean he would be able to cope in the wild.

There didn't seem to be any rush. He decided to leave it a couple of days, see how he felt after the weekend.

On Monday, however, he didn't feel any more confident. He mentioned this to Bob during their afternoon session, but Bob wasn't overly worried. "Nobody's going to push you, old chap," he said.

"I can't stay here for ever, though, can I."

Bob thought about it. "Well, no," he admitted. "This isn't a nursing home *per se*. We like to send our residents back out into the world." He made a note on the little pad balanced on his knee.

Something occurred to Michael. "What happens to the ones you can't?" he asked.

Bob raised an eyebrow. "I'm sorry?"

"You don't cure *everybody*, do you?" Michael said. "The law of averages says there must be some you can't help."

"We try not to think of it as a *cure*," Bob said genially. "I'm inclined to resist absolutism." They looked at each other for a moment, then Bob's phone rang. He looked at its screen. "Sorry, old son," he said. "I should answer this." He put the phone to his ear and said, "Yes? Yes." He looked at Michael. "Yes. Yes." He hung up. "I'm afraid we're going to have to cut this one short," he told Michael, slipping the phone back into his pocket. "Something I need to attend to. Perhaps we can pick this up again tomorrow?"

"Sure," Michael said, but in the end they never did, quite.

A few days later, he decided the situation was ridiculous. If Bob and the doctors thought there was no reason to be there any more, all he was doing was taking up a bed that someone else might need. Eventually, he went to see Aggie, there was a flurry of form-signing, and less than twenty-four hours later he was standing outside the front of the house with his possessions neatly packed into three carrier bags, waiting for a cab.

No one came to say goodbye. Not Bob nor Doctor Reese nor the Director or any of the doctors or nurses. He just stood outside the front door for five minutes and then a minicab driven by a young Asian man pulled up in front of him.

"Cab for Brookes?" the driver asked.

"That's me," Michael said, and without looking back he got into the taxi.

It was only a few minutes' drive from Mill Hill to Finchley, but it felt to Michael like the distance between the Earth and the Moon, and by the time the cab drew up outside his house beside Victoria Park he felt exhausted. He also realised, belatedly, that he had no money to pay the fare.

"Already paid for, chief," the driver said cheerfully. "All's good. Have a nice day."

The cab drove off, leaving him standing on the pavement outside the house. He looked up at it, trying to make it fit into his memories. The window frames needed a lick of paint, but someone had been tending to the little front garden because it wasn't notably overgrown. He looked both ways along the street, mentally logging parked cars and pedestrians. Across the road, beyond the park's railings, he could see pensioners and dog walkers and young mothers with prams. He stepped forward through the gate.

At the front door, he put his hand in his pocket and took out a small bunch of keys. There was a little cardboard tag attached to them with string, his name written on it in permanent marker in someone else's handwriting. The keys felt unfamiliar to him, and he had to try twice before he found the right ones for the deadlock and the cylinder lock. The door was stiff as he pushed it open.

Inside, the hallway was cold and smelled of furniture polish. On the hall stand, a stack of post almost six inches tall sat in a neat pile, and beside it a smaller pile of bills from Ania, his cleaner. Someone from the office must have got in touch with her and asked her to continue cleaning while he was away, but the courtesy clearly hadn't extended to paying her. As he put the bills back on the table, he caught sight of himself in the mirror on the wall, a tall, gangly man a couple of months short of his sixtieth birthday with washed-out eyes and brown hair shot through with grey. It was quite a startling sight; there had been a mirror in his bathroom at the hospital, but he couldn't recall actually having looked at himself in it, although, as he was clean-shaven, he assumed he must have. A barber had visited the hospital from time to time, but his hair was still longer than he remembered. There was a little calendar hanging on the wall beside the mirror, scenes from The Highlands. It was still turned to the page it had been when time stopped. Checking the date on his watch, he realised it had been five months ago. He stood thinking about that for a while.

The house felt like a slightly shabby show-home, neat and clean and tidy but lacking a sense that anyone actually lived there, and he kept experiencing brief moments of dislocation when he didn't know it at all, as if for a fraction of a second he wasn't so much recognising it as populating it with memories. He looked into the living room and dining room, opened the door of the cupboard under the stairs, walked past his study and into the kitchen, where he finally put his carrier bags down on the floor. The back garden had been tended, too; the conifers at the far end had been trimmed and topped out, the lawn mown and the flower beds weeded. A rickety fence panel, loosened by a storm a couple of years earlier, had been replaced. He wondered what else had been done to his home while he was away.

Seeing a charger sitting on one of the worktops, cable curled around it, he dug around in one of the bags and took out his phone. He had a dim memory of refusing to part with it – he thought he might have made quite an issue of it – but when he had regained himself enough to try and call someone he had found the battery was flat, and eventually it had been taken away for safekeeping. He plugged the charger into a socket, turned it on, connected the cable to the phone, and left it on the worktop while he carried his bags upstairs.

Both bedrooms were neat and tidy, the beds made, carpets hoovered and surfaces dusted. The bathroom was clean, toiletries and bottles of shampoo and shower gel arranged on the shelves. He stood in the main bedroom for a while, looking out through the net curtains into the street, then he turned and went back to the spare bedroom and put his bags on the floor.

Back downstairs, he took a key from a cupboard and walked down the garden to the shed. Here, again, was that faintly maddening sense of neatness. Whoever had been looking after the garden had cleaned and racked all the tools; the mower was hanging up on its pegs with its lead coiled around the handle. All the old bottles of weedkiller and boxes of grass seed were in a row on the back shelf, arranged according to size. Not even a cobweb. He took it for granted that he would be under observation, given the circumstances, but this was ridiculous. He was beginning to feel a distant sense of what might have been outrage that someone had been in his house and tidied everything up. Bob had told him that emotional reactions to situations were a good sign, although he seemed to recall that this had all started with emotional reactions in the first place.

He suddenly felt very tired. He locked the shed and went back into the house, clicked the television onto one of the news channels and stretched out on the sofa with a cushion under his head. When he woke up again it was four hours later and it was starting to get dark and for a few alarming moments he had no idea where he was.

Apart from three cans of Guinness, the fridge was empty. The only food in the house was either in the freezer or in tins, and he didn't feel like cooking anyway, so he ordered a pizza, and when it arrived half an hour or so later it was delivered by Ismail himself, owner of the takeaway.

Ismail was a tall, solemn man wearing a skull cap and jeans and a leather bomber jacket. "Been away, have we, Mister Brookes?" he asked.

"Overseas posting," Michael told him, which was what had been suggested he say to anyone who asked.

"Thought we hadn't heard from you for a while," Ismail said, wrestling the pizza box out of its insulated bag and handing it over. "Anywhere nice?"

"Bonn. Very dull." Michael gave him two ten pound notes from the household budget jar in the kitchen. "Don't worry about the change."

Ismail nodded. "That's very kind of you," he said, pocketing the money. "Enjoy your meal. And welcome back."

Michael found that he wasn't terribly hungry after all, and he only ate a couple of slices washed down with a glass of water. He closed the pizza box and got up and finally went into the study.

He turned on the light and stood in the doorway, looking around. There was the same sense of recently cleaned neatness. Desk at the window with his laptop on it, bookshelves, two small wooden filing cabinets, an armchair, an Aeron chair at the desk, half a dozen prints on the walls, West Country landscapes, mostly. Obviously, someone had been in here – there was no dust on the filing cabinets – but had anyone *been* in here? The keys to the filing cabinets and his desk were on the fob in his pocket, along with all his other keys, and they had been in safe keeping at the hospital with the rest of his possessions for five months, but Ania had a spare key to the front door and someone had obviously had access to the garden, so there was no knowing who had been tramping through the house. He supposed, considering what had happened, he would have to assume it had been searched, and he found the sense of invasion was not as great as he might have expected. There were, he had found down the years, procedures for everything. It wasn't anything personal.

He sat at the desk and unlocked the drawers and opened them one by one, but it was impossible to tell whether anything had been rearranged; he honestly couldn't remember how they'd looked before he went away. In the bottom drawer was an envelope containing a thousand pounds in twenty pound notes. He took two hundred pounds out and put the rest back. He looked at the laptop but didn't open the lid. It could wait till tomorrow.

On one of the bookshelves was a framed photograph. In it, he was wearing jeans and boots and a waterproof jacket. There was no grey in his hair, and he was laughing. To his left there was a great expanse of rough, whitecapped sea, and to his right a cliff path wound away into the distance through gorse and heather. He had a little rucksack slung over one shoulder, and he remembered it had contained a thermos of coffee and two ham sandwiches made with doorsteps of fresh crusty white bread. Standing beside him was a short, sandy-haired woman. She was wearing walking gear as well, and she was grinning. They'd stopped a stranger, another walker on the path, to take the photo.

"What we must never underestimate," Bob had told him, "is the *grief*."

Two

The doctors at the hospital encouraged all the residents to have a balanced breakfast, even those, like Michael, who had spent their entire working lives starting their day with nothing more substantial than a slice of toast. Breakfast ran from half past six till nine, but if you went downstairs late you found that the food had been sitting under heat lamps for over an hour and was dried out and horrible, so he had grown used to waking early, and when he opened his eyes the next morning he experienced a moment of profound dislocation. Where was his room? Why did his bed feel different? Why was the light coming from another direction? He blinked, and blinked again, and felt most of the parts of the world settle into place.

He sat up and swung his legs out of the bed, flexing his toes against the carpet. It felt disquietingly different to the carpet in his room at the hospital. He reached out for his meds, two small brown bottles on the bedside table, and tipped a tablet from each into his palm, one red and one blue . Meds were always taken first thing in the morning before food, never during or after. There were thirty pills in each bottle; the labels only had his name printed on them, no dosage instructions or what the medication was or even the date and he had not been given a prescription form. He presumed that towards the end of the month, when his supply ran low, someone would be in touch to tell him what to do, although nobody had given him any guidance. He washed the pills down with a gulp of water and waited for a few minutes. As always, the pills had no discernible effect, and as always he wondered what would happen if he skipped them, just once. This had been a harmless little thought experiment while he was at the hospital and there were doctors available at a moment's notice in case anything went wrong. Now, though, it just made him aware of how alone and unsupported he was.

He showered and shaved. He microwaved a slice of pizza for breakfast, drank a cup of coffee with it, rinsed his plate and cup and put them in the dishwasher, and was walking along Ballard's Lane towards Tesco by nine o'clock.

Finchley had not changed at all while he was away, which was vaguely disappointing. He had been away almost half a year; he should have been greeted by a wall of skyscrapers and a monorail system, but it was just the same shops struggling gamely along in the face of whichever financial clustershambles was gripping the country at the moment, the same people putting a brave face on things, not because they were necessarily brave but because they had no other choice. Restaurants and cafés were offering lunchtime specials and all-you-can-eat Happy Hours. Traffic was busy and there seemed to be more people out and about, although that could have been his imagination. Some people were still wearing masks, but not very many.

He stopped off at his bank and withdrew three thousand pounds in cash, and in Tesco he spent forty minutes or so pushing a trolley along the aisles, picking up essentials and other odds and ends. He was sorting through a tray of broccoli when he heard music coming from somewhere, the same few bars of an irritating tinny jingle repeated over and over again. He looked up, thinking it was coming from the store's public address system or something, but it seemed closer to hand, and now fellow shoppers were giving him glances as they passed by, and he suddenly realised it was coming from his phone. He hadn't heard it ring for five months and he'd entirely forgotten what it sounded like. He took it out of his pocket and looked at it for a few moments as if it was a baffling ancient magic charm. He touched the little green phone icon.

"Old son," Bob said. "How are you?"

"I'm okay, I think. Just doing some shopping."

"Excellent. How's that going?"

Michael looked around him at the other shoppers. "It's going all right, I suppose. It's only Tesco."

"Don't knock it, it's a considerable advance. No anxiety? Disassociation? Memory lapses?"

"How would I know?" He heard Bob sigh. "I'm okay, Bob. It's all going very well."

"How about sleeping? Did you sleep all right?"

He hadn't felt able to use the main bedroom, so he'd spent the night in the spare bed. "Like a top," he said.

"Good, good. Sleep's very important; we underestimate it."

"I've never underestimated sleep, I promise you."

"Great. Look, the reason I called, someone's going to be popping by, just to introduce herself. Name of *Jo*. Jo does *outreach*. She'll be the point of contact between you and us."

"Okay," Michael said, although he didn't see any need for a point of contact, particularly; he could walk to the hospital from here in an hour or so, if he set a good pace and took some shortcuts.

"Good. Lunchtime work for you?"

"I suppose. I won't be doing anything."

"Great. Okay, you take care. I'll be in touch again soon."

When Bob had hung up, Michael went back through the store to pick up a small carton of milk, in case his visitor took it in her tea and coffee.

Bob's idea of 'lunchtime' was not quite the same as Michael's; he was still putting his shopping away when the doorbell rang, and when he answered it he found a young woman wearing jeans and a hoodie standing outside.

"Hi, Michael?" she said. "I'm Jo." She held out a laminated card. "Bob called about me?"

Michael leaned forward and read the card without touching it. It had the logo of the local hospital trust, and the usual out-of-date photo, and the name JoAnne Charnley. It gave her job description as 'social worker'.

"Is this a bad time?" she asked. "I can come back."

He looked at her. She was about his height, and she had short brown hair, and she was carrying a cheap leather-effect document case under her arm. "No, it's okay," he said. "I wasn't busy. Come on in."

She put her hand in a pocket of her jeans and pulled out a piece of cloth. "Do you want me to mask up? Some people do."

The only people he had seen wearing masks in the hospital had been members of staff passing through the keypad-protected door to the Acute wing. "You don't have to," he said. "I've had my vaccinations."

"That doesn't mean anything," she told him. "My Gran's had it twice and she's had all her jabs."

"I've just spent threequarters of an hour wandering around Tesco's and there wasn't a soul there wearing a mask," he told her. "I don't mind if you don't."

She looked at the piece of cloth. "I should," she said. "Healthcare professional and all that." She suddenly came to a decision and stuffed the mask back into her pocket. "But some things work better if people can see each other's faces." And she stepped through the door.

As he led the way down the hall towards the kitchen, she said, "I'm sorry I wasn't there yesterday; I should have been, just to say hello, but I had a bit of an emergency."

"Oh, that's all right," he said. "There wasn't a lot of ceremony."

"Let me guess. They just put you in a cab, didn't they."

"Yes."

He heard her sigh. "I'm sorry. I keep telling them. It's such a simple little thing but it makes such a difference. Oh," she said, seeing the groceries on the worktop. "You've been shopping."

"There wasn't any food in the house. Please, sit down. Tea or coffee?"

She pulled out a chair and sat at the kitchen table. "Only if you're making one."

"I was just about to sit down with a cuppa," he said, switching the kettle on.

"I'll have a coffee, then," she said. "Black, two sugars, please." She settled the document case in her lap, unzipped it, and dipped a hand inside. "Before I forget, I want to give you this." She put a business card on the table. "It's got my phone number and my email address, in case you want to get in touch."

"Thanks." He spooned grounds into the two-cup cafetiere, took a couple of mugs out of the cupboard.

"Did Bob tell you what I do?" She put a spiral notepad and a pen on the table and propped the document case against her chair.

"He said something about outreach."

She pulled a face. "Kind of. I'll be popping in once or twice a week, as often as you want, just to see how you're doing, if you need anything, that kind of thing. I'm not a probation officer or anything. Just someone to chat to, if you need a chat."

"All right," he said. "Thank you."

"It can be a bit of a shock, leaving somewhere people have looked after you. If you have any trouble coping, you must let me know."

"I will," he promised. The kettle boiled. He poured water into the cafetiere, gave it a stir, popped the plunger on and brought it over to the table with the mugs. "So," he said, sitting down across from her.

24

"I'm employed by the local hospital trust," she told him, "but I'm also on a retainer from your employers, so I'm fully vetted. But my clearance isn't very high, so you should be careful what you tell me or we'll both be in trouble."

"And we wouldn't want that. Don't we have our own... um... outreach workers?"

She shrugged. "Once upon a time, maybe. Outsourcing's gone through a lot of industries like a bad dance craze. I'm not complaining, particularly; the money's not bad. It's the paperwork that kills you."

He smiled and pressed down the plunger on the cafetiere, poured their coffee, nudged the sugar bowl towards her. "So, what do we do? Word association? Rorschach tests?"

She shuddered. "Gods, no. I'm not a psychiatrist. I'm just a social worker, like it says on the badge." She spooned sugar into her coffee and stirred it. "How are you?"

"It's still a little early to tell, really. It's all a bit of an adventure at the moment."

"I know it's a bit of a cliché, but you really have to be kind to yourself. Take it at your own pace. Have you been in touch with your employers?"

When his phone had recharged, he had checked and found there were no messages or emails or missed calls at all, from anyone, which seemed rather sad. He said, "Not a word."

"Well, there's no rush. Do you need anything?"

He shook his head. "I don't think so."

"I know you'll be okay for medication because you only left the hospital yesterday. When things are going well the temptation's going to be to think you don't need them any more." She saw the look on his face. "You've been thinking about it, haven't you. Well, don't worry, everyone does. But you have to watch out for it."

"I plan to be a good boy," he said, putting sugar in his own coffee. "One day at a time, right?"

She looked at him. "I won't kid you and say it gets easier, because a lot of times it doesn't. It's a long, hard slog."

"Everyone seems determined to be rather downbeat," Michael told her, remembering some of the things Bob had said.

She thought about that. "It's important that we're honest,. Try to be optimistic without just patting you on the head and telling you everything's going to be all right."

"I don't mind being told everything's going to be all right. So long as it turns out that way."

She smiled. "Well, let's try to make sure it does turn out that way." She sipped her coffee. "It's important to remember that this isn't a test. There's no right or wrong way to do it, and there's no prize at the end."

"Not even a certificate?"

She shrugged. "I can knock you up a certificate, if you want. I could probably find someone mildly important to sign it, too."

He smiled. "There's no need. I'm not really motivated by rewards."

"That makes you unusual, these days. Also, I should tell you that there's no cut-off date, so we're not working to a deadline. I'll be available as long as you think I'm helping; when you think you're ready to knock it on the head, just let me know. I won't take it personally."

"What if you don't think we're ready to knock it on the head?"

"Then I'll give you my opinion and we'll take it from there, but there's no point in me turning up twice a week if you don't want me here. It wastes my time and it wastes yours."

He thought about it. "Suppose I decide I want to knock it on the head right now?"

She gave him a long stare. "Michael," she said, "are you going to be one of the *awkward* ones?"

He laughed and sat back. "No," he said. "I promise. I just want a quiet life."

"Good," she said, opening her notebook to a blank page. "That's all any of us want." She wrote the date at the top of the page and said, "So. How are you feeling?"

He thought about it. "Unmoored," he said. "A bit adrift, really."

She made a note. "That's entirely normal when you've just left an institution." She stopped and thought about it. "That sounds awful, doesn't it? *Institution*? You've just spent five months in a place where everything's been taken care of for you and help was never more than a few seconds away. Now you've got to rely on yourself, and that can be a bit dislocating. It will pass, I promise." She glanced at the shopping bags on the worktop. "You did your shopping, which is good. You identified a problem and set out to solve it. You'd be surprised how many of my clients just sit at home, completely frozen, waiting for somebody to come along and sort it out for them."

"Acclimatisation," he said.

She raised an eyebrow. "Excuse me?"

"At the hospital, they made us practice doing everyday things like shopping. They call it Acclimatisation."

She nodded. "Well, it seems to work, so that's good." She made a couple more notes.

"What happens to those?" he asked, nodding at the notebook. "Do you file reports?"

She looked up. "In triplicate, usually," she said. "One copy to the referring authority, one to the Trust via my line manager, one for my files. In your case it's a little different. Just the one copy, to the referring authority, which is your therapist, Doctor Bentley."

"Bob."

She shrugged. "I don't know anything about him. As far as I'm concerned he's just a signature at the bottom of a memo."

"So what happens to your notes?"

"I write up my report and then I shred them." Jo clasped her hands on top of her notebook. "I don't know who you are or what you do, and I don't want to know. What brought you here doesn't concern me, although obviously I'm sorry it happened to you, whatever it was. I'm just here to help you with... *this*." She gestured at the kitchen and the wider world outside. "To be honest it's a pain having to get rid of my notes. Fortunately, I only have a couple of clients at the moment, so I can work from memory."

"I'm sorry," he said. "It's none of my business; I shouldn't have asked."

"You have every right to ask, Michael," she said seriously. "You have agency. You mustn't ever forget that."

"All right," he said.

"Okay." She looked down at the notebook again. "Is there anything you need?"

"I can't think of anything right now. It might be useful to know what my status is with work, but that's not vital for the moment."

Jo jotted another note. "Haven't they written to you?"

He thought of the pile of letters on the hall table. "Maybe. I haven't checked yet."

Another note. "They should have done, but if not, let me know and I'll give them a poke."

The thought of anyone below Cabinet Office level giving the department a 'poke' was rather charming. Michael thought he would like to be a fly on the wall when that happened. "I'll check later."

She nodded, still writing. "Let me know either way, yeah?"

"Will do."

She put down her pen, sat back, and smiled at him. "Well, it's still early days, but it's a promising start."

"Is it?"

"As I said, some of my clients are like rabbits caught in the headlights for the first few days. I have a feeling you won't be one of those."

"Well, that's good to hear."

"There was one more thing I wanted to ask. When I get a client, the Trust sends me a sheet with a potted bio – name, address, age, stuff like that – and on yours the next of kin box is blank."

"Yes," he said.

She tipped her head to one side. "No one?"

"Not a soul."

"No uncles or aunties?" Michael shook his head. "Cousins? In-laws?"

"Sorry, no."

"That must be weird," she said. "I've got an extended family the size of a small country. You should see us at weddings."

"In practice, if anything happened to me, a flag would go up somewhere and Human Resources would be notified," he said. "I don't think I'm breaking the Official Secrets Act telling you that."

"It must feel lonely. Just you and HR."

"Not really. I'm surviving." They both knew that not so long ago this had not been remotely true.

"Well," she said, closing the notebook. "Let's see if we can get you doing better than just *surviving*, eh?" She took a swallow of coffee. "This is really good; what brand is it?"

Michael shrugged. "I can't remember. I probably got it from Tesco's."

"Let me know if you ever find out." She put her notebook back in her document case and took out a diary, bulked out with many inserted pieces of paper and post-it notes. "When can I visit again? Wednesday all right for you?"

"Wednesday's fine," he told her.

"Okay." She opened the diary and leafed through it until she found the right page. "Same time?"

"That's good for me."

"Good. Wednesday about half past ten." She made a note, closed the diary, zipped it and her pen into the document case, and sat smiling at him. "So, I'll be off if there's nothing else."

"I'm sorry I couldn't give you more to do."

"Oh, don't be." She stood up. "I like a nice quiet client. But if there's anything at all…"

"I'll be in touch," he said, getting to his feet. "I promise."

He walked her to the door and watched her go down the path and out the gate, and she crossed the street to cut through the park and onto the main road. When he closed the front door the silence of the house seemed to lean down on him again.

"I know it sounds like a cliché, but keeping busy can really help," Bob had told him. "Simple, repetitive tasks are good and they can give you a sense of being in control of the world around you. Even an hour or so doing the hoovering can be therapeutic."

The house wasn't exactly in need of cleaning, but there was stuff he could keep himself busy with. The clothes he'd brought back from the hospital smelled of whatever industrial detergent they used in the laundry room, so he put them in the washing machine. He washed up the mugs he and Jo had used and tidied the kitchen. That brought him up to lunchtime. He made a sandwich and another jug of coffee. Then he washed and tidied up again.

He took the vacuum cleaner out of the cupboard under the stairs and hoovered the living room and the hallway and the stairs. He didn't hurry. He waited for the promised therapeutic effects to kick in, but they never did. Maybe he was doing it wrong. He sat for a while watching the news. The economy was in crisis. The Prime Minister seemed not to have a clue what to do. The Bank of England was floundering. It was as if he'd never been away. A minor Royal he'd never heard of had driven their Range Rover into the front of a branch of Argos in Canterbury, whether by accident or design was not discussed. Some kind of natural disaster had occurred on the Dutch coast, but he couldn't make sense of the aerial footage and nobody seemed to have been hurt. A mass shooting at a mall in Sacramento. A teenager stabbed to death in West London. The search for a missing care worker in Shropshire was in its second week. He had always suspected that the news they were allowed to see in the hospital was carefully curated so as not to upset the residents, and it was a bit of a shock to encounter the raw unfiltered product again. He didn't suppose it was doing him any good. On another channel a scientist was explaining to a journalist, who was boggling mildly on the audience's behalf, that there was a nontrivial chance that the Cosmos was a colossal simulation.

"The whole Universe and everything in it and all its backstory could have suddenly come into existence eight months ago, and we wouldn't be able to tell," he said.

"How's that different from God?" asked the journalist.

"This has nothing to do with God," the scientist said sternly.

No, Michael thought, that would not have gone down well with the residents at the hospital, for many of whom Reality was already troublesome. He turned the television off.

At around five, he went back into the kitchen, heated up the oven and put the chicken in to roast. Later he ate a leg and a wing with potatoes and green beans. Afterwards, he did the washing up, removed the remaining leg and wing from the chicken, and put them in freezer bags along with the breasts. If he was careful and mildly inventive he could make a chicken last almost a week, and he could boil up the carcass with some vegetables for soup.

He took the pile of post from the hall table into the study and sat at his desk sorting through it. Junk mail – the majority of it from local estate agents – went straight in the bin. Utilities were all on direct debits and standing orders, but he was enough of a dinosaur to like having paper bills for his records. He opened the envelopes, and it seemed that the gas and electricity companies were still determined to suck the country dry before their associated hedge funds moved on to another unsuspecting nation. There was indeed a formal letter from HR acknowledging the status of his sick leave; it was so devoid of human warmth that it might as well have been written by a machine. A couple of letters from his local health centre asking him to get in touch to arrange an appointment. A letter from a hospital trust in Northwick Park inviting him to take part in a bowel cancer screening study. Not much, really, for five months.

He put most of the money he'd withdrawn that morning into an envelope to pay Ania, wrote her name on the front, and propped it up against the desk lamp, then he sat back in the chair and looked out of the window. Outside, shadows were gathering under the trees at the bottom of the garden. The sky was a pale, translucent blue streaked with clouds lit orange with the sunset. A squirrel bounded across the lawn, took an impossible-looking leap at the fence, and was gone into next door's garden.

There was an unopened half-bottle of Famous Grouse and a glass in one of the drawers. He took them out and put them on one side of the desk. The surface of the glass was clean and shiny, not a mark on it. He turned on the lamp and then leaned down until his cheek was resting on the desktop. Looking across the surface, he thought he could make out a single faint smear on part of the desk he hadn't touched since he got back, where someone had missed polishing the wood quite properly. When, he wondered, did one surrender wholly to paranoia?

The next morning, after breakfast, he mowed the lawn, and while he was weeding one of the flowerbeds – not that it really needed it, whoever had been looking after the garden had done as thorough a job as whoever had looked after the house – Jill from next door came out and stood looking over the fence.

"I thought I heard you moving around in there," she said.

On his knees at the edge of the flowerbed, Michael sat back and looked at her. "Yes, that's me back, Jill. Been on a business trip."

"Anywhere nice?"

"Not really. Five months in Bonn." He performed a comic shudder that made her laugh. "Very dull. How's you?"

"Not so bad, thanks. Oscar was poorly for a little while, but he's okay now." Oscar was Jill's cat. Jill was a stout, white-haired woman in her late sixties. Her husband, the mildly racist Gavin, had died the previous year. Michael remembered having attended his funeral, but could remember no details about it, and he thought that was a sign that storm clouds had been gathering, even back then. He got slowly to his feet, hating the stiffness in his knees.

"I didn't know what to think when I saw that black boy in your garden," Jill volunteered, reminding him that she wasn't exactly PC herself. "I almost called the police."

"I'm sorry about that," he told her. "I should have said something, but it was all a bit of a rush. A colleague over there fell ill and they needed someone to fill in. You know how it is."

Jill had no idea how it was, but she thought he worked for the Treasury – which was technically true – and that had built a picture in her mind. "He was lovely, actually. Loz," she said. "He came over and pruned the trees at the bottom of the garden for me."

"Loz," Michael agreed. "Salt of the earth. Just like the chaps who did my decorating."

Jill beamed. "Oh, they were lovely," she said. "Ever so polite, and not noisy at all, not like some of them. I hardly knew they were there. One of them did me a quote for my front room."

Michael didn't know the standard operating procedure – one heard rumours, but one could never be sure of rumours. Considering the circumstances, he could see that his employers might think it reasonable to send in the quiet and polite decorators to check if he had been playing fast and loose with things he should not, and the lovely Loz to take care of the garden and make sure nothing of note had been buried there. It would be funny if the decorators were actually moonlighting as decorators, though.

They wouldn't have found anything, because there was nothing to find. The closest he came to bringing work home was a subscription to the *Financial Times*. True, there were gaps in his memory where he might have done anything, but if that had been the case he doubted whether he would have been allowed home.

One of the doctors at the hospital had counselled a technique for dealing with abstract situations. "Either you can rage against them, or you can accept them," she'd said, unwilling perhaps to recognise a third alternative, which was to simply run away. It was just a tarted-up version of something Michael had read years ago: *I'll have to get over this sooner or later, so why not do it now?*

So, how to react to this invasion of his home? Rage would be pointless, and running away would be counterproductive and rather melodramatic. Which left acceptance. Shrug. Carry on. Be English.

"Actually, it's a form of oppression," another doctor had said when the subject came up in conversation. "Be English. Stiff upper lip, don't make a fuss. We've been doing it for so long there's a vast pit of buried anger and resentment. It's no wonder we're all so sick."

Jo turned up on time on Wednesday morning, and they sat in the kitchen chatting and drinking coffee. Michael still couldn't remember what brand it was, and he found himself having to be careful that it didn't become something of an obsession.

"Exercise is good," Jo told him when he mentioned the housework. "But maybe you should go out a bit too."

"I walked up to Whetstone yesterday afternoon," he said.

She made a note. "Is that far? Sorry; I'm not from round here."

"A couple of hours, round-trip." It was actually the furthest he'd walked in one go since going into the hospital, and his legs still hurt a bit.

Another note. "Not too shabby. Plenty of fresh air?"

"The outward leg was up the Great North Road, so not really. I came back along the Dollis Valley, though."

"Nice walk along there? Green? Woody?"

"Mostly, yes. Quiet, anyway."

"Green and woody is good. I always find it soothing. How did your interactions with other people go? No sense of panic or anything?"

"It was fine," he said, although he hadn't interacted with anyone, really. No more than anyone in London did, anyway. "I thought you weren't a therapist."

Jo looked up from her notes. "I'm not."

"It feels like you're asking therapist questions."

She put down her pen, clasped her hands together on the table, and asked seriously, "And how do you feel about that?" Then she laughed. "The look on your face." She shook her head. "Some people who've spent a long time in hospital can have feelings of agoraphobia when they leave, and that's within my brief. But it sounds like you're okay so far. Have you tried public transport yet?"

"Not yet."

"Well, that can be a bit of a shock sometimes; it's bad enough for those of us who have to use it every day. Take it easy, like with everything else." She took up her pen and made another note. "So, is there anything you need?"

"I don't think so, no. I found a letter from HR, by the way. Just a form thing."

She nodded. "That's something, at least. You should be getting another letter soon, now you're out of hospital. That'll just be a form thing too, so don't worry about it. Eventually they'll invite you in for a chat, and don't worry about that either, it's a formality."

"All right."

"There's an awful lot of law and precedent on your side, no matter how hard the government's trying to shred it. I have the feeling your employers are going to play it straight, but if they don't you're not alone."

"You know," he said, "I wasn't worried about this before, but now I am."

Jo waved it away. "Employers will try to take the piss; it's axiomatic. That's why it's handy to have someone like me who knows their way around the legislation. But like I said, I think your people are going to be straight. I wouldn't lose any sleep over it."

"Okay. If you say so."

"I do say so." She took out her diary. "Will Monday next week be okay? About the same time?"

After Jo had gone, he went into the living room and sat down in front of the news. A Parliamentary Private Secretary had been suspended pending investigations into a groping complaint from a researcher. The King and Queen were in York, where it was pouring with rain. The Prime Minister was dodging questions about some issue or other. A boyband Michael had never heard of had announced they were splitting up.

It occurred to him, because his mind was idling, that he had never finished *The Heart of the Maze* and it had never crossed his mind to bring it home with him because that would have felt like stealing. He went into the study and booted up the laptop, but it wasn't available on Amazon, and Google offered him a bewildering list of results which weren't remotely relevant. It seemed that it was one of those minor cultural artifacts that fell through the cracks in the internet. Try as he might, he couldn't recall the author's name. He wondered if he could contact the hospital and ask to borrow it, but then he had a few woozy moments when he wondered what would happen if they said they'd never heard of the book, if it turned out that he had imagined it.

Best not to dig too far into that. He went back into the living room and sat down again, mind boggling mildly at daytime television.

At some point, he became aware of that irritating jingle again, but this time he couldn't quite work out where it was coming from. He stood up and listened, but it seemed to be everywhere. He went out into the hall and it seemed louder. Looking down the hall, he saw his phone, its screen all lit up, on one of the worktops, where he'd left it plugged in to the charger. He made a mental note to change the ringtone, and wondered what had possessed him to use that one in the first place.

He went into the kitchen and picked the phone up and thumbed the answer icon and said, "Hello?"

"Mike," said a woman's voice. "It's Martine. How are we doing?"

"Oh, not so bad, thanks."

"Good, good. Look, how about coming in to the office tomorrow for a bit of a chat?"

He thought about his earlier conversation with Jo, and wondered why there hadn't been a letter. Maybe it was on its way.

"You still there?" she said.

"Yes," he said. "I'm still here."

"So, how about it?"

"Well…" he said doubtfully.

"Terrific," she cut in. "Eleven o'clock be all right for you? Excellent. See you then." And she hung up.

He stood looking at the phone, feeling a vague numbness in his hands and feet. He supposed he should mention this to Jo, but he didn't want to phone and find she was in the middle of a visit with another client, so he texted her to call him when she had time, and five minutes later the phone rang again.

"Michael," Jo said. "Are you okay?"

"I'm not interrupting something, am I?" he asked.

"No, I'm on a bus. What's up?"

"HR called. They want to see me tomorrow."

A silence, while she thought about it. He heard people chatting in the background, the sound of someone pressing the button to stop the bus. "How do you feel about that?" she asked.

"I don't know."

"You don't have to go, you know. You can put it off for another day."

He considered that. "Better to get it over with, though, surely."

"There's something to be said for that, of course, but it depends how you feel. There's no rush, and they're not allowed to stampede you. You only got out of hospital on Monday."

It seemed impossible to choose. He felt the first stirrings of panic. "I'll sleep on it."

"That sounds like a good idea," she told him. "But don't forget, there's no right or wrong answer, no win or lose. You decide what's best for you, not for everybody else."

"Okay," he said. "I'll let you know what happens."

"Good. Got to go; my stop's coming up. Talk to you soon."

They hung up and Michael stood where he was, that sense of being *unmoored* starting to wash over him again.

Three

He almost didn't go. After a night of broken sleep, he woke up late the next morning and lay in bed staring at the ceiling, telling himself that there was nothing at all to stop him pulling the duvet up over his head and blocking out the world. And that, he supposed, was the danger.

Eventually he got up and went downstairs to sit eating toast and jam while looking out the window at drizzle falling on the garden. Periodically, he glanced at the clock on the cooker as it counted down towards the time when he ought to get ready if he was going to make the appointment. The time came round and he was still sitting there in jogging bottoms and a teeshirt, and he let it pass. *Too late to go now,* he thought. *Ah well.*

Ten minutes later he was back upstairs, dressing in jeans and a polo shirt, and fifteen minutes after that he was standing on the southbound platform at Finchley Central watching a train clatter down the track towards him, a little baffled that he was there at all.

With rush hour out of the way, the train was almost empty. There were just a couple of people sitting at the other end of his carriage, and they paid him no attention. He stared at his reflection in the window above the seats opposite and told himself that he could get off at any point and return home. That, he supposed, was what Jo had meant by *agency.*

It was axiomatic that if you were on the way to an appointment that you really *wanted* to be on time for, you would be faced with an insurmountable combination of failed points, missing drivers and broken-down trains, whereas if you weren't in a hurry or were actually reluctant to reach your destination the London Underground would operate like a gigantic well-oiled machine and get you there ridiculously early. The train he had caught was fiendishly efficient, by Northern Line standards, and hardly anyone got on between Finchley and Central London, and though he did have a couple of wobbly moments, Michael actually made it to his destination.

There was a narrow little street near the southern end of the Tottenham Court Road, or near the eastern end of Oxford Street, depending on which direction one approached it from. It cut across the corner behind the junction in an uneven curve. It wasn't a very long street – you could walk unhurriedly from one end to the other in a minute or so – and like a lot of London's tiny little alleys and sidestreets it was easy to miss. Towards the Tottenham Court Road end a lot of the buildings had been converted or redeveloped into smart little offices or expensive little flats, but the Oxford Street end was a parade of cramped shops and restaurants and casting agencies. There was Arno's Trattoria (est. 1954) which no one in living memory had ever been observed to enter or leave. There was Cherished Vinyl (est. 1986) for all your pre-loved record needs. There was Bloom's kosher deli, which served the best hot salt beef sandwiches in London, and The Jamaica Kitchen, which did you a massive plate of curried goat and rice and peas for less than a fiver. There was a deeply suspicious little bookshop with painted-out windows whose clientele only turned up after dark when there was less chance of being recognised, and a dance studio which had recently retooled itself as a fitness club for the unemployed, and between these there was a narrow brown wooden door with flaking varnish and a column of bell-pushes mounted on the wall beside it.

Every weekday morning for twelve years, until the onset of his illness, Michael had come out of Tottenham Court Road station, crossed Oxford Street, stopped off at Bloom's to pick up a coffee, and stood in front of this door without consciously thinking about it. It had been like a reflex, and now that reflex was gone and all of a sudden the door seemed at once familiar and unfamiliar, like architectural *déjà vu*. He could still change his mind; the cameras mounted unobtrusively on nearby buildings would be showing him standing there, but there was nothing to stop him simply turning and walking away. Nobody would even blame him. He sighed and pressed the second bell-push down, the one with the faded handwritten label that read *Lohman Film Editing*, and it might have been his imagination but it seemed that he heard the electronic bolts withdraw before he'd even driven the button fully home.

Beyond the door was a steep, dingy staircase of cracked and uneven lino just wide enough for one person. Halfway up, the stairs doglegged to the left and there was a less obtrusive camera mounted on the wall looking down at anyone coming in from the street. There was also, it was said, a backup camera, but Michael had never been able to find it.

At the top of the stairs, on the first floor, there was a small reception area. When Michael had first come through the front door, it had been shabby and a little forbidding. It had been manned by John, a retired sergeant of Special Branch who regarded everyone who came up the stairs as if he thought they were going to steal the petty cash. The walls had been covered with unpainted hessian that attracted dust and wouldn't let it go, John had stood behind a high wooden counter, and the chairs had been the kind of hard seating you used to find in 1970s works canteens.

Still, Michael remembered, back then you could just walk through the front door, nod hello to John, and, if he recognised you, you could carry on past the counter towards the lifts without breaking stride. That had changed, gradually, in time with a series of redecorations. The hessian was painted over and new flooring laid, and a memo came down that all visitors had to sign in and remain accompanied by an employee at all times. The hessian was stripped off the walls and replaced with textured paint that also attracted dust, and another memo required all employees to sign in and out of the building. The textured paint was melted off with hot-air guns, an operation which took days and left a smell of burning paint that lingered for weeks; in its place pale oak veneering went up, the counter was replaced by a glass-topped desk, and staff were issued with identity badges which had to be shown and logged in and out.

New lighting was installed, and a wall of potted palms appeared behind the desk, leased from and tended by an enterprising and thoroughly vetted firm of horticulturalists which provided plant life for half the offices in the City. John, who would have hated all this, was long gone by this time. His replacement, another former Special Branch officer, lasted about a year, and then the department recruited the first in a long line of cheerful, efficient young women to staff the front office. A little box appeared on the desk, for staff to touch their identity cards in and out and save them the bother of signing a register. And then, in a final burst of activity a couple of years ago, the veneer on the walls had been peeled off and replaced with translucent blue edge-lit glass panels, marble tiling was laid on the floor, the palms were removed and a long planter of indoor ferns brought in, and a glass and metal security gate not unlike the ticket gates on the Underground installed between reception and the short corridor that led into the building.

The old glass desk had also been retired. Now there was something that looked like a decorator's pasting table, but made of polished teak. On it sat a little computer monitor and a combination telephone/comms centre with more buttons than the cockpit of an airliner, and behind it in a complicated-looking and ergonomic chair, sat the latest receptionist. She was brown-haired and neatly suited, and she had joined the office around the time Michael's life began to go out of shape, and he hadn't had time to commit her name to memory. Alice? Angela? They'd exchanged a few polite words, but they were strangers. Held under the table by clips were a couple of flash-bangs and a taser, in case of emergencies. Nobody was seriously expecting an emergency, but the weapons came with the office's status. Back in the late 1930s the War Office had requisitioned a bewildering range of properties for various uses, and they didn't give them all back after VJ Day. No one knew what the office had been used for back then, but it came with a firearms requirement and none of its subsequent residents had ever seen the need to give that up. Rob, Michael's line manager, kept a Glock in his desk; he'd shown it to him one afternoon during a terminally dull discussion of Estonian banking data.

With the firearms requirement came mandatory firearms training. Michael remembered a day's small-arms instruction at Aldershot that had left him with aching wrists, a stamped certification, and the words of the instructor ringing in his ears. *"We mustn't be glum, sir, not everyone suits a sidearm. Have we perhaps thought of trying a shotgun?"*

Well, quite.

As he waited on one of the comfy seats against one wall of the reception area, it occurred to him that he had never really spent much time here. He'd only ever passed through, going in or out of the building. It felt strange to be sitting here; there was that weird sense of *déjà vu* again, that feeling of it being simultaneously familiar and unfamiliar. Alice/Angela kept glancing over at him, as well she might. From her point of view, he had never left the building. She'd seen him arrive one morning five months ago, and after he'd become unmoored in Rob's office on the third floor he'd been sedated and then taken out through the back of the building and put in a van waiting on Hanway Place. As far as she was concerned, he'd simply vanished, logged in and never logged out again, as if he'd been swallowed by the building. He wondered, for the first time, what the office gossip about him was like, and found himself settling into a very English cringe on his seat.

"Mister Brookes?"

Michael looked round, saw a young man standing on the other side of the security gate. "Yes?"

"You're here to see HR?"

"Yes."

"Hi, I'm James. I'll show you upstairs."

Michael got up. "I know the way."

"Sorry," James said. "Rules." He touched his pass to the reader on the gate to let Michael through.

When Michael arrived at the department, HR had been called Personnel, and they had consisted of a crabby old lady named Meg who occupied a pokey little office on the ground floor at the back of the building. It was Meg to whom you submitted your expenses and your holiday dates, and Meg who issued stationery supplies. She organised flights and hotels for staff visiting overseas offices, and she kept, in a row of scratched and dusty filing cabinets, files on every member of staff employed by the office for at least the past twenty years. There had been a running joke that without Meg the entire department would be unable to function. And then Meg had simply not been there one day. Found dead by her sister, rumour had it, in her little flat in Wood Green, her cat starved half to death while it sat beside her waiting to be fed.

The office did not seize up, but a hurricane of change did blow through it, presaged by the arrival of a team of consultants, four men with an officer-class look to them, who set up shop in a spare office on the third floor and ignored the staff for six weeks before departing again.

The result of their labours was that Meg's empire was split up and a whole new management tree planted. New departments dealing with Travel and Office Supplies appeared. Expenses and Office Maintenance were wholly subsumed into Finance. And Meg's filing cabinets fell into the hands of a new Human Resources department.

HR arrived one day in the earthly form of Martine, who favoured charcoal-grey business suits and pale blue silk shirts and a sniper's stare. With her came a staff of five, and although it was never quite explained what they all did, or why it took six of them to fulfil a role which Meg had ably – if not contentedly – managed to carry out on her own for many years, it was clear the old Personnel office was too small for them all, so they were promoted upward through the building to the top floor, where a suite of offices next door to the little-used Conference Room had lain empty for as long as anyone could remember.

Teams of cleaners and decorators were brought in to make the offices habitable, and a great deal of flat-pack furniture and almost two dozen brand new filing cabinets with digital combination locks went up in the lifts. When the refurbishment was over only the HR staff, to anyone's knowledge, ever entered the offices again.

In the years that followed, although the department experienced the kind of churn familiar to any office environment, the personnel of the HR department remained unchanged. Sightings were few and far between, except in times of crisis, when they made their presence known like a band of bureaucratic Furies.

James led him from the lift to the door of the Conference Room, knocked, then opened it without waiting for a reply. Inside, Martine was sitting at the head of a long oval mahogany table, a stack of folders in front of her.

"Mike," she said without getting up. "Hello."

In a moment of weakness some years ago, Michael had confided to Martine that he disliked being called 'Mike'. He said, "Hello."

Martine waved at the other end of the table, where a notepad, ballpoint pen, glass and carafe of water had been set in front of the only other chair in the room. "Have a seat."

Michael sat and looked at Martine down the polished expanse of the table. She studied a folder open in front of her. "How are we doing?" she asked without looking at him.

"We're doing all right," he said.

"Sure about that? Still taking the pills? Fully engaged with the outside world again? No more temper tantrums?"

"All of those," he said.

She glanced at him, went back to the folder. "It's been decided to waive disciplinary procedures," she said.

"Okay." He hadn't been aware that disciplinary procedures were even being considered. Just how bad had his Bad Moment actually been?

Martine turned a page in the file. "Wouldn't be appropriate," she said. "And it would leave us open to an unfair dismissal claim."

"That would be bad," he agreed.

She looked at him. "Do I detect a return of the famous Brookes deadpan humour?"

"I don't know," he told her. "I can't remember."

"It's a promising sign, whatever," she said, returning her attention to the file and making a notation with a silver propelling pencil. "Not that you'd do that anyway," she added. "A team player, that's our Mike. Loyal to a fault."

His memory was still littered with blank areas, like blind spots, places that disappeared if he looked directly at them, and he found that this was one. Was he a team player? Was he loyal? No more or less than anyone else, he thought, but he couldn't be sure.

"Still," she said, laying down her pencil and looking at him. "There's the question of what to do with you, isn't there."

"I rather thought I'd come back to work, when I was well enough," he said. "If I was well enough."

"Retirement's always an option," she told him. She closed the folder, set it aside, opened another one. "Pension pot's not spectacular, but that's the civil service for you." She took out a sheet of paper and looked at it. "Mortgage is paid off, no other big debts. Ought to last you well into your twilight years." She raised an eyebrow at him. "We could put some consulting work your way, if you want to keep busy, or even find you something in academia, if you're that way inclined. Although I can't promise it would be in the Home Counties, so you might have to move."

"I'm sorry," he said, "am I being made redundant?"

Martine shook her head. "Not at all. Just trying to cover all the bases, that's all."

"I should really be discussing this with Rob," he told her.

"Rob?"

"My line manager."

"Rob's gone," she said, putting the sheet of paper back in the folder. "Not a name round here any more."

"Gone where?"

"Private sector. One of those dodgy think tanks on Tufton Street."

"I've only been gone five months."

"Well," she said. "Five months is a long time, isn't it. It's the difference between winter and spring, although Christ knows it's hard enough to tell them apart these days."

"I've never had a problem telling winter and spring apart," he said. "Is this some kind of test?"

Martine blinked at him and took up another file. "So," she said, "the question is, what do you want to do? Do you want to retire?"

"No." For some reason, the prospect terrified him.

She picked up her pencil and made another note. "We could sign you off again, say for another five months, contingent on doctor's advice, see how you feel at the end of that."

The thought of drifting around the house for another five months was almost as scary as retirement. "I want to come back to work," he told her. His brain suddenly caught up with what he'd just said, and he added, "Eventually."

Another note. "And we can be sure you won't blow up again? No more fits of the screaming habdabs?" She looked seriously at him. "I have to think of your co-workers."

"I'm not dangerous."

She tipped her head a little to one side. "You don't remember, do you." And then she watched as he tried to remember, but it was another blind spot.

"I'm not dangerous," he said again.

She looked at him a moment longer, then looked down at the documents in the folder. "Get on all right with the Dutch, do we?"

"Beg pardon?"

"The Dutch," she said. "People from Holland. The Dutch." She sighed and laid her pencil down and looked at him. "Amsterdam Office," she said. "Good working relationship there? Any friction? Get on the wrong side of anybody?"

"I was there last year," he told her, wondering where this was going. "They're a good bunch. Friendly, professional."

Martine gave him a look which told him all he needed to know about what she thought of *friendly, professional*. She looked down at the folder again and turned a page. "Somebody over there dropped a bollock and now the Dutch economic unit aren't talking to us."

For a moment, his mind refused to parse this sentence. "What do you mean, not talking to us?"

"I mean not talking to us. They turned off the tap; no data, no cooperation, they're not even answering the phone."

"Why?"

She looked up and rubbed her eyes. "Well, that's just it, Mike. We don't know. Amsterdam Office say they didn't do anything wrong, and the Dutch aren't saying anything at all."

Michael thought about it. "How far up has this gone?"

"Our Service has talked to their Service, but according to them it's a departmental matter, which is a euphemism for 'sort it out among yourselves'. This has been going on for the last forty-eight hours; I figure we've got another day or so until some dickhead in Cabinet Office hears about it and decides to use it to make his name, and then it'll be out of our hands, and you know what that means."

He nodded. Heads would roll, and nobody would be too particular whose. It occurred to him to ask why Martine was telling him all this, but he realised with a sinking heart that he already knew. He said, "Isn't there anyone else who can go?"

"Sure," she said. "*I* could go, if push came to shove. But you're a familiar face. You know old man van Hoebeek." She mangled the pronunciation.

"We've met a couple of times at conferences," he pointed out. "It's a bit of a stretch to say I know him."

"Doesn't matter. You're a familiar face; he knows you have some seniority. He'll know we're taking this seriously if you turn up." She gave him a serious look. "Right now, this is a row in the corner of the playground, but it's only a matter of time before Teacher notices, and then we'll all be in detention."

"It's a cute metaphor," he said. He looked around the conference room. "Why can't I do it over Zoom or something?"

"Because we can't talk to them to set up a Zoom meeting, Mike. Try to keep up."

"If we can't set up a Zoom meeting, how am I supposed to organise something face-to-face?" But he thought he already knew the answer to that too.

Martine started to sort through her folders. "Well, we've sort of presented them with a *fait accompli*."

"You've already told them I'm coming."

"We've sent them a message to expect you," she said. "Ball's in their court now. Either they'll agree to see you or they won't."

"I still haven't said yes."

She looked at him. "Come on, Mike. Your country needs you. Go and talk to the old man. Find out what's got their knickers in a twist. Come back and tell me all about it. How hard can that be?"

"It could be very hard. Do you think I'm well enough to do this?"

"Do *you*?"

He shrugged.

"If you don't think you're up to it, we'll think of something else."

"Like what?"

"We still have some moves left before questions get asked in committees, but we want to keep this in-house if at all possible." She looked at him and raised her eyebrows.

Michael didn't say anything. This was what Jo had warned him about. He was being *stampeded.*

Martine took a white envelope from one of the folders and slid it across the table. "You're on the half past three flight from Gatwick, coming back tomorrow evening. That's your ticket and itinerary. If they decide to keep you waiting we'll change the return date for you."

He looked at his watch. "I won't have time to go home and get my passport and a change of clothes."

She put another envelope on the table. "We took possession of your passport when you had your mad moment," she said. "Standard procedure, nothing personal." She reached down beside her chair and lifted an overnight bag and showed it to him. "Suit, shirt, tie, underwear, shoes. You'll have to get yourself toiletries at the airport." Another little envelope came across the tabletop towards him. "There's a line of credit, but don't go mad in duty-free and I'll want all the receipts. You're booked into that hotel near the DNB." She slid a final envelope across the table. "Anything else?"

He said, "I'm not sure I'm up to this, you know."

"Look," she said reasonably, clasping her hands on the tabletop in front of her. "Go and listen to Theo's gripes and woes, then come back and tell me what he said. That's all. Tell him we're keen to get this sorted out, but don't make any promises. You can do that, can't you?"

He opened one of the envelopes, tipped it over, and his old maroon EU passport fell into his hand like a relic from a mythical civilisation. "I can't promise it'll help."

"It doesn't have to help," she told him. "So long as we're talking, that's a start."

In his passport photograph, he looked untidier than he remembered, hair uncombed, eyes a bit wild. Not a great advertisement for a British civil servant on a diplomatic mission. He put the passport down in front of him and sighed.

That was all the answer Martine needed. Suddenly she was all movement, gathering her files and folders together and standing up. "You'd better make a move," she said. "It takes ages to go through Security these days. At least nobody's on strike right now. Don't forget this." She gave him the overnight bag. "Stay away from the Embassy except in emergencies, and don't go near Amsterdam Office; as far as the Dutch are concerned they're toxic right now."

He picked up the envelopes and put them in the bag. "Right," he said.

She looked him up and down and beamed. "That's the way," she said. "Couple of days away, do you the world of good. Text me if the meeting's on; otherwise I'll wait till you're back for your report."

"Right," he said again.

She held the folders to her chest. "And after you get back we'll see about signing you off for another couple of months, give you a chance to have a nice rest, and we'll take things from there." She gave him a last long look and then started to move towards the door. "So, I have to be somewhere else. James'll be in shortly with a couple of forms for you to sign, then he'll take you down to Reception. We can find our way to Gatwick okay, can't we?" She smiled. "Course we can. See you tomorrow." And then she was gone, no handshake, not even a thank you, leaving him sitting there feeling as if he had accidentally fallen into a spin-dryer.

He might have had a breakdown, but he wasn't stupid. Heading through Surrey on an almost-empty Gatwick Express, he opened the overnight bag and took out a rather sombre grey suit in its own garment bag, a white shirt, two pairs of underpants, two pairs of socks, a plain blue tie, and a pair of black shoes. He checked the inside of the bag and its side-compartments, but there was nothing else there.

He put everything back in the bag and started to transfer the contents of the envelopes around his coat pockets. There was a credit card issued by a small private bank, the details of his flights, a sheet of paper with the name and address of the hotel they'd booked him into, along with the booking code. It all seemed perfectly blameless, but he felt the edges of a superstitious dread. He took out his phone and dialled Jo's number.

"Hi," she said when she answered. "Michael."

"I just wanted to let you know I'm going away," he said.

"Going away?" She sounded flustered.

"Work asked me to do something for them. Can they do that?"

"Well, they can *ask*. You're still officially signed-off. Did they bully you into it?"

"Not exactly, no. Kind of."

He heard her sigh. "Where are you going?"

"I can't tell you that. If everything goes well I should be back tomorrow evening, but it might be a few days. I didn't want you coming to the house and finding me gone."

There was some background noise that sounded like traffic, then she said, "Okay. How do you feel about it?"

Well, that was the question, wasn't it. He looked out of the window; the train was rattling through a little station out in the countryside, but it was going too fast to focus on the signs. "I'm not sure," he said.

"You're within your rights to say no, you know," she told him. "They can't make you do anything."

"It'll be all right," he told her. "It's nothing difficult."

"If it's nothing difficult they could send someone else."

"It turns out I have a certain set of skills."

More traffic noise, then the beep-beeping of a pedestrian crossing. "Well, thanks for letting me know," she said. "Have a good trip. If you need to talk, you can call any time. Otherwise, I'll talk to you when you get back. And take care."

He leaned out a little to look up the aisle, but from where he was sitting the carriage seemed to be deserted. "Will do. You too."

In the end, the journey was less of a challenge than he might have expected, considering that a few weeks ago he had been unable to cope with something as simple as buying a newspaper. He'd never exactly been an International Business Traveller, but he supposed he had travelled enough, down the years, to develop a set of reflexes, and he found that they took over if he relaxed enough.

So he made it through the crowds to the transit system for the North Terminal, and he navigated the passport gates and security without having a meltdown. He bought himself some toiletries and a couple of newspapers, and sat and had a coffee and a sandwich at one of the catering franchises while he watched the rest of the passengers. By the time he'd done all that, his flight was being called, and not long after that he was buckling himself into his seat.

And there he sat, looking out of the window at the terminal buildings and airport vehicles, suddenly conscious that finally there was no turning back. He could have turned round at any point and got a train home. Now, the doors were closed and he was locked into a metal tube with several hundred other people, and short of causing a major scene there was no way out. As the engines wound up and the aircraft started to move away from the terminal, he found himself gripping the armrests and bracing himself to wake up suddenly in a cell with no memory of how he'd got there.

Somewhat to his amazement, it didn't happen. Maybe he was stronger and in better shape than he'd thought. Watching the Sussex countryside drop away below the plane, he actually found himself rather enjoying it.

It helped that the journey wasn't a long one. It took longer to get from Finchley to Gatwick than it did to get from Gatwick to Schiphol. The cabin crew barely had enough time to serve drinks and sandwiches before the afternoon flight was banking over the enormous Tata Steel complex on the Dutch coast and lining up for final approach. Sitting near the back of the plane, Michael reset his watch to European time and reflected that six hours ago he had been sitting in his kitchen eating a slice of toast and trying to persuade himself not to go in to the office.

He always forgot how huge Schiphol was. It was a seemingly endless trek along corridors and up stairs and down escalators just to reach passport control, where he was met by a sea of bodies untidily herded into queues by moveable barriers. Half the electronic gates were taped off, apparently out of order, and the ones that were working had been allocated to EU passport holders, so Michael found himself in a queue with third-country passengers, of which there were many, shuffling towards a line of desks, only two of which were manned. The couple in front of him – New Zealanders, judging by the little flags stitched to their rucksacks – were wearing sunglasses and baseball caps, and the young Marechausee officer at the passport desk had to tell each of them to take these off before she could process them.

When his turn came, Michael stepped up to the desk and handed over his passport. The officer scanned it, typed on her keyboard, looked at him, looked at her screen again. "One moment," she told him. She leaned back in her chair and caught the eye of an older officer who was standing a little way along the line of desks. He came over and they had a brief, quiet conversation. She showed him the passport and pointed at the screen. Then they both looked at Michael.

"Purpose of visit?" the older officer asked.

"I'm here for a business meeting," Michael told him, which was true. "At De Nederlandsche Bank." Which was, strictly speaking, untrue.

"And how long will you be staying?"

"It depends on the meeting," Michael said. "It could be several days, but if all goes well I'll be leaving tomorrow."

The officer looked at his passport one last time, then handed it back to the younger officer. "Well," he said, "let's hope all goes well. Have a pleasant stay." And with a nod he went back to take up his place behind the desks.

The younger officer stamped his passport and held it out. "Thank you," she said.

"Thank *you*," Michael said, taking it and tucking it into his pocket. "Have a nice day."

There was another walk, and then – it was always a bit of a surprise – a pair of automatic doors disgorged him at one end of a modern, brightly lit shopping mall. At other airports, you came out of Arrivals and you were still recognisably in an airport, but here it was as if you'd stepped through a magic portal and there was a little branch of Albert Heijn right in front of you.

He walked along the mall to the railway station concourse, bought a three-day GVB travel ticket, checked the departure boards, then went downstairs and got on a train. The relatively new Noord-Zuid Line on the Metro would have got him to his destination perfectly well, but he preferred to take the route he'd always used since first visiting the city, so he left the train at Amsterdam-RAI and caught a tram, settling back in his seat to watch the brick buildings and shops and traffic and cyclists pass by outside.

It wasn't a long journey, but it was starting to get dark as he got off the tram at Frederiksplein, and by now the whole day was beginning to sit down on him. Feeling tired and heavy, he walked across to

Weteringschans and stood for a few moments at the junction looking across at the tower of the Dutch national bank, all lit up in the early evening. This was the part of Amsterdam that he was most familiar with, and seeing it again somehow made the tension drain from his shoulders in a way that returning home from the hospital had not. He thought that this whole day had been something of an achievement for him. *"Little victories,"* Bob had told him. *"We have to learn to count our little victories."* So he would count this one. Maybe there would be more tomorrow.

The hotel occupied two of the tall, narrow townhouses that lined Weteringschans, and while the layout was still familiar it had experienced a refurb at some point in the past couple of years and it seemed brand new. He'd been booked into one of the cheaper rooms on the street side of the building, rather than at the back overlooking the canal, but he found he didn't mind that so much. The room was clean and comfortable, and he wasn't a tourist.

He hung the suit up in the wardrobe in the hope that the wrinkles would relax out. He put the shirt and tie and underwear into a drawer of the little dresser against one wall, and took his purchases from Gatwick into the granite-lined ensuite shower room and arranged them by the sink, all the little 100ml tubes of soap and shaving gel and deodorant and toothpaste that were deemed safe for air travel. *"If people knew how much damage you can do with a couple of hundred mils of the right chemicals, they'd never fly again, sir,"* his firearms instructor had scoffed, apropos of nothing, that day at Aldershot.

He went back into the bedroom and switched the television on, and after a bit of experimentation he managed to find the BBC news, where the Chancellor of the Exchequer was making the latest in a series of what were carefully not referred to as emergency statements to the House of Commons. Michael thought the man was starting to look a bit ragged, but it was hard to work up any sympathy. He put his meds on the bedside table, one bottle for the red pills, one for the blue, alongside a little bottle of water from the minibar. He opened a little packet of chocolate biscuits from the tray beside the kettle and sat nibbling one while he read the room service menu.

The phone by the bed rang. He sat looking at it for a few moments, and when he answered it a man's voice said, "Mister Brookes?"

"Yes," Michael said.

The voice told him an address and a time, and Michael had to get him to say it again so he could write it down. Then the voice hung up.

He sat down on the end of the bed again, looking at the piece of hotel notepaper he'd scribbled the instructions on. How did one pass a message when someone wasn't talking to you? Well, not talking did not imply not *listening*. The office had told the Dutch he was coming and where he would be staying, and his passport had set off some kind of flag at the airport, so they knew he was in the country. All they had to do was give him a couple of hours to get through Immigration and arrive at the hotel and then phone up. It was hardly a magic trick.

He texted Martine to tell her a meeting had been set up. He didn't give details, but he signed off with *see you tomorrow*. There was no reply. He put the phone down on the duvet beside him and went back to watching the news.

About five minutes later, the room's phone rang again. This time when he answered a different male voice said, "Remember that bar?"

"Yes," he said. "I remember." The caller hung up. Michael looked at the television and sighed. He'd been planning to have room service send up a club sandwich and then have a shower and turn in early.

As clandestine meets went, it was hardly a classic of tradecraft. Café Kale was only a minute down the street from the hotel, and even if the Dutch had him under surveillance, why should they care? It was also a favourite watering hole for senior staff from the bank, and this early in the evening there was a better than even chance that there would be someone there he knew.

He pushed open the door and stood for a moment letting his eyes adjust to the low lighting. The little bar was busy, but the only person he recognised was a tall fair-haired young man sitting over in a corner with a glass of Amstel and a little plate of chicken satay in front of him. Michael went over and sat down opposite him.

"Do you want a drink?" Seb asked. "Something to eat?"

Michael reached out and took one of the chicken skewers from the plate. "I've been told to stay away from you," he said. "*Toxic* was the word used." He bit one of the pieces of chicken off the skewer.

"Have a beer," Seb told him as one of the bar staff came over.

"Maybe a coffee," Michael told the waitress. "An Americano?"

"And another one of these," Seb said, indicating his glass. He watched her go back to the bar, then he said, "What are you doing here talking to me, if you've been told not to?"

"I thought it might be useful to find out what the fuck's going on."

"It's been a little *lonely* here lately, Michael, that's what the fuck's going on. Nobody wants to talk to us, nobody wants to know us. Have you come to shut us down?"

"I don't have that authority. I've just been sent to talk to van Hoebeek's people and find out what their problem is."

Seb sat back in his chair and looked at him, and Michael suddenly realised how tired he looked; as if he hadn't slept in days. "We've been cut off," he said. "Ordered to close the office and go home and wait. Nobody's telling us anything. We're already looking for new jobs."

Seb had joined the office straight out of the economics department of Utrecht University, and he wouldn't have any trouble finding work in the private sector, unless London put obstacles in his way, which wasn't beyond the realms of possibility. Michael said, "What happened, Seb?"

"We don't *know*, Michael," Seb told him in a quiet voice, leaning forward a little. "We don't *know*. We sat down in the office and had a post-mortem and we did *nothing wrong*."

The waitress returned and put a cup of coffee, a bowl of sugar cubes, a little jug of milk, and a glass of water, in front of Michael, and another Amstel in front of Seb. When she'd gone again, Michael said, "What happened?"

Seb drained his original glass, set it to one side. "We don't know when it started," he said. "We don't live in their pockets. The last time we had a contact with them was a fortnight ago, and everything was fine then. Last week was the scheduled monthly meeting, and they didn't turn up. We stooged around for a bit, then we tried calling them, but they weren't answering their phones. So I went over to Theo's bank and they wouldn't let me past the front desk. The receptionist said nobody was available to see me." He took a skewer from the plate, but didn't take a bite. "We thought there must be some kind of flap on, something above our clearance, it wouldn't be the first time. We rang around and World War Three wasn't happening, but we decided to drop it for then." He looked at the skewer as if suddenly realising it was there. He put it back on the plate and took a big drink of beer. "We tried again the next day, and it was the same thing. Nobody taking our calls, nobody available in person."

"When did you tell London?" Michael asked, dropping a sugar cube into his coffee and stirring it.

Seb picked up the skewer again and started to tap the sharp end on the edge of the plate. "Not for another two days," he said. "Don't look at me like that, Michael, we were trying to find a way to fix it."

"I'm not judging you," Michael said, although whatever this situation was, it had been going on for much longer than Martine had told him. "What did you do next?"

"I told you, we sat down and tried to figure out what we might have done to make them cut us out, and we didn't come up with anything. We've always been on good terms; we had a couple of bumpy moments after Brexit, but we got over that and they've never held it against us."

Michael tried his coffee, dropped another cube of sugar into the cup. "But you do have a suspicion, don't you," he said.

Still rattling the end of the skewer against the edge of his plate, Seb looked out across the bar. "There's a guy on their team," he said. "I've known him for years. I went to his home and put a note through his door and he came round to my flat and put a note through *my* door, that's how mad things have become. He said he'd meet me, but here's the thing, he wouldn't meet me in Amsterdam. I had to go to Den Bosch, which is an hour on the train." He shook his head. "It was like something out of a bad spy novel. I had to go to such-and-such restaurant at so-and-so time and sit at a table at the back and wait, so I went down there yesterday, and I waited and I waited and I almost gave up and came home, but after an hour or so he turned up. No apologies, no excuses. He didn't even shake hands, just sat down in front of me and told me not to get in touch with him again." Abruptly, he pulled a piece of chicken off the skewer and put it in his mouth.

"So why was he there?"

Seb took another mouthful of beer. "Maybe for some people friendship still matters. I don't know." He dropped the skewer on the plate as if faintly disgusted by it. "They have a new special adviser, a Danish guy called *Claes*. Claes is a specialist in conflict economics. My friend says things started to change after he arrived. Claes this, Claes that. Claes is a monster."

"He said this Claes was responsible for them cutting off contact with us?"

"Not in so many words. But listen, I'd already heard of this guy. He's properly crazy. He published a paper for the University of Roskilde about wartime economies. How to prop them up, how to knock them over. Danish Intelligence made it disappear almost as soon as it came out, but I've seen an abstract, and it's scary stuff. It's basically a new handbook for economic warfare."

Michael thought about this. It was the first he'd heard of it. "Do we know about this?"

"I sent a report, must have been this time last year. I never got a response, but that's situation normal."

Michael drank some coffee. "So how did he turn up here?"

Seb shook his head. "Don't know. He's the sort of guy you lock up in a think-tank and let him come up with wild and crazy ways of destabilising nations; you don't let him just wander around Europe looking for work."

"Have you told London about this?"

"I'm telling them now."

Michael sat back. "It seems a bit of a stretch," he said.

Seb shook his head. "We're not spies, Michael. We're *accountants*. We spend all day looking at spreadsheets. This guy I met with yesterday, I knew him at university, and he was *terrified* just being in the same room as me, I could see it in his body language. Whatever stinky word this Claes has been whispering in the old man's ear, it's put the fear of God into everybody."

Michael dipped another piece of chicken in the little bowl of peanut sauce and ate it. "I was rather hoping you'd tell me someone had insulted Theo's wife or run over his cat or something."

Seb stared at him. "Can you fix this?"

"It's not my job to fix it," Michael said. "I'm just here to listen to what they have to say and report back."

"Are they going to see you?"

He nodded. "Tomorrow morning. I'll be back in London by the evening."

"At least they're talking to you." Seb lifted a finger and stabbed it down on the tabletop. "But we did *nothing* wrong," he said, a little too loudly for Michael's taste. "Tell London that we did nothing wrong and they're treating us like *total* criminals."

"They're just trying to cover their backs," Michael said. "You know what they're like."

"You've done enough business here to know the Dutch," Seb told him. "We're pretty relaxed about stuff, but we're professional. We can be stubborn but we'll always be straight with you. Whatever's going on here, it's just not... *Dutch*."

Seb had a very idealistic view of the world, if he thought that. In Michael's experience, people did whatever it took to survive, regardless of national stereotypes. The English liked to think of themselves as a compassionate, commonsense sort of people, animated by the Blitz Spirit, but they would lose their shit entirely if someone holding an Extinction Rebellion banner sat down in front of their car.

He said, "I think the best thing you can do is keep your heads down until this is sorted out. Try not to make any waves, because you'll only wind up making things worse."

Seb snorted. "Sit down and shut up."

"If that's what it takes. Whatever this is, London don't want it to escalate. They'd prefer it to be sorted out without attracting too much attention."

"Are you going to tell them you've spoken to me?"

Michael sat back. "Oh, I don't know, Seb. They told me not to. If anyone asks I'll have to put my hands up to it, but for now let's let them think I had an early night."

Seb considered that. "Okay," he said. He drained his glass and took his coat from the seat beside him. "But if it does come up, tell them we did nothing wrong, yes?"

Michael watched him stand. "All right."

Seb struggled a little putting his coat on, and Michael wondered how many drinks he'd had while he was waiting here. "Nothing wrong," he said again, more quietly.

Michael watched him push through the doors and out into the evening. He sat and finished his coffee and ate the rest of the skewers to give Seb time to get clear. When he called the waitress over to settle his bill, he discovered that Seb had left him to pay for the food and beer as well.

Four

The three hundred-year-old bank owned by Theo van Hoebeek's family was in an ancient building down a narrow street not far from Dam Square, but they didn't want to meet there. The address the caller had given the previous evening turned out to be a big anonymous glass-fronted block about ten minutes' walk from Amsterdam Zuid station. Crossing the marble-floored foyer, the place felt cold and empty, as if the building was deserted.

Michael was showered, shaved and suited. He'd slept surprisingly well and he'd even managed a rasher of bacon and some scrambled eggs for breakfast, but he felt weirdly unprotected attending a meeting without a briefcase. His shoes pinched a little, and the brand-new soles lacked just enough grip on the floor of the foyer to make each footstep feel slightly uncertain.

A brisk young woman in a business suit met him at the front desk. She checked his passport, to make sure he was who he claimed to be, and took him up to the fifth floor in the lift. Following her down silent corridors, the sense that the place was unoccupied grew stronger. There was none of the background noise of a busy office building, no sounds of conversation from behind the closed and unmarked doors they passed, no one else about. The whole place smelled of new carpeting.

The fifth floor was a maze of identical corridors that led finally to a pair of big double doors. The young woman knocked gently, and without waiting for an answer opened one of the doors and stepped aside to let Michael through.

The room beyond was large and windowless and well-lit. In the middle was a big circular conference table ringed with comfortable chairs. In front of each place was a notepad, a silver propelling pencil, a glass, and a carafe of water. Sitting in an arc around one side of the table were half a dozen people. Three of them were middle-aged and well-suited and well-fed, and Michael tagged them as government lawyers and tuned them out. One was van Hoebeek's general manager, a tall middle-aged woman named Lieke, with whom Michael had always got on well. Beside her sat a small, unassuming and slightly untidy man in his thirties who was fiddling with his propelling pencil.

And in the centre of the arc, like an ancient king, was Theo van Hoebeek himself, last surviving child of Johann, Resistance hero and legendary rascal. He was almost eighty now, tall and broken-nosed and built like a church door, magnificent in a tweed three-piece suit with a gold watch-chain looping across his stomach, his thick white hair swept back and expensively barbered.

Michael paused in the doorway for a moment, trying to read the room. The lawyers were regarding him like a team of surgeons deciding where to make the first incision. Lieke favoured him with a sad smile. The man beside her glanced at him, nodded hello in an amiable, distracted sort of way, and went back to his examination of the pencil. Theo was looking off into some vast distance. He seemed to have been carved from some very hard wood, like a totem.

"Good morning," Michael said. "Thank you for agreeing to see me."

Lieke pointed at a chair. "Sit down, please."

Michael sat and faced them across the table, feeling his heart rate start to accelerate. There was a silence while they all looked at each other.

Finally, Michael said, "It seems there has been a breakdown of trust."

The lawyers looked at him as if he had somehow said something obscene in Dutch. Lieke smiled thinly at him. The small, unassuming man had begun to disassemble his propelling pencil. Theo just sat there regarding his faraway vista.

Michael took a breath and soldiered on. "We're eager to repair things, but first we need to know what's happened."

Lieke asked, "Are you empowered to make any commitments?"

"No. I'm just here to find out what's gone wrong." He tried a joke. "I imagine it'll be up to smarter people than me to work out what to do." Nobody smiled. Theo gave no sign that he was even aware of anyone else in the room.

Lieke glanced at the others on her side of the table and nodded fractionally. One of the lawyers reached down into a briefcase by the side of his chair and came up with an A4 sheet of paper, which he skimmed across the table towards Michael.

It was a photocopy of part of a newspaper article, from the *Guardian*, judging by the typeface and layout. Just a couple of column inches about an economic forecast for Germany's arable farming industry. Michael read it, read it again, looked up and raised his eyebrows.

"Some time ago," Lieke said, "we embarked on an exercise to test our security and that of our partners. We added some doctored figures to the data we shared. It's all harmless material, and the figures were only slightly changed." She nodded at the photocopy. "Those figures are from data we shared with your colleagues here in the Netherlands."

Michael looked down at the article again. The figures seemed perfectly blameless, barely even relevant to anything. "I have to ask," he said carefully, "are you sure?"

"We altered the data differently for each partner we shared it with. The information in that article came from you. Someone in your organisation is leaking to the media, and if they're leaking to the media they could be leaking to anyone else."

Michael looked at them. The lawyers were giving him the hard stare. Theo still seemed to be away with the fairies. The little man had arranged the pieces of his propelling pencil on his notepad. There seemed to be far more pieces than necessary for such a simple device.

"When did you carry out this exercise?" Michael asked.

"Three months ago."

All of a sudden, Michael saw why they had agreed to meet with him. He'd been in hospital during their 'exercise'; he'd never been near the altered data. "This didn't necessarily come from us," he said. "Our material gets sanitised and circulated fairly widely. Treasury and the Foreign and Commonwealth Office, to name but two."

"It's still a breach of trust," the little man said without looking at him. His English was almost accentless.

"You could have said something."

"To whom? Who can we trust?"

"As Claes says," Lieke told him. "It seemed less dangerous to simply break off contact."

So that was Claes. Claes the economy-destroyer. He had begun to put his pencil back together. "If you don't mind me saying," Michael said, "this could have been handled... better." Claes glanced up at him, smiled, and went back to his pencil. "If this is true, all you've done is tipped off the person responsible for the leak that you're on to them."

"We want to see your distribution list," Lieke said.

Michael sat back in surprise. "Well," he said, "I'll pass on your request, obviously. But I can tell you right now the answer will be 'no chance'. How would you feel if we asked to see *your* distribution lists?"

"We can't be sure you'd give us the real lists anyway," Claes mused. He screwed the end onto his pencil, clicked it until the lead emerged, and drew a line on the pad in front of him. "No offence."

"This is a serious situation," Lieke said. "If we can't trust you, we won't cooperate."

"If we don't sort this out between ourselves, our respective parent Services are going to step in and start slapping people," Michael pointed out. "Then our respective governments will get involved and that's just going to make everyone unhappy."

"We're *already* unhappy," said Claes, drawing more lines on his pad.

"I'm sorry, who are you?"

Claes looked up from his doodles and narrowed his eyes. "Who are *you?*"

"Gentlemen," Lieke said, stepping in smoothly. "Everyone has been behaving like an adult so far, which is refreshing, to be honest. Let's not spoil it." She looked at Michael. "It's understood that you have no authority. You're a messenger."

"Yes," said Michael.

"So I think we're done here. When are you due to return to London?"

"I'm booked on the late afternoon flight."

Lieke nodded. "Go back and tell your superiors what we've told you. After that, it's up to them. We will not cooperate until the matter is resolved. You've behaved in an exemplary manner. Thank you."

Nobody moved, but it seemed he had been dismissed. He picked up the photocopy. "May I take this?"

"By all means. We have plenty of copies."

He folded it up and tucked it into the inside pocket of his jacket. Still, nobody had moved. The lawyers were whispering among themselves, Claes had gone back to doodling on his pad, Theo had still not acknowledged that there was anyone else here.

He stood up. "Thank you for agreeing to see me," he said again. "I hope this gets sorted out as soon as possible."

"So do we," she told him with a thin smile. "This is at least a start."

He took a last look around the table, trying to work out what was wrong with the picture, then he went back out into the corridor, where the young woman in the business suit was waiting to show him out.

He took the Metro back to the station near the Rijksmuseum, but instead of walking down Weteringschans to the hotel and picking up his luggage, he turned towards Dam Square. He didn't have to be at the airport for three hours, and he felt as if he needed to decompress a bit and process what he'd seen and heard in that room.

It was a bright, breezy afternoon and he walked through the square and just wandered from street to street, faintly amazed that he had survived being yanked out of his home and sent to the other side of the North Sea to do a job he didn't even understand, and now he was walking through crowds of shoppers and tourists and workers in a foreign city. A week ago, he had been sitting in the hospital agonising about whether or not to go home. And the amazing thing was, he felt all right. He'd had a couple of moments in the office in Zuid when he'd felt a slowly building weightlessness, but they'd passed quickly. He had coped. He wondered if Bob would be proud of him.

He gradually turned back towards the hotel, and on an impulse he stopped at a canalside bar. The bar was on the first floor of an old building, with a steep flight of stone steps leading up to the door and another set of wooden steps into the bar itself. Inside, the bar was quiet and almost empty, its wooden floor uneven and a long counter that stretched almost from end to end of the room. Michael ordered a coffee and *bitterballen* and took a table by the window, where he could look down along the canalside at the people passing by.

When the barman had brought his coffee, he texted Martine to let her know the meeting had taken place and that he would be back in London by the evening. He knew he'd have to go straight to Hanway Street to be debriefed, and he imagined he wouldn't leave until around midnight. He wondered whether the office would spring for a car to take him home. He dithered over adding details of the meeting – Claes, for instance – to the text, but decided against it.

A young couple with the look of tourists came into the bar. Almost immediately behind them was an older man, grey-haired and heavyset, in working clothes. They all went up to the counter. The young couple started to read the bar menu; the older man just nodded to the barman, who started to draw him a beer.

Michael sipped his coffee and resumed looking out of the window. Down below, in the middle distance, a stout well-dressed little old lady was making her way along the street beside the canal, towing behind her on a lead a white West Highland terrier. Michael opened his phone's contact book and thumbed Jo's number.

The phone rang a couple of times, and when she answered she sounded, if not flustered, then busy. "Michael. How are you?"

"I'm not interrupting anything, am I?"

"No, no." From the ambient noise around her voice, it sounded as if she was in a confined space, a small room or something. "Where are you?"

"I can't say, I'm afraid, but I'm on my way home. I think I just actually had a good day."

"Well, that's a promising sign. No, no, turn left."

"What?"

"Not this left, the next one." He heard a strange distorted sound in the background which might have been someone speaking. "Sorry, Michael, I'm in a car. Yes, this one."

Down in the street, the little old lady had almost drawn level with the bar. Michael saw that two fit-looking young men in casual clothes were following very close behind her. Way too close. He tipped his head to one side.

"I don't care, drive down here," he heard Jo say. "Are you still there, Michael?"

"Yes," he said. "I think there's going to be a –"

One of the young men reached into his jacket and took out a huge pair of scissors. In one smooth movement, he half-bent down and snipped the dog's lead. The other one opened a big denim bag and dropped it over the dog, picked it up, turned on his heel, and started to walk back the way he had come. A moment later, a man on a motor scooter pulled up briefly. With the bag in his arms, the young man hopped onto the pillion and the scooter drove off.

It had all happened too quickly for Michael to make any sense of it. The young man with the scissors had peeled off and vanished into the crowds. The little old lady was plodding along, still unaware that anything had happened.

Michael said, "I think there's just been a –" and then two black SUVs drove up and jerked to a stop outside the bar. All the doors opened, and seemingly dozens of large men jumped out. They were all dressed alike, in jeans and dark blue windcheaters and those sunglasses favoured by cricketers and security contractors.

Sensing movement in the bar, Michael looked round and saw Jo coming towards him looking flushed and out of breath, as if she'd just run up a flight of stairs. He looked dumbly at her, then at his phone, then at her again.

"Michael," she said as she reached him, "you have to go right now."

"What are *you* doing here?" he asked. He thought it was a perfectly reasonable question.

"Get up, Michael," she told him. "Those people down there are coming for you."

The big men in the windcheaters were almost at the bottom of the steps. One of them shoulder-charged a passer-by out of the way.

Jo grabbed his arm and hauled him to his feet. "Dammit, Michael," she said. "Come with me if you want to live."

All of a sudden, everybody seemed to be moving. Jo pulled Michael away from the table and the young tourist couple stepped away from the bar and stood in their way. The older man stepped up behind the tourists, grabbed them by their collars, and jerked them backward, pulling them to the floor. Meanwhile, everyone else in the bar – the barman included – had crowded into the doorway in an attempt to get out.

By this time, Jo had dragged Michael stumbling to the other end of the room, pulled open a door, and thrust him through it onto a small landing at the top of another set of stairs. "Down," Jo said. "Go go go go. There's a door at the bottom, go through that."

As they reached the bottom of the stairs, the bar erupted in crashing and shouting. Michael found the doorhandle and pushed, and stepping out into the street behind the bar, beside a parallel canal. A silver hatchback was parked by the pavement a short distance away, its rear door opened. Jo marched Michael over to it and all but threw him into the back. "Keep your head down," she said and slammed the door.

She trotted around to the passenger side of the car and jumped in. "Go," she said to the driver, a burly man with a ponytail, and the car set off.

Curled up on the back seat, all Michael could do was listen to Jo giving directions. At one point, the car stopped so suddenly that he was tipped onto the floor behind the front seats.

"No," Jo said, "don't stop, don't stop."

"It's fucking traffic lights," the driver said with exaggerated calm. "Do you want us to kill somebody?"

"Just be careful," Jo told him. "Go right here, then left, then right and over the bridge."

"Did they see us?"

"I don't know." She turned in her seat and looked out through the rear window as Michael clambered back onto the seat. "I can't see anyone following. We'll have to change cars anyway." She looked down at Michael. "Are you okay?"

"'Come with me if you want to live'?" he said.

She shrugged. "First thing that came into my head."

"What are you doing here?"

"That," she said, "is a long story." She looked out of the window again. "Hello, by the way. Stay down."

"What's going on? I have to go back to London."

"That's another long story," she told him. "Arno and I just saved you from a world of grief."

"You're welcome," Arno said from the driver's seat.

"Who were those people in the bar?" Jo asked. "The ones who tried to get in our way. Were they your people?"

Michael tried to replay his memory of what had happened in the bar, but none of it made any sense. "I don't know," he said. "Listen, thank you for whatever that was, but just take me to the airport."

"No can do," she told him. "Someone wants to talk to you."

"Who?"

"You'll see."

Michael sat up in the back seat and tried to open the door, but the central locking was on and the handle wouldn't work.

Jo sighed. "Head down, Michael. Please."

"Will this person I'm going to see explain all this?" he asked.

"He'll tell you what's happening," Arno mused. "Whether he'll be able to *explain* it…" He sucked his teeth and shook his head.

"Is this some kind of prank?" Michael asked. "Because if it is, it's not very funny."

"I'm afraid not," said Jo. "It's very real. Just not in a way you're going to believe. Here," she said to Arno. "On the left."

The car slowed abruptly, made a sharp turn, bumped over something, and drove down a steep ramp into a resonant space where the engine was suddenly very loud. The car stopped, reversed, stopped again, and Arno turned off the engine.

"Okay," Jo said, turning to look at Michael again. "Are you going to do anything silly?"

"At some point, we're going to have to have a conversation about which of us is doing something *silly* here," he told her.

She sighed. "All right. Get out."

As Arno released the central locking, Michael sat up. They were in an underground garage. Not a big public one, more like the kind of thing you found under an office building. Most of the spaces were occupied. Jo and Arno got out of the car, but Michael sat where he was.

"Come on, Michael, don't be an arsehole," Jo said, bending down close to the window. "I've had a really frantic couple of days and my patience is running out."

"No," he said.

"I know what you're thinking," she told him. "You're thinking that if you sit there long enough some innocent bystander's going to come along and see us here and they'll rush off and call the police. But nobody else is coming down here for hours. Eventually you're going to need a wee and you'll have to get out anyway."

Michael had his phone out and was trying to call Martine, but there was no signal. "Who *are* you?" he said.

"I'm your fucking *social worker!*" Jo yelled. She closed her eyes momentarily and took a deep breath. "Look," she said more calmly, "come and talk to this person, and we'll try to get you to Schiphol in time for your plane. If we can't do that, we'll put you on another flight. The worst that's going to happen is you might wind up at Stansted or Luton instead of Gatwick."

Michael thought about it. Then he got out of the car. Arno blipped it locked and went off to another part of the garage.

Jo put out her hand. "Phone."

"No."

"Hand it over, Michael. I'll make sure you get it back."

"No."

She told him in a calm but serious voice, "I'm half your age, I'm very fit, I'm faster than you, and I have medals for Taekwondo. Now give me the phone before I get violent."

He held his phone out and she took it, removed the back, took the battery out, and put the pieces in separate pockets. Meanwhile, Arno pulled up at the wheel of another hatchback, this one dark gray. Jo took a folded bundle of cloth from another pocket and offered it. "Get in the car and put this on."

Michael took the bundle. It was a hood. "You're not serious," he said.

"If you don't put it on, I'll duff you up and put you in the boot," she told him.

He glanced towards the entrance ramp of the garage, but it wasn't that close and he didn't doubt that she could run him down before he'd even gone halfway. He got into the back seat of the car and pulled the hood over his head. He heard Jo get into the passenger seat. "Lie down back there," she told him. "And no peeking."

They drove back out onto the street, and then took what felt like a somewhat tortuous route for about twenty minutes. In films, kidnap victims would memorise every bump and turn, every passing sound, and miraculously reconstruct the journey of their abduction. But that was in films. Michael had no idea where he was, or where the garage had been, and within a couple of minutes he had entirely lost track anyway.

Eventually, the car came to a stop, then moved forward again slowly. It bumped over what felt like a kerb, drove forward a few more metres, then stopped again. Arno turned off the engine, and Michael heard Jo getting out and opening the back door.

"All right, Michael," she said. "Leave the bag on and step out slowly. I'll help you."

He shuffled along the seat until he was able to half-turn and put his feet on what felt like stone paving outside. With Jo's help, he got out of the car and stood up, and when he had his balance she guided him forward.

"There's a set of five steps here," she said. She took hold of his hand and put it down on a narrow metal rail. "That's the handrail. Just walk up slowly and everything will be fine."

Step by hesitant step, he walked up, and at the top he felt that he was in a narrow space. Jo kept walking him forward.

"Ten steps ahead there's some stairs. They're steep and there's a lot of them." She put his hand on another banister, this one of polished wood. "Go on up. I'll be right behind you."

He took the stairs slowly, one by one, and it seemed to take a long time to reach the landing at the top. "That's great," Jo said. "Nearly there." She turned him to the left and guided him forward. "Okay. Stop here and don't move." A moment later he heard a door close behind him and a key turn in the lock.

He stood where he was for almost a minute before he swore under his breath and pulled the hood off, to find he was standing, quite alone, in what appeared to be someone's living room.

The room was small and well-appointed, with a sofa and a couple of armchairs and a low table with a vase of flowers. All the light came from a tall standard lamp in one corner because the windows were covered with blackout blinds. Michael went over and examined one of the blinds. Its edges had been glued to the window frame.

He wandered around the room, looking at the pen-and-ink drawings on the walls, most of them bleak landscapes, beaches, winter fields with a solitary windmill breaking the horizon. He tried the door, examined the lock, although he hadn't the first idea how one would go about picking it. There was a small television mounted on one wall, but no sign of a remote control. Its standby light was out, and he couldn't find a manual power switch.

Back at the windows, he ran a finger down the blind. There was a length of dowelling at the bottom, to weight it down and keep the blind straight, and he managed to get his fingertips under one end and pull it away from the frame. This let him get a good grip, and then it was just a matter of pulling back and up and ripping the blind away from the frame. The glue took the paint off the woodwork underneath, but that wasn't his problem.

When he'd freed enough of the blind, he ducked behind it and found himself looking out from the first or second floor onto one of the city's broader canals in bright sunshine. On the far side, tall old buildings leaned against each other, some of them painted in pastel colours, many of them festooned with window boxes full of flowers. A big glass-roofed tourist boat was making its way up the middle of the canal past moored houseboats, and the streets on either side were full of people. It looked like a scene from a tourist board film. There were locks on the window. He stood there, looking out, trying to work out what to do. James Bond would have got the window open and climbed down the outside of the building in a few moments, but he wasn't James Bond. He was an economist in his late fifties and he was still recovering from a breakdown, and he had never climbed down the outside of a building before in his life.

He'd never had any training for a situation like this. One heard of other departments being offered away-days during which they would be introduced to various techniques of tradecraft, streetwork, and strategies to counter abduction and interrogation, but that had always seemed like too much hard work to no purpose. When was he ever likely to need stuff like that? He'd only done the gun course because of the office's vestigial firearms requirement, not because he'd particularly wanted to; it was rare for economists to get into shootouts.

Still, not so long ago the events of the past couple of hours would have put him in the Acute ward. This, of course, didn't help him understand what was going on. Was it something to do with what he'd been told by the Dutch earlier? He reached into his jacket and touched the folded photocopy that was, as far as he could work out, the only evidence that there was a leak in his department. What should he do with it? Hide it somewhere? Eat it? He leaned forward and rested his forehead on the window, trying to look straight down at the street in front of the house. There must be a back way in; if he'd been brought in through the front door half of Amsterdam would have seen him being led out of the car with a bag over his head.

And what the fuck was Jo doing here?

He heard the door being unlocked, two men entered the room. One was short and trim in a good suit; the other was taller, wearing black cargo trousers tucked into high lace-up boots and one of those olive-drab fleeces made fashionable by Ukrainian politicians. The short one was wearing a rubber Boris Johnson mask; the taller wore a Donald Trump mask.

"You see?" said Trump in Dutch, his voice muffled by the mask, gesturing at Michael. "I told you. Now he knows where we are."

"I have no idea where we are," Michael told them.

"I told you we should have put him in a basement somewhere," Trump said.

"Nobody's being put in a basement," Johnson said. "We're not the French." He switched to English and said, "I have to apologise for this situation, Mister Brookes. We just want to ask a few questions."

"You're not the only ones," Michael said angrily.

The two masked men regarded him calmly for a few moments, then Johnson turned to Trump. "Perhaps I should speak with Mister Brookes alone, Anton," he said.

Anton's shoulders slumped when he heard his name. "Why don't you give him my *address* as well?"

"It'll be okay," Johnson assured him. "Lock the door behind you. Mister Brookes is a civilised man." He looked at Michael. "Aren't you?"

"No," said Michael.

Johnson reached out and gave Anton's arm a squeeze. "It's fine," he said.

Anton stared at him a few moments longer, then he glared at Michael and turned and left the room, closing the door behind him. Michael heard the key turn in the lock.

"Right," Johnson said after a pause. He indicated the seating. "Shall we sit down, please?" When Michael didn't move, he said, "I really do just want to talk. You're not going to be harmed. I'm sure you could incapacitate me, but what are you going to do then? The door's locked."

"I could put one of those armchairs through the window," Michael told him. "That might attract some attention."

"Oh, don't do that," Johnson told him, walking over to one of the chairs and sitting down. "We're only borrowing this place. Please, sit."

Michael perched himself on the edge of the sofa. He wasn't planning to launch himself across the space between them, but it didn't hurt to make it look as if he was.

"So," Johnson said. Then he stopped. "I'm sorry, this is ridiculous. Just a moment." With a bit of a struggle, he peeled the mask off. He was in his forties and a little red-faced and sweaty, his brown hair rumpled up, and he had a neat goatee. "Ridiculous," he said again, holding the mask up and looking at it. "Have you got rid of this embarrassing man yet?"

"Not entirely, no."

Johnson shook his head and laid the mask on the floor beside his chair. "Please forgive all this cloak-and-dagger business. We've never done anything quite like this before."

"Kidnapping, you mean?"

"It's a little outside our competencies. We've been improvising. Anton decided we shouldn't let you see our faces, so he went out to a sex shop and bought us a couple of gimp masks. I had to make him take them back and get something less absurd."

"Because a Donald Trump mask is perfectly sensible."

"Quite so." He put his hands up and smoothed down his hair. "My name is Thijs," he said.

"Are you Dutch Intelligence?" Because it was – just – possible that the instruments of the Dutch state might have temporarily lost their minds.

Thijs settled back in the chair and clasped his hands over his stomach. "No, we're very far from being Dutch Intelligence. No. Tell me, Mister Brookes, have you ever heard of a man named Franc Brossard?"

"No." There were so many holes in his memory that this might well have been a lie, but the name didn't ring a bell.

"He likes to style himself 'Franc Le Métro'."

"I've never heard of him. Who is he?"

"He's an academic. As am I." Thijs thought about it. "As are we all, to a greater or lesser extent. Can you think of a reason why Brossard would want you abducted?"

"You still haven't told me why *you* wanted me abducted."

"We've been rationalising it as a *rescue* rather than an abduction. We're not sure that it's entirely safe for you to be out on the streets at the moment; those people who turned up at the bar were there for you."

Michael thought of the seeming army of men that had erupted from the two SUVs. "Why?"

"We don't know, and frankly we'd like to find out why they were pulling a stunt like that on our territory."

Michael shook his head. "I'm sorry… *territory*? Who *are* you?"

Thijs regarded him calmly. "I'm unsure quite how to approach this," he said. "Most of us come to it from a very different direction." He thought for a while. "I represent a small group of academics and researchers here in the Netherlands, and Brossard represents a similar group in France. We have an informal agreement not to trespass on each other's turf without prior consultation, and today the French broke that agreement, and I think I'd rather like to know why."

"I don't *know* why," Michael told him.

"The French tried to snatch you from a bar in the middle of Amsterdam, in broad daylight," Thijs told him. "We've had some difficulty with drugs gangs here in recent years, and I have to tell you, even *they* wouldn't do something like that, even the *really* crazy ones, because they're too smart."

"They didn't do it very well," Michael said. "They didn't cover the rear exit."

"Well, that's the French for you," said Thijs. "Always letting their hearts rule their heads. The point is, by our terms of reference, they were prepared to commit an outrage to get their hands on you." He tipped his head to one side and smiled at Michael.

"Well," Michael said, "this is all very interesting, and I do appreciate your help, but I'd like to go now."

Thijs looked thoughtful. "I am tempted, you know," he said. "If only to see how far you get. My guess is not very far; the French have already destroyed our relationship, they're not just going to give up now."

Michael wasn't so sure about that. All it would take was one call to Martine, if he could get to a phone. He wondered what level of response he would get; the attempted abduction of a government employee by a foreign power should at least merit the deployment of some SAS blokes. A brisk extraction from here, wherever this was, breathless dash in a convoy of armoured Range Rovers to the RNLAF base at Eindhoven, a quick flight in an RAF transport plane. He could be back at Hanway Street by teatime. Or maybe not. That kind of thing only happened in films.

"I don't know how many people they've deployed for this," Thijs went on, "but I would imagine they'll be keeping an eye on ports and airports. Certainly they'll be watching the British Embassy in Den Haag, and the Consulate here. If they suspect we've become involved – and they have to, really, it's a logical assumption – they'll be watching *us* too."

"So they'll be watching this place."

"Maybe not. We've never used this house before, and everything was moving very quickly. We might have slipped through."

They sat and looked at each other for a while. Michael said reasonably, "At the moment, this is just you and me having a nice chat. But if I don't get off the plane at Gatwick this evening, or contact my employers with a good reason why I haven't come back, wheels are going to start turning. Eventually – quite quickly, possibly – this is going to involve our respective governments at some level, and once that starts it'll be impossible to stop."

"It's a good pitch," Thijs agreed. "If a bit apocalyptic." He thought about it. "I said that most of us come to this from a different direction," he said. "And perhaps I should have explained that at the beginning." He leaned forward slightly, looked Michael in the eye, and said, "Mister Brookes, do you believe in miracles?"

Michael felt his eyebrows go up. "I'm sorry, what?"

"Miracles. Do you believe in them?"

"Water into wine? Parting the Red Sea? That kind of thing?"

"More at the water into wine end of the scale. Although lately it's hard to be certain."

Michael was entirely baffled. "No," he said. "Of course not. I'm not remotely religious."

"This has nothing to do with religion." Thijs thought again. "Has anything *extraordinary* ever happened to you? Something so far outside your experience that you might with some justification regard it as a miracle?"

"No, of course not." For all the gaps in his memory, Michael reasoned that he would have remembered a miracle.

Thijs tipped his head to one side. "Why 'of course not'?"

"Because there's no such thing."

Thijs smiled at him.

"And what does it have to do with you kidnapping me?"

"I told you, we prefer to think of it as a rescue. The French are trying to kidnap you."

"The only people who've done any kidnapping today are you," Michael said. "All I saw back at that bar was a lot of people getting out of cars, then I was hustled out of there and somebody put a bag over my head." He stopped. "Where's Jo?"

"Jo's busy right now," Thijs told him. "You can see her later."

"How's she mixed up in all this?"

"It might be better if I let her explain that." Thijs shifted in his chair. "What I need to know is that, for the moment at least, you won't try to cause any trouble."

"I'm not sure I can promise that."

"I'd really prefer not to keep you locked up, you know," Thijs told him. "It sort of defeats the whole object."

"How long is this going to last, then?"

Thijs thought about it. "Well, until I can be sure Brossard's people aren't going to abduct you, at least."

"That makes you no better than them." Michael got up, went over, grabbed the bottom of the blackout blind, tore it entirely away from the window, and dropped it on the floor. Bright afternoon sunlight flooded into the room.

Thijs hadn't moved from his chair. "Did that make us feel better?" he asked.

Michael didn't move from the window. Outside, the real world was going about its business as usual. It might as well have been on the moon.

Thijs came and stood beside him. He looked at the places where paint had come off the windowframe and tutted. "I told you, we're only borrowing this place," he complained. He shook his head. "If we'd let the French have you, you really *would* be in a basement somewhere right now. Probably cable-tied to a chair."

"Let me speak to my employers," Michael said. "They'll be able to protect me from whatever this is far better than you can."

"Yes," Thijs said, "Jo said you worked for the British Government." He clasped his hands behind his back and looked out of the window while he thought about it. "No, I'm sorry. I think I prefer to resolve this amongst ourselves. And besides, we've already caused an international incident; how much worse can things be if we look after you for a few more days?"

"I need to talk to them, at the very least. It's important."

Thijs smiled and shook his head, and they looked at each other, and if this was the moment when Michael might have decided to try and fight his way out of there, it passed.

"So what happens now?" he asked.

Thijs shrugged. "It's possible that the French will just fold their tents and go home now, in which case we can have you back in London after the weekend. I'd like to talk further with you and try to work out what they want. Either way, we'll have to move you; you'll be safer outside the city and we only have this place for a few hours, anyway." He added, "And you might want to consider how the French knew you would be here."

Michael thought he might also want to consider how Thijs and his friends had known he would be here. But there were more pressing things to worry about. He was alone, he was completely cut off from support, he had no resources – not even a phone – and when you came down to it he wasn't a field agent, he was just an economist waiting for his pension to come over the horizon. And, he had to admit, he wanted to know what was going on here. It would perhaps be easier to just wing it and hope that the opportunity to contact Martine would present itself at some point.

"If I'm not back in London on Monday," he said, "I'm going to cause trouble."

Every Day Has Its Dog

Five

They put the hood back on, took him downstairs, and put him in the car. They drove for about fifteen minutes, then the vibration of the tires on the road smoothed out, the sound of the engine echoing off surrounding buildings faded away, and the car accelerated.

After another half an hour or so, the car slowed and made a right-hand turn onto a bumpy road, and then slowed further onto what felt like an unmade track. It came to a stop, and he was helped out and into a building. He heard a door close and then someone pulled off the hood.

"You know," he said, "this is starting to get monotonous."

"Sorry, Professor," said a voice behind him. "Just following orders."

He turned and saw a tall, fair-haired, cheerful-looking young man in jeans and a sweater standing there folding up the hood. "I'm not a professor," he said.

The young man held up his hands. "Hey, no offence. That's just what I was told. I'm Piet."

"Michael," said Michael. He looked around and saw that he had been delivered into the kitchen of what seemed to be an old house. The floor was stone flags, the walls whitewashed plaster. There were cupboards and chests of drawers and a big kitchen table with half a dozen chairs. To one side there was an Aga, and under the window was a deep sink. He walked over and looked out of the window, saw a wire fence, and beyond that green fields that seemed to extend all the way to the horizon. "Where are we?"

"I'm not supposed to say." Piet laid the hood down on one of the worktops. "But you're still in Noord-Holland, obviously."

"Obviously." He turned from the window. "Are you my jailer?"

Piet smiled amiably. "Babysitter is probably closer. I'm just here to make sure you don't get hurt. And before you ask, no, I don't know what's going on."

"You just do what you're told."

Piet's smile broadened. "Thijs said you'd be grumpy, but you don't have to be. Think of this as a weekend break. Some people pay good money for that." He walked over to the Aga and set a kettle on the hotplate. "Do you want tea? English people like tea, yeah?"

Michael checked his watch. He had about an hour to get to the airport for his flight. Could he still manage that? Say he managed to overpower Piet and escape from the house, what was he going to do then? He'd heard the car drive off, so he had to find his way on foot to a main road, flag down a vehicle, get a lift back into Amsterdam, and then make his way out to Schiphol. It seemed unlikely. He pulled out one of the chairs and sat at the table. "Tea would be lovely, thank you."

"Excellent." Piet opened one of the cupboards and took out two mugs. "There are some things I've been told not to talk to you about, I should warn you."

"Does that include the French?"

Piet glanced over his shoulder. "The French?"

"They tried to kidnap me a couple of hours ago, apparently."

Piet's eyes widened. "Franc Le Métro's people? Wow. Those guys are pretty crazy, but I didn't think they were *that* crazy."

"Thijs said you have some kind of agreement with them."

Piet turned from the range and looked at him with his hands in his pockets. "This maybe sounds like some of the stuff I'm not supposed to talk about. I know Thijs wants to explain it all properly." He shrugged. "But, yeah, we do have a sort of informal agreement to respect each other's turf. Kidnapping?" He shook his head. "That's way out of line."

"So what will you do?"

Piet looked thoughtful. "Complain, I guess. Withdraw cooperation. Doesn't sound like much, does it."

Michael shook his head. "Suppose they come here for me?"

Piet smiled. "They have to find you first. The Netherlands isn't a big country, but it's still a lot of space to search."

"They seemed to know where to find me earlier."

"Ah, now," Piet said, turning back to the range, "that's something I don't know anything about, so I can't help you." He opened a metal caddy from the worktop and popped a teabag into each of the mugs. "I'm more of a coffee drinker and I don't take milk, so I don't have any right now, but I've got lemon."

"Lemon's fine," Michael said. "May I use your lavatory?"

Piet gestured towards the kitchen door. "There's a loo in the hall. Second door on the right."

Michael got up and went out into the hall. It was wood-floored and the walls were panelled. He tried the first door on the right and found himself looking into a cupboard containing a hoover and shelves of cleaning products. He ignored the second door and carried on down the hall. He paused at the front door and peered out through the pebbled glass panel at the top, but the outside world was just a green and grey blur. Very slowly and quietly, he turned the handle, but the door was locked, and he moved on. At the far end of the hall, he gently pushed open a door and stood looking at a neat, old-fashioned sort of living room or parlour. There were windows at each end, but all he could see was more fields. He could not, from a quick glance round the room, see a phone.

He went back into the hall. The toilet was tiny and cramped, with a washbasin the size of a handkerchief and one of those continental lavatories with a landing stage. He used the facilities and went back into the kitchen, where Piet was just putting a mug of tea on the table.

"I was going to give you the tour later," he said.

"Just curious," Michael said. He sat at the table and picked up his mug. It had the words *europe's my cup of tea* on the side. He put a couple of lumps of sugar into it from a bowl on the table, and stirred it. "How long have you lived here?"

Piet brought his own mug over to the table and sat down. "All my life, apart from university," he said. "And my parents before that, and my dad's parents before *that*. And so on."

"How do you know Thijs?"

Piet sipped his tea. "Maybe Thijs should tell you that, if he thinks it's something you should know."

"But you're one of these... academics he told me about?"

"Academics?" Piet shrugged. "Sure."

Michael looked around the kitchen. "How long am I going to be here?"

"That would be up to Thijs," Piet said genially. "Hey, you're not vegetarian, are you?"

Michael shook his head.

"Excellent! I've got a couple of really nice steaks in the fridge. We can have them for dinner."

"Excellent." Michael took a sip of his tea. "Do you believe in miracles?"

"Miracles?" Piet beamed. "Sure."

The steaks were, as advertised, excellent. Piet fried some potatoes and made a huge bowl of salad to go with them, and they ate in the kitchen. They were just finishing when they heard the sound of a car pulling up outside. They looked at each other for a few moments, then Piet got up and went out into the hall.

Michael heard the front door open and close, and the sound of a quiet conversation, then Thijs came into the kitchen. He had a serious look on his face and a bulging overnight bag in his hand. "How are you?" he asked from the doorway.

"I missed my flight," Michael said, pushing his plate away. "So you're now in a *lot* of trouble."

"Hm," Thijs said. "Can I have a word, please?" He went back into the hall.

Michael got up and followed him into the parlour. Thijs closed the door behind them and they sat in armchairs facing each other. Michael saw Piet go past the front window, smoking a cigarette and chatting to Arno.

"I'm afraid I'm the bearer of bad news," Thijs said.

"Good," Michael said deadpan. "Because I was just sitting here wondering how much worse this could get."

Thijs gave him an awkward look. "Quite," he said. "Relations between ourselves and the French seem to have completely broken down. We reached out to them and asked them to leave, and they refused. They've apparently hired a ridiculous number of security contractors."

"The people at the bar."

"Just so. Former Foreign Legion, SAS, whatever. Very serious people. This is completely outside our experience, and we have no idea how to respond."

"You could hire your own contractors," Michael mused.

Thijs stared at him. "This isn't funny."

"And here I was laughing my socks off." He sighed. "Surely your police will take care of this? Someone will have reported what happened at the bar, they'll at least want to investigate."

"And that's another thing," Thijs noted. "We normally prefer to remain below the radar; we'd really rather not attract the attention of the authorities."

"That decision seems to have been taken out of your hands," Michael pointed out. "So what are you going to do now?"

Thijs spread his hands. "I don't know. I genuinely don't. Nothing like this has ever happened to us before. Some of our more excitable people want to go to Paris and cause an outrage there, in revenge."

"Put me in a car," Michael said reasonably, "and take me to The Hague and drop me off outside the British Embassy. Then all your troubles will go away."

Thijs shook his head. "The repercussions of this will last for years. Decades, maybe. I want to know why the French seem to have entirely lost their minds."

"I don't *know*, Thijs. How many more times? All I want to do is go home. I've been in hospital for the past five months, I only got out on Monday."

Thijs looked at him for a while. "What if I told you that miracles exist?"

"I'd say you were crazy."

Thijs put a hand into a pocket of his jacket and brought out an old tennis ball, grey and scruffy, all its fluff worn off. "Not Biblical miracles, not raising people from the dead or feeding five thousand with a couple of fish and a loaf. Small things, things which mostly seem to have no purpose whatsoever but nevertheless are impossible according to our current understanding of the universe."

"I'd say you were even crazier."

Thijs looked at the ball, weighing it in his palm. "It happened to Franc Brossard," he said. "Twelve years ago he was a teacher at a *lycée* in Paris, and one evening he was travelling home on the Métro and he saw something *impossible*, something which should not exist." He tossed the ball in the air and caught it again. "We don't know what it was because he's never described it, which is something of a breach of etiquette among our community but it's hardly the worst thing he's ever done. Catch." He pitched the ball casually at the floor and bounced it in Michael's direction. Michael jerked back in surprise and caught the ball without thinking, and everything changed, all at once.

One moment he was sitting in Piet's parlour. The next, he was sitting in a huge chilly space full of thick fog, as if the room had suddenly become impossibly large. There was the smell of a bonfire in the air, and a woman's voice calling from a distance. The woman laughed, and Michael heard a dog barking. There was a small, dim disc of light, low down and to his left, and as he looked at it he suddenly realised it was the sun, close to the horizon and shining weakly through the fog. He was actually *outside*, but he was still sitting in the armchair and he could see the carpet under his feet. He felt an enormous sense of *longing*. Then he let the ball tumble from his fingers and the room blinked back to normal and he was left sitting there in shock.

The ball rolled across the floor and stopped by Thijs's chair. "So what would you say now if I told you miracles were real?" Thijs asked.

Michael stared at him wide-eyed.

"We have no idea what this is," Thijs told him. "Is it a memory? Is it a recording? Is it *still happening*, somewhere? We don't know." He leaned down and picked up the ball. "We've never been able to identify the language the woman's speaking. Although we're about eighty percent sure the dog's a golden retriever."

"Do it again," Michael said without thinking.

Thijs smiled and shook his head. "It's incredibly powerful, isn't it? That feeling of wanting to be there forever? It can be quite addictive, if you let it." He looked at the ball one last time and put it back in his pocket and looked seriously at Michael. "The ball isn't the miracle; it's an innocent bystander, a side-effect. The miracle is what *made* it this way. Very few people have ever seen that, not directly, but Franc Brossard did, that night in Paris, and he's become dangerously obsessed."

Michael found he was still trembling. He supposed a very good theatrical technician could have rigged the room with special effects, but how could that account for the almost physical ache he felt now it was over? Could he have been drugged somehow?

"Are you okay?" Thijs asked. "It's a lot to take in."

A lot later, it occurred to Michael that they didn't give him time to process what had happened. Thijs took him out to the car. Piet was waiting in the hall with the hood, but Thijs just shook his head. "We're not going far," he said. He glanced at Michael. "And I don't think we need to worry about him seeing where he is any more."

Outside, Michael stood beside the car while Thijs put the holdall in the boot. The day had clouded over, and a breeze was blowing across the fields, and the house really was in the middle of nowhere. He couldn't see another building anywhere. He smelled damp earth and vegetation, and water somewhere nearby. Really, though, he was still *there*, in that foggy autumn moment, that vast outdoors in Piet's parlour with the sun shining from an impossible distance. He looked at the house, and it was just a ordinary brick-built house with a couple of big sheds at the back, no sense at all that for a few moments it had enclosed a... He shook his head.

Pulling out onto the road, Michael saw that the house sat on a broad strip of land between two canals. The whole landscape was like that, long fields divided by a gridwork of waterways over which the road crossed on little bridges. They stayed off the main road, driving for about twenty minutes further into the flat, almost featureless countryside. Michael saw other farms, widely spaced and isolated, and once a commuter train on a low embankment heading in the direction of Amsterdam, its windows lit up in the deepening twilight.

Eventually, they turned off onto a bumpy track and pulled up outside another farmhouse with a couple of quadbikes parked outside. It was a lot cooler now, and Michael felt a faint spit of drizzle against his face as he got out of the car. It seemed absurd that it was still the same day; he felt as if he had travelled a very long way since leaving for his meeting in Amsterdam-Zuid that morning.

The house was newer than Piet's, and it felt snug and warm. Thijs had brought the holdall in from the car. "I got you a change of clothes," he said, putting it down in the hallway. "And some toiletries. I had to guess the sizes, I'm afraid."

Michael looked at the bag and wondered if he would ever see his own clothes again. "Thank you," he said.

A door opened along the hall and Jo stepped out looking slightly bashful. "Hi," she said.

"Hello," said Michael.

"I'm going to leave Mister Brookes with you for now," Thijs told her. "I have a lot of phone calls to make."

"How does it look?" she asked.

"It looks like a mess," he said gravely. "I'm trying to call a conference."

"Here?"

He shrugged. "Anywhere. It's still early days." He turned to Michael. "You'll be okay here," he said. "Get some sleep and we'll try to make sense of all this tomorrow."

"You don't sound very confident that that's possible," Michael said.

Thijs smiled ruefully. "Well, let's try, anyway." He nodded to them and went back out to the car.

"Poor sod," Jo said when he was gone. "He doesn't need all this bullshit. His kid's in hospital, too." She looked at him. "Come on into the kitchen. Have you had something to eat?"

Picking up the holdall, he followed her down the hall. "Yes, thanks. Piet cooked. Steak and potatoes."

"How are you feeling?"

That was a good question. How *did* he feel? Like a paper boat being carried along on a flood. "I've got to talk to London. It's very important."

"We can't let you do that. Not until we have an idea what this is all about. You've suddenly become of interest to some of the weirdest people on the planet and we have to know why, because that's important too."

The kitchen was modern, all marble worktops and stainless steel surfaces and mysterious black appliances and a wooden central island with a tiled top and four tall stools set around it. "I mean national security important," he said, putting down the bag.

"Me too, sort of," she told him. "Coffee?"

"Yes," he said. "Please."

Jo went over to one of the worktops and pressed a button on a black cube the size of a shoebox. The front of the cube lit up with rows of numbers, and it started whispering to itself. She opened a cupboard over the worktop and took out two cups. "So, he showed you the tennis ball, yeah?"

"How do you know?"

"I've seen that look before."

"Do I have a look?"

She nodded and set the cups down beside the cube. "I bet he didn't give you any warning, either."

"It was a bit of a surprise, yes."

"He shouldn't have done that. You've been ill; the first time *I* saw it I completely freaked out."

"It's quite something."

"Yes, it is." She turned and leaned back against the worktop and looked at him. "And it's completely useless, like pretty much all of them."

He raised an eyebrow. "There are more things like that?"

"Oh, Christ yes." She shook her head. "What's Thijs told you?"

"Some confused story about miracles."

Jo sighed and waved at the island. "Sit down, Michael, you've had a long day."

He went over and perched himself on one of the stools. The cube stopped whispering and began making a subdued chiming sound. Jo flipped up a door on its side, put one of the cups inside, pressed another button, and the smell of coffee started to fill the kitchen. "Didn't Piet tell you anything?"

"He said Thijs would explain."

Jo swapped the cups over and pressed the button again. "Piet's a lovely bloke, he really is," she said. "But he's not big on initiative." She brought the cups over to the island, collected a sugar bowl and a little milk jug and a couple of spoons, and put them in front of Michael. Then she sat down opposite him and rubbed her eyes. "It's really hard to know where to start."

"We can assume I don't believe in miracles," he said. "If that helps."

She gave a wan smile. She looked, Michael thought, worn out. "Gods, me neither." She shook her head. "Okay, let's ease you into this slowly. Thijs and Piet and I – in fact, everyone you've met since you left that bar – are part of an informal network of people who investigate… weird stuff."

"Weird stuff. Like the tennis ball."

Jo nodded. "Like the tennis ball."

"So you're paranormal researchers."

"No. Not exactly, because this stuff isn't paranormal. It's not *any* kind of normal. There are groups like us everywhere." She thought about it. "I can't think of anywhere in the world where there aren't at least a few of us." She thought again. "Maybe Antarctica, although I wouldn't swear to it."

"All right," he said. "You're everywhere and you investigate weird stuff. With you so far." He spooned sugar into his cup and stirred the coffee.

"That's the easy bit," she said. "It's probably going to take a bit of an effort to get your head round what's next."

"Thijs has a tennis ball that makes you think it's autumn," he said. "How much harder can it be?"

She wrinkled her nose. "You'd better strap yourself in." Then she stopped and looked down the kitchen to the window at the end, where the last light of this very long day was barely illuminating the fields beyond. She stayed silent for so long that he began to wonder whether she'd forgotten he was there. "There are other things like the tennis ball," she said finally. "We don't know how many; we assume not all of them get found. But they're very rare. There are sixteen that we know about. A couple of them do stuff that's useful, but most of them are just pointlessly weird. The Italians have got an old dessert spoon that plays the first few bars of a piece of music if you tap it on a hard surface, which is pretty cool the first time you hear it, but that's all it does. Nobody's ever been able to work out what the music is; I think it sounds a bit like the *Ode to Joy*, but it's not." She looked at him, trying to read his expression, but he didn't say anything. "Anyway," she went on, "the reason they're like that is because they were all nearby when something happened."

"A miracle," Michael said.

Jo scowled. "Yeah, well, some people call it that. The truth is, we don't know what it is, and we've been studying it for *years*. Maybe it's a field of energy, maybe it's a crack in space-time, no one knows. For a long time, people thought it was God. We call it *the Essence*."

Michael raised an eyebrow.

Jo took a swallow of coffee. "Every so often, completely at random, the Essence... interacts with the world somehow, and even more rarely it does something to objects that happen to be there at the time. It's like they become radioactive or something." She saw the look on his face and added, "They're *not* radioactive, obviously, otherwise we wouldn't be carrying them about. They're not *physically* different, in any way that we can measure – the tennis ball's still a tennis ball – but something happens to them. They get superpowers. Mostly really crap superpowers; I mean the tennis ball's *amazing*, right? But it's no practical use at all." She shrugged helplessly. "Anyway, we study this stuff."

They sat looking at each other for a while. Finally, Michael said, "You can't possibly expect me to believe that."

"I said it would be an effort."

"Why have I never heard about this before?"

"Events only happen very, very rarely," she said. "They don't last long, and they're mostly easy to miss. All we see is the artifacts that get left behind, and there are only a handful of *them*."

Michael heard someone moving about upstairs. He looked at the ceiling.

"Dan and Josine," Jo said. "This is their house. They're giving us some space for the moment, but I'll introduce you in a while. They're lovely."

Michael thought about what she'd just told him. "All right," he said. "Assuming I believe any of this — which I don't, but let's assume for a moment — I don't see what it has to do with me. Why are the French trying to kidnap me? Why have *you* kidnapped me?"

"We haven't —"

He raised a hand. "You haven't kidnapped me, you've rescued me. Yes, I know. But you'll have to forgive me for not being able to tell the difference."

She shook her head. "We don't know, Michael," she said, and he didn't quite believe her. "Whatever it is, it's serious. Franc Brossard's got a reputation for being a complete arsehole, but they've driven a coach and horses through agreements and understandings that go back decades. Centuries. They wouldn't do that unless it was something big."

"It's mistaken identity, then," he said. "They've got me mixed up with someone else."

"That doesn't change anything; they still want you, and we still need to know why."

"Just let me call the office, Jo," he said. "They'll have me out of here in a few hours and then the French will go away and you can all go back to your lives."

"We need to know, Michael," she said seriously. "Nothing like this has ever happened before." She looked at the expression on his face. "You're still not convinced, are you."

He shook his head. "Really not," he said. "Sorry."

"Okay," she said. She got off her stool. "Leave your coffee; I want to show you something."

He followed her out of the kitchen and upstairs, then up another flight of stairs into the attic, which had been converted into two big rooms. The first had cardboard boxes stacked neatly against one wall and an exercise bike standing in the middle of the floor. Jo went and opened the door to the next room and beckoned Michael through.

For a moment, he couldn't work out what he was seeing. The floor and walls and ceiling of the room were covered in what looked like fine metal mesh. It even covered the skylights. A sort of little path of carpet offcuts had been laid on the floor, leading to a waist-high cage of more metal mesh, and in the cage there was a little white dog. The dog kept jumping up and bouncing off the wall of mesh, sitting for a moment, then jumping again.

Jo stepped into the room and closed the door, and Michael saw that the mesh covered the inside, overlapping the frame so that it made contact with the mesh on the wall. "Come on," she said. "Come and meet Archie."

As they approached the cage, Michael saw that the dog was a West Highland terrier, and something about the way it was enthusiastically jumping at the mesh didn't make sense; it was like there was some kind of optical illusion. Then he realised that the dog wasn't jumping; it was *disappearing* and then reappearing almost instantaneously at the edge of the cage, then walking back to the middle and doing it again. Michael stopped and tipped his head to one side.

"Yes," Jo said, walking around him to get to the cage. "Archie has a superpower. Hey, Arch. Come and say hello to Michael." She unlatched the cage's door and pulled it open, and the dog toddled out, tail wagging and tongue lolling. It looked at Michael, seemed to consider for a moment, then gathered itself, ran towards him, and sprang into the air. For such a plump little dog, it managed quite a lot of altitude.

Michael took a shocked half-step back and held out his arms to catch the dog, but it wasn't there any more and a moment later there was a soft thud behind him. When he turned and looked he saw the dog sitting on the floor with its nose right up against the mesh-covered wall of the room, a baffled look on its face.

"Sorry," Jo said, rummaging in a pocket. "Should have warned you." She brought out a bone-shaped dog biscuit and knelt down, waving it in front of her. "Hey, Archie. Look what I've got." The dog waddled over, took the biscuit, and flopped down on his stomach to eat it. "I shouldn't really give him these things," she said. "He's way overweight; Christ only knows what the old lady's feeding him."

Michael said, "Did he just…?"

"Teleport? Oh yes, Archie can teleport. Can't you, baby? That's a *good* boy." She scratched behind the dog's ears; he looked happily at her for a moment, then went back to crunching at his treat. "I don't think he understands any English," she said. "He speaks *biscuit*, though."

Michael touched his chest. He had the bizarre sense that the dog had jumped *through* him.

"Not so long ago, Archie and his mum, Mrs de Keyser, had a little holiday on the coast," Jo said. "And while they were there they walked right through an Event. The old lady probably didn't even notice it, but Archie picked up his little... talent. Yes, you *did*, didn't you?" The dog rolled over on his side, tail thumping, to let Jo rub his tummy. "Thing is, all he really wants is to be with his mum, so he's always trying to go home. Which is why he's in a Faraday Cage for the moment."

All of a sudden, the picture sorted itself out in his head and he saw Archie toddling along on his lead behind a little old lady outside the bar, moments before the French had arrived. "You stole him," he said in wonderment. "I watched you do it."

She glanced up at him. "Yeah, I wondered if you'd seen that," she said. "We've just *borrowed* him for a few hours, that's all. We're not going to hurt him. Take a little blood, some DNA. We should put him on a diet, really, but he won't be here long enough. In a little while, I'll open the door and he'll just..." She made a fluttering gesture with her hand.

"I don't know about all the other stuff you believe, but you people certainly have a lot of euphemisms for kidnapping."

"There are people who *would* steal him, if they knew about him," she said seriously. "And they wouldn't give him back; they'd take him to pieces without even thinking twice about it. As far as we know, this is the first time the Essence has turned a living thing into an artifact." She scratched the dog under the chin. "If only you could talk, eh?"

"Well, thank the gods you have scruples." He looked down at Archie. "How can you be sure he'll go back home?"

She smiled. "Archie *always* goes home. Don't you, you clever boy?" She looked at Michael again. "About a week after he got back from his holiday, he fell in the canal at the back of Mrs de Keyser's house. I think he was chasing ducks and just forgot to stop. The next door neighbour heard the old lady shrieking out in her backyard and looked out of the window, and he saw her standing there and Archie sort of bobbing around in the water. The neighbour had a rowing boat and he came out to rescue Archie, but Archie wasn't there any more. The neighbour thought Archie had gone under, but when he and Mrs de Keyser went back into the house they found him standing in the living room along with about a gallon of water. Mrs de Keyser said he must have got out of the canal on his own and slipped back inside in all the excitement, but the neighbour didn't see any water anywhere else in the house. Just in the living room. As if Archie had fallen out of the ceiling."

"And you stole him because of *that*?"

She sighed. "A few days later they're walking in the Vondelpark and Archie catches sight of a couple of parakeets and goes haring off after them. Archie loves chasing birds. Mrs de Keyser loses sight of him. She searches for hours. I mean, *hours*, she loves this dog. People join in, trying to help. A couple of dozen people wandering through the park shouting, 'Archie!' Finally she gives up and reports it to the police and she comes home and guess what?"

"Archie's sitting in the living room waiting for her?"

She smiled and rubbed the dog's tummy again. "*Clever* boy."

"Archie seems… accident-prone."

"Nah, he's just got an adventurous spirit."

"And the neighbour's one of you."

"A friend of a friend. Word got back to us."

"And you decided to steal him."

"Duh? *Teleporting dog*?" She grinned. "It wasn't easy. Have you any idea how hard it is to get hold of this much copper mesh?" She gestured round the room. "We didn't even know if it would work. We lined a bag with mesh, like one of those RFID wallets, but we didn't know whether he'd just vanish the moment we dropped it over him."

Michael thought about it. It seemed to him that he was coping remarkably well with all of this. He said, "It's a bit of a stretch, isn't it? Going from a story about a lost dog to assuming he can teleport?"

She shrugged. "How did he get back into the house the second time? It's not like he has a key." She got to her feet, bent down, and took Archie in her arms. "You know how it is. If you've got a hammer, every problem's a nail; if you're an essencehead everything's a potential Event. We look for this sort of stuff." She went back to the cage and popped the dog inside. "Anyway, as I said, we'll let him go home in a little while. We want to set up some cameras in here first to film him when he goes."

"Suppose you discover he's out of range and he can't go home?"

Jo pushed the door of the cage shut until the catch clicked. "We'll just drive him back into Amsterdam and let him go there. Also it'll be useful information to have." She looked at him. "We didn't just fall out of a tree, you know."

"You did from where I'm standing," he said. "How did *you* get mixed up in all this, anyway?"

She shook her head. "You don't get to hear that story yet." She walked past him towards the door. "Come on, I'll show you where you're sleeping."

The holdall Thijs had brought from the car contained two pairs of jeans, two plain black teeshirts, two pairs of socks, two pairs of boxer shorts, a grey sweater, a grey sweatshirt, a pair of trainers, and toiletries including a little bottle of an aftershave called Horse, which turned out to be surprisingly pleasant.

He stood in the little ensuite bathroom of the small, cosy bedroom and stared at himself in the mirror, wondering if he should start growing a beard as a disguise. He'd never had a beard before, and he wondered how it would look. Would it be enough to fool the French? He shook his head and undressed before getting into the shower. The water was very hot and at a decent pressure, and he stood there for a long time with it pounding on his shoulders, waiting for it to ease the stress in his muscles, but it didn't help all that much.

When he came out, he heard people going up the stairs to the attic, and a few moments later he heard them moving about in the rooms above his head.

Thijs might have been thoughtful enough to include aftershave in his bag of goodies, but he'd forgotten pyjamas or any kind of nightware, so Michael put on a pair of boxer shorts and one of the teeshirts. He hung his suit up in the little concertina-doored wardrobe, stuffed his dirty shirt and underwear in the holdall.

He sat on the end of the bed and stared at the wall, going back over the day in his head. It was a technique Bob had recommended, a way to put everything in its place before going to bed, try to detect any blank spots in his memory. Everything about the day had made perfect sense until around lunchtime when he had gone into the bar. Even the news that someone had been leaking classified material wasn't impossibly weird; it was a constant hazard, familiar from any number of

Westminster scandals and spy novels. After that, everything was a blur of hooded car journeys and safe houses and tennis balls and teleporting terriers and a frankly ridiculous story about a mysterious force that caused miracles, and it was hard to put everything in order. He was sitting here in Dan and Josine's comfy little house in the middle of the great dark silence of the Dutch countryside, so he supposed that much of what he remembered had happened, but none of it made any sense.

Still, the fact that he had survived it all – so far, at least – without becoming unglued was a significant achievement, and he chalked that up as a little victory. He'd amassed quite a few of them over the past few days, but that didn't mean he should relax and assume everything was all right. Something as trivial as a bad cup of coffee could still tip him over and put him back in the Acute ward. Except the Acute ward was inaccessible right now. He was out in the middle of this insanity without a safety net.

Best not to think about that. He wondered what was happening in London. He was small fry as far as the Intelligence community was concerned, but he had been sent on a significant mission. He'd said he was coming home, and the fact that he hadn't turned up at Hanway Street would have been noticed by now. What would they do? Check the flight, obviously. Check the hotel. Check his house, probably. Alert the Dutch police. Send a crash message to Theo van Hoebeek, something he couldn't possibly ignore. He looked at his watch. He wasn't hugely overdue, and there would be a period of decision-making; some of this would still be going on, some of it wouldn't have happened yet. *Something* would be happening, though, and in time more things would happen, and eventually all he would have to do was wait for his chance and walk up to a policeman and say his name and this lunacy would be over. He wouldn't have to put on his new clothes, climb out of the window, and flee into the night, which he had considered. And in the meantime, he could try and work out what was happening. That sounded good. It almost sounded like a plan, if he didn't think too much about it.

More footsteps in the attic. He listened to them coming downstairs. Presumably, Archie had gone home to his mum.

Six

The next morning, he washed his meds down with a handful of water from the bathroom tap, congratulating himself for having had the presence of mind to put the pill bottles in his pocket yesterday rather than leaving them at the hotel. He showered and shaved – a beard probably wouldn't suit him anyway – dressed in jeans, teeshirt and sweater, and followed the smell of frying bacon down to the kitchen.

Dan and Josine were an affable middle-aged couple with the look of vaguely reformed hippies, and they were both standing at the stove in the middle of an admirably coordinated exercise in cooking.

"Hey," Josine said with a smile when he came into the kitchen. "How did you sleep?"

"Very well, thanks," which was the truth. "It's a very comfortable room."

"We're just making breakfast," Dan said. "Go and sit down and I'll bring it through. You're not a vegetarian, are you?"

"Not remotely, no," Michael said.

He went into the dining room, where one end had been set with two places for breakfast. A few moments later, Dan came in and put a plate in front of him. "We thought we'd try to do a Full English," he said. "Did we get it right?"

On the plate were a couple of sausages, bacon, black pudding, baked beans, a little pile of fried potatoes, and scrambled eggs. Michael didn't have the heart to tell him that his breakfast usually consisted of a slice of toast and a cup of tea, even when he was travelling. Maybe a croissant, if he felt adventurous. Even in the hospital, where dieticians were constantly evangelising about the importance of a proper breakfast, he hadn't eaten a lot. "It's brilliant," he said. "Thank you very much."

There was a cafetiere of fresh coffee on the table. He poured himself a cup and set about his breakfast. It occurred to him that these people did not match his usual image of kidnappers. They were in fact rather kind people; Thijs had brought him some fresh clothes, Piet had cooked dinner for him, Dan and Josine had produced a slap-up breakfast. Nobody was in the least bit interested in handcuffing him to a heavy piece of furniture and hitting him. If anything, judging by Thijs's body language last night, they were rather embattled. He didn't know what to think about that, but the food was excellent.

Jo came into the room, sat down, and poured herself some coffee. Her hair was still wet from the shower. "Sleep all right?" she said.

"Fine," he told her. "Yourself?"

"Sorry," she said, "I'm usually a bit bleary in the morning before I've had my coffee." Dan came in with another large breakfast and put it on the table in front of her. "Bless you, Dan," she told him. "You're a lifesaver."

"I had a call from Thijs," he said. "You're to stay here today."

She nodded. "Yeah, he texted me. Thanks. Did he say how Anneke is?"

Dan shook his head. "Does he ever?"

When Dan had left the room, Michael said, "Who's Anneke?"

"Thijs's kid. She's not very well."

He waited for her to expand on this, but she just started ploughing into her breakfast, so he asked, "Did Archie get away all right?"

"Yup. Everything went like clockwork. The neighbour saw them going out for a walk this morning; she's got a new lead for him, one of those chain things."

They ate for a while in silence. Jo refilled her cup. Michael said, "I was a bit confused by everything yesterday, but in bed last night it occurred to me to wonder how everyone knew where I would be."

"I guess that would be because everyone was following you," she said without stopping eating.

"But how did everyone know I'd be in Amsterdam in the first place?" he went on patiently. "Even *I* didn't know until lunchtime the day I left."

Jo looked at him, knife and fork clutched in her fists.

"The only people who knew I was coming were HR, me, and the people I was meeting with."

Jo pointed her knife at him. "Airline. Hotel staff."

"I'm just a name on a booking form," he said. "If my name was Brad Pitt or Frank Sinatra or Madonna I can see that raising an eyebrow or two, but I'm not famous."

"The French think you are."

"I can't shake the feeling that things were moving before I even left home on Thursday."

She went back to her breakfast. "Yesterday was a bit of a shock," she said. "Now you've had time to settle you're coming up with questions, but I'm afraid some of them are going to have to stay unanswered."

"You sounded really busy when I called you on Thursday," he said. "Were you on your way here?"

Jo didn't answer.

Eventually, he said, "So, what's the plan for today? A trip to Atlantis? A visit to an alien autopsy?"

"I know it all sounds ridiculous," she said without looking at him, "and you're welcome to laugh all you want, but you should keep in mind that there are people out there who want to take you somewhere nice and quiet and beat you up until you tell them what they want to know. Brossard's not going to give up just because his contractors missed you yesterday." She laid down her cutlery, picked up her cup, and looked at him. "So, yeah, keep up the jokes."

Michael looked at her for a few moments, then he dropped his napkin beside his plate and got up. "I think you need a lot more coffee," he told her, and he went out.

The hallway ran all the way through the house, from front to back, with a door at each end. He walked down to the back door and tried the handle. It was unlocked, so he opened it and stepped out into the paved yard behind the house.

It was another bright, breezy day, huge billows of fluffy white cloud sailing across the sky above a seemingly infinite vista of flat green fields. Michael could see another house, about a mile and a half away, and he wondered how long it would take him to run there. Longer than it looked, probably; if it was on the other side of a canal he'd have to keep going until he found a bridge, and that might not be until he reached a road.

He heard a footstep on the paving behind him, and Jo said, "I'm sorry. It's been a rough couple of days, for all of us."

"How long do you think it takes to put together a kidnapping?" he asked without looking at her.

"Don't know."

"Let's try an easier question, then. How long does it take to put a team of security consultants together? Bearing in mind you can't just order a dozen up on Amazon for next-day delivery."

She thought about it. "Brossard's supposed to have connections in the French Security Services," she said. "That might make a difference."

He shook his head. "They've known for days that I was coming. Maybe since I got out of the hospital." He turned and looked at her and raised his eyebrows.

"We didn't have that much lead time," she said. "And that's all I'm going to tell you. Sorry, Michael."

He turned back and looked out over the fields.

"What Thijs thinks is that you saw something or heard of something in London, before your breakdown," she said. "Brossard heard about it somehow, but by then you'd disappeared into the hospital. Then he heard you were coming to Amsterdam, and he decided to take his chance and snatch you."

It didn't sound any crazier than everything else that had happened to him since Thursday. "I don't remember anything," he said. "Certainly not anything big enough for someone to go to all this trouble."

"It doesn't have to be something big," she told him. "It might have been so far out of context that you wouldn't even have realised what you were seeing."

Michael put his hands in his pockets and shrugged. "Brossard's going to be out of luck, then. My memory's more holes than not."

"That won't stop him."

He looked at the distant house and wondered who lived there.

Thijs turned up late in the afternoon. He was carrying a laptop bag and he looked exhausted. "It seems the contractors have scattered," he told them in the dining room. "A couple of them were arrested trying to get on the Harwich ferry, but they're not talking. I'm guessing the rest left the country by road. They'll be in Germany and Belgium and France by now."

"What are the police holding them for?" asked Michael.

"Public disorder. There was quite a fight in the bar after you left. But really the police don't know what they're dealing with. All they have is eyewitness statements and street camera footage of a group of men getting out of a couple of cars and going into the bar." Thijs took the laptop out of its bag and opened the lid.

"It won't be the only team," Michael said. Thijs and Jo looked at him, and he shrugged. "That's how we'd do it." Was it? He couldn't remember. It sounded plausible, at least.

Thijs opened a folder and clicked on a file. He turned the laptop so they could see the screen, which showed an image of a tall, thin man with slicked-back hair and a big nose. "Do you know him?"

The man was walking along a narrow, crowded street. The photograph had been taken from the other side, over the roofs of cars. Michael shook his head. "Never seen him before."

"Well," Thijs said, "he knows you. This is Franc Brossard. Someone spotted him quite by chance in Amsterdam yesterday and managed to get this shot."

Michael leaned closer to the screen. It wasn't a great photograph, but Brossard looked a few years younger than him. He was wearing a light brown overcoat over what looked like a good suit, and he was striding along as if he didn't have a care in the world.

"Where was this taken?" Jo asked. "It looks familiar."

"De Pijp." He looked at Michael. "Just a few minutes' walk from your hotel."

"I don't suppose it's any surprise he's here," she said. "Although he's got a fucking cheek. Do we know where he's staying?"

Thijs shook his head. "We're asking around, but I'm not hopeful."

"There," she said to Michael, pointing at the screen. "Does that look like somebody who's just going to give up?"

He had no idea; it was impossible to tell. "I get the message," he told her. He looked at Thijs. "So what now?"

"I don't know," Thijs said. "At the moment I'm at a loss regarding how to keep you safe in the long term."

He sat back in his chair. "Well, *that's* reassuring."

"Brossard's an extremely wealthy man," Thijs told him. "His family owns chemical plants all over Europe and the Far East, he's well-connected politically; his sister sits on the French Council of Ministers. He can keep this up for years, if he chooses to."

"I thought he was a teacher."

"He was until his dad died a couple of years ago and left him the family business," Jo said. "It's complicated."

"Can't we just *tell* him that I don't have what he wants?"

"He wouldn't believe it."

"We could at least try."

"I've called him," Thijs said. "His phone cuts to voicemail. I sent him a strongly worded email."

"Excellent," said Michael. "Very good."

"What about the conference?" Jo asked, stepping in before someone started shouting.

"I've been talking to people," Thijs said. "It's not going to be easy to get everyone together; the last time there was a conference was in 1971 and it was a disaster. There was bad blood for years afterward."

"Why have I never heard of you people?" Michael asked wearily. "You can't move these days for flat-earthers and antivaxxers and climate change deniers, but you? Not a word."

"That's because essenceheads are some of the most intensely paranoid people on the face of the Earth," Jo said. "They don't trust the internet *at all*. No email, no message boards, no chat rooms, nothing. A lot of them won't discuss it over the phone. Some of them won't even write *letters* to each other because they think the Post Office is reading their mail."

He glanced at Thijs, who was sitting with a pained expression on his face. "How do they communicate, then?"

"Word of mouth," said Jo. "Couriers. Face-to-face meetings. You'd be surprised how quickly you can get a message from one end of Europe to the other without using the phone or the internet or the postal system."

"People have been studying the Essence for a long time," Thijs said. "Nobody's certain how long. But there was a time when essenceheads were burned at the stake for heresy. That kind of thing can make you want to keep your beliefs to yourself."

"I still find it hard to believe it hasn't leaked."

"Oh, I don't doubt it has. But seriously, can you imagine any newspaper editor ever running a story about it? Really?"

"And you're seeing it from the inside now," Jo pointed out. "From the outside, there's nothing to see. There's a war going on between us and the French right now, and all there is to see from the outside is a fight in a bar."

"It's not a war," Thijs said.

"What Brossard did yesterday was a declaration of war, Thijs," she said seriously.

"It's not a war," he said again. "And please don't go around spreading that kind of talk. It's not helpful."

"Yeah," she said, crossing her arms grumpily. "Heaven forbid we should take this seriously."

Michael rubbed his eyes. "You people are giving me a headache."

"You've come to the attention of a super-secret bunch of conspiracists," she said. "Everything else is just details."

He wasn't certain he could think of a mysterious force which caused miracles as a 'detail'. "And this is all very jolly, but it doesn't really help me get my life back, does it."

"It's still early days," Thijs told him. "We'll think of something." But he didn't sound as if he believed it.

Josine announced that she was going into the nearest town for some shopping, and Jo went with her. With Dan outside in one of the sheds tinkering with the quadbikes, Michael and Thijs sat at the island in the kitchen drinking coffee and failing to make smalltalk.

"There's something else I wanted to show you," Thijs said eventually, putting his laptop on the tiles in front of them and opening the lid. "I think I told you that it's incredibly rare for someone to witness an Event, but it's even rarer to get documentary evidence." He clicked open a file and sat back on his stool.

The window on the screen showed a video of an Amsterdam tourist scene. A cloudy day, a makeshift flower stall beside a tram stop, a canal, crowds of people on foot and on bicycles. Judging by the clothes, it wasn't a particularly warm day. The sound was tinny, distant, the conversation of passers-by and traffic. The camera panned to follow one tall woman as she cycled by, and before it panned back Michael saw a little family group coming along the pavement, mother and father and a little girl in a bright-yellow coat.

All of a sudden, something happened to the colour balance of the video, as if the light had changed abruptly, and at the same time a strange noise came from the laptop's speakers. The viewpoint of the camera dipped and swooped and he heard someone shout, "What the fuck?" When the image steadied it was looking at the flower stall. It wasn't much of a flower stall, just a few buckets half-full of water with bunches of tulips sitting in them, but as he watched Michael saw, with a skin-crawling sensation at the back of his neck, all the flowers turn their heads in unison to look straight at whoever was holding the camera. They were all making the same high-pitched screaming sound.

It only lasted a few seconds. The flowers stopped screaming and their heads drooped, flopping in all directions, and the colour returned to the world. The camera viewpoint swooped around again to show people shouting and running across the road to see what all the fuss was about. When the camera turned back to the flowers, they were visibly rotting away, and a few moments later all that was left were some scraps of browning vegetation.

The video stopped, and Michael and Thijs looked at each other. "September the tenth, 2001," Thijs said. "The Prinsengracht tram stop. It was all over so quickly that nobody knew quite what they'd seen, and if anyone went to the media about it, well, the events of the next day buried it completely. Amazing, isn't it?" He closed the video file. "The stallholder just emptied the buckets and whatever was left of the flowers into the canal, which you're really not supposed to do, but all the physical evidence was gone."

Michael didn't know what to think. "Why isn't this all over the internet?" he said.

"Oh, I don't doubt there's a blog post from a bystander somewhere that mentions it, in some dusty corner," Thijs said. He closed the lid of the laptop. "It just didn't seem to get any traction. And as I said, it was overtaken by events. It took us years to track this footage down; it turned out a Hungarian tourist filmed it."

"How did you get hold of it?" Michael asked. "Show him the tennis ball?"

Thijs sighed. "That thought does you no credit. And yes, that's what we did. There have never been many essenceheads in Hungary, for some reason, but now there's one more."

Even if you took away the Essence, and Archie, and the tennis ball, and buckets of screaming tulips, this was all so unimaginably weird that it crossed Michael's mind that he might have had a relapse and been taken back to the hospital, there to suffer massive hallucinations. He said, "Still doesn't help me. Sorry."

"None of it looks familiar?"

Michael shook his head.

Thijs put the laptop back into its bag and set it on the floor beside his stool. "We don't have many first-hand accounts of Events," he said, "but the ones we do have all mention a sudden change in the light just before it happens."

"I've never seen anything like this before."

"Well, it's a mystery to me." Thijs considered what to say next. "Could your employers have discovered something?"

Michael sighed. "I'm not a spy, Thijs, I'm an economist. I produce classified economic forecasts, and they're only classified because of where the raw data comes from and the customers they go to. I can't imagine any circumstances in which my department could have discovered anything of interest to this man Brossard, unless it was relevant to his business. And even then it would hardly cause this much trouble."

Thijs pulled a face. "It was just a thought. We've been studying the Essence for centuries, and we still have no real understanding of its nature. Some of us have made quite a convincing case for it being responsible for all paranormal phenomena. UFOs, ghosts, Bigfoot, basically the entire Fortean canon. There are some who even believe it explains all Biblical miracles, although we do not. Someone who had made a breakthrough would be of enormous interest to us."

"Maybe so," Michael said. "But I'm not that someone."

They were still sitting there when Jo and Josine came back with bags of shopping. Jo looked at them while Josine went back to get the rest of the bags from the car. "Are we all right?" she asked.

"We're still trying to work out what to do," said Thijs.

"Well, that's a surprise," she said. She put her bags on one of the worktops and started to take tins and packets out. "We got stuff for a stir-fry."

"I should be going," said Thijs.

"At least stay and have something to eat," she told him. "When was the last time you had a proper meal?"

Josine came back with a carrier bag in each hand. "There's a car parked at the top of the track," she said calmly. "They must have followed us from town."

They all looked at her, then at each other. "Go," Thijs said to Michael. "Call Jo when you can."

Michael hesitated for a moment, then ran out of the kitchen and down the hall to the back door. He ran across the yard, between the sheds, and out into the field beyond. There was no sound at all apart from his breathing and his feet crushing down the plants and pounding into the damp soil. There was just enough light left for him to see where he was going, which was useful because he didn't want to run full tilt over the edge of a canal. In the distance, to his right, he could just see the shape of the neighbouring house. A bright light came on outside. An intruder light? He wasn't going there, anyway; his first instinct was to get away from any kind of habitation until he had the situation under control.

He kept going, trying to pace himself and thanking God that he'd kept up with his exercise while he was in hospital. He glanced over his shoulder, but nobody seemed to be following.

And then the vegetation in front of him seemed to rear straight up out of the ground in a huge vaguely human shape and there was no time to dodge round it. He ran into something solid and he felt a sting in his side and the world went away.

Seven

He woke up with a banging headache and a bag over his head, and his first thought was to wonder what it was with these people and hoods. Was it some kind of fetish or merely because they'd seen kidnappers use them in films?

He was lying on his side on a soft surface, a bed or something, and when he tried to move he found that his wrists had been secured behind his back. Not cable-ties, something more substantial, like a pair of handcuffs. He rolled awkwardly over on his back, then shuffled his feet to one side until they reached the edge of the bed. He got first one, then the other, on the floor, and managed to lever himself up into a sitting position. Which didn't help his situation a lot, but it was a start.

He heard a door open, and someone came into the room. "I demand to be taken to the British Consulate," Michael said, and his voice sounded dry and croaky. He said it again in French.

There was no answer. Instead, a hand roughly the size of a steam shovel gripped his upper arm, hauled him to his feet, and walked him none too gently out of the room and down a corridor. They stopped, another door opened, and he was urged into another room and then forced down onto a chair. One of the handcuffs was unlocked, his hands brought round in front of him, and his wrist cuffed again. Then, all of a sudden, the hood was pulled off, to leave him squinting under fluorescent light.

He had been expecting Franc Brossard to be in the room but instead, on the other side of a table, was a big, unamused man wearing a polo shirt. Behind him, the door closed again as whoever had brought him here left the room. He tried to sit up properly and found that his handcuffs had been slipped through a loop of chain, the ends of which were bolted to the floor. The chain was a little too short, so he had to sit crouched forward.

The room was small and shabby, its walls and ceiling covered with acoustic tile, and the man on the other side of the table didn't look very impressed to be there. He was grey-haired, in his sixties, and broad-shouldered, and his face and arms were tanned in a way that spoke more of years spent in the field in bad parts of the world than a sunbed.

"I want to talk to the British Ambassador," Michael said in French. "I'm a British citizen and I demand to be released."

The big man regarded him sourly for a few moments, then he said in English, "You see, once upon a time that might have worked. But being British isn't what it used to be." He had an American accent.

"You're not French," Michael said.

"No," the big man said. "I am not. Were you expecting the French?"

"Who are you?"

"My name is Stilwell," he said. He reached down beside his chair and came up with a cardboard folder that was almost two inches thick. He dropped it on the table in front of him, and in the quiet of the room it sounded as loud as a pistol shot. "And now you belong to me, Mister Brookes."

"What's going on?"

"Well." Stilwell scratched the side of his nose. "Some people would say that I have rescued you from the clutches of a dangerous group of deluded radicals."

"You know what?" said Michael. "I'm getting a little tired of being rescued."

"You've just spent two days in the company of a bunch of essenceheads. I'm surprised you're not thanking me."

Michael sighed.

Stilwell reached out and tapped the folder. "This is what we have on you," he said. "Actually, we have it all on computer; we like to be as paperless as possible. I had this printed up specially, for the sound effect. I've seen guys roll over just hearing the sound of their file hitting the table."

Michael stared at him.

Stilwell took a pair of half-moon spectacles from his breast pocket, perched them on the end of his nose, pulled the folder towards him and opened its cover. "So what do we have here?" he said, looking down on the top sheet. "Name. Date of birth, yadda-yadda. Place of birth – how do you pronounce this?"

"Droitwich," Michael said.

Stilwell nodded. "That's what I thought." He took out a fountain pen, uncapped it, and made a notation, then he set the page aside and looked at the next one. "Parents, education, blah blah blah et cetera and so on." He looked at Michael over the top of his spectacles. "I'll level with you, we've only got a page and a half on you. The rest of this –" he picked up the folder and gestured with it, "– is just blank paper."

"For the sound effect," said Michael, although a page and a half was still too many.

"Right." Stilwell put the file back on the table in front of him and closed the cover. "What I can't decide is whether you're really smart, or really stupid."

"I would have thought it was fairly obvious," Michael said. "Who are you?"

"Me? I'm an Air Force Colonel whose life has taken a *very* strange turn over the past six years."

"CIA?" Michael asked, blinking at him.

Stilwell shook his head. "Nothing quite so straightforward. Ultimately I answer to the President, but for the day-to-day stuff there's a very small and very discreet Senate committee. We're a small team, but very fast and agile, and we have a lot of autonomy. We're tasked with investigating the Essence and evaluating any threat it poses to the national security of the United States."

"Oh for God's sake," Michael said wearily.

Stilwell tipped his head to one side and regarded him steadily. "Can you tell me why Franc Brossard wanted to abduct you?"

Michael sat up as far as he could. "No. I have no idea. And before you ask, neither do the Dutch essenceheads."

"He must think you know something important," Stilwell mused.

Michael looked at him. "I'm really tired of having this conversation, Colonel," he said. "I came here on Thursday for a meeting, and then everything became totally insane and I have *no idea why*. All I want is to go home."

"There's no need to shout," Stilwell told him. "Nobody's going to hear you."

"If you'd had the couple of days I've had, you'd be shouting too."

Stilwell settled back in his chair and crossed his arms. "So if you can't help me, I guess we have to ask ourselves what I'm going to do with you."

"You could let me go home," Michael suggested. "With a few quid for my trouble."

"I could," Stilwell agreed, "but you don't have a passport."

Michael scowled. Of course they'd searched him while he was unconscious. His passport was still in his coat pocket at Dan and Josine's house. More to the point, he realised that he'd left his tablets behind too; he could picture the two little bottles on top of the chest of drawers in his room.

"How long was I unconscious?" he asked.

Stilwell consulted a surprisingly dainty watch. "I make it about thirteen hours. Why?"

"I'm on medication," Michael said, feeling a slow gathering of panic. "If I don't take them every morning I'll get sick."

Stilwell narrowed his eyes. "Sick how?"

"It's hard to explain. I had a breakdown."

"What are you taking?"

"I don't know, nobody's ever told me."

Stilwell looked sceptical. "Okay, we can have you checked over and get you some more meds, that shouldn't be hard."

"So long as I cooperate."

"Hell, we'll do it anyway. You're no use to anybody if you're sick." He leaned forward. "I don't want to know who you've been with because we know who they are and where they live and what they do when they're not chasing around Europe looking for Events. I'm not interested in them; I'm interested in what Brossard wants from you."

"Maybe you should have kidnapped him instead."

"Something's got the crazies all het up," Stilwell told him. "And it's not Zandvoort, it's something else. Maybe it's you."

Michael frowned. "What's Zandvoort got to do with anything?"

Stilwell ignored him. "No one knows what the Essence is. Is it an energy field? Is it an expression of the collective unconscious?" He was gesturing with one hand. "Is it a natural thing or is it something that's been created? If it was created, was it by accident or by design? Is it sentient? Is it *intelligent*?" He crossed his arms again. "I've got guys who study this thing all day long and some of them think it doesn't even exist, they think it's some sort of mass hysteria."

Michael thought of the tennis ball, the footage Thijs had shown him, Archie. He didn't say anything.

Stilwell took off his spectacles, folded the arms, and laid them down on top of the file. "It's rare for anyone to witness an Event," he said. "Nobody even knows how many there have been. We figure most of them take place in uninhabited places – out at sea or somewhere in the stratosphere or in the middle of the Sahara or something. The various groups all disagree, which is just one of their problems. All you get is a bunch of objects that people say were at the scene. The essenceheads think they've got magical powers."

Michael sagged back as far as he could go on his chair.

"You're the only civilian we've come across who's got this close to the crazies, and that makes you of interest," Stilwell told him. "That's not your fault, and it's not mine. We'll talk to you for a while and then we'll see about sending you home. You won't be harmed, not physically or mentally or emotionally or reputationally. You'll just talk to us." He put his spectacles back in his pocket. "Now, you don't have to do that. You've broken no laws, that I know of; you can get up and walk out of here and nobody's going to stop you."

"I have no passport and I only have about a hundred euros in my pocket," Michael reminded him. "Even if I could find a Consulate on my own, how the hell am I going to explain what happened?"

"Okay," Stilwell allowed, "you can't do that." He beamed and clasped his hands together in front of him. "I guess we're stuck with each other, then."

Michael raised his hands and gave the chain a tug, but there was no give in it at all. "Does my Service know you've got me?"

Stilwell shook his head. "Nope. And we're not going to tell them; that just complicates things too much."

"What about the Special Relationship?"

Stilwell chuckled. "Special Relationship? Oh my." He smiled. "The US got into the game late with the Essence and we've been playing catch-up ever since. We regard it as a potentially existential threat and I have carte blanche to lie, cheat, threaten, steal, kidnap, suborn and murder in order to protect my country."

"Well, you've done at least two of those to me already. Are we going to work through the list?"

"What we're going to do," Stilwell said, "is move you somewhere and have a proper chat with you. This place is okay but it's not ideal."

"Not ideal for waterboarding?"

"We don't waterboard," Stilwell said gravely. "The paperwork is…" He sucked his teeth theatrically.

"That's funny."

Stilwell got up and went over to the door. "First we'll get a doctor to take a look at you and sort out some medication." He opened the door and spoke quietly to someone standing outside, and when he came back he had another big man with him, this one younger with a military haircut and almost no neck. He unlocked one of the handcuffs, removed the chain, and closed the cuff again.

"Come on," Stilwell said. Michael got up, hands in front of him, and walked over to the door. "Just a second." Stilwell took an overcoat from a hook by the door and draped it over Michael's hands to hide the handcuffs. "No sense in attracting attention."

Michael didn't think people seeing the cuffs would have made much difference. Two more big military-looking men waited outside, dressed like Stilwell in tan slacks and black polo shirts. As if they hadn't stood out like sore thumbs already, they stationed themselves behind and to either side of him. With Stilwell leading the way, they all walked down a corridor with Michael in the middle. Stilwell paused at a security door, typed a code into a little keypad, and pushed through.

Only then did Michael realise they were in an airport. He saw coffee and fast-food franchises, and crowds of people with luggage, and over to one side a line of check-in desks. Surrounded by the Americans, he walked across the concourse, following Stilwell towards a wall of glass through which he could see a line of taxis. Almost every head in the place looked at them as they went by, and Michael wondered what would happen if he started shouting for someone to call the police.

As he was wondering this, he noticed a young woman wearing a baseball cap and overalls with the logo of a cleaning company on the front. She had a big denim bag slung over her shoulder and she was pushing a trolley laden with bottles of cleaning products and rolls of paper towels. She was moving more or less towards them, but there was something wrong with the wheels of the trolley because it kept wanting to go off in a different direction and she had to wrestle with it. The Americans kept having to adjust their course because every time the young woman wrangled the trolley it wound up heading straight at them.

There were a lot of people on the concourse, either queueing up for coffee or the check-in desks or just standing around with their baggage around their feet and looking at the display screens, and the young woman with the trolley was between the Americans and the exit doors. No matter how much they changed course the trolley was always somehow aimed directly at them. It was quite comical to watch.

In the end, she got the trolley steered sufficiently that it was only heading for the American on Michael's right. He tried to move to the left, but there was nowhere to go because they were just passing a big group of teenagers with too much luggage and bristling with skis and snowboards. Up ahead, Stilwell kept ploughing on, and the Americans behind and to his left kept going, but at the last moment the one on the right had to step away in order to avoid the trolley. The bag the young woman was carrying looked heavy, and Michael thought he saw whatever was inside moving around.

As the American stepped around the trolley and it passed Michael, the young woman unzipped the bag, put her hand inside, and reached out and clasped his wrist with the other hand. All of a sudden he was standing in someone's living room.

"Well," Jo said, letting go of his wrist and taking off her baseball cap. She blinked out and reappeared a few feet away on the other side of the room. She tutted and took her hand out of the bag, unslung it, and lowered it to the floor. Archie popped his head out, tongue lolling happily, then he toddled out and looked about him. Jo gave him a couple of treats and an ear-scritch, then she looked at Michael, put a finger to her lips, and beckoned him to follow her. Michael stood where he was, unable to believe what had just happened. One moment he had been in an airport, the next he was here. There had been no transition, no flashing lights, no noise or dramatic music. He'd just been instantly somewhere else.

"Michael," Jo said quietly from the door, "will you get your fucking act together and come on?"

Michael watched Archie walk over to a little footstool. The dog jumped up, turned around a couple of times, and then curled up contentedly.

"Michael!" Jo hissed.

He followed her, wondering if this was what it felt like when his meds wore off. They went along a short hallway and down a couple of steps to a chaotic little kitchen with a door that opened onto some more steps down to a small brick-floored yard enclosed on two sides by high fencing. On the third side, the yard ended at the edge of a canal, beyond which Michael saw a line of houses and a quiet street, and moored houseboats.

Jo locked the kitchen door behind them and walked across the yard to the edge of the canal, where Arno, the driver from Michael's first kidnapping, was waiting in a rowing boat. She stepped in and sat down, and after a moment Michael did likewise and Arno rowed away.

Michael stared at Jo. "Did you just do what I think you did?"

"If you think Archie and I just rescued you, then yes." She sounded delighted. She carefully rolled the Faraday bag up and laid it across her knees. "We didn't even know it would work."

"We'd have all looked really stupid if it hadn't."

She wrinkled her nose and waved the comment away.

"I have," he said, "*so* many questions."

"I know," she said, looking happily about her. "But not now, eh? Today has been full of win, for a change. Just let me bask in the moment."

There was a car waiting for them at the top of a set of steps not far from Mrs de Keyser's house, and Arno drove them out of the city again. This time they drove a long way, to an old house on the edge of a village almost within sight of the Friesland coast, where there was an air of triumph which Michael couldn't share.

"We really didn't know if it would work, you know," Thijs told him as they sat around a picnic table in the house's big garden.

"Yes," Michael said. "Jo mentioned it." There had been a brief detour to a lockup garage in a part of Amsterdam which was not remotely touristy, where a little old man with an attaché case full of exquisite jewellers' tools had removed the handcuffs. Michael had kept Stilwell's coat, though. The pockets contained nothing apart from a ballpoint pen, half a roll of mints, and a folded piece of paper with the word *not* written on it.

"Extraordinary," Thijs said, shaking his head in wonderment. He seemed to have recovered some of his bounce. "Absolutely extraordinary. It was all Jo's idea." On the other side of the table, Jo raised her glass of beer, clearly still basking in the moment.

"I'm not entirely clear how you knew where to find me," Michael said. He had, apparently, just been teleported out of Eindhoven airport.

"Stilwell and his people flew in a couple of weeks ago," said Thijs. "They've been headquartered there ever since. Once we realised who had you, we checked our sources in Eindhoven and they said he and his men had turned up at the airport with someone who seemed very drunk in the back of their car."

"That could have been anybody."

"We were winging it, Michael," Jo said.

"How did you know it was Stilwell's people?"

"Because Stilwell knocked on the door after you'd legged it." She took a drink of beer. "I'll give him credit, at least he does his own dirty work, not like Brossard."

"So you know him?"

"We hadn't met before, but we know of him," said Thijs. "We've seen photographs. He was very polite, but obviously he just wanted to keep us talking while his men rounded you up."

"So on that evidence you stole Archie again and drove for a couple of hours to Eindhoven with him in a bag."

"He loved it," Jo said. "Snoring his little head off all the way, bless him."

The level of smugness in the garden was starting to annoy him. On the other hand, he had been reunited with his medication and his passport and what he was starting to think of as his luggage, so there was at least the hint of a silver lining. "So, as well as the French, now I have an arm of the US government willing to kidnap me," he said.

Jo raised her eyebrows. "An arm of the US government?" she said. "Is that what he told you?"

Michael nodded.

"Stilwell's group is privately funded," Thijs said. "Mostly by the religious Right. They're very well-connected politically, but they're not officially a government agency."

"Amateurs," Jo snorted.

"That's all very well," Michael said, "but it doesn't change the fact that there are now two groups of people in the Netherlands who're prepared to kidnap me. Three, if we include you." There was a faintly embarrassed silence around the table. "Who else?" he asked wearily.

Thijs and Jo glanced at each other. "We were discussing this while you were away," Thijs said, making it sound as if Michael had just returned from a relaxing weekend break. "Word's got around among the community, obviously, because I've been speaking with other groups and trying to drum up support. I've had some requests to speak with you. People have started to offer us artifacts."

Michael looked at them and didn't say anything.

"Artifacts are incredibly rare," Jo said. "They only change hands now and again, and for *fantastic* sums of money. We had somebody offer us forty million euros for the tennis ball once."

"I confess I was tempted," Thijs added.

"People don't just hand them over for the chance of half an hour's chat with an English economist," Jo went on. "If they're prepared to do that, they're prepared to snatch you."

Michael thought about it. "Well, that's wonderful," he said. "And speaking of which, how did Stilwell know where to find me?"

Jo and Thijs looked at each other again. "Apart from us three, the only people who knew we were at that house were Dan and Josine," said Jo. "So…"

"It doesn't mean they told him," Thijs said. "They may have mentioned it to a friend. Or it may have been a coincidence that Stilwell's people saw the two of you when you went shopping."

Jo snorted. "Yeah, right. They just happened to be outside the Albert Heijn having a cigarette when we came out."

"Anyway, I've sidelined them somewhat until I can work out what happened. I don't like the implications at all, though; it means I can't trust anybody."

"Welcome to my world," Michael said with a humourless smile. "Anyway, does anyone have any ideas what to do? Because Stilwell's *really* not going to give up on this."

Thijs shook his head and went into the house.

"Can't you give him a break?" Jo said in a low voice. "Seriously?"

"He doesn't have half the developed world queueing up to kidnap him," Michael pointed out. "I can't keep running around the Netherlands for the rest of my days, Jo. Why won't somebody just talk to the French and tell them I don't have what they want?"

"They're not taking calls. And they wouldn't believe us anyway."

Michael looked around the garden. He thought he could smell the sea, just a couple of miles away. He said, "What if I meet with Brossard? Try to convince him?"

Jo thought about it. "It would probably solve a lot of our problems, because we'd never see you again." She held up a hand to stop him replying. "And before you say it, I'm not riding to the rescue with Archie again. The poor little sod's had enough adventures for one week. Not to mention it's cruel to the old lady."

They sat quietly for a while. Michael couldn't see out of the garden because it had a high fence around it, but he could hear the occasional car passing through the village. It all felt very peaceful.

He said, "How did you know it was safe to go back to Mrs de Keyser's house? We might have appeared right in front of her."

"She was next door; the neighbour was keeping her busy with coffee and cakes. And that's another reason why I don't want to use Archie again; right now she thinks he's going missing under his own steam, but if we keep snatching him she'll get suspicious and word will get out and one day someone else will put two and two together and he'll go missing and he won't come back. I'm not having that."

"Why do you have a key to the house?" he asked.

Jo shrugged. "Just in case."

In a normal world, all this would have been outrageous. But the world wasn't normal any more, and if the essenceheads were to be believed it never had been. Maybe he should just go with the flow. He put his head back and looked up into the clear, cloudless sky.

"You know," he said, "there's another way I can talk to Brossard."

She looked at him, but he didn't say anything more, and after a while she said, "Seriously?"

"It has the advantage of being unexpected," he mused.

She thought about it for a while. She said, "That's crazy." Then she smiled. "I like it."

Thijs didn't want to let them go.

"This is a very bad idea," he told them. "It's not safe for either of you to be out on the streets." He nodded at Michael. "Particularly him."

"It's only a bit of a drive," Jo assured him. "We'll be gone for a couple of hours. We're both going stir-crazy cooped up here."

"You've both just got back from a trip to Eindhoven," he pointed out.

"That was hardly a relaxing day out. Come on, Thijs, just give me the keys."

"I should go with you."

Jo shook her head, and they embarked on a brief staring contest, which ended with Thijs putting his hand in his pocket and bringing out the car keys. "You're going to see *him*, aren't you," he said.

"No we're not," she told him.

"Stay away from him," he said. "He's nothing but trouble."

"We're just going for a drive, Thijs," she said.

"I won't be able to help you if anything happens," he said.

Jo held out her hand, and after a few moments Thijs put the keys in her palm.

The three of them went out to the car, and Thijs watched glumly as Jo and Michael got in. Jo started the engine. "Who are we supposed to stay away from?" Michael asked.

"The person we're going to see," Jo said, putting the car into gear.

They drove for about forty minutes until they reached the outskirts of Groningen, then they drove around for a bit while Jo checked out the area for any suspicious parked cars before pulling up in front of a dilapidated-looking house across the road from a little light-industrial estate. The house was almost hidden behind a big overgrown hedge, and to one side stood a garage that had been almost completely covered in graffiti. As Jo pushed open the gate, Michael saw that a big crack wandered diagonally up the front of the house, held together by metal strapping and rivets.

Jo marched up the front path, and as he followed her it crossed Michael's mind – it was pretty much automatic by now – that he could make a run for it. If he could make it as far as one of those industrial units across the road he could ask to use the phone, or at the very least make so much of a nuisance of himself that someone would call the police. But he didn't.

The door was answered by a very tall man of indeterminate middle age. He was completely bald, and his head and what was visible of his face were tanned the colour of a hazelnut. The rest of his face was almost entirely concealed by a huge untended beard, from which a bulbous drinker's nose protruded below a pair of tiny, angry-looking eyes. He was wearing jeans and a painter's smock covered with what looked like oil stains.

"Hey," he said.

"Hey," Jo said, stepping forward and giving him a hug. "This is Michael. Michael, this is Wim."

Wim looked at him. "Hey," he said.

"Hello," said Michael.

The little eyes squinted at him. "You're the guy, huh?" he said in English.

"I'm *a* guy, certainly."

Wim looked at him a moment longer. "Come on in, then," he said.

The house smelled of pipe tobacco and fried fish and the hallway was stacked almost waist-high with books and bound magazines. There were more books – on floor-to-ceiling shelves, in stacks on the floor, scattered over the furniture – in the living room, along with old pizza boxes, piles of dirty clothes, broken guitars, loose sheets of paper, and an annoyed-looking Persian cat which watched them from the space it had cleared for itself on a cluttered coffee table.

"Still haven't got a cleaner, then," said Jo.

"If you leave it long enough it stops getting worse," Wim told her as he picked his way across the room. "It's good to see you and everything, but what brings you here?"

"We were just passing."

Wim grunted and said, "Lol," which may have been the first time Michael had ever heard anyone say 'lol' out loud. Wim flopped into a splay-legged armchair. "Does he know you're here?"

Jo was clearing books and newspapers off the sofa so they could sit down. "I didn't actually say it out loud, no."

"I bet he tried to stop you."

She shrugged and perched herself on the edge of the sofa and motioned to Michael to sit beside her. "You heard about Anneke?"

Wim nodded. "It's a shame. She's a sweet kid."

"You could get in touch and tell him that yourself, you know."

He shook his head. "He'd either throw it back in my face or ignore me completely," he said. "I'm done with all that." He looked at Michael. "I've been hearing a lot about you."

"No offence, but that's not remotely reassuring."

"That's what happens when you attract the attention of conspiracists, I'm afraid. How much do you know about the essenceheads?"

"A lot more than I'd like."

Wim snorted. "Yes. That sounds about right; I'm sorry this is happening to you." He looked at Jo. "I'd love to think this is a social visit, but it isn't, is it."

She sighed. "When did you last talk to Franc Brossard?"

"Franc?" Wim shook his head. "Quite a while. He's no fun any more. He got weird."

Michael wondered how strange an essencehead would have to be for another essencehead to call them 'weird'. He said, "Weird how?"

Wim looked at him. "He thinks the Apocalypse is coming."

"That's quite weird," Michael admitted.

"It's a cultural thing, mostly," Wim said. "The French have always thought the Essence is an expression of the Divine. Me? Not so much."

"Essenceheads are crazy," Jo said. "Some of them are actually stand-in-the-middle-of-the-road-barking-at-cars crazy, but they're all crazy. They argue all the time. They get together and they argue about details so nitpicking that you'd need an electron microscope to even see them. Some of them think something's going to happen, some kind of paradigm shift."

"What about you?" Michael asked Wim. "Do you believe that?"

Wim wrinkled his nose. "Nah. The Essence has been manifesting for centuries. Thousands of years, depending on who you believe. If it was going to do something spectacular, it would have done it already. Like Jo says, essenceheads love to argue. This is just something else to argue about."

Michael looked at the cat, which was staring at his knee with an expression that suggested it had violence on its mind. Or maybe it always looked like that. He said, "If they think I know anything about this, they're wrong." He was getting tired of saying it. Nobody seemed to want to believe him, except maybe Jo, and sometimes he wasn't even sure about her.

"Could you contact Brossard?" Jo asked. "If you wanted to?"

Wim sat back in his chair and blew out his cheeks. "I doubt he wants to talk to us right now."

"He's not talking to Thijs," she said. "But he might pay attention to a message from you."

Wim regarded them levelly. "If you want me to tell Franc to leave you alone, that's not going to work," he said. "You know what he's like."

"That's not what we want you to tell him," Michael said. And then he told Wim what they really wanted.

When he'd finished, Wim sat and thought about it for a while. "That's quite mad, you know," he said eventually.

"I said something like that," said Jo.

"Franc's people aren't amateurs," Wim said. "He's got some ex-*Deuxieme Bureau* guys working for him, they're not assholes."

"But in *theory*..." Michael said.

"Oh, well." Wim crossed his arms. "In *theory* you can do anything. In *theory* I could become Prime Minister one day."

"Wim," said Jo. "Is it doable?"

He scratched his beard. "There would be blowback."

"We'll cross that bridge," she told him.

"What's Thijs's view on it?"

"Thijs doesn't know."

Wim stared at her. "Well, shit," he said. Then a sly look crossed his face. "Bragging rights would be *awesome*, though."

"So?" said Michael. "Can you help?"

Wim sniffed. "What about resources?"

Jo folded her hands primly in her lap.

"Shit," he said again. He sighed. "Let me sleep on it. Can you come back tomorrow?"

"It's best we don't stray out into the open too often," Jo said.

Wim nodded. "I guess you're at Sofi's old place?"

"Yeah."

"It's not going to take Franc long to find you there, you know. He's *been* there." He got up and ambled across the room and started to sort through a pile of rubbish.

"I know, but we're not a fucking intelligence agency," Jo told him. "We're running out of safe houses."

"You could take him into Germany," Wim suggested, still moving bits and pieces of stuff out of the way. "Maxi Zimmermann would be happy to babysit for a while; Franc wouldn't dare go near him there."

"It's not a matter of babysitting," Michael said. "I want to know why everybody's chasing me around the Netherlands."

"Are you sure knowing's going to help?"

"It would be an enormous step forward for me."

"We'd rather keep Michael close to hand," Jo said. "Maxi and her family are lovely, but I don't want to be driving to Bremen every time I want to talk to him."

"And you want to limit access. Ah." He straightened up holding a videotape.

"That too." Jo got up.

"Where are you going?" Michael asked.

"I'm going to make some coffee," she told him. She nodded to where Wim was moving piles of books off an old video recorder. "I've seen this before and I don't like it. It's creepy. But you might as well see for yourself."

When she'd gone, Michael said, "You don't… seem like an essencehead, if you don't mind me saying."

Wim was standing in the middle of the room, looking around. "That's because I'm something of an apostate. Thijs and I had a bit of a disagreement a while ago and now we don't talk."

"What did you disagree about?"

"Oh, this and that. Can you see the remote control anywhere?"

There followed several minutes of searching before they finally found the remote control under the cat, which was unwilling to give it up and had to be lifted spitting and hissing out of the way. "Persian cats are supposed to be chilled couch potatoes," Wim said. "Don't believe it; this one will have your eye out if you give him a chance."

"Let's not give him a chance, then," Michael said, watching the cat settling itself on the coffee table again.

"Damn right. Okay." Wim waded through the mess on the floor to the video recorder and slotted the tape into the front. "I presume Thijs showed you the Amsterdam footage?"

"Yes."

"And what did you think about it?"

"I honestly don't know. I've seen the tennis ball, too."

Win snorted. "Magic tricks." He pointed the remote control at the big wall-mounted television and pressed a button. Nothing happened. He tried again. Nothing. He slapped the remote control against his palm a couple of times, and this time when he pressed the button the television came on with an alarming crackle.

"As I'm sure Thijs and Jo have told you, there's not a lot of footage of Events, and it's hard to find," Wim said, returning to his armchair. "Thijs and I had to go to Esztergom to get the Amsterdam one, and we practically had to promise our firstborn to the little shit who had the tape before he turned it over." He pointed the remote control and pressed another button. "And then there's this."

The screen lit up slowly, a sickly off-blue, distorted along the top and bottom.

"It's a copy of a copy of a copy," Wim said, "so the quality's not great, but it's good enough to give you an idea."

The screen flashed white a couple of times, then filled with blobs and scratches and flickers of static. After a few moments, they settled down and a series of numbers came one by one, counting down from five, and Michael realised he was looking at a piece of ciné film transferred to tape. The numbers counted down to one, then the screen filled with static, out of which a group of figures slowly emerged.

At first, it was hard to work out what was happening. The figures were standing on a beach somewhere, with the sea behind them. There were about twenty of them, mostly men, in baggy suit trousers and shirts, with their sleeves rolled up. A couple of women were wearing old-fashioned and rather drab sun dresses. Several of the men were setting up a huge old film camera on a low platform, while others were fiddling about with cables and bits of archaic-looking equipment. One of the women approached whoever was filming the scene with a huge grin on her face and performed a little curtsey.

"August the seventeenth, 1965," Wim said. "On the Baltic coast of Poland."

The scene cut to a close-up of the men fiddling with the film camera. One of them glanced over from the platform and waved good naturedly, then the scene panned away down the beach and Michael saw some old buildings in the distance, some houses and beyond them the tower of a church.

"It's an East German film crew," said Wim. "They're filming a thriller called *The Unknown Man*, it's basically an American *noir* transplanted to East Berlin. A piece of propaganda, really; the hero's a former *Volkspolizei* officer turned private detective, the bad guys are all American gangsters and crooked West German politicians. It was never going to win an Oscar."

Another cut, and this time the focus was on a couple walking along the beach towards the camera. One was a short man with a rodent look, wearing a suit and tie and a fedora, the other a tall woman with long brunette hair in a plait. She wore a sun dress that was considerably less drab than the ones the female crew members were wearing. They were deep in conversation as they approached, smoking cigarettes and looking serious, the sea rolling gently against the beach behind them.

"Matthias Weber and Hannelore Huber," Wim said. "Our hero and his femme fatale. They called Weber 'The German Bogart', which flatters him considerably. Hannelore, though," he shook his head, "she had real talent."

"I've never heard of them," said Michael without taking his eyes off the screen.

"You won't have. It was a long time ago. They were big in the East for a while, though."

A gust of wind blew Weber's hat off and bowled it across the sand, and Hannelore put her hand over her mouth and laughed as she watched him scuttling after it. Weber managed to catch the hat before it reached the water's edge, and he came back brushing sand off it and smiling ruefully as if happy to be part of the joke, but Michael thought he was only playing for the camera. He had the look of someone who didn't take kindly to embarrassments, no matter how small and harmless.

Another series of cuts. The crew setting up the camera. There was an old-fashioned van parked on the beach behind them, with cables coming out of its back doors. Weber and Huber sitting in folding chairs, shaded by umbrellas, leaning close to each other as they discussed a script that Weber was holding. Huber looked up at the camera and smiled. Huber in another chair having her makeup touched up by one of the girls in summer dresses. An older man in shirtsleeves and wearing a tie, deep in discussion with a stout middle-aged man in a suit.

"Our director and our producer," Wim said. "Lorenz Bohrer and Hans Ehlers. Ehlers was an ex-Luftwaffe mechanic, went home to Halle after the war and set himself up making low-budget thrillers. Bohrer was an utterly useless director, but one of his relatives was a higher-up in the Party so nobody dared tell him."

Jo came into the room with a mug of coffee in her hand, but she stopped in the doorway. "Not finished yet?"

"Just getting to the good bit," Wim said.

She pulled a sour face, shook her head, and went back into the kitchen.

"I shouldn't have said that," Wim said. "I've watched this thing so often I've probably become a bit disassociated; I sometimes forget these were real people."

On the screen, Ehlers suddenly realised the camera was there, and he waved it away irritably. There was another cut, and the camera was watching the two men from further away, people walking through shot carrying bits of equipment.

"Here it comes," said Wim.

Cut to a viewpoint behind and off to one side of the film crew, everyone looking in the same direction along the beach. Bohrer standing on the platform beside the film camera. Slow pan out to where Weber and Huber were walking towards the camera, acting an animated conversation. All of a sudden, the light seemed to change and the colours of the scene became weak and watery. Something flickered behind the two actors, something so fast that it almost wasn't there at all.

And then Matthias Weber was gone.

"Wait," Michael said. "What?"

Huber turned her head and looked confused to find herself suddenly alone. She looked towards the film crew, and then she was gone too.

Michael sat forward on the edge of the sofa. On the screen, members of the film crew were running towards where Huber and Weber had been. Then one of them was gone, then another. The others came to a stop and turned and ran back towards the camera, and the subliminal flickering came up the beach after them and they disappeared one by one. The scene yawed alarmingly and suddenly blacked out.

There was a long silence in the living room.

"What was that?" Michael asked.

Wim pointed the remote control at the video recorder and wound the tape back. "Watch," he said.

The beach came up again, Weber and Huber walking along. Wim pressed a button and they slowed down, slowed down again, slowed down again, until they were barely moving.

There was something on the beach behind them.

It was hard to make out because even with the tape slowed down to a near-standstill it was still moving almost too quickly to register. Like a visual migraine, a blind spot with a razor-thin kaleidoscope line of multicoloured light curled around its leading edge. It touched Weber and he simply wasn't there any more, as if he'd been edited out. Wim sped the tape up a little and Huber realised something had happened and started to turn jerkily. She slowed again, and the light touched her and she was gone.

Wim paused the tape. "It got them all," he said. "Twenty-two people, gone in a few seconds."

Michael got up, picked his way over to the television and leaned towards the screen. Even with the tape paused, the blind spot was still barely there at all. "It's a trick," he said. "Special effects, editing."

Wim shook his head. "I've had the film looked at by an expert. No edits, no splices, no manipulation."

"So what happened to them?"

"I don't know. Nobody knows." Wim put the remote control in his lap and scratched his beard with both hands. "No one saw it happen. Some locals came along the beach a while later and found all the film gear and the vans, but there was nobody there. It was as if they'd just abandoned everything and gone home."

Michael looked at that thread of light again. "You're saying *this* is the Essence?"

"I'm saying I don't know. It was nearly sixty years ago, there were no eyewitnesses." He nodded at the television. "This is the only evidence we have. Presumably the crew filmed what happened to Weber and Huber, but that footage is gone. Maybe it'll turn up one day, it's not impossible, but I'm not holding my breath."

Michael looked at him, at the screen, back to Wim. "I have no idea what to say."

Wim grunted. "Anyway," he said. "Somebody must have called the police eventually, and they came and poked around and didn't know what to make of it all, so they called in some Party official or other, and *they* didn't know what to make of it either. The disappearance of twenty-two East German citizens on a Polish beach was a potentially huge embarrassment for the Polish government, so the Poles dithered for a little while before they contacted Berlin. By that time, bits and pieces of gear, including the ciné camera that filmed all this, had been spirited away by the locals. The police found most of it later and some people went to jail, but the authorities didn't know the camera had been there so they weren't looking for it, and even if they had been, someone had already developed the film, and *that* disappeared for... well, ever such a long time."

"It's in very good condition," Michael said.

"Yes." Wim nodded. "Well spotted. It's a bit scratchy, but it's hardly degraded at all. The guy who examined it for me said it looked about five years old, at most."

"Maybe it is."

"It's not, I had a little bit tested. It really is about sixty years old. Which makes me wonder if that makes the film an artifact."

"How did you wind up with it?"

Wim shrugged. "It got passed down from person to person until it eventually reached somebody who realised what it might be, then he sat on it for a decade or so, and when he died his son found it among his possessions along with a note to send it to me."

"Why you?"

"Ach, we'd been friends for years. He never told me he had the footage, though, the fucker."

Michael looked at the screen again. "What happened to Weber and Huber and the others?"

"Oh, they were never found." Wim picked up the remote again. "It was a big problem for the DDR and Poland, so in the end they decided to just cover it up. There was some wild story that the film crew had decided to defect en masse, that they'd been rowed out to a submarine or something, but nobody in their right mind believed that. Twenty-two people picked up off a beach in broad daylight?" He shook his head. "Nah." He stopped the tape and started to wind it back. "They hushed it up, told the families that the crew had been killed in a road accident, staged funerals with empty coffins. I went to Leipzig and talked to Weber's daughter a few years ago; she still believes it."

"That's awful."

"Yup. Not the worst thing the Communists ever did, either." He got up and started to rummage among a pile of old cardboard folders. "Your Dutch is pretty good; how's your German?"

"A bit rusty. It used to be better. Why?"

Wim pulled a folder from the bottom of the pile; the rest toppled over. He came over to Michael holding it out. "You can have that to read. It's not the original; I've got that in a safe deposit box. And the film's in another one."

Michael opened the folder and took out a couple of hundred pages of photocopies. The top sheet said *Der Unbekannte Mann*. "You found the script?"

"At a film memorabilia auction in Deventer, would you believe. I was there looking for something else. You can hang on to that; I've got a couple of other copies."

Jo came back into the living room. "Is the afternoon matinee over? We should be going before Thijs starts tearing his hair out."

Wim looked at her. "Get some burner phones," he told her. "Then send someone over here with the number of one of them and I'll call you."

"Okay."

"Don't come here again until this is over; if we have to meet I'll think of somewhere."

"Do you think you can help?"

"I will certainly give it thought." He turned to Michael and put out his hand. "Good to meet you."

Wim's palm was uneven with callus. "Thank you, and you."

Wim walked them to the front door, but as Jo went out to the car he put a hand on Michael's arm and stopped him. "You should get out of this right now, you know," he said quietly.

"I would if I thought there was somewhere I could go," Michael said. "I'm afraid I don't know who I can trust at the moment."

Wim sucked his teeth. "Remember I told you Thijs and I had a row about some things?" he asked.

"Yes."

"Well, one of the things was what we should do about the Essence."

"That sounds like a fairly fundamental disagreement," Michael said. "Considering it seems to occupy a large part of your lives."

Wim looked sourly at him. "He and the others are completely blissed-out by it. They think it needs to be kept secret so they can spend the rest of their lives studying it. I think we should be warning everybody about it as loudly as we can."

"You think it's that dangerous?"

"I think it's worse than that," Wim told him. "I think it doesn't even know we're here. And if it did, it wouldn't care."

Standing on the path, Michael looked up at the crack in the front of the house. "What happened?" he asked.

"Earthquake."

Michael looked at him, but there was no indication that he was joking. "Earthquake," he said.

Wim nodded. "We have the dubious fortune to be sitting on quite a large natural gas deposit here." He stepped outside and stood beside Michael and looked at the house. "So someone started extracting it, and we started to get earthquakes." He shrugged. "We're still waiting for the government to sort out compensation."

"Good lord."

"It's been quite the scandal over here. I'm not surprised you haven't heard of it, though."

That wasn't the problem. The problem was that he *should* have heard of it, if only in passing. It was another black hole in his memory, and he had no way of knowing how many more of them there were.

Eight

He thought about what Wim had said all the way back to the house. Jo detoured through a number of little towns on the way and stopped off at a mobile phone shop in each of them, and by the time they got back they had half a dozen burner phones, each one preloaded with fifty euros of credit, the sort of thing you used to plan a drug deal or a murder and then dropped down a mineshaft.

Thijs was grumpy and didn't do much more than grunt hello when they got back. Anton had turned up while they were away, and the two of them took themselves into the study at the back of the house and shut the door. For want of anything else to do, Michael made a couple of omelettes and he and Jo ate in the kitchen.

"Who's Sofi?" he asked.

Jo looked at him. "Why?"

"Wim said this was her house."

She nodded, remembering. "Thijs's wife. She died last year."

"I'm sorry."

"Why? You didn't know her."

He shrugged. "I'm still sorry."

She looked at him for a while. "I was only given a sketchy background for you, but it said your wife died too."

He nodded.

"You don't have to talk about it if you don't want to."

"It's okay," he said, wondering as he said it if it was, really. It occurred to him that he had been trying very hard, ever since he regained himself at the hospital, not to think about it. "Her name was Christina. She was diagnosed with a brain tumour last year but by then it was already inoperable. So, rounds of chemotherapy and radiotherapy, and they didn't work, and, yes, she died."

"I'm sorry."

"Why? You didn't know her."

Jo reached out and punched him on the arm, a little more forcefully than necessary. "And that's why you had your breakdown."

"I've always assumed so. I can't remember. I remember going back to work and trying to carry on in the days after she died, but then everything gets confused. The next thing I remember properly is being in the hospital."

"What was it like? The hospital?"

He shrugged. "It was all right, I suppose. A bit run down, but isn't everything these days? Everyone was very kind."

"I'd never even heard of it before," she said. "It comes under the local hospital Trust but it's not part of it. Weird kind of setup. Feels a bit like an NHS version of *The Prisoner*."

"Best not to think too much about it. They got me back on my feet; I suppose that's the important thing."

"And you haven't had any relapses? Moments of absence? Giddy spells?" He looked at her and she shrugged. "I'm still your social worker, technically."

He smiled. "I've felt a bit odd a couple of times, but just for a few moments. The medication seems to be working."

"Yeah," she said. "I was meaning to talk to you about that. Could you let me have a couple of pills? One of each?"

"Why?"

"I know somebody who can test them for me, see what they are. I'd like to get you another supply, just in case; you can't exactly get a repeat prescription right now and I'd rather not wait till the last minute."

Michael laid down his fork. "I've got a month's supply," he said. "If this isn't over by then, medication is going to be the least of my problems."

"It might not be your *only* problem, but it won't be the least of them, I promise you; there might be withdrawal symptoms, you might relapse, anything. It's just a worst-case scenario, that's all."

He thought about it, then he took the bottles out of his pocket – he didn't let them out of his sight now – and put one blue pill and one red pill on the table. Jo wrapped them in a clean piece of kitchen paper, made a neat little parcel, and buttoned them in her shirt pocket.

"Who *are* you, actually?" he asked. When she raised an eyebrow, he added, "One minute you're my social worker, the next you're running all over the Netherlands and you've got chemists at your beck and call analysing drugs for you."

"He's not at my beck and call," she said. "We were at school together." She finished her omelette and dabbed her lips with another piece of kitchen paper. "Okay. I'm Dutch on my mother's side, born here, spent my first few years living here. My dad was posted back to his company's head office in Leicester for a while, then they sent him back here when I was thirteen. Dad died when I was eighteen and I decided to go back to the UK to university, which was probably a mistake but it's too late to whine about that now. Mum stayed here and I'm not going to tell you where she lives because it's none of your business." She folded her hands in her lap and looked primly at him. "Your turn now. Can you tell me what you were doing in Amsterdam?"

He shook his head. "Official Secrets Act, remember?"

"You said something about national security, though."

"I might have exaggerated a little, but I still can't tell you. How did you know I was coming?"

She thought about answering for a moment, then said, "One of the French got in touch with us and said Brossard was going to do something; I guess maybe their conscience got the better of them, although they didn't give us a lot of warning."

"What did they say?"

"Brossard was on the warpath and he was going to snatch an Englishman in Amsterdam the following day, basically."

"And they knew my name?"

"Oh yeah. Name, the flight you were coming on, the hotel where you were staying. Had a description of you, too. And they had my name. And before you ask, no, I wasn't planted on you. I'm part of a pool of social workers and we're assigned clients at random. I'm as pissed off about this as you are."

He doubted it was even possible to be as pissed off as he was. "It's a hell of a coincidence, Jo."

"Yes," she said wearily. "Yes, it is."

Anton finally left around six, and shortly afterward Thijs took the car and drove off without telling them where he was going.

"I'm going to need to build some bridges," Jo said when they heard the car drive away.

"You're going to need to tell him what we're going to do," Michael told her.

"He probably knows already; I wouldn't put it past Wim to phone him and gloat while we were driving back. I love Wim to death but he can be such a bellend sometimes."

"Where do you think he's gone?"

"Hospital, to see Anneke." She glanced at him. "She's got a brain tumour."

He thought of chemotherapy, radiotherapy, huge ticking machines, doctors, nurses, the smell of hospitals. "Ah," he said.

"Whatever else this is about, I'm never going to forgive Brossard for putting him through this right now," she said.

"Brossard probably doesn't know."

She shrugged. "I don't care."

Later that evening, someone turned up to take the number of one of the burner phones to Wim. Jo didn't let them into the house. After that, there was nothing practical to do; everything depended on Wim and whatever resources he could get together.

Jo went into the living room and watched television. Michael drifted from room to room, looking out of windows, waiting for the sound of black SUVs screeching to a stop outside and large numbers of big men running towards the house.

He sat drinking a cup of tea while looking at the little pile of mobile phone boxes on one of the worktops. It would only take a couple of minutes to set up one of the burners and text Martine, and then all this would be over. He would probably never find out what it was all about, but was that really such a bad thing? Most people went through their whole lives in ignorance of the hidden machineries of the world, and it didn't seem to make them particularly unhappy. The majority of them, he thought, would actually rather not know.

Still, he left the phones in their boxes. If someone in London had alerted the French that he was coming to Amsterdam, making contact would probably be a mistake. He couldn't think of any circumstances in which they would want him to be kidnapped by a gang of French conspiracists, but that didn't mean it hadn't happened. The thought made him feel very alone.

He took the folder Wim had given to him into the study, made himself comfortable in an armchair under a floor lamp, and took out the photocopy of the film script. *Der Unbekannte Mann*. The next page had an address in Berlin – he assumed in the East, he didn't know the city – and the one after that, it seemed to be an insert typed on a different machine, was a list of cast and crew.

He sat and read down the names. Hannelore Huber as Marthe Braun, Matthias Weber as Josef 'Joe' Becker. He thought of Weber, 'The German Bogart', his ratty face under that ridiculous fedora. Did people in mid-1960s East Berlin really dress like 1930s American detectives? He wondered how Weber had felt seeing Huber's name above his on the cast list.

The next page opened *Pankow, 1950*. The audience, if there had ever been one, would have been seeing the office of Joe Becker's detective agency. Weber got almost a page of sub-Chandler voice-over, mostly scene-setting – it was a hot Berlin summer, there was a sense of violence hanging over the city, that kind of thing. Joe had a part-time secretary, Liselotte, whose purpose seemed chiefly to be, by reminding Joe that numerous bills were overdue, to inform the audience that his agency was not a great success, although Joe didn't seem outwardly bothered. They exchanged tough-guy banter.

To escape from his financial straits, Joe went to a bar – it was just called *bar* in the script, and Michael assumed that Lorenz Bohrer, who was listed as director, screenwriter and originator of the story, had intended to come up with a name later – where he had a run-in with two former *Volkspolizei* colleagues which ended with him being beaten up in an alleyway. It was all rather familiar and clunky. Joe and Liselotte and the two Vopos were stereotypes, the dialogue was excruciating. Michael had a dark thought that if the Essence was responsible for the film crew's disappearance, it had at least spared East German cinema audiences from seeing the film.

He wondered how the film would have gone down. Wasn't American cinema regarded as decadent in the DDR? He couldn't remember. Would it have made a difference if it was an East German imitation of an American film? 1965 was four years after the Berlin Wall went up, but the film itself was set a decade and a half earlier, when Germany had still only just begun its long march towards postwar reconstruction. Did it even matter?

He looked up from the page and saw Jo standing in the doorway. "Is it any good?" she asked.

"No," he said. "No, it's terrible."

"I got a text from Thijs. Anneke's had a turn for the worse so he's staying at the hospital tonight. They're going to give her a scan in the morning."

There came a point where scans were less a diagnostic tool and more a way of reassuring the patient and their relatives that the doctors were still trying, against all the odds. "Okay."

"If I turn in, can I trust you not to do a runner?"

He smiled sadly. "Where would I go?"

She looked at him for a few moments without speaking. "We'll get this sorted out, Michael."

It seemed a rash promise to make, considering, but he said, "Yes, I'm sure we will. How's Thijs?"

"Hard to tell, from a text. At least he's talking to us." She shrugged. "Okay. There's some booze in one of the kitchen cupboards, if you fancy a nightcap. See you tomorrow."

"Yes," he said. "Goodnight, Jo."

After she'd gone upstairs, he went into the kitchen and checked the cupboards, eventually finding several half-full bottles of Scotch and gin and vodka, along with one lonely unopened bottle of Pernod. He stood looking at them for a little while, then closed the cupboard and went over to the back door and stood on the step.

There was no indication from upstairs that, if she had heard him open the door, Jo was going to do anything to stop him walking down the garden and going over the fence, but he stayed where he was, listening to the night and thinking about the footage Wim had shown him, the blind spot outlined by a curved razor-line of light dancing along the beach as it overtook Weber and Huber and came for the rest of the film crew.

Wim was right; if the Essence could do that, somebody should be warning the world about it. But how did you go about doing so? You couldn't show the tennis ball to everybody, and if you posted the footage online all you'd get would be hordes of 'experts' examining it minutely and trying to outdo each other in coming up with clues to prove it was fake. It could only make things worse. And anyway, how was anybody supposed to defend themselves against it?

On the other hand, Brossard and Stilwell at least claimed connections with their respective governments. Did that mean the authorities already knew and were taking it seriously? Was there some obscure and obsessively concealed department within SIS charged with combing the world in search of artifacts, fearful of winding up on the wrong side of an Artifact Gap?

He sighed, suddenly nostalgic for the days when his biggest concern had been getting downstairs to the hospital's dining room before the breakfast sausages dried out. That felt like a very long time ago, and he experienced a momentary wave of vertigo, a need to shout and break things. He reached out to the doorframe to steady himself, but the feeling had passed before he touched it. He closed his eyes and took a deep breath, tried to concentrate on the ground beneath his feet the way Bob had taught him. "It's probably just mumbo-jumbo, old son," Bob had said, "but it'll take your mind off things until you feel better."

And he did feel better, after a few moments, but he couldn't kid himself any more. He might be coping, after a fashion, but he was still some way from being well.

He woke the next morning with a vague feeling that he'd had a terrible nightmare about hospitals. He shaved and showered and took his pills and went downstairs to make some toast and a cup of tea. He looked out of the windows, but he couldn't see the car.

He'd almost finished breakfast when Jo came into the kitchen and made a beeline for the coffeemaker.

"Any word from Thijs?" he asked.

She shook her head.

"What are we going to do if he doesn't come back?"

"No thinking now, Michael," she told him. "Coffee now. Thinking later."

He made himself another cup of tea, and they sat in silence at the kitchen table.

Jo was beginning to look slightly less bleary when the one unboxed burner phone rang. She took it from her pocket and held it to her ear. "Hey," she said. "Yeah? How? Yeah, fair enough, I'm still not properly awake." She glanced at Michael. "Sooner would be better," she said. "We can't let this go on much longer. Okay, where do you want to meet? Thijs isn't back from the hospital yet so I'll need to organise a car from somewhere. No, I don't know. He hasn't been in touch. Okay. See you later. Bye."

She hung up and put the phone on the table. "He thinks he's had an idea," she said. "He wants to meet us later to talk about it."

"That sounds hopeful."

"Well, let's hear what it is before we get all excited."

"I'm not sure we should stay here much longer," he said. "Stilwell said he knew who all the Dutch essenceheads were and where they lived."

She snorted. "Stilwell is full of shit. If he knew that, he'd never leave us alone." She finished her coffee and went to get a refill. "Unless someone grasses us up, we're as safe from Stilwell here as anywhere else. It's Brossard I'm worried about."

"Wim said he'd been here."

"Yeah." She came back to the table. "He used to be happy to join in with everybody else; he and Thijs even co-authored a paper about the tennis ball. I figure he was just playing along so he could pick our brains. I never trusted him."

"But Thijs did."

"Thijs has a good heart, bless him, always sees the best in everyone. Sofi was the cynic; she could smell bullshit a mile off." She took a drink of coffee. "Brossard will assume we've got you and sooner or later it'll cross his mind to check here."

"We'd better do something soon, then."

"Oh yeah," she said. "We're definitely going to do something."

Piet drove up to Sofi's house, and Jo and Michael used his car to drive to a little park near Groningen University for their meeting with Wim. It was late afternoon before they got back, and Thijs's car was still not at the house. Michael started to worry that the French had abducted him at the hospital, but after dinner Jo received a text.

"He says something's happened," she said. "He's staying there tonight and maybe tomorrow too."

"Does he say why?"

She shook her head. "It's got to be bad news, though. It's been nothing but bad news since Anneke got sick."

"Maybe we should put this off," he said. "Until he gets back, at least."

She looked at him. "You really mean that, don't you."

He shrugged.

"Bless you, Michael," she said. "But no, we can't put it off. It's time we took control of this thing."

Nine

He thought he was starting to get used to the landscape, the enormous sky full of drifting cloud, the endless flat fields separated by drainage canals and ditches, the occasional road on a low embankment, the sense of the North Sea not far to the West, just waiting for the one catastrophic storm that would let it reclaim the land. It seemed calm and uncomplicated, just a few simple elements arranged in a rather pleasing manner. It reminded him a little of his life in the hospital, just breezier and with fewer home comforts.

He looked at the ruggedized military-surplus walkie-talkie on the shelf in front of him, but Jo said, "They'll call us when he gets here."

Several of the radios, a pair of binoculars, and a rather nice tripod-mounted telescope had been delivered to the house shortly after dawn, along with some camouflage clothing in roughly the right sizes, a couple of packets of sandwiches, and a flask of coffee, which he thought an admirable attention to detail.

He bent over the eyepiece of the telescope. A mile or so away a road ran across the landscape on an embankment, and from here he could pan quite a long way along it in both directions; though at the moment the telescope was trained on where Piet's car was parked all on its own near where the road crossed a canal, its driver's door wide open.

"I'm not sure I could live out here," Jo said, looking through the window with the binoculars. "It's kind of spooky. Looks like a location for an episode of *Doctor Who*."

"I rather like it," he said. "Reminds me a bit of East Anglia."

They were on the upper floor of a two-storey boathouse beside one of the larger canals that divided the landscape. Michael thought it might be some kind of maintenance headquarters; the lower floor was open on one side and comprised berths for a couple of boats, and the upper floor was divided into two rooms. The smaller one had a couple of camp beds and the larger appeared to be some kind of office, with desks and chairs and ranks of shelved box files. There was a huge, detailed map of the area's waterways on the back wall, and the front wall was almost all windows. It smelled of wood and water and old dope. It was impossible to reach directly from the road; you had to drive about three miles before you came to a side-road, then cross several little bridges and culverts before you came to a farm track that doglegged back another three miles or so. When Wim had explained his plan in the park in Groningen the previous day, Michael hadn't been sure about the boathouse; it seemed an obvious place for any French advance team to check out, but now he was here it seemed so isolated and far from the road that he thought nobody would bother.

The radio on the shelf made a staticky noise, then a quiet voice said, "Car coming." Michael looked through the telescope again, and a minute or so later a grey hatchback came along the road. It passed Piet's car without stopping and went on its way.

"Locals," Jo said.

"Won't they report the car parked there?" he asked.

"They're used to seeing cars parked on that stretch of road," she said. "Farmers, water engineers, fishermen, maybe someone who's just stopped for a piss. It'd have to be there for a couple of days before anyone batted an eyelid."

Michael, who lived on a street where an unfamiliar vehicle was likely to be reported to the local Neighbourhood Watch if it was parked there more than an hour, found this unlikely, but hopefully they wouldn't be here very much longer.

The radio crackled again. "Car coming," said the voice.

This time, the car was a black SUV that stood out like a sore thumb. Jo said, "Are these people addicted to black SUVs or something?"

"It's a signature look," Michael said, watching through the telescope. "Hard to let go."

The car slowed as it passed Piet's car, then it pulled over to the side of the road and stopped, and three men in jeans and windcheaters got out. They stood looking about them for a few moments, then they walked back to Piet's car. They peered inside, looked underneath, opened the boot and the bonnet. One of them stood in the road scanning the area with binoculars while the others checked either side of the embankment. Through the telescope, it felt to Michael as if he could reach out and tap them on the shoulders.

"Another car coming," said the voice on the radio. "It's stopping not far away. Driver and three passengers. Okay, they've parked it across the road."

"Now *that'll* get the attention of the locals," Jo said.

Apparently satisfied that the scene was secure, the three men got back into their car and drove off. A minute or so later, another voice said, "They're stopping here. Parking across the road. They're staying in the car."

"That's very naughty," Jo said. She picked up the radio and pressed the talk button. "Okay," she said, "they've blocked both ends of the road so it looks like it's happening. Stay on your toes and let me know if they make a move."

"Someone's getting out," said the first voice. "One man on his own, tall, long brown coat. He's just standing there. Okay, now he's walking."

Jo and Michael looked at each other. There was another radio on the shelf; Michael picked it up and cradled it in his hand as a figure came into view walking up the middle of the road. Whoever it was, they weren't in a hurry; they sauntered along the road, hands in the pockets of their coat, as if they owned the place.

"Cocky bastard," Jo said.

"Is it him?" Michael asked. "He's not close enough for me to tell yet."

"It certainly *looks* like him."

"*Looks like him* isn't good enough," he said. "We have to be sure."

"Calm down, Michael," she told him, watching through the binoculars as the figure moved along the road. "This is fun. It's like spy stuff."

He didn't tell her that, in his admittedly limited experience, the majority of 'spy stuff' consisted of reading reports compiled from material collected by people you never met, and then sitting in endless meetings arguing about it with people you didn't necessarily like. He kept the telescope trained on the distant figure as it walked down the middle of the road. Slicked-back hair, big nose. It certainly *could* have been the man he'd seen in the snapshot from Amsterdam.

It took the man ten minutes to reach the parked car, and by then Michael was sure it was Brossard. Under the long cashmere overcoat, he was wearing grey chinos and a black turtleneck. Michael had never seen anyone who looked more out of place.

Brossard stood by the car and looked about him. He went to the edge of the road and peered down the embankment into the field beyond. Michael pressed the talk button on his radio several times, and watched Brossard startle as if at a sudden noise. Michael pressed the button a couple more times, and Brossard walked over to the car and looked inside. He went round to the driver's side, reached in through the open door, and took out the walkie-talkie that had been sitting on the seat. Michael saw him raise it to his lips.

Michael's radio crackled, and a voice said, "Are you there, Mister Brookes?" in lightly accented English.

He pressed talk. "Monsieur Brossard."

"I was told you would be here." Brossard sounded faintly amused.

"You were also told to come alone," Michael said.

"Does that mean we're not going to meet after all? I'm *so* disappointed."

"He's *so* fucking punchable," Jo said.

Michael pressed the button. "What do you want from me, Monsieur Brossard?"

Through the telescope, he watched Brossard go to the edge of the road and gaze out across the fields as if looking for where the transmission might be coming from. Unfortunately, he was looking in the wrong direction. Maybe the boathouse wasn't so obvious from the road, after all.

"If you want to know that, Mister Brookes, we'll have to meet face to face," Brossard's voice said.

"Well, that's not going to happen."

Beside him, he heard Jo say calmly, "And *go*."

"You know that eventually I'll catch up with you," said Brossard. "It must be better for us to stop this ridiculous chasing around." Michael saw the figure of Piet emerging from hiding in the field and scrambling up the embankment.

"I can chase around as long as you can," he said.

Brossard laughed. With his back turned, he never saw Piet coming across the road towards him, never knew what was happening until Piet dropped a bag over his head and then manhandled him down the other side of the embankment and out of sight.

Michael didn't see what happened next, but a few moments later a Zodiac crewed by Wim, which had been hiding under a camouflage net in a side channel, emerged from under the bridge with Piet and

Brossard on board. Once he was out in the open, Wim opened the engine up and the Zodiac pointed its nose at the sky and practically took off. Before long, it was passing the boathouse, still going like a bat out of hell. Brossard was crumpled in the bottom of the boat, not moving.

"All right," Jo said into her radio. "Everyone go home, you've been absolute stars. If somebody could come back later and get Piet's car, that would be great, but check first in case they leave someone behind. Thanks for your help, we love you all."

Michael looked through the telescope again. The two black SUVs were speeding along the road towards the place where Brossard had been. He didn't know how much the Frenchman had been paying his contractors, but he thought he was owed a refund.

"Shall we go?" Jo asked with a huge grin.

He smiled at her. "Yes, let's," and they went downstairs to where their own boat was waiting.

It wasn't quite the boat chase from *Puppet On A Chain*, but by the time the contractors could have reached the boathouse they were already several miles away in the maze of canals and waterways and there was no way anyone could catch up without using a helicopter.

Eventually, they came to a concrete slipway, where a couple of cheerful young men had already loaded Wim's Zodiac onto a trailer. "You're a bit late," one of them said. "The others have already gone on ahead."

"We were enjoying our day out," Jo told him while she tied the boat up and stepped onto the slipway. "Get these things out of sight as quickly as you can, yeah? The owners will pick them up later in the week when things have calmed down a bit." She looked at Michael, who was staring at the sky. "You okay?"

"I was thinking about drones," he said.

They all looked up at the clouds for a few moments.

"Well," Jo said, "there's nothing we can do about that." She looked at the two young men, who didn't seem quite so cheerful now the subject of aerial surveillance had been raised. "There's nothing we can do about it," she told them again. She pointed at the boat. "So get this thing on the trailer and get it under cover and keep your heads down."

"I can't believe you didn't think of drones," said one of them.

"What were we supposed to do? Buy an anti-aircraft gun?" she asked.

"You can get things that jam their signal," said the other.

"And if I did this for a living I probably would have done that," Jo told them. "But I'm a fucking social worker. Now get this boat out of the water and go home."

Walking up the slipway to the road, she said, "You think they've got drones?"

Michael shrugged. "It should have occurred to me earlier; we could have planned differently."

She glanced at the sky. "Too late to worry about it now; we'll just have to hope they're as shambolic as we are."

The slipway was on the edge of a village, and a couple of streets away someone had left a car for them and hidden the keys under the wheel-arch. A half-hour's drive brought them to the outskirts of a little town, and an abandoned factory waiting for demolition behind hoardings and high fencing. Jo drove past it twice to check the coast was clear before parking nearby and leading the way to a point where the fence had been cut in order for the mesh to be bent aside and then pushed back into place.

"You took your time," Wim said, coming across the factory yard to meet them. "We were about ready to give you up."

"Don't you start," said Jo. "How did it go?"

"Remarkably well, considering how quickly we set it all up." Wim fell in beside them as they walked towards the factory's main building, a shabby three-storey concrete cube with a squat chimney at one corner. "He had this on him," he said, holding up a taser. "He tried to use it on me, but Piet got it off him and gave him a couple of little shocks and he quieted down after that."

Michael took the taser, turned it over in his hand, and put it in his pocket. "We didn't want him hurt."

"He tried to tase me," Wim said. "He's lucky I didn't tie a rope round his ankles and tow him behind the boat."

"What about his phone?"

"Threw it in the canal, along with his wallet. Just in case."

Michael suspected Wim was enjoying this far too much. He asked, "Has he said anything?"

Wim grunted. "Christ yes. He won't *stop* saying stuff. It's mostly swearing and threats and it's all in French." He pulled open a door, and they stepped into the building.

There was no real way to tell what the factory had once made. Everything had been stripped out of the ground floor, leaving a huge empty space interrupted by two rows of raw concrete columns. There were marks on the floor where some kind of machinery had once been installed, and curls of cable hanging from the ceiling. Two chairs stood in the middle of the floor; Brossard, with the hood still over his head, was cable-tied to one of them, and Piet was sitting on the other.

"Hey," Piet said, smiling at them. "Hey, Professor."

"I'm not a Professor," Michael said.

At the sound of his voice, Brossard stopped struggling against his bonds. "I'll make you suffer for this," he said in English, voice muffled by the hood.

"At this point, I can't imagine any way in which you could make my life significantly worse than you have already," Michael told him.

"Do me a favour and keep an eye outside," Jo told Piet. "Let us know if someone turns up."

Piet stood. "Are we expecting someone?"

"My men will be here soon," Brossard said loudly, as if hoping his contractors could hear him.

"Those guys?" Wim snorted. "Those guys are still running around the countryside trying to work out what happened. They're an embarrassment. You need to complain to Mercenaries'R'Us or wherever you got them from."

"Best to be prepared," Jo said to Piet.

While Piet headed for the door, Michael took his chair and set it in front of Brossard, then he sat down and hutched forward until they were almost toe-to-toe. He sat up straight and rested his hands on his knees and looked at the Frenchman. Brossard's expensive cashmere overcoat was stained with mud and water, and his trousers and turtleneck were going to need the services of an expert laundrette if they were ever going to be useful for anything other than doing the gardening in. Wim went over and whipped the hood off his head, and he looked about him, blinking. His eyes were red and his nose was running, and his hair had escaped from its products and stuck out in all directions.

"Where am I?" he demanded.

"I'll tell you where you're not, Franc," Wim told him soberly. "You're not in Kansas any more." He folded the hood up and walked round to stand behind Michael.

"I'm extremely wealthy," Brossard told Michael. "If you let me go, I can make you very rich. All of you."

"So," Michael said, drumming his fingers on his knees. "I have some questions."

"I don't have to talk to you," Brossard told him.

"Oh, you really do," Wim said.

Brossard sneered. "You can't make me."

Michael half-rose from his chair, leaned over, and slapped Brossard twice, very hard, across the face, then he sat down again. He did it so quickly that even Brossard just sat there looking surprised.

"Whoa," Wim said quietly.

Brossard suddenly started to jerk about, trying to break the ties holding him, but they were too strong. He couldn't even move the chair, because it was bolted to the floor. Michael sat calmly and watched until he tired himself out and slumped back breathing hard, the imprint of fingers coming up red on his cheek.

"These people," Michael said, indicating Jo and Wim, "may not be your friends, but they know you. You're colleagues, of a sort. So they're not going to hurt you. I, on the other hand, have only just met you and I am absolutely not your friend, and I *am* going to hurt you. Your men don't know where you are; *you* don't know where you are. Nobody's going to come riding over the horizon to rescue you. I have all the time in the world." He smiled.

Brossard made another attempt to break free, but it was half-hearted. When he was done, he sat there glaring. "I'll see you all in court," he snarled.

"Oh come on, Franc," Wim said. "You're not going to go anywhere near the police. Those two guys of yours that got picked up in de Hoek are singing like birds to save their own skins; you'll be lucky not to wind up arrested yourself."

Michael didn't know if this was true or not, but it sounded plausible. Brossard certainly seemed to think so, because he seemed to shrink slightly within the ruins of his coat.

"So," Michael said. "First question. What do you *want?*"

Brossard glared at him, lips pressed tightly together as if he was afraid that he'd weaken and start talking without meaning to.

Michael reached into his pocket and took out the taser. "This was for me, wasn't it," he said, holding it up. "You brought it to the meeting because you were planning to shock me and abduct me."

"Like *you* did?" Brossard said.

"Do you believe in miracles?" Michael reached out and held the taser under Brossard's nose and pressed the button so a bright spark leapt crackling for a few moments between the contacts. Brossard jerked his head back. Michael sighed and pressed the taser to his chest.

"All right!" Brossard yelled, struggling to twist away. "All right! Jesus fucking *Christ*!"

Michael rested his thumb on the button for a few moments longer, not so much to scare Brossard as to have a debate with himself about whether or not to press it. He sat back, but he didn't put the taser away. Brossard was never going to know how close the decision had been.

"Something is about to happen," Brossard said. "Events are coming with increasing frequency; there was a time where we'd go years without anything, but in the past month alone there have been Events in the south of France and Lithuania and here in the Netherlands, and those are only the ones we know about. It's clear a tipping point is coming. I was told you know what it is."

"Told by whom?" Michael asked calmly.

"I don't know. I received an anonymised email."

"Saying what?"

"That you had information about a change in the nature of the Essence and that you would be travelling to the Netherlands in the near future. They gave me your flight number and the address of your hotel." Brossard nodded at Jo. "And her name."

"When was this?"

"Two weeks ago."

"That's impossible." Two weeks ago, he had still been in the hospital.

"The email's still on my phone," Brossard said. "You can check — oh, wait, you *can't* check because you threw my phone in the *river*, didn't you, you fucking geniuses."

"You kept that south of France Event to yourselves, didn't you," Wim said. "That wasn't very friendly."

Brossard made a rude noise.

"I'm sorry," Michael said, "but do you always go out and kidnap people because of an anonymous tipoff?"

"You don't understand," Brossard sneered. He looked at Wim and Jo. "*None* of you understand. You sit around cooing over your fucking *tennis ball* and writing learned papers for each other to read, and you don't see what's beyond the end of your nose. The *world* is about to change and we have to be ready."

Michael stared at him. "Is that *it?*" he said. "Is that what you've overturned my whole life for?" He sat forward and Brossard's eyes widened with alarm. "I have absolutely *no idea* what you're talking about, Monsieur Brossard. I'd never even heard of the Essence until a few days ago, and I still don't know whether I believe it or not." He reached out and tapped Brossard on the nose with the taser. "I don't have what you want."

"The email said you'd had an accident and were suffering from amnesia," Brossard said, trying to squirm away. "There are drugs we could try."

"You were going to give me *truth drugs?*" He pressed the taser against the Frenchman's cheek. "Really?"

"Why would you trust an anonymous email?" Jo asked hurriedly before things got out of control.

"I've had emails from this source before," Brossard said, his lips distorted by the taser pressing against the side of his face. "They call themselves 'Kelvin'. They've tipped me off to artifacts and they've never been wrong."

Michael sat back. "They're wrong now, Monsieur Brossard. At best, they're mistaken. At worst, they've decided to mess up my life and they've talked you into doing it for them."

"You absolute jackass, Franc," Wim said. "Coming to my country with a bunch of hired soldiers on the say-so of a *sockpuppet*."

"What language does Kelvin email you in?" Michael asked.

"French, of course."

"Good French?"

"I've never had the sense that it's Kelvin's second language, if that's what you mean."

"All right, Monsieur Brossard," Michael said, holding up the taser. "Now you have a choice. Either you can stop this right now, or I can put this thing in your mouth and hold the button down until the battery runs out. Either one would suit me."

Brossard stared at him. "You don't understand," he said. "We need to know."

"I don't *know anything*," Michael told him very seriously. "So what's it to be? Stop persecuting me, or eat the taser?"

"That's not a fair choice."

"You're lucky you're getting any choice at all."

Brossard glared at him for a long time. Finally, he nodded, but he did it unwillingly. Michael stood up and put the taser in his pocket and walked away.

"Okay, Franc," Wim said, going up to him and shaking out the hood. "In a while the guy who does security for this place is going to come back. We sent him off on a wild goose chase in town and he doesn't know us and he doesn't know what's been going on here, but he'll cut you loose."

"Don't you dare put that thing back on me," Brossard said.

"Now," Wim went on, "you can go to the police if you want, it's a free country, but you ought to keep in mind what I told you about those guys who were arrested. Also you can kiss goodbye to any cooperation from anyone in Europe. Thijs has a lot of goodwill in the community and people didn't really like you a whole lot even before you pulled this stunt."

"I'm going to make you suffer for this," Brossard told him.

"Oh, there you go with the big man talk again," Wim said cheerfully, dropping the bag neatly over his head and turning to catch up with the others.

Back outside the fence, a little old man in working clothes was waiting with Piet by the car. "Hey, Pops," Wim said amiably. "So, there's a Frenchman in there tied to a chair." He took a wad of high-denomination euros from the back pocket of his jeans and counted off about a dozen notes. "He's not dangerous, but he is angry, so you might want to leave him for a couple of hours before you go and turn him loose."

"Is he going to make any trouble for me?" the old man asked.

"Nah," Wim assured him. "He's too pissed off with us to bother with you." But he peeled off a couple more notes and handed them over.

Piet and Wim drove off in Wim's car, and Jo and Michael headed back in a roundabout way to Sofi's house. They drove for quite a while in silence before Jo said, "Well, that's an unexpected new side to you."

Michael was watching the countryside go by outside. "For me too," he said. It was no great surprise that he was angry, or that the reservoir of anger was quite enormous. The readiness – almost an eagerness – to use violence was a bit of a shock, though. He thought he might, if he'd been alone with Brossard, have hurt him quite badly, and that was something he was going to have to reflect on.

They drove on for a couple of miles without saying anything, then Jo said, "So, has all that got us any further forward? We'd already guessed they thought you knew something about the paradigm shift."

"Guessing is one thing," he said. "Having it confirmed is something else. But yes, it doesn't really explain anything, does it." He thought for a while. "I was still in the hospital when Brossard got that email. How could anyone back then have known I was going to Amsterdam at all, let alone which flight I was going to be on?"

"I don't know," she said. "But it sounds to me as if Brossard's friend Kelvin works for your employers."

Michael looked out of the window again.

Thijs's car was parked outside Sofi's house when they finally got back. "I don't know if this is a good sign or a bad one," Jo said, turning off the engine and undoing her seatbelt.

Bad sign, Michael thought. Thijs was sitting in the living room. His eyes were red from crying, and it looked as if he'd spent the past couple of nights sleeping in his clothes. Michael felt his heart sink.

"Oh, Thijs," Jo said when she saw him.

Thijs looked at them, and, unbelievably, he smiled. "It's gone," he said. "The tumour. It's gone. It's a miracle."

Mad Jack's Angel

Ten

"We need to examine the hospital," Thijs said.

"We need to calm down a little and think about this," Jo told him.

Thijs sat forward on the edge of the sofa, a serious look on his face. "They gave her a scan and it was *gone*, Jo," he said. "Just *gone*. Not a trace of it, as if she was never ill at all."

Jo glanced at Michael, who was sitting in an armchair in the corner looking attentive, but he was really trying to fit together everything that Brossard had told them at the factory. It was like a jigsaw where, every time you put a piece in place, the picture abruptly changed.

"Listen, Thijs," she said gently. "This is great news, it really is, but you've got no evidence that this was an Event."

"What else *could* it be? The doctors can't explain it." He sat forward a little further. "I was talking to one of the nurses. She said something happened to the lights the night before. I was asleep in a chair in Anneke's room so I missed it, but she said everything looked weird for a few moments. Does that sound at all familiar to you?"

Jo shook her head.

"We have to take readings," he told her. "Background radiation, ultraviolet, infrasound; this stuff persists, you know that. How often do we get the chance to examine a site so soon after an Event? And there may be artifacts; we have to check." He stopped, as if he'd suddenly become aware that he was babbling. He rubbed his eyes and started again more calmly. "I was asleep, Jo. It was *in the room with me* and I missed it." He sounded utterly bereft, like a man who had slept through the Second Coming. "It cured her, and I missed it," he said.

Jo seemed momentarily at a loss. "Where is she now?" she asked.

"Still at the hospital. The doctors want to run some more tests, they want to be sure. I just came back to get some clean clothes and some equipment; I'm going back in a little while."

"You can't just set your gear up in her room, Thijs," Jo told him. "They're going to wonder what the fuck you're doing."

"This is the third Event we've had recently," Thijs said. "It's unprecedented. Brossard's right, something's happening and we need to understand what it is."

She glanced at Michael again. "Yeah," she said. "We need to have a conversation about that."

"Stilwell said something about Zandvoort," Michael said, suddenly remembering. "He said something had got you all excited and it wasn't Zandvoort."

"Yeah, there was an Event at Zandvoort," Jo said. "Two, actually, a couple of days apart, but the second one was so big that nobody's been paying any attention to the first." When Michael looked blank, she said, "The sinkhole? On the coast? Have you been watching the news at all?"

"When I was in the hospital they wouldn't let us see news that might upset us," he said. "Since I got out..." He stopped. "There was some kind of disaster," he said, picturing the news item. "People died."

"Nobody died. But yeah, some kind of disaster."

Thijs got up. "I've got to go back," he said. "Could we keep this between ourselves? I don't want every essencehead in the Netherlands trampling around the hospital contaminating the scene."

"Hang on," Jo told him. "We've got to talk about Brossard."

"We don't have to worry about Brossard any more."

"Oh, I think we really do, Thijs."

"I got some messages last night," he told them. "The consensus among the community is that we should have a conference and discuss this situation, so Brossard's obliged to leave us alone until then. He's probably back in France by now."

Jo and Michael looked at each other. Michael glanced at his watch; it was unlikely that Brossard was even halfway back to Amsterdam yet.

Jo looked completely flatfooted by the news. "Where?" she said.

"Venue to be confirmed," Thijs said, heading for the door. "But peace has broken out and soon this will all be sorted out." He smiled at Michael. "You're perfectly safe now."

"Sneaky fucker," Jo said after Thijs had gone. "He tried to snatch you before everybody heard about the conference."

"He might not have got the message," Michael reasoned. "He might still not have heard; we did throw his phone into a canal, after all."

"Oh, he'd have heard. He'd have been the first person to be notified."

Michael shrugged. "He didn't strike me as someone who'd honour a gentlemen's agreement."

"It's not a gentlemen's agreement, Michael, it's a serious thing," she told him. "He has to leave us alone now, otherwise the French will never be welcome anywhere again. They'll lean on him to stick to the rules." He must have looked particularly unconvinced, because she added, "Trust me, he's out of our lives for the moment."

"It doesn't change anything for me, anyway," he said. "I can't go home because I don't know who I can trust, and Stilwell's still out there somewhere. I presume this truce doesn't cover him."

She snorted. "It's a miracle Stilwell manages to put his socks on in the morning; he wouldn't have found you at all if somebody hadn't grassed us up."

Michael wasn't so sure about that. Jo might not have a very high opinion of Stilwell, but she wasn't contemplating spending the rest of her life on the lookout for large Americans who wanted to drug her and cart her off to a secret interrogation centre somewhere. He had no idea how he was going to resolve that.

He said, "You don't really believe the Essence cured his daughter, do you?"

Jo took a fraction too long to answer. "It doesn't matter what I believe," she said. "It's what Thijs believes and we'll just have to work around it."

"What are we going to do?" he said.

She thought about it. "I'd better make some calls and see what's going on; if Thijs is going to be out of the picture for a while somebody'll have to organise things." She looked at him. "Are you okay?"

He nodded. "Still trying to put everything together."

She got up and took a couple of the burner phones from the worktop. "Let me know if you have any breakthroughs."

While Jo worked the phones, Michael went into the living room and sat down in front of the television. He fiddled with the remote control until he found the channel menu, scrolled down to a Dutch news channel, and pressed the button.

What came up was a studio discussion, an anchor and three guests sitting around a table. The backdrop behind them was a big low-angle aerial image of a stretch of coastline interrupted in the middle distance by a big semicircular bay. There were a couple of what looked like naval frigates anchored some miles offshore.

One of the guests appeared to be a geologist, and she was telling everyone else that the underlying rock formations at this point on the Dutch coast were not favourable to the formation of sinkholes, but as the authorities refused to allow her and her colleagues to examine the area there was no way to be sure.

The discussion cut to the same aerial image of the coast, but this time it was moving in that weird rock-steady first person shooter glide you got with a drone camera. The angle tipped up a little and Michael could see all the way down the coast to what he thought might be Rotterdam or the Hague.

The camera slid forward through the sky towards the bay, and as it drew closer it looked as if some colossal creature had come up out of the North Sea and taken a bite out of the smooth sweep of the coastline. It appeared to be about half a mile across, and perhaps a quarter of a mile deep.

One of the other guests was talking over the footage, addressing a theory that the sinkhole could have been the result of some kind of military installation left over from the Occupation, perhaps part of the Atlantic Wall or a hitherto-undiscovered complex of U-boat pens. The man who was speaking cited Wehrmacht and Kriegsmarine records, but the third guest cut in and pointed out that local people would have noticed construction on that scale and would still have been talking about it after the War. Then all three of them started talking at once.

Meanwhile, the camera viewpoint came to a halt some distance short of the bay, as if unwilling to fly out over that expanse of calm water. It panned left and moved inland, where Michael saw that a huge bite had also been taken out of the dykes that protected the coastline from flooding and the dunes behind them. Sunlight glinted on inundated scrubland.

"Quite something, isn't it?" Jo said from the doorway.

"It really is," he said. He remembered seeing this same drone footage on the BBC news the day after he came home from the hospital, and it was probably indicative of his state of mind at the time that it hadn't made a bigger impression on him. "What happened?"

"Well, nobody really knows." She came over and sat beside him on the sofa, and he pressed the mute button on the remote to silence the studio discussion. "As far as anyone can make out, it was an ordinary day on the beach. People sunbathing, walking, playing. There was a yoga class going on. The weather was calm. Then, apparently, this little hole appeared on the beach. Not very big at first, maybe the size of a football, but the edges kept falling in and it kept getting wider and wider. The people on the beach moved away from it, and they had to keep moving as it got bigger and bigger. The hole kept widening and they kept moving away and some people got hurt – twisted ankles and stuff like that, nothing serious, but there was a lot of panic. The edge of the hole reached the water's edge and the sea started to come in." The footage from the drone was repeating, and she sat watching for a minute. "That made the hole fall in faster; I saw one eyewitness being interviewed and he said it sounded like a train. A huge train. There were some little buildings up the beach, cafés and bars and so on, and they fell into the hole, and then the dyke behind them." She pointed at the screen. "It's flooded about a mile inland. Whole thing took between twenty and forty minutes, depending on who you listen to."

"It's amazing nobody was killed."

"Isn't it? It happened really quickly, but just slowly enough for people to get out of the way."

He looked at her. "You can't believe that was deliberate."

She shrugged. "Do you want to know how weird this thing is? There's a woman who was on the beach when the hole first opened up. She says she got a look into it while she was running away; she says it was a good look, but I reckon it can't have been much more than a quick glance. She says it was like looking into a big cave or something, maybe a hundred metres deep, and she says she saw people down there. *That's* how weird this thing is."

There was a long silence.

"What kind of people?" Michael asked finally.

Jo shrugged again. "She couldn't say. People running."

There was another silence. "Is that why you think the Essence did this?" Michael said. "Because somebody *thought* they saw something?"

She shook her head. "Nah. We've got three or four separate witnesses who say something happened to the light on the beach just before the hole opened up, just for a few seconds. One of them said he thought it was an eclipse or something."

"That seems to be the only thing all these events have in common," he said.

151

"That's right. And most people don't even notice; they think maybe a cloud went in front of the sun or something, if they think about it at all." She looked at him. "That ever happen to you?"

"I don't usually pay much attention when clouds go in front of the sun." He shook his head. "No, I don't remember anything like that."

"Anyway, they daren't send divers down because they're afraid the site's still unstable. The Navy tried one of those little underwater robots – you know, the ones they use to find shipwrecks? All they wound up with was a bigger hole and one less robot. Conventional wisdom is that eventually so much of Holland will have fallen into it that it'll stop collapsing. At least, that's what everyone's hoping." She looked at him. "Want to go over there? Tomorrow or the day after?"

"Really?" he said, surprised.

"Sure, why not? It's going to be days before anything happens with the conference, and Brossard's not going to bother us any more. Zandvoort's a nice town; we can make a day of it."

It smacked a little of going to visit the site of a train crash or a terrorist atrocity. "Are the authorities letting sightseers in?"

"You can't get right up to the edge of it, but you can get a pretty good view if you find the right spot. It'll be better than sitting here staring at the walls. We're owed a bit of a break, after today."

"All right." Although staring at the walls for a while actually sounded quite attractive; it felt as if he hadn't stopped moving since he left London.

She beamed. "Good. I need to make some more calls, then we can have a look in the fridge and decide what to have for dinner."

"Sounds like a plan to me," he said, smiling.

After she'd gone, he sat watching the news for a while. The drone footage was repeated several times, along with some confused phone camera video taken by people who had been on the beach when the hole opened. Most of it was of people running and shouting and screaming, but there was one striking image of a sloping-sided pit in the sand like the funnel of an ant-lion nest, visibly getting larger as the hole at the bottom yawned open. It really had happened very quickly.

Did he believe it had been caused by some unknowable force, rather than by a flaw in the bedrock underlying the beach? He supposed it didn't really matter; all the people who had come into his life recently *did* believe it, and that was the environment he had to deal with at the moment.

It felt as if, by accident or design, he had been introduced to the Essence gradually. First it had been a strange, otherworldly thing which had changed a tennis ball into something wondrous. Then it was the unknown force which had granted Archie his superpower. Then it was the Amsterdam footage, which was weird and unsettling but essentially harmless. Then it was that blank spot on the air, flickering up the beach to erase the East German film crew. Then it saved a little girl's life. Now it had the power to alter the landscape. What would it be tomorrow?

Or this could all be happening in his head. He could be sitting in Piet's front room with Thijs, the tennis ball still in his hand. He could still be in the hospital, strapped to a bed in the Acute wing. Perhaps his breakdown was still happening; perhaps he was in Rob's office right now, in the midst of meltdown.

He blinked. Ran his hand over the arm of the chair, feeling the fabric against his fingertips. He pinched the skin on the inside of his wrist and it hurt, which was what you'd expect. Could one hallucinate pain? He looked around the living room. It was hard to believe that something this detailed could be his imagination, but he supposed that was the point.

Did it make any difference whether this was real or happening entirely in his own head? He still had to cope with it somehow, either way. According to Brossard's informant, the mysterious Kelvin, he knew something about this paradigm shift or overturn or whatever it was that had the essenceheads so worked up, and that seemed extremely unlikely, but there were those yawning gaps in his memory, those places that could contain literally anything at all. Maybe in one of those empty spaces was the answer the essenceheads were looking for. He didn't believe it, but he couldn't disprove it either, and if he couldn't disprove it, this madness would never end.

He turned off the television and went into the kitchen. Down the hall, the study door was open, and he could hear Jo saying, "We can't rely on the English for anything, Stav. You know what they're like, they think everything that happens in Europe is a plot to reverse Brexit. They'll come to the conference and sit there looking smug and then they'll try to take the credit for everything."

Michael stood at the back door, looking out at the garden. It was a nice garden, quite large but well-planned and well looked-after, although he had a sense that it was a couple of weeks since anyone had paid it any attention. He checked in the fridge, but apart from half a dozen eggs, most of a packet of Jarlsberg slices, and two bottles of mineral water, it was quite empty, as was the freezer.

"There won't be much," Jo said from the doorway. "Thijs only uses this place at the weekend."

"We could have another omelette," he suggested.

She wrinkled her nose. "There's an Indonese restaurant on the other side of the village; I'll get a takeaway."

"It never occurred to me that there would be essenceheads in England," he said.

"Yeah." She smiled ruefully, sat down at the table, put the phone down in front of her, and rubbed her eyes. "There's never been a documented Event anywhere in the British Isles – nothing that's been confirmed, anyway – but the English keep trying to convince everybody that it's Essence Central. It's quite comical, really."

"Are there many of them?"

Jo shrugged. "A couple of dozen or so. Like here, I guess."

He looked at the phone. "What's going on?"

She scowled. "Everyone agrees we need to have a conference, but they can't agree where it should be. The English say they can block-book a hotel at the NEC in Birmingham if somebody else comes up with the money, the Germans say they've got a conference centre in Dortmund that'd do us nicely. The French are pissed off that they're not getting a say in it at all but fuck 'em, they can take that up with Brossard. Situation normal. Essenceheads love to argue."

"So we're just going to sit here until they make their minds up?"

"Don't worry; it won't take them long. They all want to have a look at you."

He raised his eyebrows. "Me? You're expecting me to go?"

"Sure. What were you expecting to do? Sit outside in the car?"

He hadn't really thought about it, but the prospect of spending any length of time in a building full of people who thought he was in possession of some kind of cosmic secret wasn't particularly attractive. "It does feel like a bit of a lion's den situation, if I'm honest."

"Nah," she said. "It's neutral ground; you'll be fine."

"Thijs said there was some bad blood after the last conference."

"Yeah, someone got shot." She smiled brightly. "Anyway, I'm feeling peckish. Shall I go and get some food?"

The food turned out to be one of the best Indonese meals Michael had ever eaten, and there was tons of it, which was handy because shortly after it was delivered Wim and Anton turned up. Without his Trump mask, Anton turned out to be a handsome, bookish-looking man in early middle age wearing wire-rim spectacles. He brought with him a big old canvas camera shoulder-bag that he didn't let out of his sight. Wim was still glowing with what he considered the success of the day's operation.

"Pops went in to have a look at him after a couple of hours and he was still shouting," he said, happily tucking into babi kecap and rice. "So he left him another hour or so, and when he came back Franc had quieted down and he cut him loose."

"Any problems?" Jo asked.

Wim shook his head. "First thing Franc did was demand Pops's phone. When that didn't work he offered him a *fantastic* amount of money for it. When *that* didn't work he just ran off, Pops didn't see where."

"I'm not sure I like the idea of not knowing where he is," said Michael, who had felt a lot more comfortable when Brossard was tied to a chair.

"Ach, you don't have to worry about Franc any more; he's going to be too busy getting ready for the conference to bother us. Right, Anton?"

"Yes," said Anton, who had been monosyllabic ever since he arrived.

"What if the conference decides he's perfectly within his rights to kidnap me and pump me full of truth drugs?"

Wim sat back and thought about it, fork poised in the air. "Well, I can't promise that *won't* happen," he said. "But it's pretty unlikely."

"Wim," Jo chided. She said to Michael, "That's not going to happen. Brossard's been a complete arse, nobody's going to pat him on the head and tell him he's a good boy."

"But everyone wants to know what I know," he said. He looked around the table. "I mean, don't *you* want to know what this is all about?"

"There's nothing to know," Jo said calmly. "You don't know anything; you never have. I don't know how you got mixed up in this circus, and I'm sorry it's happened, but it's not your fault."

"Have you heard from Thijs?" Wim asked.

"Thijs has a lot on his mind," she said, which was not entirely untrue. "I'm trying to coordinate things."

"Right," said Anton.

"You're welcome to do it, if you want," she told him.

He smiled and shook his head.

After they'd gone, Michael said, "What's Anton's problem?"

"Anton's never happy unless he's unhappy," Jo said wearily. "You get used to it."

"Is he going to be a problem?"

She looked at him. "No more than usual. And that's a very Security Service sort of question."

He shrugged. "I'm having to think that way, these days."

She thought about it, then she sighed. "I'm going to turn in," she said. "It's been a long day. Leave everything in the kitchen, we can sort it out tomorrow."

"Okay," he said, but when he went into the kitchen he couldn't in all conscience just abandon it, so he scraped the leftover food into the containers it had arrived in and put them in the fridge, then he rinsed the plates and bowls and cutlery and loaded the dishwasher.

When he'd finished that, he still wasn't remotely ready to go to bed, so he went back into the living room and searched through the TV channel menu until he found the BBC news. The ceiling of a school classroom in Worcester had collapsed, injuring a dozen children, some of them seriously. The Education Secretary was unavailable for comment, but the Department of Education released a statement that was a clumsy attempt to evade any responsibility at all. At another school, a right-wing protest against a Drag Queen Story Hour had descended into violence and the police had been forced to make arrests. Michael wondered why people weren't protesting against the general collapse of school infrastructure instead.

The newspaper review came on, but the guests weren't really there to review tomorrow's news, they were there to spin it, to tell people what they should be thinking, to use it as a springboard to score political points. The rolling news channels had a pool of commentators and reviewers; the same faces over and over again, and Michael thought it must be a nice little earner. A couple of hundred quid's appearance fee for an hour talking about the next day's papers; if you managed to do that once a week it would go some way towards paying your mortgage, and even if you only managed to win a handful of insomniacs over to your way of thinking it was still worth the effort.

Tonight's reviewers were the comment editor of one of the right-wing broadsheets, and someone introduced as a 'PR Consultant', although Michael remembered when she had worked for one of the far-right think-tanks that hung off Westminster like ticks.

He gathered that there was no such thing as 'truth' any more, that emotions were more important than facts, and he couldn't quite understand how people had so calmly accepted that. It seemed to him that truth was a fairly fundamental thing, but perhaps he was wrong.

In a world like that, anyone who insisted on facts was the enemy, to be dismissed or doxxed or driven out of public life altogether. Michael had noticed a disturbing upwelling of anti-science sentiment in recent years, a sowing of distrust in experts, and it produced an environment where flat-earthers could deny the world was a sphere and climate deniers could dismiss record temperatures as lies. *The scientists say this thing is true, but the scientists can't be trusted, therefore it's a lie.* How did people fall for this stuff? Was the world so awful that it was more comforting to abandon rationality and embrace superstition instead?

All of which made it remarkable that the essenceheads had managed to remain out of sight for so long. There were security services who would have envied that degree of anonymity. If Jo and Thijs were to be believed, they had kept themselves to themselves for centuries, quietly witnessing and recording the manifestations of something which challenged the common understanding of reality, and nobody in the wider world had ever heard of them. The world was ripe, in this coming age of superstition, for something like the Essence, and yet they somehow managed to keep the lid on their secret.

Even more remarkably, governments seemed to have done the same. You couldn't dip your toe into the conspirasphere for a fraction of a second without encountering Roswell and Area 51 and 9/11, but of the Essence there was no trace, even though Stilwell had claimed the Americans knew about it at governmental level. No leaks, no nothing.

Which made him wonder again how much his own government, his own Service, knew. Were they aware of the essenceheads but dismissive because they were obviously crazy? Did they regard it as a secret too dangerous to share? Jo had said that there had never been an Event in the UK, and if he had learned nothing else from his time close to government it was that the British coveted what others had. Why should those people have miracles when we don't? Was all this a possible route home? In the few days he'd been with the essenceheads he'd picked up useful intelligence, not least about Kelvin, Brossard's mysterious informant, who seemed to have a source within Michael's department. Could he leverage all that into a safe return to London? Could he make use of it to discover what was going on? Could he ignore it all and just walk off into the sunset if the opportunity presented itself?

The answer to that last one was obvious, at least. Running away was always an option, but it wouldn't solve anything. Instead, he sat where he was and watched the two guests on the television spinning a newspaper article about the harm caused by internal combustion emissions into a criticism of the weakness of the leader of the Opposition, and he wondered how anyone was supposed to know what was real any more.

Wim and Anton turned up again the next morning, and they took Wim's car to Zandvoort. Wim drove and Anton sat in the front passenger seat with his camera bag in his lap. Jo and Michael sat in the back and nobody spoke much as they drove south along the coast and then across the causeway into Noord-Holland.

They were just outside Beverwijk, still some miles from Zandvoort, when Michael started to see temporary signs erected at the side of the road, warning that they were entering a restricted area.

"Don't worry about them," Wim said. "They put those up in the first few days and haven't bothered taking them down yet. The zone's a lot smaller now."

Still, as they approached Haarlem the signs appeared more frequently, and their warnings grew stronger. Entering the town, Michael saw what looked like barricades lining the roadside. Wim reached over and took a laminated card from the glove compartment and put it on the dashboard below the windscreen.

In the centre of Haarlem, everything seemed normal. People were out shopping or going into restaurants and cafés, getting on with their ordinary lives. Wim said, "They blocked all the roads in and out when it happened. Everything from Bloemendaal to Nordwijk and from the coast out about as far as Vijfhuizen was locked down for about a week. You can imagine how happy that made everyone.

"When it was obvious nobody was going to die, they made the control zone smaller. Now it's just the town and six or eight kilometres down the coast, and that's mostly to keep control of the media and stop sightseers getting themselves hurt. Here we go."

They had turned towards the coast, through an area of grassy dunes and lakes and scrubby trees, and up ahead Michael could see military vehicles parked at the roadside. A little further along, concrete blocks about the size of cars had been placed on the road, narrowing it so that only single vehicles could pass, and just beyond these some small one-storey modular buildings had been set down on the central reservation, clustering beside a checkpoint consisting of a counterweighted metal pole. Wim slowed the car and stopped at the end of a queue of vehicles waiting to pass through the checkpoint.

"There's nothing to worry about," he told them. "I'm officially a Zandvoort resident; I've been going in and out of the zone ever since it happened."

"I thought you lived in Groningen," Michael said.

"I've got a flat not far from the beach."

Michael wondered what all these people did in their real lives, to give them so much spare time for chasing the Essence and enough money to afford second homes. To his knowledge, Jo was the only one with a job, and even she seemed to have abandoned that in a hurry. Would his employers have noticed that? Would they have tried to contact her when he failed to return home? She didn't seem particularly worried by the prospect.

He glanced out of the back window. A little white van had pulled up behind them; now, if they wanted to change their minds, Wim would have to make a U-turn and drive back along the cycle lane that paralleled the road, which was bound to attract somebody's attention.

He said, "If I'd known we were going to be passing through checkpoints, I might not have agreed to this."

"It'll be fine," Jo said, most of her attention on something she was thumb-typing into her phone.

"One of the first things my Service will have done is circulate my photograph and description among your authorities," he said, although of course there was no guarantee of that. He noticed that at the mention of his employers, Anton stiffened slightly in his seat. Wim, driving forward a few yards as the line of traffic moved on, gave no sign of even having heard.

"Even if they have, and even if these soldiers have your photograph, nobody's going to expect you to be out here," she said, still typing. "They'll be looking for you at ports and airports and railway stations, maybe using facial recognition on the street cameras in the cities, depending on how much of a fuss they want to make. Relax."

Which was easier said than done. They pulled up at the barrier and all of a sudden soldiers with assault weapons were standing on both sides of the car. One of them glanced inside, looked at the card below the windscreen, then straightened up and waved to his colleagues, one of whom raised the barrier to let them pass.

"See?" Jo said. "Nothing to worry about."

As they drove away from the checkpoint, Michael looked back . The soldiers were already attending to the little white van. It suddenly occurred to him that not so long ago he had been considering walking up to a police officer and asking for help to escape from this insane situation. Now he was worried that the authorities would spot him, and he couldn't quite work out how or when that change of perspective had happened. He'd read somewhere that Stockholm Syndrome might not actually exist, but if it did, was this how it would feel, this matter-of-fact acceptance of the life of a fugitive? Or had he just surrendered himself to the mad adventure of it all?

The road rose up a long, shallow gradient between high grassy dunes, curved past a little beach resort, and then there was the sea on his right, a narrow strip of blue-grey visible beyond a broad expanse of parking that ran along the coast all the way to Zandvoort. Restaurants and bars and apartment buildings began to appear on the inshore side of the road.

They drove into the centre of the town, past the little railway station, then Wim turned off the main road into a maze of winding little sidestreets and pulled up outside a narrow modern-looking three-storey block of flats.

"It's not much, but it's handy for the beach," he said.

They got out of the car and Michael stood looking about him. Like Haarlem, there was no real sense that anything had happened here. There was a branch of Albert Heijn across the road and it looked busy, there were plenty of people out and about. As he looked around, three soldiers in camouflage fatigues passed by on the other side of the street. Over on the other side of the car, Anton was taking from his big old camera bag a big old camera, one of the analogue motordrive monsters that paparazzi used to carry, complete with a big flashgun attached to the side with a translucent white diffuser clipped over the bulb. Anton caught him looking and raised his eyebrows, and Michael looked away.

"They're not really locking the town down any more," Wim explained as he led them down the street. "They realised that would only cause more panic and wild stories. What they're doing now is issuing residence permits so the people who live here can come and go as they please, and they're restricting access for outsiders. It's more about crowd control, because Christ knows everybody likes to travel for a couple of hours to come and look at a fucking big hole in the ground. And it's working, because fewer people are coming in to gawp; everyone's bored with it now."

"Really?" said Michael.

"Wim wrote the disaster response protocol," Jo said.

Michael glanced over at Wim. "You work for the government?" he asked.

Wim pulled a face. "I consult."

Michael thought about that. He said, "What does Thijs do for a living? If that's not a secret."

Wim guffawed. "He runs a second-hand bookshop."

"He's an antiquarian book dealer," Jo corrected patiently.

"Second-hand bookshop," Wim said again, nodding cheerfully.

Michael looked at Anton, walking along with his big old camera slung against his chest on a strap. Anton didn't seem inclined to volunteer his profession; maybe he was a particularly old-school sort of photojournalist.

They walked for a while along the backstreets, then Wim led them out into a wide plaza between tall hotels, and there was the seafront, and beyond it the North Sea itself, patiently chewing against the Netherlands as if it knew it had all the time in the world and only had to wait for a moment's inattention on the part of the Dutch.

Michael walked to the edge of the promenade. A blustery wind blew the scent of sand and rotting seaweed in his face as he looked out towards the horizon, below which hid the coast of Norfolk, a couple of hundred miles away. It was the closest he'd been to home since he'd arrived at Schiphol. Thirty feet or so below, the beach was full of people, kids playing in the sand, couples walking along hand in hand, people flying kites or walking their dogs. Against the sea wall were wooden buildings, shops, bars, cafés; many of the cafés had decking out in front with tables and chairs set on it, and all the tables were occupied. He smelled fried onions on the air.

"The whole town's economy would have collapsed if it had been kept locked down any longer," Wim said, standing beside him. "They had to cancel the Grand Prix as it was; they lost millions."

Michael had forgotten about the town's Formula One racing circuit. "How dangerous is it now?"

Wim shrugged. "Nobody knows. The collapse has more or less stopped, obviously, otherwise we'd be standing in the sea right now. The hope is that the worst is over, but there's a plan to evacuate everybody if it starts to expand again."

Michael thought about some awful void eating away at the bedrock below the promenade. The first he'd know about a collapse would be that terrible moment of weightlessness. He said, "Is it even possible to evacuate the whole town?"

Wim wrinkled his nose. "Probably not in time, if the initial collapse is anything to go by. We'd do our best."

"Jo said someone saw people, at the bottom of the hole," Michael said.

Wim grunted. "Yes, that was quite a big thing, for a day or so. Then someone discovered that the witness had a history of drug use and mental health problems and the media tore her to pieces. She's in hospital now, mostly for her own safety."

"So you don't believe she saw anything."

"Well, that's a good question, isn't it. If you're an essencehead, it's quite believable; if you're not, it's just crazy talk. Myself?" He sniffed and shook his head. "Nah. It's a bit too rich, even for me."

They stood for a while looking out at the sea. "This is what you meant about warning everybody, isn't it," Michael said. "About the Essence."

"Oh, I was banging that drum long before *this* happened. With a very few exceptions, artifacts are just silly little curiosities, and because of that maybe we've convinced ourselves that the Essence is harmless. But it can come out of nowhere and just erase people from existence, and now it looks like it can make the ground open up under our feet without warning, and if it can do that nowhere is safe. And all Thijs and the others want to do is write papers about it." He turned and started to walk away along the seafront.

The promenade was wide as a boulevard, lined with hotels and the little caravans of street-food vendors. They bought ice creams from a van and walked on. Out to sea, Michael could see the cordon of Dutch Royal Navy ships that kept inquisitive boats from getting too close to the collapse, but apart from that there was no sign that this was anything other than a normal day on the Dutch coast.

"How much does your government know about the Essence?" Michael asked.

"That's hard to say," Wim said thoughtfully. "I don't think I've ever met another essencehead with connections to the government, but it's not like we have a secret handshake or something. If they do know, it's classified a long way above my clearance. Which is quite funny, if you think about it." He finished his ice cream, wiped his moustache and beard with the napkin that had come with it, crumpled the napkin, and popped it in a waste bin as they went past. "It's absurd to think governments don't know about it, at some level. It's been going on a very long time."

"How long?"

"I don't know; nobody does. Thijs has some Twelfth Century Spanish manuscript fragments that describe something that sounds like an Event, but it's hard to be certain." He stopped again and put his hands in his coat pockets and looked out to sea.

"Do you think your government know there was an Event here?"

Wim shrugged. "They've got access to the same eyewitness reports that we do. They're treating it as a civil emergency, which is what I'd do if I wanted to avoid a panic, so it's hard to tell." He gestured along the coast. "Maybe they're just sitting down there in the Binnenhof with their fingers crossed and hoping things won't get worse."

"That's what my government usually does," Michael agreed.

Jo and Anton had walked on a little way. She stopped and turned. "Do you two want to see this thing or not?" she called.

"I saw it already," Wim said, but he said it so quietly that only Michael heard him.

They walked for about twenty minutes. The boulevard narrowed until it was barely wide enough to allow two cars to drive down it, and guest houses and what looked like private residences started to appear in the gaps between the hotels. The last hotel on the seafront was a fifteen-storey white block faced with balconies and, judging by the number of people in the lobby when they stepped through the big revolving door at the front, it was doing good business.

Jo went over to the reception desk. Over to their left was a doorway leading into a big dining room full of people. To the right, a smaller coffee bar was equally packed, and more people were using the seating arranged around the lobby. It looked as if the hotel had been taken over by a convention.

"Sightseers," Wim said. "You wouldn't think people'd come all this way to have a weekend break on the edge of a great big hole, would you? And yet here they all are."

"People don't like to be told they can't go somewhere," Anton said. It was virtually the first thing he'd said since they'd left Sofi's house

Wim made a rude noise. "Disaster tourists," he said. "A few weeks ago this place was full of journalists, but they've mostly gone now."

"I thought you said people were getting bored with it," Michael said.

Wim nodded. "But the ones who do come stay here. You'll see why in a minute."

Jo came back from the desk carrying four binocular cases by their straps. "They put the price up again, the sods," she said.

"You can't really blame them," said Anton.

"Oh, I can," she told him, handing out the binoculars. "Come on."

They took a lift up to the top floor, and Jo walked down the corridor with a key card in one hand and a piece of paper in the other, looking at door numbers, until she found the one she wanted.

It was a big room, which felt even bigger because it had been stripped of everything moveable. The bed was gone, as were any chairs and tables that had once been there. All that was left was the familiar low shelf along one wall below a big mirror. Cables dangled out of the wall to one side of the mirror, over an empty television bracket. The furniture was gone because it wasn't the important thing about the room. The important thing was the view.

Michael walked over to the windows and looked out across a huge vista of landscape. From here, he could see all the way down the coast to a vague and tiny suggestion of something industrial – chimneys? cranes? enormous buildings? – it was impossible to say what it was, but he remembered the drone footage he'd seen on the news, and thinking it might be Rotterdam or The Hague.

"The hotel's been renting these rooms out to journalists by the hour," Jo said. "For the view."

"It's pretty impressive," Michael agreed. "But won't journalists have drones?"

"Fewer than you'd think," Wim said. "And in the very early days the authorities were shooting them down." He pointed at the ceiling. "They had snipers on the roof. The big news organisations kicked up a stink about it. And the locals weren't too keen, either. You know, bits of drones falling on their heads and all that."

It was impossible to plan for something like this; the best thing any government could do was bolt together a number of existing emergency protocols and hope to wing it long enough to get on top of the situation. Michael took out his binoculars. The road along the seafront had been blocked just beyond the hotel, and he could see a lot of soldiers and military vehicles down there. Beyond the roadblock, the houses on the promenade continued for another mile or so and then came to an abrupt stop as the road curved sharply back inland.

"All the houses on this side have been evacuated," he heard Wim saying. "It's just a precaution, but a lot of people are really pissed off."

Beyond the road, the landscape was a scrubby wilderness of dunes and bushes and trees. And half a mile further on the smooth line of the coast was broken by the half-moon of the collapse, a great bite taken out of the land. It was one thing to see it on drone footage, but quite different to be looking out at it from the top floor of the hotel. It seemed much larger in real life, and it extended a lot further inland than he'd appreciated. The scrubland behind the coast seemed to be inundated for as far as he could see: a great expanse of shallow salt marsh.

"We've lost a lot of land, and it's going to take a lot of work to get it back," Jo said. "If we can even afford to do that these days. Fortunately, all of that land's a nature reserve."

"Not so fortunate for the nature," Anton mused.

"Well, no. That's true. But imagine if this had happened where we parked the car. Lots of people would have been killed; we'd have had to abandon the whole town."

"Has it got any bigger?" Michael asked.

"Not so much, since the early days," said Wim. "Maybe a few metres or so. We're trying to reinforce the sea wall."

Michael could see yellow earthmoving equipment on the coastal embankment on both sides of the bay. On the far side they were just specks, even with the binoculars, but on this side he saw tractors and bulldozers and diggers, and lots of people. He supposed they were quite brave to be so close; another collapse would pitch them all into the sea.

He said, "You don't have any evidence that the Essence exists, though, do you," and everyone stared at him. Wim gestured pointedly at the scene beyond the window. "Yes, but you've no reason at all to believe that whatever caused this also caused the Amsterdam Event." Behind him, he heard someone tapping at the door.

Wim said, "The light –"

"The light changed, yes. I know. But that's *flimsy*, isn't it? It doesn't prove that everything's connected." The tapping came again. "You might as well say the Essence caused that crack in your house."

"No," said Wim, "I *know* what did that." Another tap at the door.

"We've got the room for an hour!" Jo called out in a loud voice, but there was more tapping, and she turned from the windows and started to go over to the door. "You know," she said to Michael, "I really thought we were starting to get through to you, after everything that's happened."

Michael looked out at the landscape beyond the windows again. He heard Jo open the door and say, "What," then there was a sort of scuffling sound and when he turned to look Jo had backed up against the wall and Colonel Stilwell was standing in the doorway with one of his men behind him in the corridor.

"Hello," Stilwell said with a big smile. He was wearing jeans, a light blue UCLA sweatshirt and a Naval surplus pea jacket. "I *thought* that was you I saw in the lobby."

Michael lowered his binoculars. "We don't want any trouble," he said.

"Trouble?" Stilwell grinned. "There's not going to be any trouble." He stepped into the room, followed by his colleague, and the door closed on its springs behind them.

"This is quite a coincidence," Michael said.

"Isn't it, though?" Stilwell sounded delighted. "I just decided to come out here and look at the sinkhole, and there *you* were. Isn't life wonderful?"

"Isn't it though?" Wim said.

"You're wearing my coat," Stilwell told Michael. "That's theft; I could have you arrested."

"Good luck trying to explain how I wound up with it."

Stilwell looked at Jo. "You, I recognise," he said. "You were at the airport, and we're going to have a little chat about how you managed to pull that off."

"We're really not," she told him.

"Oh, we really are." He took another couple of steps into the room; the other American stayed with his back to the door. Stilwell looked at Wim and tipped his head to one side. "Willem van de Kamp," he said. "Do your employers know what you do in your spare time?" He still hadn't stopped smiling. He turned to Anton, who was holding his camera with both hands as if he thought Stilwell was going to take it away from him, and shook his head. "Don't know *you*. Are you new?"

"No offence to you or your associate, Colonel," Michael said, "but there are four of us and only two of you. I don't fancy your chances of getting us out of this room, let alone out of the hotel, so we're at a bit of a stalemate here."

"Well," Stilwell said, reaching behind him under his coat and bringing his hand out holding a pistol, "that's why we have these. To resolve *stalemates*." He nodded to Jo and waved her back towards the windows. Behind him at the door, the other American had taken out a gun of his own.

"It's illegal to be carrying those," Wim said.

"You're more than welcome to take them away from us," Stilwell told him. "If you can."

"Guns are really only a threat when there's the possibility that you'll use them," Michael said, and it was like hearing someone else speaking. "You're not going to shoot me, because you think I have something you want, and you're not going to shoot anyone else, because someone will hear and they'll call hotel security and you'll wind up having to fight your way out of here. So we're back to stalemate."

Stilwell narrowed his eyes. "You're a different person when you're not chained down."

"I've been on a steep learning curve."

Stilwell thought about that. He looked at the windows and jerked his chin at the outside world. "What do you make of that?"

"I don't know," Michael said. "I genuinely don't."

"You see what I meant about the Essence being an existential threat? If it can do that here, it can do it anywhere. Suppose it did it under the White House or the Houses of Parliament?"

"I imagine quite a lot of people would celebrate."

"Smartass. Suppose it was Tel Aviv or Tehran, then." When Michael didn't reply, he said, "You need to wake up to what you've got yourself mixed up in, buddy."

Michael didn't say anything. It may have been the first time anyone had called him 'buddy'.

Stilwell looked at the others. "So what's the deal? The Essence never did anything like this before; is something happening?"

Nobody said anything.

"The French guy certainly thinks so," Stilwell went on. "*Franc Le Métro* – do you *all* have superhero names, by the way?"

"Yes," said Jo, beside Michael. "Mine's 'Angry Girl'. Would you like to know why?"

Stilwell guffawed. "Why don't you teleport yourself and these guys out of here? No? Didn't bring that particular artifact with you? Tell you what, I'll give you a straight hundred million bucks for it, in any currency you want."

The last thing Michael wanted was for the conversation to go anywhere near Archie. He said, "If you have a spare hundred million to spend, you'd be better off buying yourself an island or something and retiring."

Stilwell gave him a sad look. "How can I retire when *this* is happening?" he asked, nodding at the window again. "This could literally be life or death for the human race."

He said, "It doesn't really solve your problem though, does it, Colonel? There are still four of us and two of you."

There was a certain mindset that said if you were holding the gun everybody else had to do what you told them, but if you took away the threat of actually shooting anyone a gun was just a meaningless object, and Stilwell seemed to have forgotten that. For the first time since walking into the room, a look of uncertainty crossed his face, and that was when Michael heard a faint, high, rising whine somewhere off to his left. He glanced over and saw Anton raising the camera to his face.

"Close your eyes," Jo said in a calm whisper that only Michael heard.

Michael closed his eyes and he heard Anton say, "Smile, you son of a bitch," then there was pop as the flashgun discharged and there was a flash of something that wasn't light, something so far from being light that it was unrecognisable as a natural phenomenon. For a fraction of a second, he felt it sucking his eyeballs against his closed lids, then it was gone and there was the sound of people falling over and Jo said, "Okay," and when he opened his eyes again Stilwell and his bodyguard were both collapsed on the floor.

All of a sudden, everyone was moving. Jo went over to Stilwell and started going through his pockets. "Leave the guns," she said. "Don't touch them."

Anton and Wim manhandled the other American away from the door, patted him down, and rolled him into the recovery position. Wim opened the door and glanced outside. "Clear," he said.

"Fine," she said. "Make sure you don't leave anything behind." Michael stood where he was, still trying to work out what had just happened. "We're going now," she told him. "We're not going to run or make a fuss or do anything to attract attention. These blokes are going to be out cold for about an hour, and when they wake up they're going to be in a world of trouble, so give yourself a shake."

They went out into the corridor and Wim made sure the door closed and locked behind them, then they walked along to a door with an exit sign over it and down fifteen flights of emergency stairs, which was enough to remind Michael just how out of shape he was.

At the bottom, Jo collected the binoculars. "I have to give these and the key back," she said. "There's a three hundred euro deposit on them. If you go over to the right there's a side door. Wait for me there."

The door to the stairs opened in a quiet corner of the lobby. Jo headed for Reception while Michael and the others went outside and found themselves in a little paved smoking area. Jo joined them a minute or two later, and they set off into the streets behind the seafront.

"Doesn't look like he brought anyone else with him," Jo said as they walked. "I didn't see anyone in the lobby, anyway."

"Man's an idiot," said Wim. "He thinks he's a fucking cowboy or something."

"What just happened?" Michael asked.

"Later," said Jo, taking out her phone and dialling a number. "Okay," she said when whoever she was calling answered. "Make the call." She listened. "No, everything's fine. Just make the call, okay? I'll be in touch. Thanks, bye."

Forty minutes later they were back in the car and Wim was driving them out of town on a different road to the one they'd come in on. They passed through another checkpoint, but again the soldiers on guard just waved them through. Obviously they weren't as bothered about people leaving the area.

"That wasn't really a coincidence, was it," Michael said as they drove out into the countryside.

Beside him, Jo was going through the wallets they'd taken from the Americans. "We let slip to Dan and Josine that we were going to be at that hotel today," she said.

He thought about it. "Why?"

"Well," she said, taking a wad of assorted currency from one of the wallets and counting through it, "for one thing it confirms that they've been leaking to the Americans, so that's one loose end tied up." She folded the money and put it in her pocket.

"So you were expecting him."

"Hoping, really." She rummaged in the wallet again. "We just made an anonymous phone call to the police saying that men with guns are on the top floor of the hotel," she said. "They're going to search all those rooms and they're going to find two unconscious blokes with guns and no ID." She held up a pair of blue passports and a couple of driving licences. "The Dutch authorities take that kind of thing *very* seriously. Stilwell and his people will be lucky not to wind up being deported."

"You said he was stupid."

"Oh, he is. But even stupid people can get in the way." To Wim, she said, "Stop at the next bridge, would you?"

"And that is…?" Michael nodded at Anton, sitting in the front passenger seat. He'd put the camera back in its bag, and the bag was on his lap.

"That's not ours," she said. "We borrowed it from the Austrians."

"The Austrians."

She thought about it. "When I say 'borrowed', we had to put up a *fantastic* amount of money and there's a courier waiting to take it back to Graz tonight."

"You'll notice," he said, "that I'm being surprisingly calm about the fact that you seem to have used me as bait."

She looked at him. "You're the one who was worried about him still being on the loose."

"You're the one who kept telling me he wasn't a problem."

Jo sighed. "Okay, I'm sorry," she said. "I should have discussed it with you."

"Yes," he said. "You should." And actually, he *was* surprisingly calm. His life had been deformed to such an extent that being set up by people he was starting to regard as friends was barely worth mentioning. "Do you remember that little speech you gave about me having *agency*? A lot's happened since then; it might have slipped your mind."

She gave him a serious look. "Point taken, Michael. I'm sorry."

The car came to a bridge over a canal, and Wim pulled to a stop. Jo hopped out and dropped the wallets and passports into the water.

Eleven

Wim dropped them at Sofi's house and then drove off with Anton, presumably to return the camera. With Thijs still not back from Amsterdam, the house felt cold and abandoned. They heated up the remains of the previous evening's meal for a late lunch, sat at the kitchen table to eat.

"What you were saying before Stilwell turned up," Jo said. "You're *still* not convinced about the Essence? After everything?"

"I don't know, Jo," he said, concentrating on his food. "It feels as if someone just made up an explanation for all this a long time ago, and nobody's ever questioned it. You might be studying something that isn't there at all." They glanced at each other. "Surely I'm not the first person to think that."

Jo shrugged. "Every couple of years some bright spark pops up with a paper saying something like it. I told you, essenceheads love to argue. The Essence is *orthodoxy*, Michael. People have *seen* it. Not very many, I'll grant you, and most of them didn't realise what it was, but it's been seen in action and it's the best explanation we've been able to come up with."

They ate for a while in silence. "Dan and Josine will have told Stilwell about Archie," Michael said at one point.

Jo shook her head. "They never saw him; he arrived in a bag and he left under his own steam and he was only there for a few hours anyway. We were careful."

"They must have wondered why you were covering one of their rooms with copper mesh."

"They were never in that room," she said. "And when Archie was gone we put it back the way we found it. And even if they did see what we'd done, they didn't know what we had up there." She rubbed her eyes. "I'm getting tired of having to micromanage all this, you know. Thijs's mind hasn't been on things for weeks and nobody else wants to take the responsibility." She blinked at him.

"Wim seems happy to help."

She snorted. "Wim's happy to help because it makes everyone else notice that Thijs isn't here." She glowered at her food. "I should really get those two in the same room and bang their heads together."

"What do you think will happen to Stilwell?"

"I'm *hoping* the Dutch will put him in a cell for a few days and then boot him out of the country." She shrugged. "Depends how much clout he has with the State Department, I suppose. They could lean on the Dutch to let him go."

"So today might have been a waste of time."

"No, Michael," she said. "Today was the day we *fought back*. Today was the day we put everyone on notice that we're not a pushover. It was not a waste of time."

It seemed that the Dutch essenceheads considered themselves at war with the world, and not just because of Brossard and Stilwell. He said, "You never got round to telling me how you got involved in all… *this*." He waved a hand to indicate everything.

She heaved a sigh. "Remember the Amsterdam footage?"

He nodded.

"I was there."

He raised his eyebrows.

"I was ten," she said. "We'd come over to visit my gran and we were out for a walk one day and all of a sudden the colour sort of drained out of the air. We couldn't work out what it was so we stopped and watched." She looked towards the window. "There was a lady on a bike, riding by, and she stopped too. I thought she was the most beautiful lady I'd ever seen."

You read in books about the hairs on the back of people's necks standing up, but in real life you never experience it yourself. Until you do. Michael said, "That was you in the footage." He remembered the little girl in the yellow coat, standing in the background holding her father's hand, mouth hanging open.

She looked at him. "We didn't see what happened. It only lasted a few seconds. The guys at the flower stand by the tram stop along the road were shouting, but we couldn't see what they were shouting at. The lady on the bike looked down at me and smiled, and she gave me ten guilders, told me to buy an ice cream or something, but I never did. I've still got that ten guilder note. So, yeah, I think essenceheads are weird and crazy, and they drive me out of my mind, but I believe in the Essence because I was there. I saw the light change."

All of sudden, Michael realised something which should have been obvious all along. He had fallen in with people who basically believed in the literal existence of magic. He wondered how she felt, seeing herself in the footage of the event, frozen in time at the moment when a miracle happened. Was she trying to track down that miracle, or to recapture the childhood moment when her father had still been alive and a beautiful lady gave her money for an ice cream?

He said, "Do the others know?"

She shuddered. "Christ, no. They'd never leave me alone. It's our secret, right?"

"I've signed the Official Secrets Act, remember?"

She smiled. "Anyway, years later I decided to try and find out what had happened, and one thing led to another and here I am, a fully paid-up member of the Crazy Squad."

He got up and took the plates over to the sink and ran hot water over them. "You don't seem as… committed as the others."

She sighed. "Sometimes I think they like me for that; maybe they think I'm their pet sceptic or something. But I was *there*, I don't need convincing." She took a tea towel from the back of one of the chairs and came over to the sink to dry the dishes he was washing. "It's complicated."

"A little cynicism is good," he told her. "Otherwise, like you said, you wind up being a fanatic."

"In your business too?"

"Sometimes. I'm an economist, not a spy, but I do mix with Intelligence people on occasion and now and again you meet someone who's a true believer. I usually try to avoid people like that at parties."

"A lot of essenceheads are like that. Brossard definitely. Thijs and Wim, too, in their own ways."

"Stilwell?"

"He's a fanatic, but I'm not convinced he's a believer. The people who fund him and his operation, the religious Right, *they* believe. They think the Essence is the hand of God."

"Like Brossard and the French."

"Kind of, but the Americans believe it's a literal expression of the Rapture, a sign that the End Times are coming."

He thought about that. "I got the impression that he was looking for ways to stop it."

She nodded. "I guess his relationship with his employers is a bit complicated."

"When he was talking to me in Eindhoven, he had a dossier on me," he said. "Or not a dossier, more of a go-to. Name, date of birth, where I went to school. Stuff like that."

"You think maybe Kelvin's been talking to him too?"

"I don't know. He knows who I work for, though, and that's not exactly in the public domain."

She looked thoughtful. "Have you pissed somebody off?"

"I can't remember; I can't imagine upsetting someone badly enough to do something like this, but I suppose anything's possible. Whoever's done this, they work for my employers and they're someone senior enough to be part of the decision-making process that came up with the idea of sending me to Amsterdam." He thought of Rob, his line manager, who had somehow decamped to one of the think tanks that provided opinion-makers to the news organisations. Had he done something to monumentally offend Rob?

"And they're an essencehead," Jo pointed out. "Brossard said Kelvin was tipping him off about artifacts. Does that sound like anyone you know?"

He shrugged. How was he supposed to recognise an essencehead? Wim would never have fitted in at the department, and Brossard would have lasted about a week, but Jo and Thijs and Piet and even Anton wouldn't even raise an eyebrow unless they started spouting madness about Events and artifacts, and he was fairly certain nobody he knew had ever done *that*.

He shelved it for the moment. "You said there was an earlier Event at Zandvoort," he said. "Was that when Archie got his superpower?"

She nodded. "We think so, yeah. A few of the eyewitnesses to the second Event said they'd been at the beach a couple of days earlier and they saw the light change then too. Mrs de Keyser likes to take Archie to the seaside at weekends if the weather's good; we checked with her neighbour and she was there that day."

Michael was beginning to feel rather sorry for Mrs de Keyser, what with people kidnapping her dog and her neighbour gossiping behind her back. "Was it the same part of the beach?"

"Exact same spot and same time of day, as far as we can judge. One of the eyewitnesses was the owner of one of the bars that fell into the hole; she said she saw the light change both times."

He wasn't sure how much credibility he gave that change in the light thing, but Archie was real and so was the hole in the coast; *something* had happened on that beach, and it had happened while he was still in the hospital. Everything had happened while he was still in the hospital, and he was blundering around in the aftermath.

Jo went into the village to get some supplies, and Michael drifted around the house for a little while before finding himself back in the living room looking at the folder Wim had given him. He sat down and took out the script of *The Unknown Man* and looked at the title page, thinking about a force that made gave West Highland Terriers the power to teleport, miraculously cured little girls, did something indescribable to tennis balls, turned cameras into stun-guns, and created huge voids under Dutch beaches. Not to mention making a bucket of cut tulips scream, ever so briefly. There was no pattern to it, no sense of logic. It manifested at random and sometimes left behind fetish objects. It was completely inexplicable and it was hard to believe in, but he'd seen Archie in action and watched the footage of an East German camera crew being erased from existence, and *something* was doing all that. Did it really matter, for the purposes of his life as it currently was, if he thought of the cause as the Essence?

He leafed through the script until he found the place he'd got to the other day. He turned a couple of pages and Joe was back in his office, having his cuts and bruises tended by Liselotte. There was more tough-guy dialogue; she was of the opinion that he needed to find a new line of work, and he was inclined to agree.

This cosy little scene was interrupted by the arrival of our femme fatale, Marthe Braun. Michael had no idea what the actress playing Liselotte looked like, but he could quite easily imagine Hannelore Huber completely outshining her. He pictured her coming into the office wearing expensive clothes, high heels, a hat, and carrying a little purse, completely cool and in control.

But for all that, she was a lady with a problem. Her husband, Erich, a businessman, had gone missing in the British sector of the city. The authorities had drawn a blank – or more likely, she thought, had simply ignored her. She'd heard, though, that Joe Becker was a man with many connections across Berlin, a man with his ear to the ground. There was more hardboiled dialogue. It was becoming clear that Joe was the classic sap, the shady character down on his luck who was primed to respond to flattery. He was also vulnerable to Marthe's promise of a large amount of money to retain his services, and an even larger one if he managed to find Erich Braun.

Joe travelled to the British Zone, visiting his various contacts. Michael presumed that, by the time Lorenz Bohrer came to make *The Unknown Man*, it would have been impossible for him to get permission to film in what by then was West Berlin, but it didn't matter because it was all bars and dives and meetings on street corners, and they could have filmed that in the studio or in the East. Joe's British Army contact, a Corporal Smith, was an intriguing collision of classes, given to exclaiming the German equivalents of 'cor blimey, guv'nor' and 'what ho! Jolly good!' But that was okay because he was less a character than a plot device, a conduit for information which would move Joe further into the story.

Michael wondered if any of the cast were still alive. Only Weber and Huber had been on location on the day of the Event, so the rest presumably would have been back in East Germany. Maybe some of them had already completed work on the film and gone on to other projects when news came through about the deaths of the stars and the crew in a 'road accident'. And that led him to wonder how much of the film had actually been completed before the Event brought production to an end. Had it been almost finished, just a few location scenes left to be filmed? It raised the intriguing possibility that there might still be an almost-complete film somewhere, only waiting to be edited. It was unlikely, but stranger things had happened. Stranger things had happened to *him* in the past week or so.

The socially fluid Corporal Smith was a virtual fountain of information, revealing that Erich Braun had been a member of the Nazi Party from the early days of its rise to power, and his fortune was founded on postwar black marketeering, allegedly in partnership with an American Colonel named Jones. Corporal Smith was of the opinion that Braun had been enthusiastically profiteering the whole time Hitler had been in power, and had simply moved in a slightly different direction after the war.

It was a monumental piece of exposition; it was very poorly written and occupied an entire page of the script, but it didn't get Joe any closer to finding Erich Braun. It also meant that Marthe Braun had been somewhat economical with the truth when she'd briefed him about her missing husband.

Joe was walking down the street, processing this new information, when a jeep screeched to a halt beside him and its occupants – in American uniform – got out and beat him up. Then they threw him in the back of the jeep, drove to the nearest checkpoint, and dumped him on the pavement.

Some time later, with the help of a former Vopo colleague, Joe returned to his office to find the door smashed open and his rooms in ruins.

And there, Michael assumed, ended Act 1, with Joe standing in the wreckage of his office, knee deep in a mystery involving Nazis, corrupt Americans, and black marketeers. It was hardly groundbreaking stuff. In fact it was absurdly familiar; he could picture Bogart and Bacall in the lead roles, although he doubted they would have put up with the crappy dialogue. And maybe Orson Welles would have been available to play Erich Braun, because he suspected that Act 3 would swerve into *Third Man* territory. Welles could have sorted the script out too, while he was at it.

He heard the front door open and close, and a moment later Jo looked into the living room. "I thought I'd knock a bolognese together," she said, holding up a shopping bag. "We can do a proper shop tomorrow."

"Sounds good to me. Can I help?"

She shook her head. "I can do a bolognese with my eyes shut." She nodded at the pile of typescript in his lap. "Is that getting any better?"

"I'm afraid not, no. Have you heard from Thijs?"

"No. We could be waiting here a while, you know."

"To be honest, it's nice to have a break," he said. "Things have been a bit too hectic for the past few days."

She looked sadly at him. "We *will* sort this out, Michael. We just have to stamp out the fires one by one."

He smiled. "Of course," he said, although even if Brossard and Stilwell could be neutralised, it still only scratched the surface of the profound insult which had been dealt to his life. The real problem was Kelvin, the source of all his woes. He was currently coming round to the view that Kelvin had leaked the Dutch data to the media, plunging him into this nightmare to throw the leak investigation into disarray. It seemed rather extreme, for a couple of column inches in *The Guardian*, so presumably the leak was more serious than that. It didn't help, though. Kelvin could be anyone who'd had access to that data; they could conceivably be more than one person. He still didn't know who he could trust.

He took up the script again. He wondered how Joe would react to a situation like this. It would probably involve a bar at some point, followed by a punch-up from which he would inevitably emerge worst. Joe, for all his world-weary wisecracking, had no more agency than he did. They were both being propelled by circumstances they could only vaguely understand. Michael presumed that by the end of the script Joe would have taken control and turned the tables on his adversaries; he had rather less confidence that would happen to him.

Joe visited Marthe Braun's home – described in the script as 'opulent', whatever that meant in the context of 1950s East Berlin – to confront the femme fatale about her husband's background. Marthe, confident and drily amused, denied nothing. The pair engaged in hardboiled flirting, with Marthe running rings around Joe. Again, it was a conversation which could have come from any of a dozen noir thrillers, so derivative that he felt he'd read it before.

At the bottom of the page, Marthe said, "At least you're alive."

Michael said, "It's the little things that make a difference."

He turned the page, and Joe's next line was, "It's the little things that make all the difference."

He stared at the line for a long time, then he turned forward a few pages. Joe visited a psychic who styled himself 'Mesmer'. Mesmer's room was full of esoteric articles, a goat's head mounted on the wall, a human skull sitting on a table with a black candle stuck to it, Tarot cards, a crystal ball, a silver dagger, the withered hand of an Egyptian mummy.

"They're just props," Michael said. "I get them for a few bucks apiece from antique stores; the customers love them."

Mesmer's next line, on the following page, was, "It's all just set dressing, Herr Becker. Like in the theatre. I get them for a few marks at the flea market; my clients expect a certain atmosphere."

Michael felt a cold fingertip touch the back of his neck. The script didn't describe Mesmer's room, beyond saying it contained *esoterica*, but Michael could picture it because he *had* read a description of it somewhere. There was a drifty, woozy sensation of rising panic. Had the script been on the beach that day? Was it an artifact that somehow induced a powerful sense of *déjà vu*? No, Wim had said this was a copy; the original was in a safety deposit box somewhere. But Michael had read this before, he felt the story beginning to surface in his memory. Which was impossible. He read the scene again, and he could almost see himself sitting somewhere else, reading a slightly different version in different circumstances. Mesmer hadn't been called Mesmer, though; he'd been called... Stainforth? Stockwell? *Stanage*. He'd been called Stanage. And suddenly Michael knew what he was reading.

Script in hand, he went into the kitchen, where Jo was chopping onions. "Can I borrow your phone, please?" he asked, feeling weightless.

She looked at him. "What for?"

"I want to call Wim," he said.

She narrowed her eyes. "What about?"

He waved the script. "Please, Jo. You can dial the number if you want."

She looked at him a few moments longer, then she laid the knife down on the chopping board, took her phone from her back pocket, scrolled down the contact list, and thumbed the call icon. "Are you okay?" she asked, holding it out.

"Yes," he said, taking the phone, but he wasn't, because more memory was surfacing. Joe Becker hadn't been Joe Becker; he'd been Joe Sharky. Marthe Braun had been Maria Broward. "Hello?" he said, holding the phone to his ear. "Wim? It's Michael. I'm reading the script."

"Hey," said Wim. "That's good news, obviously, but you might want to be careful about using names in future, just in case."

Michael didn't care about that, right now. "It's based on a novel called *The Heart of the Maze*. Not just based on, Bohrer lifted big bits of dialogue nearly verbatim."

There was a silence at the other end, while Wim thought about that. "Are you sure?"

"Yes. I was reading it recently in – back in London." He felt as if he was levitating. Was this the kind of epiphany conspiracists hoped for? This moment when two unrelated things seemed to connect and proved that there really *was* an underlying order to the universe? "Or maybe the book's based on the script. Maybe the person who wrote the book saw the script first."

"Who wrote it?" Wim asked calmly, as if he was trying to calm down a dangerous drunk.

Michael shook his head. "I can't remember, and I don't know when it was written."

"Shouldn't be hard to check. *The Heart of the Maze*, you say?"

"I tried to look it up before, but there's no novel of that name."

"Just because it's not on the internet, doesn't mean it's not there," Wim said amiably. "Stuff falls through the cracks all the time. But thanks for this; it's always good to get some more background. Was the author English, by the way?"

Michael tried to focus, but it seemed as if that memory had never been there in the first place; he just hadn't bothered to notice who had written it. "I don't know. I'm sorry."

"Doesn't matter. I'll see what I can find out. And thanks again."

They hung up. Michael handed the phone back to Jo, who had been watching his side of the conversation with a look of increasing concern. "Are you sure you're okay?" she asked.

"Yes," he said, but he wasn't. Wim hadn't said, "Wow, *that's* a coincidence," but it was. It really was. It was a ridiculous coincidence.

"Maybe you should go and sit down," she told him.

He looked around the kitchen, and for a moment he thought he saw faint halos of light around the furniture. "Maybe," he said.

"You've been running on adrenaline for days," he heard her say. "It's all starting to catch up with you."

He went back into the living room and sat down, and a moment later she followed him in. "Do you want anything?" she asked. "Cup of tea? Glass of water?"

"I'll be fine," he told her. "It'll pass."

"How do you feel?"

"I'll be fine," he said again, but he had a very real sense of tectonic movement, of things rearranging themselves in his mind. It should have been alarming, but somehow it wasn't; the act of remembering *The Heart of the Maze* had closed a switch somewhere in his head, and other memories were coming up out of the background noise. He suddenly remembered that he had a cat.

"I'll make you some tea," Jo said, and she left the room.

The cat had turned up one day, a young stray tabby, sitting outside the back door when Christina came back from work at the local school.

She'd opened the door to say hello and it had walked in, looked around, shat on the dining room floor, and then walked back out again.

But it had come back the next day, and the next, patiently waiting at the back door, until one evening she weakened and opened a tin of tuna and put some on a saucer, and the cat had more or less inhaled it and then gone on to have seconds, and after that it hardly left the house, apart from to sit out on the little patio area keeping watch for Oscar, next door's cat. Christina named it Walter, and Walter had grown up to be plump and lazy and, as far as they could tell, perfectly happy to eat and sleep and occasionally approach one or other of them for cuddles. It was as if he had always lived with them.

Walter had known there was something wrong when Christina got ill; Michael remembered him being unusually clingy, and after she went into the hospital he was always waiting by the front door for her to come home, but she never did. After she died, he spent evenings curled up in Michael's lap, either looking for comfort or looking to give it.

Jo came back with a mug of hot, sweet tea with a slice of lemon floating in it, and when she was sure that he wasn't going to melt down through the floor she went back to the kitchen.

Walter had been a great companion for him, in those early days after Christina's death. How could he possibly have forgotten that? After the funeral, he'd tried to get his life back on its wheels, and it had meant a lot to him to find someone waiting for him when he got back from the office, even if Walter had just wanted a bowl of tuna or some Dreamies or someone to scratch behind his ears. The simple act of having to care for someone else had somehow carried him through those early days.

He'd been determined to carry on as normal. Maybe he'd been afraid to take the period of leave that HR had suggested; maybe he'd been afraid that everything would overwhelm him if he didn't occupy himself with mundane things like work. Maybe he'd thought he could process what had happened bit by bit rather than having to do it all at once.

He remembered going in to the office, day after day during the week. Shopping and gardening at the weekends. Looking after Walter. Simple things, the familiar, comforting tracks of his existence. All of a sudden he remembered meetings and reports and conferences. It was, he recalled now, customary for Rob to go down to the Treasury on Thursday afternoons to brief the Chief Secretary's senior staff on matters of note, and sometimes he went along for moral support or to clarify some arcane point. He remembered that Rob, who usually presented at the office in jeans and a shirt and trainers, kept a suit and a Guards tie specially for those meetings.

His last day at the office had been a Thursday, and he remembered that he had decided to make an effort to match Rob's protective colouration, and he was wearing the three-piece suit he'd last worn for a reception at the Dutch Embassy. He hadn't been able to find a Guards tie, so he wore his old Trinity College one. He stopped off at Bloom's as usual for a coffee, then went up the stairs to Reception, where he'd said hello to Alice/Angela, swiped his pass against the gate reader, and passed through to the lift.

For some reason, the lift wasn't working. He remembered now that he'd stood there foolishly pressing the button, but nothing happened. He remembered Alice/Angela leaving her desk and coming towards him. She was smiling and holding something out in her hand, offering it to him, he couldn't picture what it was. And then...

And then he woke up in the Television Room at the hospital. Weeks of his life had simply gone in the blink of an eye, without him even being aware that they had disappeared.

He drank some tea, feeling the newly dislodged memories starting to settle themselves. Someone must – he hoped – be looking after Walter, and he couldn't understand why nobody had mentioned that to him. And he couldn't entirely understand why, in all his cleaning of the house, he had not found any cat food, or a cat bed, or a scratching post, or a litter tray and bags of litter, or food and water bowls, or cat toys, or cat hair, or any sign at all that a cat had ever been there.

Jo was still in bed when he got up the next morning. He took his pills and went downstairs and made himself toast and a cup of tea, and he was sitting at the kitchen table eating and watching rain lashing the garden when she came into the kitchen and squinted blearily at the window.

"Urgh," she said, and went to make coffee. "How are you feeling?"

"Better," he said.

"You're sure?"

"Yes," he said, and he was. He did feel better; if the memories of Walter and the weeks after Christina's death could come back to him, others could too, if he gave them time. They'd talked about it last night, over dinner, and Jo was of the opinion that it was a sign that he was finally healing. At some point, a memory would surface which would explain everything that was currently happening to him. He just had to be patient. She had not, though, been able to cast any light on the whereabouts of his cat.

When Jo's blood caffeine level finally reached the point where she was capable of human interaction, she said, "Any plans for today?"

"I thought I'd go back to Amsterdam and get a flight home," he said.

"Funny." She took another big swallow of coffee. "I was thinking we should maybe get you checked over."

"Checked over by whom?"

She shrugged. "There's an essencehead in Utrecht, he's a psychiatrist. It's a bit of a drive, but not much further than Zandvoort."

Michael shook his head. "No."

"Suppose you have another... episode like last night?" she said. "I was really worried about you there for a while."

"If it means more of my memory comes back, I'd be happy to have another *episode*." He shook his head again. "No, let's not."

She sighed. "I should have thought about it sooner," she said. "You're still not properly well; they should never have let you out of the hospital."

"Oh, they should," he said.

"Maybe by *their* terms, but you've been under a lot of stress. I don't want you to relapse."

"I'm not going to relapse."

"We can't be sure of that, Michael."

"It's too late to worry about that now," he told her. "I can't go back to the way things were when I came home; we'll just have to deal with it."

She didn't look convinced. "Okay. But I want you to tell me if you start to feel weird again. The moment it starts to happen, yeah? Don't try to muddle through hoping everything will be all right."

They heard a car pull up outside, then a few moments later the front door opened and closed and Thijs walked into the kitchen. He looked fresh and rested and back in control of things, but there was a grave look on his face. "I gather you've been busy," he said.

"We've had an eventful few days," Jo said carefully. "How's Anneke?"

"Don't change the subject," he said. He went over to the worktop and started to make himself a cup of coffee. "Franc Brossard's screaming his head off about you kidnapping him. Did you kidnap him?"

"A bit," said Jo.

He glanced at her. "A bit?"

"Quite a lot, actually," she allowed. "Pretty much completely."

"Whose insane idea was that?"

"Mine," Michael said.

"Not Wim's?"

Michael looked at Jo and she shrugged. "He helped," he said. "But the whole thing was my idea."

Thijs turned and leaned back against the worktop and put his hands in his pockets. "Well, Brossard's saying this negates any complaint we have against him. He says it demonstrates we're just as bad as he is and he wants the conference to either sanction both of us or drop the whole thing." He raised his eyebrows and waited for a response.

"It's my fault," Michael said.

"No," said Thijs. "It might have been your idea, but the *fault* lies elsewhere." He looked at Jo. "And I got a text from Felix Ehrenfels. You borrowed the Austrian camera."

"Rented," Jo said glumly, like a teenager caught out shoplifting.

"Rented," he said, tipping his head to one side. "And where did we get the money for that?"

"The usual place."

"Oh, for Christ's sake," he muttered.

"You weren't here," Jo told him, colour rising in her cheeks.

"Oh no." He raised a warning finger. "You don't blame me for this. I might have had things on my mind, but you didn't bother to even try to discuss it with me."

Jo surged to her feet. "Let's talk about this in private," she said angrily.

They went into the study, and one or other of them closed the door more forcefully than necessary. Michael got up from the table and went to make himself another cup of tea. From down the hall, he heard muffled shouting. It went on for a long time.

After about twenty minutes, he heard the study door open, then the front door opened and was slammed shut, and a few moments later

Thijs came into the kitchen. He crossed to the worktop, emptied the coffeemaker, filled it with fresh water and grounds, and switched it on.

"I'm not angry with you," he said without looking at Michael. "You wouldn't be human if you didn't want to do *something*. Jo should have known better, though. She's burned through resources and goodwill that took us years to build up, and for what?"

"She only wanted to help." Michael was aware how lame it sounded, even as he said it, but that didn't make it any less true. "I'm not going to criticise her."

Thijs sighed. "We had the moral high ground," he said, turning to look at Michael. "We were the injured party. I could have gone to the conference and argued that Brossard should be sanctioned, perhaps even expelled from the community. How can I do that, now we're just as prepared to use violence as he is?" He turned back, put a cup into the coffeemaker, and pressed the button. "And this thing with Stilwell? It might have seemed like a jolly little adventure at the time, but now we'll *never* be rid of the man. He's going to haunt us till the end of our days, just because we made a fool of him." He shook his head and took the cup out of the coffeemaker and brought it over to the table. He rubbed his eyes. "I'm sorry," he said. "I've been trying to resolve this situation and everyone's been running around in the background making it worse."

As far as Michael knew, Thijs had spent the past couple of days examining a hospital in Amsterdam looking for signs of the Essence. He said, "We found out why Brossard wanted to abduct me."

"You found out that he doesn't *know* why he wanted to abduct you," Thijs pointed out tiredly. "An anonymous source told him that you know *something*. You don't know any more than you did before you snatched him; it's meaningless."

"Well, speaking as the object of Brossard's attentions, it felt good to actually do something, rather than sitting around bemoaning my situation."

Thijs shook his head and said, "Short-term gratification."

Michael thought that he might start shouting, himself, if they stayed on this subject much longer. He said, "Has there been any word about this conference?"

"Oh yes," Thijs said. "That's why I came back this morning. We've decided on a neutral venue. It's in Poland."

Twelve

Getting there was awkward. The nearest airport to the conference venue was fifty miles away at Szczecin, but even if it had been right next door flying was out of the question because Michael's passport would be flagged the moment he tried to book a ticket. Getting there by train was also awkward, involving several changes. It was doable, but it was also very public.

"Fucking typical," Jo grumbled. "We would have been within our rights to have the conference in Amsterdam; we're the ones the French invaded. But no, we have to have it halfway across fucking Europe."

"It could have been worse," Michael told her. "It might have been in Estonia. Or Finland."

"Yeah," she said. "The Finns are batshit crazy. Lovely people, but batshit crazy. Mind you, so are the Poles."

Michael's parameters of batshit craziness had been somewhat reset over the past week or so. He said, "I still don't see why I have to go."

"Well, it's *about* you, for one thing."

"What difference does it make whether I'm there or not, though?"

"People are going to want to hear your side of the story," she said seriously. "And these are people who can make things happen, not like me and Thijs. These are people who make decisions for the whole community."

"What can they do, though? Realistically? Take away Brossard's essencehead badge?"

"You'll see," she told him.

Thijs flew on ahead, partly to help set the conference up, but mostly because things were still tense between him and Jo. Michael and Jo went into Groningen and bought a couple of proper changes of clothes for him, and a new coat, and a suitcase to transport it all. He felt as if he was accreting a new life, the way caddis fly larvae built themselves a protective cocoon out of bits of gravel and sand.

"I don't want to sound as if I'm complaining," he said as they left another clothes shop laden down with plastic bags, "but who's paying for all this?" He couldn't use the credit card Martine had given him because it would send up an alert, so Jo was buying everything for him.

"There's a central fund," she said, leading the way back to the car. "We all put a few quid into it. We also have a sugar daddy."

"Who?"

She shook her head. "He likes to keep his head down."

"And he gave you the money to hire the camera."

"Yup."

"You said it was a lot of money."

"It was." She didn't seem inclined to discuss the subjrct further, so he dropped it.

While they were in Groningen they popped in to see Wim, and discovered that he had been barred from attending the conference.

"Bloody Thijs," Jo fumed. "This is because you helped us, it's just pure spite."

"Ach, I think it's rather funny," Wim said genially. "Fuck 'em."

"I'm going to pull his fucking ears off when I see him," she said.

Wim's living room was not noticeably tidier than the last time they'd been here. The cat was in its accustomed place on the coffee table, staring at Michael's knee as if delighted to have a second chance at it.

"I found out who wrote *The Heart of the Maze*, by the way," Wim said.

Michael sat up straight. "Oh?"

Wim nodded. "It's not a great surprise you couldn't find out anything about it; it's a vanity publication, there probably weren't more than a couple of hundred copies. Man named Neville John Hallam."

"Oh, *him*," Jo said.

Michael looked at her, then back at Wim. "You've *heard* of this chap?"

"Mad Jack," Jo said, nodding.

"Neville John Hallam," Wim said. "Also known as Mad Jack Hallam. He was a bomber pilot with the RAF, and late in the War he ran into a flight of Messerschmitts over the Dutch coast and he came down outside Alkmaar. He was pretty banged up, but the Resistance managed to smuggle him home. He got some medals, but he never flew again."

Michael looked at them again, his heart sinking. "He was an essencehead, wasn't he."

Wim nodded. "Kind of. I thought I'd heard the name of the book before, so I did some digging in my files." He held out a tattered photocopy. "He wrote *The Heart of the Maze* sometime during the Fifties, probably couldn't find a publisher who'd take it, so he set up his own publishing company to do it himself."

The photocopy appeared to be of a newspaper article; it was smeared and blurry, and it was impossible to make out the text, but at the top was a photograph of a rather fierce-looking man of indeterminate age with Brylcreemed hair, a handlebar moustache, and a patch over his left eye.

"Mad Jack was kind of a minor legend among the postwar Dutch essencehead community," Wim went on. "Sort of a Don Quixote figure. He swore that when he was shot down his life was saved by an angel. Nobody paid him much attention; he lost an eye and one of his legs and he took some shrapnel in his chest when he bailed out, and he was probably suffering from PTSD or whatever they were calling it back then. He came back to the Netherlands and bought himself a flat in Alkmaar and made a nuisance of himself looking for his 'angel'. The essenceheads sort of kept an eye on him and hummed and hahed about whether or not to take pity and let him in on the secret, but in the end they decided they couldn't trust him to keep it to himself."

"So he never knew about the Essence?"

Wim shook his head. "Not from us, anyway."

Michael looked at Jo. "You knew about this?"

"Every Dutch essencehead knows about Mad Jack, the poor old sod," she said. "I'd never heard about a book, though."

"So what happened to him?"

"The book was published in 1960," said Wim. "It was totally ignored, didn't make a ripple; I don't think it was even reviewed. He seems to have travelled a lot after that, I guess he was looking for more stories about angels. He was on a visit to Berlin in early 1964, and he fell under a tram."

"You're kidding."

"So I suppose what we have here is two ends of the same story. There's a book nobody's read, and a film nobody's seen, and unless you put them together they look like completely unconnected things."

Michael looked at Jo. "That can't be it, can it?"

She thought about it. "I can't see how," she said, but she didn't sound sure. "Kelvin told Brossard you knew something about whatever the Essence is going to do. What's this got to do with that?"

"I don't know. I thought I knew nothing about the Essence, but now it turns out I was reading a book by an essencehead."

"Hallam didn't know he was an essencehead," Wim pointed out.

"Okay, so you read his book," said Jo. "But it's a cop thriller set in LA in the 1930s; it's got nothing to do with the Essence." She thought about it some more. "It is fucking weird, though, I will give you that."

"Still," Wim said, "it's an angle on the East German footage that we've never had before. People are going to be writing papers about this for years; I might write one myself, just to put Thijs's nose out of joint." He grinned happily.

Michael wasn't listening. He was thinking of Neville John Hallam tumbling out of his crippled Lancaster into the night over Noord-Holland. What had he seen that would make him come back after the War to look for it again?

In the end, they decided to drive to Poland. "It's no worse than driving from Southampton to Aberdeen," Jo said. "Although why would you want to do that?"

On the morning they left, he got up early, took his meds, showered and shaved, and went down to make breakfast. His few possessions, including the suit Martine had given him in London a thousand years ago, were already packed in his suitcase and holdall, all of these things that had been bought for him, that didn't actually belong to him.

He found himself wondering if he would ever see Sofi's house again. He liked it here; it had been an island of calm in a life that had suddenly been overtaken by storms. It occurred to him that he had never had a chance to settle after leaving the hospital; he'd thought that he had been returning to normal life, but actually he had been launched into a series of temporary spaces. He hadn't even been at home for more than a few days, hadn't had a chance to get used to being there again. His life, he realised belatedly, was never going to be normal again; it had stopped being normal the moment he caught that tennis ball. He wondered how the essenceheads coped. He supposed that for them, this *was* normal. For them, something as absurd as the Essence was as normal as the sun coming up in the morning. Was that true of all conspiracists? He supposed that if you had a moment's doubt, a moment's awareness of how abnormal it was, the whole structure of conspiracy fell apart, although Jo seemed to manage to keep both positions in her head perfectly happily. Would there come a time when he would regard all this as normal too? Had that already happened?

Jo came in and clattered around moodily until her blood pressure had risen to operational levels. She kept checking the time on her phone and muttering to herself, obviously eager to get moving.

Arno and Piet arrived an hour or so later in a dark blue fourth-generation Espace with Belgian numberplates. One thing the Dutch essenceheads seemed to have no shortage of was cars. Jo made a check of the house to make sure she hadn't forgotten anything, then locked up, and they drove off. As they turned onto the road, Michael looked back at the house. Another part of his new life left behind.

Piet drove the first leg, around Groningen and out through flat countryside crisscrossed by electricity pylons and dotted with windfarms and fields covered with solar panels. According to a road sign, Bremen was a hundred and thirty-five kilometres away.

The German border came and went without any fuss; one moment they were in the Netherlands, the next they were in Lower Saxony, and there was no change at all. The countryside looked the same, and the houses Michael could see didn't look appreciably different. He supposed there had been, once upon a time, a border crossing here, a place where vehicles passing in either direction had been checked and passports examined, but if there were any signs of it he had missed them. You crossed a little river, and all of a sudden you were in a different country and all the road signs and the graffiti under overpasses were in another language.

Gradually the countryside changed, became a little less flat, a little more wooded, a little wilder than the Netherlands. They passed more windfarms. The road dipped into a long tunnel under the River Ems, and somehow when they came out the weather had changed and a faint spit of rain misted the windscreen.

The countryside continued to get woodier, and by now there was no danger of mistaking it for the Netherlands. They passed through Oldenburg, but all Michael saw from the car was trees and the occasional building peeking over an unbroken line of graffitied fencing erected to protect nearby residents from traffic noise.

Finally, a couple of hours after leaving Sofi's house, Piet pulled in to a service station outside Bremen to top the car up and let everyone stretch their legs. They sat in the little cafeteria with coffee and pastries and Michael looked out of the window and watched cars navigating around the car park.

"North or south?" Jo asked.

"There's not a lot in it," Piet said.

"North," Arno mused. "There's a lot of roadworks around Berlin."

"We wind up on the same road across the border anyway," Piet added.

"Okay," said Jo. "North it is. I'll drive the next bit. We'll stop off somewhere near Lübeck for lunch; we'll be about halfway there by then, yeah?"

There was general agreement. They used the lavatories, bought snacks and drinks in the service station's shop. Jo also bought one of those little U-shaped travel pillows, and she handed it to Michael as they crossed the car park. "You look as if you need a nap," she said.

"I'm fine," he told her, but he took the pillow anyway and slung it around his neck as they set off towards Hamburg.

He didn't sleep, though. He sat watching the countryside going by, even though it had become rather dull and samey. Just fields and trees, the occasional stretch of acoustic fencing when the road passed near habitation. The landscape was low hills rising from poor sandy soil, and where it wasn't cultivated it looked scrubby around the edges. If it hadn't been cultivated at all, it would probably have reverted to heathland dotted with pine trees; he saw a sign for the Lüneburger Heid, once upon a time the largest military training area in Europe.

The sun tried to break through the clouds, failed, tried again, then gave up. It rained for a while, but they outpaced it. An almost-imperceptible change in the noise of the tyres against the road surface announced that they had crossed from Lower Saxony into the Hamburg Metropolitan Region. They crossed the southern branch of the Elbe, skirted around Hamburg, crossed the northern branch of the river, but all Michael saw of the city was the upper floors of distant apartment blocks over the trees beside the road, and then they were back into the country.

At some point – Michael missed it – they passed into Schleswig-Holstein. Not far from Lübeck, Jo took a turnoff and a few minutes later they found themselves in the middle of a huge out-of-town shopping mall whose considerable acreage enclosed, according to the enormous sign at the entrance, a five-screen multiplex, a bowling alley, all the fast-food franchises Michael had ever heard of and some he hadn't, and enough shopping opportunities to keep the average person occupied for several months.

"Where do we want to eat?" Jo asked, driving around the car park looking for a space.

"I don't mind," said Arno. "Just try to park somewhere near civilisation."

For Michael, the day was starting to take on a hallucinatory quality. They had climbed the coast of northern Europe on a ladder of old Hanseatic cities and were now standing more or less on what had been the border between West and East Germany, and he found himself in a vast field of vehicles ranked around several enormous buildings.

Inside was even worse: a small city of shops and restaurants on three levels under a tessellated glass roof. He hadn't seen so many people in one place since he'd been snatched out of Eindhoven airport, and he felt himself start to wobble fractionally.

They walked a very long way, Jo dismissing each restaurant they passed as too expensive or too crap or too ideologically unsound, until Arno announced he'd had enough and marched into the nearest fast food outlet, which turned out to be a branch of Kochlöffel. They sat round a table and ate chicken and bratwurst and burgers. "Not the currywurst," Jo warned them. "I'm not driving the rest of the way to Poland with all the windows open." At the next table, a couple was having an energetic argument about whether or not to buy a new bed while their children threw fries at each other, and Michael wondered how German law would feel about him assaulting one or all of them with one of Kochlöffel's signature blue spoons.

It took them a long time to escape the mall. Michael found himself wondering, statistically, how many people in the crowds surrounding him were essenceheads, how many of them lived in a world where miracles were literally real, where bomber pilots bailed out of their stricken aircraft into the arms of angels and lines of light snapped people out of existence. Or did they believe something even weirder? Because if you boiled off the lightweights, the antivaxxers and the climate deniers and the 9/11 truthers, there was a depthless seam of belief systems so utterly crazy that not even the most rabid right-wing rabble-rouser would want them as recruits. Were any of *them* here? Was that man going into the sports shop one of them? That woman coming out of the Apple Store? Any of these faces pressing in around him?

He stopped and closed his eyes and took a deep breath and tried to feel the ground beneath his feet. After a few moments, he heard Jo's voice close by say, "Michael? Are you okay?"

"I'd like to get out of here, please," he said, opening his eyes.

"Yeah, me too," she said, a concerned look on her face. She glanced over at Piet, who was pointing at a sign that said *Ausgang*. "Let's try that way, yeah?"

Outside, beyond a double set of automatic doors, it was spitting with rain. Maybe it was the same rain that they'd outrun near Bremen. The mall was so huge that the car park was apparently on several bus routes, because there was a bus stop not far from the doors. Michael went and sat down on the bench, rested his elbows on his knees, and stared at the pavement between his feet.

"Any better?" Jo asked.

He nodded, suddenly very tired. "Too many people."

She looked back at the building. "Yeah, I should have thought about that. I'm sorry."

"Not your fault."

"Mind you," she added, looking about her, "I have no idea where the fucking car is. I don't even know if we're on the right side of the building."

"I saved the GPS coordinates," Piet said, holding up his phone. "I'll bring it round."

Arno went with him, while Jo sat on the bench beside Michael. She looked out over the sea of parked cars. "Didn't expect I'd wind up doing this the first time I met you," she said. He looked at her, and she smiled to show she was kidding.

"Won't your employers be wondering what's happened to you?" he asked.

She shook her head. "I told them Mum was poorly and I had to come over to take care of her. They're pretty good about stuff like that."

"Ah," he said.

"It's not the first time, anyway."

"I'm sorry."

She shrugged. "Old age sucks, what can I tell you? She's had a bumpy couple of years, but she's doing okay at the moment, and she's got good care over here. Still, the time's coming when I'm going to have to decide whether or not to move back here permanently."

He thought about it. "Will that be a wrench?"

She wrinkled her nose. "Nah. I'll be glad to get out of there, to be honest. The whole fucking country's lost its mind."

They were quiet for a while, and Michael wondered just how far away the car was. He said, "When did you first hear about all this?"

"That Thursday morning," she said. "Thijs phoned me while I was having breakfast and asked if I knew anybody called Michael Brookes. I said yes, and he said you were coming to Amsterdam and Franc Brossard was planning to snatch you off the street."

"So you knew before I did."

"Not *long* before. I was just leaving the house for the airport when you phoned. I was only a couple of flights behind you."

"And you didn't think to warn me."

"We didn't know what was going on; everybody was panicking."

"So the French knew I was coming, and they knew you knew me."

"Seems so, yes. And I take that personally."

Michael sat back and rubbed his eyes. Who in London knew both those things? The obvious suspect would be someone in HR, but he didn't know who else had access to his file. He said, "You were following me."

She nodded. "We mobilised every fucking essencehead in Amsterdam. We even got some people up from Utrecht. Followed you from the airport, kept an eye on the hotel, followed you to that office building in Zuid. I guess the French were following you, too, although we never spotted them."

He chewed his bottom lip and thought about that. "How did you know they were going to try and take me in that bar?" he asked. "I only went in on impulse."

She looked at him.

"You were on your way to the bar when I called you," he said. "You were practically outside; you got there more or less at the same time as the French. How did you know? I'd been there about ten minutes. I ordered a coffee and some food and I texted the office to say I was coming back and I phoned you and I watched Archie being stolen and then all of a sudden you and the French were there."

"I got a call to say the French were making their move," she said. "Arno and I were on our way to the hotel; I'd decided it was time to talk to you and find out what the hell was going on, but I got a call to say where you were and that the French were going to snatch you."

"Who from?"

She stared into space. "I don't know," she said finally. "I assumed it was someone who was keeping an eye on the French." She took out her phone and swiped through a couple of menus, then scrolled back a long way through her call logs. "There," she said, showing him the screen. "There's you calling me that morning."

He looked at the list of calls. The one before his had no caller ID; it had come in ten minutes before he phoned. "And you don't know who made this call."

She shook her head. "I didn't recognise the voice, but I didn't know everyone we had on the street. Like I said, some of them were from out of town. I tried calling the number back a few days ago, but it's dead."

He thought about it, but there was something wrong with the picture. He said, "Three people came into the bar after me. There was a young couple who looked like tourists, and an older man in working clothes."

"I don't know who they were."

"The young couple tried to get in our way as we were leaving, but the older man stopped them," he said, remembering now how the older man had pulled them off their feet. "And then everybody in the bar tried to get out of the door at once, but what they actually did was block the way in for the French. They gave us time to get away."

Jo looked at him and shrugged helplessly. "I remember those two, but I don't know anything about an older man."

It was almost as if there was someone else in play. Not the French, not the essenceheads, someone else. Of course, everything had been very confused; there had been a lot of people running about, and he might not be remembering things entirely accurately. There could be a perfectly rational explanation that didn't involve a third party. Maybe the call Jo had received had come from Thijs's French informant. But why hadn't they called Thijs? Why would they have Jo's number?

He sighed. Bob had warned him about something like this. *The world doesn't make sense, old son. Sometimes you'll get coincidences that make it look as if it does, but it really doesn't. You have to watch out for that.* Perhaps he was seeing patterns that didn't exist. And to be honest, who could blame him if he did? Virtually nothing since he walked into that bar made any sense. He'd kidnapped a French industrialist and threatened to put a taser down his throat; it would be hard to convince anyone that was rational.

"I don't know," he said, watching the car pull up at the bus stop with Arno at the wheel. "It feels as if this is more complicated than we thought, but I can't work out how."

Jo got to her feet. "I hope you're wrong," she said. "I'm not sure I can cope with it being any more complicated."

Back on the road, he rested his head against the window and dozed, a weird half-sleep in which the sounds of the real world – the tyres on the road, the engine, music on the radio, quiet conversation between the others, the voice of the GPS patiently counting down the kilometres – felt like parts of a dream.

He opened his eyes. His neck was stiff, and all the road signs were in Polish.

Jo glanced over the seat in front of him. "Hey," she said. "Welcome back. Do you know you snore?"

He blinked blearily. "Where are we?"

"Just the other side of Szczecin," she said. "We're going to stop at the next petrol station and top the car up, maybe get a coffee."

Remarkable. He'd slept across the whole of eastern Germany. "Okay." He struggled upright. He hurt all over and there was a terrible taste in his mouth. "I think I'm getting too old for long car journeys."

"You and me both," she said. "Not much further, though. Another couple of hours."

There was a solid wall of birches and pines on either side of the road, and the daylight was just beginning to take on a late-afternoon quality. "It's a long drive."

"Have you ever been to Poland, Professor?" Piet asked from the front passenger seat.

"Yes. It was a long time ago, though."

"You can translate for us, then," Arno said. "None of us speaks Polish."

"It'll be a miracle if I remember more than a few words," Michael told him.

His only overseas posting, not long after joining the Service, had been to Poland, the year before the fall of the Berlin Wall. Second Assistant to the Deputy Commercial Secretary or something, the kind of title that was sometimes given to undeclared intelligence assets, but in his case it was true. He'd spent his time sitting in an office at the Embassy in Warsaw reading reports and writing reports of his own, and that was the extent of his intelligence work. He met the head of Warsaw Station once at a cocktail party, but he never saw any of the operatives who passed through the country because they never went near the Embassy. He'd thought at the time that it was just a way of blooding him as painlessly as possible; someone had given him a brief speech about not getting involved with the local girls and not letting anyone do him any kind of favour and he'd been handed a little booklet containing useful Polish phrases and a couple of emergency phone numbers, and that had been the extent of his induction into the secret world.

It turned out, though, that a lot of the Polish he'd learned during that year had stuck, and in the café of the Orlen filling station he found himself quite easily holding up his end of a conversation with the girl behind the counter.

"How many languages do you speak, by the way?" Jo asked as they sat at a table with their coffees.

He looked out of the window at the fields and trees beyond the car park. "More than I thought, obviously," he said.

Piet drove the final leg to the coast. Looking out of the window as they reached the crest of a long incline, Michael saw a landscape that mostly seemed to be forest. Signs for Gdańsk and Świnoujście went by. The trees beside the road withdrew to accommodate a nearly deserted road intersection almost a mile across, then closed in again. Where the trees had been cut back, the ground was sandy and scrubby. Sofi's house and the fields and canals of the Netherlands felt a long, long way away. At Goleniów, a huge chunk of forest had been cleared and he saw a line of landing lights and in the distance the control tower of Szczecin's airport, where Thijs had arrived several days earlier after a journey of not much more than an hour. Michael thought about that; the flight would barely have time to reach cruising altitude before it started to descend again towards final approach. He thought about flying over Groningen, Bremen, Hamburg. You might look down, flying over Lübeck, and be able to make out the tiny shape of an out-of-town shopping mall. You'd just have time for a coffee and then the tyres would be bumping onto the concrete. It would be as if you'd hardly travelled at all.

A few miles beyond Goleniów the landscape opened out, the forest replaced by flat fields and little villages. It occurred to him that these little groups of red-roofed houses nestled in the Pomeranian countryside were virtually the first signs of human habitation he'd seen since leaving Lübeck. Even the filling station they'd stopped at had seemed to be out in the middle of nowhere. It was as if he'd nodded off and woken in another world.

He started to see signs for Kołobrzeg, and finally, as the light was starting to fail, Piet turned off the motorway and onto a series of narrow country roads. At a roundabout, he ignored the *Centrum* sign and went in the opposite direction. He turned off onto another narrow road and through a complex of big hotels, and then, all of a sudden, there at the end of the road was the sea.

Their hotel, a huge blue glass slab, appeared to be more or less on the beach. Piet found somewhere to park near the main entrance and they got out of the car, stretching their legs stiffly and looking about them. Michael walked down to the end of the road. To either side, a cycleway ran off into the distance, and on the other side of that a little berm had been constructed by piling up sand and planting it with clumps of grass. Half a dozen steps climbed the berm, and he walked up and stood at the top, looking out over the beach.

Far away, the sun was setting over the calm surface of the Baltic, a hazy patch of bright yellow that shaded towards brass and bronze and orange and dark blue at the edges. There were still a lot of people on the beach, packing up windbreaks and picnic coolers and chairs as the sun went down and the air grew chilly.

"Not bad, is it?" Jo said, coming up the steps beside him.

On the horizon, there was a fuzzy patch where clouds discharged their rain; the sunset turned it momentarily into a veil of gold. "It's a long way to come to see the sun go down," he said.

She smiled. "It's all about the journey, not the arriving. Come on, let's get checked in. I could do with a long hot shower."

They had barely stepped through the front doors of the hotel when Thijs approached them across the lobby. He looked clean and well-rested and dapper in a three-piece suit. Michael glanced at Jo and the others and it occurred to him that the four of them looked like the remnants of a very small nomadic tribe that had just crossed a terrible desert.

Thijs's first words were, "Where on earth have you been? I expected you ages ago."

Jo didn't bother stopping. "We've been driving for ten fucking hours, Thijs," she told him as they towed their suitcases past. "Don't you *dare* start."

The lobby was busy. People were sitting chatting, wandering about, heading towards a set of doors through which Michael could see a dining room. Were these all essenceheads? Or were they civilians? There was no way to tell. He assumed the families with children were civilians, but he couldn't be sure.

They checked in and went up to the third floor, where Michael's room was at one end of a corridor and Jo and the others were down at the other end. Michael let the door of his room close behind him and leaned back against it, feeling the day catching up on him. So here he was again, in another temporary space.

The room was clean and comfortable, if a bit on the small side, but it had a couple of chairs and a little coffee table and a television. He pulled back the net curtain and looked out of the window, and saw in the last light of the day that his room looked out across a big patch of bushes and small trees to another hotel. Well, he wasn't here for the scenery.

There was a knock on the door, and when he opened it Thijs was standing there. "You'll want to rest after your journey," he said, "but I wanted to let you know what's going to happen."

"Can't it wait?" said Michael. "It's been a long day."

Thijs considered carrying on anyway, but seemed to come down on the side of leaving things alone. He said, "All right. I'll see you in the morning."

"Is Brossard here?"

"He's staying in town; you may not see him at all. This is neutral territory, he won't try anything here."

"I got the impression he doesn't care very much what you people think about him, so long as he gets what he wants."

"Try not to worry. Just be careful, and don't go wandering off on your own. I'll see you tomorrow."

Try not to worry. Well, that was easier said than done. He wasn't convinced that this essencehead circus was going to improve his situation in any substantial way. Even if they could put a stop to Brossard, he still couldn't go home.

He stood under the shower with the water dialled up as hot as he could bear for a long time and felt some of the grime of the journey wash off. Later, wrapped in the room's complimentary bathrobe, he ordered a club sandwich and chips and a Coke from room service, and he sat eating while he navigated his way around the television's menu. The BBC news had items from as far afield as Belize and Nepal, but not much from home. CNN had an economics briefing so incomprehensibly hamfisted that he skipped over it. A German channel had one of the later Star Wars films dubbed in German, he didn't know which one. The Polish national broadcaster was running a rather shouty studio discussion about LGBT rights; at least two of the panel seemed to think there shouldn't be any. Unexpectedly, he landed on a channel where a man with a beard was ranting in English about some colossal conspiracy involving fifteen minute cities, the World Economic Forum, the Mayor of London, digital currency, low traffic neighbourhoods, vaccines, and the United Nations. With the addition of each successive element, the conspiracy grew more and more insane.

"You should spend fifteen minutes as me, mate," Michael said to the television. "If you want fucking conspiracies."

Thirteen

He woke late the next morning, stiff and achy from the journey, and he had to stand under the hot shower again before he felt even remotely ready to face the day. He hated growing old; twenty – even ten – years ago, he would have rolled out of bed and got on with life, but now it took him ages to get moving, even if he hadn't spent ten hours in a car the previous day, and the really depressing thing was that it wasn't going to get any better.

It turned out that breakfast was not in the restaurant he'd seen the previous evening, but in a room on the other side of the hotel. This was par for the course, pretty much; on your first day your hotel was an impenetrable maze of mysterious corridors and rooms, but by the third day you knew where everything was and all the little shortcuts between places. Michael wondered if he would be here long enough for the place to become familiar.

The breakfast room was half-empty, a few families and couples widely scattered around the tables. Waitresses in black uniforms moved through the room clearing plates and cups and cutlery and wiping tables down. Beyond the floor-to-ceiling windows people walked or cycled along the seafront, but the little sand berm blocked the view of the sea. It looked like a bright, breezy morning.

After examining the warming pans of sausage and bacon and hash browns and baked beans on offer, he settled for a slice of toast, a ladleful of scrambled eggs and a mug of tea. He'd only just sat down at a table near the window when Jo came up with mug of coffee in hand and sat down opposite him.

"Morning," she said. "How did you sleep?"

Michael looked at her.

"It's okay," she said. "I've been up a couple of hours." She held up the mug. "This is my third."

"You shouldn't drink so much coffee, you know. It's not good for you."

She wrinkled her nose at him. "You're not my mum."

He tore the foil off a little tub of margarine and spread it on his toast. "I slept all right, I suppose. What's going to happen today?"

"Nothing much until this evening; some people still haven't turned up yet, apparently. They're flying in later."

"Well, there's no rush," he said, using his knife and fork to pile scrambled egg untidily on the toast.

"Don't be snarky; it's a miracle this thing got organised at all at such short notice. It's the biggest conference we've ever had; there's essenceheads here from all over Europe, and some from further afield. It takes a while and nobody wants to miss anything."

He cut off a corner of toast and egg and put it in his mouth.

"There's a system for conflict resolution," she said. "It'd be anarchy otherwise, people stealing each other's artifacts, keeping Events to themselves, trampling all over everyone's turf. In a situation like that, a dozen or so people with seniority get together and listen to everyone's side and then decide if there are going to be sanctions."

"Seniority?"

"It's complicated. You get seniority by being an essencehead for a long time, or by publishing some important research, or just by being very rich. They'll talk to you and Brossard and Thijs and they'll probably want to talk to me too. Then they'll argue among themselves about whether or not to do something about it, and if they do decide to do something they'll put it to a vote of the essenceheads here."

"So the French could overturn any decision just by packing the vote."

She shook her head. "The French have decided to throw Brossard under the bus; they haven't turned up."

"I'm still not clear what these seniors could possibly do to him. Brossard's very wealthy and he doesn't care what anyone thinks of him."

Jo looked out of the window and thought about it. "We're a community," she said. "We argue and sometimes we rub each other up the wrong way, but we cooperate, we lend each other a hand when necessary. I can go to pretty much every country in the world and there'll be an essencehead there somewhere who'll put me up for the night; Zandvoort was full of essenceheads in the days after the Event, and we welcomed them with open arms. The seniors can put a stop to all that. No cooperation, no help, nobody talking to you. They can basically make it impossible to be an essencehead. You'd wind up like Mad Jack Hallam, convinced that *something's* going on but completely out of the loop." She took a swallow of coffee. "Sure, Brossard's rich and he doesn't give a shit about anything but himself, but he won't be part of the community any more, and that's important."

He shook his head, still not convinced.

"Morning," Thijs said, walking up to the table. "Did we sleep all right?"

Jo scowled into her coffee. Michael said, "Sleep certainly happened."

Thijs was wearing jeans and a white shirt with a blue pullover draped over his shoulders, and he was holding a glass of orange juice. "We should get together and have a quiet chat about what's going to happen," he said.

"Jo's been explaining it to me," Michael told him.

Thijs seemed to deflate fractionally. "Okay." He looked at Jo. "They're going to want to speak with us tomorrow morning. You first."

"Fine," she said.

"They'll probably schedule you for the afternoon," he said to Michael. "So if you could keep yourself available that would be great."

There was no point revisiting his doubts about what was happening; the essenceheads were going to stage their convocation of wizards whatever he said. He was just a passenger. "What should I do until then?" he asked.

"Relax," Thijs told him. "Have a look around, enjoy the seaside. The hotel's got a spa."

"I'm not on holiday, Thijs."

"I know." He looked sad. "But we have to make the best of the situation, no? It'll soon be over. I'll see you later."

When he'd gone, Michael said, "Thijs and I have *very* different ideas of what 'over' is."

"Yeah," Jo said sourly. "We're not exactly covering ourselves in glory here."

"How far do you think I could get on a hundred euros?"

She raised her eyebrows. "Is that all you've got?"

He reached around to the back pocket of his jeans and took out the money he'd changed at Gatwick. "A hundred and thirty," he said, counting it. "And about fifty quid in Sterling."

"That's not too bad in złotys." She thought about it. "You could probably reach Lithuania with that. What were you thinking of?"

"I thought I'd go to Warsaw and hand myself in at the Embassy."

She looked at him. "No," she said. "You haven't gone through all this just to give yourself up. How come that's all you've got?"

"I was only supposed to be in Amsterdam for a few hours, remember? I paid for everything by card; the cash was just for bits and pieces."

"And you can't use your cards now?"

"They'd be flagged up," he said. "The office would know where I was; *Kelvin* would know where I was."

"You think he's that senior?"

"He seems to have had access to stuff that not a lot of people knew about."

She thought about it. "Maybe you should have a quiet word with the English essenceheads; they might have a clue who he is." Something else occurred to her. "Maybe he's *here.*"

The thought had crossed his mind. "Maybe it's best if I steer clear of the English."

"Good luck with that," she told him. "*They're* going to be looking for *you.*"

"Anyway, Kelvin could be anybody. He might just have a source in the office. He could be Dutch or Polish or German. He might not even exist; Brossard could have made him up."

"You were threatening to tase his tonsils; I don't think he was making anything up."

"Hm. Perhaps you should downplay that bit tomorrow."

She smiled at him. "Well, at least you still have a sense of humour." She reached into her back pocket and took out a wad of cash. "You could have this," she said. "It's what's left of the money I took off Stilwell."

He thought about it, but in the end he shook his head. "What would I spend it on? How much trouble are *you* in, out of interest?"

"Oh, I don't know. Lots, probably." Jo finished her coffee and stood up. "The difference is, I'm not that bothered. I've got a life."

After breakfast, he went outside, crossed the cycleway and stood at the top of the little set of steps again. The beach was already full, a field of windbreaks and beach chairs and pasty swimsuited bodies shining with sun cream. Out on the calm surface of the sea, beyond the swimmers and kayakers, a kitesurfer whipped back and forth, arms raised over their head. Compared to the North Sea, the Baltic was hardly tidal at all; Zandvoort's sea wall was thirty or forty feet high, but here it barely came up to his waist, and he could see places further along the seafront where there was no wall at all, where the beach was level with the cycleway.

The seafront was basically a wall of hotels. He counted nine of them before some trees cut off the view, all of them different designs and all of them very large. Further along the coast, a couple of miles away, he could see the buildings of Kołobrzeg town and the tower of a lighthouse. He had a faint sensation of déjà vu, a niggling feeling that the scene was familiar. Could he have been here before? He remembered day-trips to Sopot and Gdańsk, both times in the company of English businessmen who already had an eye out for post-Communist opportunity. They had been chaperoned by Polish apparatchiks who seemed more concerned about their own future, and he remembered a terrifying moment when he was convinced that one or more of them were winding themselves up to defect to him. In Gdańsk, one of the businessmen wouldn't stop asking whether they would be visiting the Hel peninsula because he wanted to be able to go home and tell his friends he'd been to Hel and back. Michael remembered cringing every time he mentioned it, but he couldn't remember coming to Kołobrzeg. He couldn't remember even hearing the name until a few days ago.

He walked along the seafront for half a mile or so, but there wasn't a lot to see apart from the beach and the sea and the line of hotels. The place seemed popular, particularly with Germans; half the people he passed were speaking German. The seafront was lined with kiosks selling amber and ice cream and soft drinks and slices of pizza. A lot of the amber was of low quality, cloudy or almost opaque, carved into teardrops or animal shapes, but there were one or two clear pieces among them, and he saw one that contained what seemed to be the preserved wing of a small dragonfly, the rest of the insect gone many hundreds of thousands of years ago.

It occurred to him that this was the first time he'd been out on his own since that afternoon in Amsterdam when he'd walked into the bar and his life had jumped the tracks. He could walk the rest of the way into town, change all his cash for złotys, get a train or a bus, and just disappear, leave his passport and his few belongings behind. There was nobody here to stop him. A week or so ago, he would have done it without a second thought, but now it seemed absurd, like running away to join the circus. Also, around the end of the month his medication would run out, and what was he going to do then?

"Thinking about making a run for it?" asked a voice, and when he turned round he found Wim standing behind him.

"I thought you'd been banned," he said.

"Nah." Wim was wearing a spectacularly ugly Hawaiian shirt and mirrored sunglasses and holding a slice of pizza on a paper plate. "They changed their minds, fuck 'em. They decided they wanted to talk to me after all."

"Well," Michael said. "I suppose it's good to get the old gang back together."

Wim snorted. "Have you seen Franc?"

"He's staying in town, apparently. When did you arrive?"

"A couple of hours ago. This is breakfast." He held up the pizza. "I'm staying here." He gestured at the hotel behind them, a black stone monolith sitting mysteriously behind a screen of trees, like an ancient temple.

"What's it like?"

"Don't know; I've only spent about ten minutes inside. Yours?"

"Seems all right. It's got a spa."

"This one too, according to the brochure in my room. They do that thing where someone pours oil on your head. A hundred and fifty euros for a treatment. Imagine coming all this way to pay somebody to pour oil on your head; you'd be better off staying at home with a bottle of Jumbo."

"There's probably more to it than that," Michael mused.

Wim looked at the hotel and shook his head. "A hundred and fifty euros," he said again. He took a bite from the slice of pizza.

Michael looked around. "Why are there so many Germans here?"

Wim shrugged. "It's a nice place, the border's not far, your euros will go a long way here if you give the hotel spa a miss. And it *was* Germany, once upon a time." He watched the people passing by. "Some of the older ones are probably here for a look at the ancestral home. Some of the *really* old ones probably used to live here."

"That must feel weird."

"A lot of Europe's like that. You wouldn't understand; you Brits haven't been invaded since 1066."

"1688."

Wim thought about it. "Oh yeah," he said mildly. "I forgot about that. That wasn't really an invasion; you invited us in."

"William brought twenty thousand men with him," Michael pointed out. "It probably *looked* like an invasion."

Wim grinned. "Hey, that was probably the last time anyone sane was running your country."

"Standards have certainly slipped recently," Michael agreed. "When are you being questioned?"

"No idea. You?"

"Not till tomorrow afternoon. People are still arriving, apparently."

Wim snorted. "We could have done this on Zoom and got it over with, but nobody trusts the internet."

"How did you cope during the pandemic?"

"Well, there wasn't a lot of fieldwork. There might have been an Event near Zaragoza towards the end of 2020, but nobody could get there to investigate so we're still not sure. Mostly we just kept our heads down, like everybody else." Wim finished his pizza and folded the paper plate into quarters and looked around for a rubbish bin. "Anyway, I'm going to walk into town. Maybe I'll bump into Franc; want to come along?"

Michael shook his head. "I don't think that's a great idea, but you go ahead. Try not to get in any trouble. See you later?"

Wim grinned. "Oh yeah. I can't wait to see the look on Thijs's face when I turn up." He set off along the seafront, and Michael walked back to the hotel.

Maybe he was wrong to characterise the essenceheads as conspiracists. Conspiracists protested at Davos, took to social media, ran podcasts, did their best to gather as many followers as they could. They wanted to be heard; it was impossible to miss them. The essenceheads, on the other hand, jealously protected their secret. Unlike the conspiracists, they had actual tangible proof of something extraordinary and, with a very few exceptions, they didn't want to share it with anyone. They were more like an intelligence service or a secret society, the kind of thing conspiracists would have theories *about*, and he thought that was sort of remarkable and probably not sustainable for much longer. The world was becoming too febrile, changing too quickly. If the Essence *did* exist, and *was* winding itself up for some mega-Event or something, the secret would be out. Then you'd get Essence deniers and the whole sorry mess would just get worse.

Jo was in the lobby when he got back. "You shouldn't go off on your own, you know," she told him.

He was starting to get tired of being told what to do. "Wim's here," he said. "I just saw him."

She scowled. "Oh, that's great," she said. "Now I've got to worry about keeping him and Thijs apart too."

"He's gone into town. I think he's hoping he'll see Brossard."

She sighed. "Maybe they'll do us all a favour and punch each other senseless. What were you planning to do now?"

"I was just going upstairs. Why?"

"I thought I'd introduce you around, meet some of the others."

He shook his head slowly. "I don't know; I was kind of hoping to keep a low profile."

"Once people work out who you are they're going to start pestering you anyway," she said. "I was hoping we could get ahead of that."

Most of the essenceheads, it turned out, seemed perfectly ordinary, friendly and polite but perhaps with an edge of shyness, and they didn't ask any unanswerable questions. A few, though, seemed as exotic as tropical birds. One tall, white-haired woman wearing a black ballet tutu, biker boots, and a leather jacket, was introduced to him as Maxi Zimmermann.

"We should be thanking you," she told him with a smile. "We haven't had one of these gatherings in years."

"I gather someone was shot last time," he said.

She widened her eyes at the memory. "Yes! That was a *wonderful* weekend." She patted him on the cheek. "Don't worry; everything's going to be fine."

"Maxi and Brossard don't get on," Jo said as they walked on. "They were married for a bit."

Michael glanced over his shoulder. Maxi was striding across the lobby towards the dining room. "I keep expecting someone to run a geiger counter over me or something," he said.

"Some of the crazier ones would probably do that," Jo told him. "But they'd ask permission first. Most of them, anyway. But you see?"

There's nothing to be afraid of, they're not going to mob you wanting an autograph."

He was starting to suspect that he was actually something of a sideshow. A lot of the essenceheads seemed to have brought their families and were treating the whole thing as a holiday, a chance to catch up with old friends and discuss matters Essencey. He'd already seen them, sitting in little groups in the café on the first floor and the big lounge beside the restaurant, various documents and papers on the table in front of them, deep in earnest conversation, which seemed a little at odds with Jo's description of them as some of the most paranoid people in the world. Maybe they felt more comfortable here, among friends. It would, he thought, be mildly diverting to study the group dynamics of these people, but he was hoping he wouldn't be here long enough.

Back in his room, he discovered that if he opened one of the windows and leaned out over the railing outside and turned his head to the left, he could just see a narrow wedge of sea over the band of trees and scrubby bushes that separated this hotel from the next one.

He used the room's little kettle and made himself a cup of tea and sat down with the script of *The Unknown Man*, but he felt strange about reading it now that he knew its source. He found himself thinking about Mad Jack Hallam returning to the Netherlands in the hope of unravelling the mystery of his wartime survival. The circumstances of the writing of *The Heart of the Maze* would probably remain unknown for ever – why would a former RAF bomber pilot write a detective novel set in 1930s Los Angeles? – and he doubted anyone would ever discover how the self-published book had found its way into the hands of Hans Ehlers and Lorenz Bohrer in East Germany. What did seem likely was that, after Hallam's death, Ehlers and Bohrer had decided to go ahead with the film anyway and simply leave his name off the finished work, passing it off as their own. Which was definitely naughty, but after all this time, who would care? Had they contrived to have Hallam killed so they didn't have to share the profits with him? That seemed absurd. The film was never going to make anyone rich, and surely Bohrer and Ehlers were bright enough to realise that.

Nobody would ever know; it was sixty years ago and even if anyone involved with the film were still alive, memories grew misty and uncertain at that distance. The families of the lost film crew still thought they'd died in a crash somewhere out in the Polish countryside on the way back to Berlin.

He paged forward through the script and found the beach scene near the end. EXT. BEACH. HAMBURG. DAY. It was only a page long.

Marthe Braun was saying, "I had to get away. He would have killed us all. He still might."

"How did you dispose of the body?" Joe asked.

"I have friends in State Security."

"Of course you do."

Michael thought of Matthias Weber and Hannelore Huber walking along the beach, delivering their lines. He thought of Weber's hat blowing off and bowling along the sand and Huber putting a hand to her mouth to stifle a laugh as he ran to rescue it. He thought of the town with its church tower in the distance, and that curl of bright kaleidoscope light coming after the two actors faster than any predator. He sat back and frowned across the room, trying to picture the church tower.

Leaving the script on the bed, he went downstairs, walking across the lobby, out of the main door and across to the beach. He stood there, looking west along the coast. He trudged through the sand towards the water's edge, stopped and looked along the coast again, seeing the buildings of Kołobrzeg town and its lighthouse in the distance. The sounds of the holidaymakers all around him seemed to fade away and he felt a shiver go through him.

He'd only glimpsed the buildings in the footage for a moment, and he'd thought it was a church tower, but it hadn't been. It had been a lighthouse. It was *that* lighthouse, in the distance. He looked back towards the seafront and remembered it being an unbroken line of trees in the film Wim had shown him; the hotels hadn't been there in 1965, but this was the same beach. Not only the same beach, it was the same *spot*. This was where Bohrer and the film crew had set up their camera. Huber and Weber had been right over *there* when they were erased from existence, and then the Essence had come for the rest of the crew. Right where he was standing.

"I can't believe nobody told you," Jo said that evening at dinner.

Michael sat staring at her.

She'd decided to try the roast pork and apple sauce with dumplings and a salad of pickled red cabbage, and she carried on eating for a few moments before she realised he hadn't said anything. She looked up from her meal.

"I'm sorry," she said. "I just assumed somebody would have said something. I should have mentioned it."

"It was here," he said.

"Oh yes." She went back to her meal. "The Kołobrzeg Event, the biggest documented Event in Europe, until Zandvoort. Of course, we were never able to investigate it properly; for years and years all we had were rumours. The Poles tried, but they hardly had any equipment and they had to be careful about attracting the attention of the secret police, and by the time the Wall came down and we could travel here freely there was no point, it had been over for almost thirty years. The footage didn't even surface until 2001 or 2002."

He looked down at his own meal, beef goulash on a big potato rösti with a dollop of pickled cabbage on the side. "And it doesn't strike you as weird in any way to have your conference here?"

She looked at him. "I told you, this is neutral territory. Nobody's going to try anything here; the rest of us wouldn't stand for it. It'd be disrespectful. Like taking a dump on somebody's grave."

It was also, he suspected, a place of pilgrimage, like the Germans coming here to see where their families had lived before the War. He looked around the dining room, wondering how many essenceheads were here because of the conference and how many had just taken the opportunity to come and have a look at the site of the Event. The room was almost full, and he still couldn't tell most of the essenceheads from the ordinary guests.

He said, "You know, every time I think I've got my head round what's happening, you go and do something like this."

She raised an eyebrow.

"Have you *any* idea how weird this is?" he asked, loudly enough for people to look over at their table.

"There's no need to shout," Jo said.

Michael looked past her and saw Thijs making his way between the tables towards them. "You're lucky I haven't been shouting ever since this started," he said.

Thijs reached their table and stood at Jo's shoulder looking around the dining room. "Everything okay?" he asked, nodding and waving hello to someone at another table.

"Everything's great," Jo said. Whatever Thijs had said to her after their day out in Zandvoort, it must have hurt, because she was still barely talking to him.

"Well, everyone seems to have arrived," he told them. "Everyone who's coming, anyway. We'll be starting in the morning. They want to see you first." He looked down at Jo.

"Fine," she said, although the look on her face suggested it was anything but.

A disruption in the colour balance of the room announced the arrival of Wim, wearing yet another eye-wrenchingly awful Hawaiian shirt. He stood by the door for a moment, looking around; then he spotted Thijs standing by their table and a big grin crinkled his beard as he set off towards them. Michael sighed and went back to his dinner.

"Hey," Wim said, still grinning, when he reached the table.

"Hey," Jo said.

"Willem," said Thijs without quite looking at him.

"I was sorry to hear about Anneke," Wim said. "How is she?"

Thijs looked slightly uncomfortable. "Thank you," he said. "She's doing as well as she can. Sofi's sister's keeping an eye on her while I'm here." Michael realised he still hadn't told the rest of the essenceheads about the presumed Event at the hospital and his daughter's miraculous recovery. He wondered how much longer Thijs would be able to keep it quiet.

"Did you find Brossard?" Jo asked.

"Franc?" Wim shook his head. "Nah. He's probably in a room somewhere trying to decide what he's going to wear tomorrow."

"I'd prefer it if you didn't make any more trouble," Thijs said.

"Oh, you'd *prefer* it? Okay. Got that." Wim looked around him. "Nice hotel. The old man paying for everything, is he?"

Thijs didn't answer.

"I've had to pay my own way," Wim went on. "So this had better be good."

Thijs cleared his throat. "I still have some calls to make." He looked at Jo. "Tomorrow, ten o'clock. Try not to be late; you know what they're like."

"Yes," she said. "Yes, I do."

Wim watched Thijs leave the dining room, then he said, "That went well."

"How long is it since you last spoke to each other?" Michael asked.

Wim thought about it. "A couple of years."

"I swear to God, I'm going to take the two of you into a corner and have a quiet word," Jo said wearily.

"Oh, hey," he said, looking across the room. "Constanza's here. I haven't seen her in years. Back in a minute." And he set off between the tables.

"It's like dealing with five-year-olds," Jo said.

Michael watched Wim being greeted enthusiastically by a table full of people he'd earlier tentatively tagged as civilians. He dropped his napkin beside his plate and stood up. "I'm going to turn in," he said.

Jo looked at his plate. "Something wrong with the food?"

"I'm not all that hungry," he told her.

Fourteen

He didn't see Jo the next morning; presumably she'd already inhaled a couple of mugs of coffee and was preparing for her testimony. The breakfast room was about half full, and people he'd never seen before kept nodding hello to him while he waited for his bread to make its way through the toaster. He found himself a table in a corner, surrounded by people he thought were tourists. At least, they didn't pay him any attention, which he would settle for. Through the big windows, it looked as if the weather was on the turn; the sky was grey and cloudy, although there were still a lot of cyclists and pedestrians going by outside. At one point Thijs came to the door and stood there as if he was looking for someone, but he turned and left again.

After breakfast, he went outside and stood on the beach again, looking towards the town. There was a chilly wind, and the sea was choppy. To the north, in the general direction of Sweden, a lid of dark cloud had settled on the horizon, but the tourists were still staking out their places on the sand, setting up their windbreaks and chairs and picnic coolers, completely unaware that they were sitting in the spot where something terrifying and inexplicable had happened decades before. Others, standing solemnly having their photographs taken, were obviously essenceheads, people who'd seen the footage and knew exactly what had happened here. He found himself wanting to run across the sand waving his arms and shouting to drive them all away. Instead, he walked along the beach in the direction of Kołobrzeg.

He hadn't planned on walking very far, but an hour or so later he found himself standing at the base of the red-brick lighthouse, looking out over the twin breakwaters that angled Kołobrzeg's river out into the Baltic. Down below in the seafront plaza in front of the lighthouse, there were boards advertising a catamaran service to Bornholm, and he thought very hard about that. If he wanted to, he could buy a ticket and just walk aboard, and a few hours later he'd be in Denmark. From

Bornholm he could go pretty much anywhere as long as his money lasted, which wouldn't be long. If he wanted to.

He walked along the quayside into the Old Port part of the town. He stopped at a Kantor and exchanged half his euros for a satisfyingly large wad of złotys, and wandered on until he found himself in the middle of what appeared to be a busy farmers' market in front of the Brick Gothic fortress of the Town Hall. A little further along, he spotted a café and he went in, bought himself a coffee and a chicken salad sandwich, and sat at a table near the window. They were the first things he'd bought, under his own steam and with his own money, since the bar in Amsterdam, and he thought about what Jo had said – centuries ago, it seemed – about him having agency. He found it hard to remember ever having agency; it felt as if he'd been swept along like a drowning man in a flooded river for so long that he barely even noticed any more.

Looking out of the window, he saw Thijs and Brossard standing across the street having an argument. He couldn't hear what they were shouting at each other, but there was a lot of hand-waving and finger-pointing going on. There was a third person with them, but Michael couldn't see who it was because Thijs was in the way. He was fairly confident that none of them could have spotted him; he was sitting too far back from the window, and they weren't paying a lot of attention to their surroundings. A taxi pulled up beside them, then a delivery van stopped outside the café, blocking his view, and when it moved off again they and the taxi were gone.

Michael carried on eating his sandwich. Obviously, there were any number of reasons why Thijs and Brossard should be standing in the street yelling at each other; he found himself broadly in favour of *anyone* shouting at Brossard in the street, it should be obligatory. But he did wonder what all that had been about.

Back at the hotel, Jo was standing in the lobby looking annoyed, which was a default setting that he had long ago stopped noticing.

"Where the hell have you been?" she asked. "I've been looking all over for you.

"I had a walk into town," he said. "I thought I had plenty of time."

"You do," she said. "Thijs has only just gone in." She took him by the upper arm and started to steer him back towards the doors. "There's something I want to tell you."

She said it with such a weight of foreboding that he let her walk him outside and along the side of the hotel before she stopped and said, "You remember I sent some of your medications to be tested?"

To be honest, he'd forgotten all about it. "Yes," he said.

"Well, I got the results back while I was in there talking to the old farts, and they're not."

He frowned. "Not what?"

"Medications. They're not medications. They're sugar pills, with a bit of food colouring."

Michael thought about that. He felt his mind slowly going blank. "That's ridiculous," he said.

"I've got the results on my phone," she told him. "I'll get the hotel's Business Centre to print them out for you." She took a breath and looked him in the eye. "There's no detectable active ingredient in either of the pills I sent to be tested. They're placebos, Michael."

"It's got to be a mistake," he said.

Jo shook her head. "My friend's a bit of a space cadet, but he's a good chemist and he does a lot of public health analysis. If he says there's nothing there, there's nothing there."

All he could think of was the vast range of pills and tablets he'd been given at the hospital, how the combinations kept changing, how they had been winnowed down, week after week, until he was left with just two, one blue and one red. "Why would anyone do that?" he asked.

"I don't know." She looked about her, at the trees surrounding them, the people walking down the road towards the seafront. "It'd be a handy way of stopping you wandering off; you'd have to keep coming back every month to get your prescription refilled."

"Unless it occurred to me to get them analysed." Which it hadn't, he reminded himself. It had been Jo's idea. He took one of the little brown pill bottles from his pocket and looked at it.

"Are you okay?" she asked.

"Better than I thought, apparently," he said, although there was a part of him that didn't buy it, that still thought these pills were all that stood between him and a catastrophic relapse. He put the bottle back in his pocket. "I'll need to think about this. How did your thing go?"

She looked at him a moment longer, as if uncertain about his reaction. "Well, there are some people in there who won't be putting me on their Christmas card list," she said. "But that was never going to happen anyway." She checked the time on her phone. "I don't think they'll get round to you today; Thijs'll be in there for a couple of hours, then they want to see Wim, and it's possible they'll want a word with Piet too. They might decide not to do you and Brossard until tomorrow."

He sighed. "This is ridiculous, Jo."

"There's another thing. Thijs and I decided not to tell them about Archie. Well, I decided. I had to talk him into it."

"How did you do that?"

"I threatened to tell them about Anneke."

Michael wondered if there would ever come a point where this whole thing got less complicated. He asked, "And how am I supposed to have got away from Stilwell?"

"I told them you gave him the slip in Eindhoven and called me and I came to pick you up."

He looked at her. "Nobody in their right mind is going to believe that."

"I don't care, I'm not giving Archie up; he didn't ask to be given a superpower."

"I didn't ask to be kidnapped, but here I am." He rubbed his eyes. "Did I happen to tell you how I gave Stilwell the slip?"

"I left it vague," she told him. "I told them I picked you up at the railway station. I thought you could fill in the blanks."

He should have got on that boat; he could have been on his way to Denmark by now. "I suppose I'll have to think of something, then."

"You're a star, Michael." She reached out and squeezed his arm. "Just a little bit longer, then we'll see what we can do."

If he was honest, the prospect of anyone doing anything seemed to be receding with every day that passed. "All right," he said.

He stayed in his room for the rest of the day, flicking through channels on the television, but nobody came to summon him to give testimony, and in the evening he went down to the dining room and sat on his own with a plate of steak and chips. He didn't see Jo, or Thijs, or any of the essenceheads he'd been introduced to, although a tableful of loud West Midlands accents on the other side of the room suggested that the English essenceheads were here. He kept his head down and concentrated on his dinner.

He was just finishing when Wim came in, said, "Hey," and sprawled in a chair across the table from him.

"Have you only just finished?" Michael asked.

Wim nodded and filled a glass from the carafe of water in the middle of the table. "Some people aren't happy unless you tell them how many angels are dancing on the head of a pin, *and* all their names."

"I won't ask how it went, then."

Wim took a sip of water. "It went," he said, "*exactly* how I expected it to go." A waitress came over to see if he wanted to order something, but he shook his head and she went away again. "What's the food like here?"

"It's all right."

"The food at my hotel's terrible, but the room service menu is *terrific*. I've been living on burgers and club sandwiches. Fish and chips. They do a *remarkable* room service fish and chips, but if you order it in the dining room it's barely edible. How do you explain that?"

"I've mostly given up expecting an explanation for anything. Have you seen the others?"

"Piet and Arno just got a cab into town, they said something about checking out some of the bars. I haven't seen Jo or Thijs."

"How about Brossard?"

Wim shook his head. He drained the glass and refilled it. "Hey," he said as something occurred to him. "Has anyone shown you the Greatest Hits tape yet?"

Michael thought about it. "I don't remember anything like that."

"I've got it on my laptop back at the hotel. Why don't you finish your dinner and come over and see it?"

Why not? It was better than spending the rest of the night in front of the television. "I'll get my coat."

"Excellent. I've got a bottle of Scotch, too."

There was a line of lamp-posts along the seafront, casting pools of white light on the cycleway, but Wim's hotel sat a little way back in the trees and it seemed kind of sinister, even with half its windows lit up. His room was on the second floor, and Michael braced himself for a scene of apocalyptic untidiness, but when Wim opened the door the only sign that it was occupied were a wheeled suitcase in one corner and a rucksack sitting on a chair.

Wim unlocked the case and took out a battered old laptop and put it on the table, and while it was booting up he took a bottle of Famous

Grouse from his rucksack and brought two tumblers in from the bathroom.

"Events happen very rarely, and they happen completely at random," he said, pouring them each a measure and handing Michael one of the glasses. "There's no way to predict them, although Christ knows people keep trying."

Michael took a sip of Scotch. "Stilwell said most of them probably happen in uninhabited places, or up in the sky or something," he said. "Places where nobody ever sees them."

"That's probably a factor, yes. It also may be the only intelligent thing Stilwell has ever said." Wim clicked through a series of folders on the laptop's screen. "Anyway, the point is, footage of Events is *incredibly* rare. You need to have someone filming in *just* the right place, at *just* the right moment, and it's always accidental. The earliest footage we know about is from out there." He waved vaguely in the direction of the beach. "1965. This is the next earliest. 1972." He clicked on a file and a window opened on the screen.

There was a very brief, grainy, and jittery shot of some people walking across a field, then the image cut to what seemed to be a tablecloth spread on the ground. On the tablecloth were plates and glass tumblers and Tupperware boxes of food – chicken drumsticks, potato salad, some other things Michael couldn't quite make out – and bottles of wine. Then the camera pulled back and there were half a dozen young people sitting on the grass around the tablecloth, laughing and waving hello. They were old enough to be college students, three boys and three girls, in jeans and teeshirts and flowery dresses and old-fashioned haircuts. The camera pulled back further and panned across what Michael realised was a park, with a screen of trees in the distance. And then the colour of the scene became weak and watery, just for a moment, before coming back to normal. The camera carried on filming for a few moments, then the clip ended.

"What happened?" Michael asked with a rising sense of panic.

"Relax," said Wim. "Nobody got hurt. None of them even noticed it happened."

"I don't understand," Michael said. "Is that it?"

Wim clicked on the little slider at the bottom of the clip and pulled it back about halfway. "Watch carefully."

He started the clip again, and Michael watched the colour drain from the world and return, and the clip ended, and he was still none the wiser.

"Watch carefully," Wim said again, setting up the clip one more time. "Above the trees."

Michael leaned down close to the screen. "Where is this?"

"Munich. It was someone's birthday party or something. Watch."

The clip started, the colour went out of the world and came back, and now Michael saw a large bird, a crow or something maybe, flying along just above the line of trees at the edge of the park. Except there was something wrong with it, and it took him a moment to work out what it was.

"Oh," he said. The bird was flying backwards.

"*That's* something you don't see every day," Wim said.

The thing was, three weeks ago he would have assumed that either something was very wrong or the footage had been manipulated somehow. Now, he was so used to the general weirdness that he hadn't even noticed it. The bird flapped solemnly in reverse for a few hundred feet, then it suddenly seemed to realise what it was doing, performed a confused and ragged somersault, pointed its beak in the right direction, and flew off out of shot.

"You wouldn't believe how many papers have been written about that bird," said Wim.

Michael shook his head, because he absolutely would believe it.

The next piece of video appeared to be a surveillance camera in a small factory at night, a high view over rows of lathes and workbenches and upright drills. It was in black and white, but something still happened to the light when the Event occurred, something changed in the greyscale of the image, and then, for a few seconds, all the machines sparkled as if they had been scattered with tiny stars. Then it stopped.

"Just outside Madrid, 1980," Wim said. "We didn't see this clip until about three years later, though. Thijs and I went down there to take a look anyway, and by that time the workshop had gone out of business and all the machines had been sold and the building was waiting to be demolished. But that's where we found the tennis ball, just sitting in a corner." He shrugged. "There's no way to tell if an Event will leave behind artifacts, or what they'll turn out to be. You have to check everything, just in case."

"I still can't believe none of this is on the internet," Michael said. The essenceheads' informational hygiene was astounding.

"I've thought of putting it up, myself," Wim told him.

"Why don't you?"

Wim looked at the screen and shrugged. "Don't know. Habit, I suppose; it wouldn't seem right. And what would be the point, anyway? Nobody would listen." He shook his head.

The next clip was from some holidaymakers in Tenerife in 1990, just a moment when the colour left the scenery. And a similar one from Durban in 2002. In 2004, a French traffic camera watched water rising from the surface of a road and then draining away again, and in 2007 a hiker in the Black Forest caught, just for a moment, a tree lurching forward as if it had suddenly decided to take a step and then thought better of it. And in every clip something happened to the quality of the light; in some it was so subtle that it would have been easy to miss, but it was always there.

"All right," Michael said. "They all have something in common. That doesn't prove the Essence exists."

"A lot of us would disagree, of course," Wim said. "But that's not why I showed you these clips. Did you spot anything else?"

Michael thought about it. "They're coming more frequently," he said finally.

"Well, maybe they are and maybe they're not." Wim paused the video on a sudden shower of flower petals that had fallen out of a clear blue sky in Mexico in 2010. "What you're actually seeing is the increase in cameras in the general population. Street cameras, surveillance cameras, phone cameras, dashcams, doorbell cameras. I don't think Events are necessarily happening more often, it's just that the opportunities for recording them have increased." He topped up their drinks. "Now, for us that's great because we have more documentary evidence and we can never have enough of that. But it makes it look as if the Essence is winding up to go into overdrive, and I don't think that's true."

"So Brossard's wrong and all this has been for nothing."

Wim shrugged and took a big swallow of whisky. "I think so, but that's just my opinion. You'd never convince Franc of that. And don't forget, the community's already in a flap because of Zandvoort. They're getting all millennial, they're ready to believe anything."

It seemed to Michael that just being an essencehead involved a certain willingness to believe in stuff that most people would regard as utterly mad. The thought of them descending even further into craziness was quite scary. Had they been obsessively searching for the Essence for so long that it wasn't *enough* any more? He said, "Thijs said something about some of you thinking the Essence is behind ghosts and UFOs and stuff like that."

Wim nodded. "I don't buy it, myself. Too neat; the world doesn't work like that."

"But if it *is*," Michael went on, "that would mean Events are much more common than anyone realises. Which would mean they're not becoming more frequent at all, so Brossard and everyone else who's expecting a paradigm shift is wrong."

"You see?" Wim waved vaguely at the laptop. "We've been studying the Essence for centuries and we're no wiser now than when we started; we just wind up with more questions. You and I have been sitting here for about an hour and we're already splitting hairs about some arcane detail of lore. And you don't even *believe* in the Essence." He topped up their glasses.

"Do you think it's God?"

Wim raised his eyebrows in surprise. "Me? No. People used to, once upon a time. Some still do; fundamentalist Americans, some of the French."

"Brossard?"

"Ah, it's always been hard to tell *what* Franc believes. Mostly he just believes in Franc."

"Thijs said he's never told anyone what he saw in Paris."

"That's true; at least, not that I ever heard about, anyway. And that's unusual; your average essencehead would never shut up about it if they saw an actual Event."

Michael thought about Jo, keeping that childhood day in Amsterdam to herself, and wasn't so sure. He said, "I assume there weren't any essenceheads on the beach at Zandvoort."

"No. And we were never able to examine the site because it's under water." He smiled. "And now you're going to tell me that if we can't examine the site we can't be sure it was an Event."

Something had certainly happened at Zandvoort, if not on the day of the collapse then the day before, because Archie was real enough. Although there was no real reason to think the Essence had granted the dog his superpower; for all Michael knew, he'd learned how to teleport on his own.

"Look," Wim said, "your life's never going to be quite the same again. How could it be after all this? And I don't hold out a lot of hope that this circus is going to improve your situation much. But you never know, there's always an outside chance someone will come up with an idea how to fix things."

There was, Michael thought, more chance of Elvis touring again. But he supposed it didn't hurt to hope, every now and then. He drained his glass and held it out for a refill. "Let's drink to that," he said.

Fifteen

Michael woke the next morning to a fuzzy head and a dull, rainy day. He took his medication without thinking about it, and only realised what he'd done afterwards. He sat on the edge of the bed staring at the rain-streaked window and supposed that at some point he would have to skip the pills to see if Jo's friend was right, but he wasn't ready to do that. He still didn't know what to think about the whole thing. Granted, he'd never experienced any sense that the meds were actually doing anything, but he'd supposed that was the whole point; they weren't meant to make him feel superhuman. He still couldn't work out why the hospital would send him out into the world with a pocket full of sugar pills, unless, as Jo said, it was to keep him coming back. And why would they do that? He'd more or less assumed that regular checkups were in his future.

Downstairs was a faint air of siege. People sat around the lounge looking miserably out at the pouring rain. Kids were running around, expending energy that they would have been using up on the beach, and every now and again little groups wearing flimsy transparent plastic ponchos over their holiday clothes went out to waiting taxis, presumably on their way to some indoor sightseeing. After breakfast, he went upstairs to the café for another cup of coffee and sat near the window. The beach was empty, apart from some hardy dogwalkers, and the sea was choppy and whitecapped. Down on the seafront, the kiosks had opened, but it was probably more out of hope than anything else. Maybe the weather would ease off, although looking at the dark sky and racing clouds it seemed unlikely.

Going back down the curving stairs to the ground floor, he saw Brossard coming through the front door, wearing a long black coat with the collar turned up. The Frenchman went straight across the lobby to the front desk, spoke briefly to one of the receptionists, and then disappeared down the corridor leading to the lifts.

Michael found a seat in a quiet corner with a good view of the entrance, but Brossard didn't seem to have brought any contractors with him; the only people who came through the doors after him were a drenched-looking couple with two small children wearing brightly coloured wellingtons and carrying buckets and spades, who tracked sandy footprints on the marble floor all the way across the lobby. Of course, that didn't mean Brossard had come here without backup. There could be dozens of large, professionally violent men waiting in guesthouses in town for the opportunity for another abduction to present itself.

He didn't see anyone he knew; no Jo, no Thijs, not even Piet or Arno. Wim was probably still at his hotel struggling with a hangover. Some faces among the other guests were beginning to look familiar, and he recognised others as having been introduced to him as essenceheads, but he found that he felt rather lost and isolated. He couldn't really have a conversation with any of these people. It was as if he was experiencing a sort of low-level nightmare in which he had become a game token for solving everyone else's problems while his own were entirely ignored.

Back upstairs, he lay on the bed and flicked through the television channels. CNN was doing another incomprehensible economic briefing. He settled on the BBC, but the news items about home seemed as far away and irrelevant as the one about nomadic horse herders in Central Asia. The Zandvoort Event seemed to have dropped off the news agenda. He assumed that it had become a matter of civil engineering now, which was not particularly sexy; the Special Correspondents had flown in at the beginning, discovered that there were no bodies to point at and no weeping refugees to interview, and flown off again without realising they'd missed the story of a lifetime. The most significant thing to happen in Europe for decades – if you believed the essenceheads – and it was too dull for the disaster tourists.

Conscious of the possibility of bumping into Brossard downstairs, he ordered a room service burger and chips for lunch. The burger, of course, was a four-inch wad of meat and salad crammed between the inadequate halves of a toasted brioche bun and held together by a bamboo skewer, but the chips were good.

He dozed for a while, and when he opened his eyes the room was dark, even though by his watch it was still only midafternoon. He got up and pulled back the net curtains and looked out on a scene of black cloud and driving rain, the trees outside whipping back and forth in strong gusts of wind. The hotel opposite was lit up like an ocean liner.

He had another shower and brushed his teeth and put on the last of his clean clothes, and he was just consulting the instructions for the hotel's laundry services when there was a knock at the door and Jo was standing outside.

"You're up," she said.

The conference room hired by the essenceheads was at the end of a corridor on the first floor, and Michael found himself getting nervous as he approached it, although he couldn't explain why. This wasn't a board of inquiry or a Treasury committee, or even a performance review. These people could do nothing to hurt him, and he was coming to the conclusion that they couldn't do anything to help him either. They were people who believed in a crazy thing, cosplaying as a Star Chamber. They were perfectly harmless.

He knocked on the door and opened it and found himself in a room a little larger than his. There was a rectangular table in the middle, with comfortable chairs for about a dozen people, all but one of them occupied, a roomful of expectant faces turned towards him. But he hardly noticed them because seated at the head of the table was Theo van Hoebeek.

Michael's mind went so completely blank for a moment that he forgot where he was and what he was doing there.

"Mister Brookes," Theo said. "Please, sit down." He gestured to the other end of the table, where there was an empty chair.

Michael sat, and felt the world start to click into place around him again. Of course Theo was chairing the meeting; he was the Dutch essenceheads' sugar daddy, the man who had come up with the money to rent the camera, the man who was paying for the hotel. It made perfect sense. It did not explain why Claes the Economy Killer was sitting in the chair to Theo's right, so completely unassuming that he was barely in the room at all.

He said, "I don't understand," and he saw Claes smile faintly.

"Before we start," Theo said, "I'd like to thank you, on behalf of us all, for agreeing to give us your perspective on this sorry matter."

Michael blinked. "You're welcome," he said. "But I wasn't given a lot of choice."

"Yes," Theo said heavily. "I apologise for that."

The concept of Theo van Hoebeek apologising to anyone for anything was so absurd that Michael was struck dumb. He looked around the table, and none of the people here presented as particularly crazy. Apart from Claes, they were all middle-aged or older; some were wearing suits, others were in casual clothing. Even Maxi Zimmermann, seated halfway along the table, was dressed down in a long-sleeved black teeshirt and jeans. Apart from her, he was fairly certain he had not seen any of these people in the hotel until right now.

"In a spirit of disclosure," Theo addressed the room, "Mister Brookes was in Amsterdam for a meeting with myself and my team on a commercially sensitive matter. Until today, that was the only time we had met." Clearly, Theo's connection with Dutch Intelligence wasn't common knowledge, and he didn't want to advertise prior meetings with Michael. "I understand he was actually on his way back to his hotel after the meeting when the incident took place. I'm prepared to recuse myself, of course, if anyone thinks this means I can't chair this meeting without prejudice."

Some people around the table looked annoyed, but most shook their heads. "This is the second time you've offered to recuse yourself," a big brown-haired man in slacks and a grey shirt joked. "Are you sure your heart's in this?"

"Stop being so fucking noble, Theo," Maxi said, and Michael had to clench his jaw to stop his mouth dropping open at anyone speaking to Theo van Hoebeek like that. "Let's get on with this." She looked down the table and smiled. "I can't wait to hear Mister Brookes's side."

"You can't wait to hear about Franc being beaten up," said a woman in a black business suit.

"Oh Christ, yeah," Maxi said. "That's never going to get boring."

Theo raised a hand before the meeting became unruly. "All right," he said. "Well, if everyone's in agreement, perhaps Mister Brookes could tell us his name and profession."

"Is my profession relevant?" Michael asked.

"In English, please," the business-suited woman said. "Not all of us speak Dutch."

Michael hadn't even realised he'd spoken in Dutch. "Sorry," he said in English. "I was wondering what my job has to do with this."

Theo gave him a stern look. "We don't know yet. Please?"

Michael sighed and looked around the table. "My name's Michael Brookes, and I'm an economist. I work for the Treasury in London."

"You have my sympathies," said the grey-shirted man, and there were some smiles and chuckles around the table.

Theo raised his hand again. "Can we keep our minds on the matter at hand?" he asked. When everyone had calmed down again he said to Michael, "Perhaps you could start by telling us what happened to you after you left our meeting."

"Franc Brossard tried to have me kidnapped."

Theo clasped his hands on the table in front of him. "Mister Brookes," he said, "you're not a stupid person, and neither are we. What did you do after you left our meeting?"

So Michael described his journey from Amsterdam-Zuid to the bar beside the canal. He edited out seeing Archie being stolen. He managed to get as far as the arrival of the French contractors before anyone interrupted.

"Why did you go to a bar instead of going back to your hotel?" asked a woman with long grey hair and a Spanish accent.

He shrugged. "I don't know," he said. "It was a nice day, I didn't have to be at the airport for several hours. I just felt like a walk, then I decided to have a coffee and something to eat."

"Why that bar in particular?" asked the man in the grey shirt.

"No reason. I just happened to be walking past when I felt peckish."

"You didn't tell anyone you would be there?"

Michael shook his head. "It was a spur of the moment thing."

"How did you know you were about to be kidnapped?" asked a tall old man wearing jeans and a turtleneck sweater.

"I'm sorry?"

The old man had been industriously writing in a little notebook. He moistened a fingertip and turned back a couple of pages and checked what he had written. "You said you saw two cars pull up and a number of security contractors get out." He looked at Michael. "How did you know they were security contractors?"

It was a reasonable question. "They looked like security contractors," he said.

The old man looked at him with interest. "Really? Is there a recognisable type?"

"Large muscular men with shaved heads, all wearing the same clothes."

"That could equally describe a rugby team."

"It wasn't a rugby team."

The old man nodded and consulted his notes again. "What made you think they were there for you?"

"I didn't. I didn't know what was going on. They pulled up outside and started to come into the bar, then Jo was there telling me I had to get out."

"And Jo told you they were there to kidnap you."

"Yes."

"So you don't know for certain who they were and why they were there. All you saw was some people getting out of a couple of cars."

Michael looked at the faces round the table. "Is Brossard denying it? Is that it? He's saying he didn't try to have me abducted in Amsterdam?"

Several people started talking at once, but Theo rapped his knuckles on the table and when it was quiet again he said, "All we want to know is what you saw. There seems to be a lot of confusion surrounding what happened in the bar, and we'd like to clear that up, if possible."

Michael sat back in his chair and crossed his arms and didn't say anything.

Theo sighed. "You're under no obligation to be here," he said patiently. "You can get up and walk out and leave the hotel and go wherever you want. Nobody will try to stop you. But as representatives of our community, we have a duty to maintain the peace, and in order to do that we have to hear everyone's story. All we want is to hear what you saw and heard."

Michael scowled. He said, "I have no idea why any of this is happening. I came to Amsterdam to have a meeting with you and I was supposed to go home the same day and now my life has been completely upended. I've been chased around the Netherlands and driven halfway across Europe. That's *my* story."

There was a silence around the table. The old man in the turtleneck said, "So you don't know what happened in the bar. You just know what people told you."

"Yes," Michael said tightly. "That's right."

There was another silence. Theo said, "Did you get the impression that someone else in the bar might have been involved in the situation?"

"A young couple came into the bar just after me," Michael said. "And an older man came in behind them. When we were trying to leave, the young couple seemed to get in our way and the older man stopped them. That's what it looked like to me, but everything was very confused."

"And you hadn't seen any of them before?"

Michael shook his head.

Theo looked at him for a long moment. "All right," he said. "Let's move on to your encounter with Colonel Stilwell, shall we? Your first encounter, I should say." He glanced around the table. "I hope nobody's going to quibble about whether this was an abduction or not?" Nobody said anything. "I gather you were drugged and taken to Eindhoven airport."

"Yes."

"Why Eindhoven airport?" asked someone near the other end of the table.

"Stilwell's organisation is renting a suite of offices there," said someone else. "You'd have to ask them why."

"I presume the Colonel questioned you," Theo said.

Michael nodded. "He wanted to know why Brossard was so interested in me."

"Which you were unable to tell him."

"Which I was unable to tell him, because I didn't know. I still don't know, not really."

"You managed to get away from them," Claes said with a dreamy little smile. "How did you do that?"

Michael looked at him. Seated among the seniors, he looked like a vaguely malevolent work experience boy. "They were inattentive," he said deadpan.

Claes raised an eyebrow. "That must have been quite some inattention."

"I saw an opportunity and I took it," Michael told him without breaking eye contact. "I got away from them and I called Jo and she came to get me."

"Why?" asked the Spanish woman.

"Why what?"

"Why did you call Ms Charnley and not the police?" There were murmurs of agreement from some of the others. "You'd been spirited out of the bar in Amsterdam, moved from house to house, drugged and taken to Eindhoven, and you'd finally managed to escape. If that was me, I'd have found a policeman as soon as possible."

"In fact," said the old man in the turtleneck, "as far as we can see you've had a number of opportunities, and not once have you tried to contact the authorities or your Embassy or anyone at all."

"I don't know," Michael said tiredly. He thought about it. "I honestly don't know. Sorry."

There was another silence in the room. Theo said, "Would you like to take a break?"

Michael shook his head. "I just want to get this over with."

Theo nodded. "All right. So, you evade the Americans and return to the fold, so to speak. Whose idea was it to kidnap Mister Brossard?"

"Mine."

"Because it probably won't surprise you to hear that both Jo and Wim have taken credit for it."

Michael shook his head. "It was my idea. I wanted to know what was going on, and he didn't seem inclined to explain things willingly."

"It seems a bit... extreme," said the burly man in the grey shirt.

"I was also very angry."

"Evidently," the man in the turtleneck said, making a note.

"Did you really put a taser in Franc's mouth?" Maxi asked.

"I threatened to." He added, "I'm not especially proud of myself."

She beamed at him. "*I'm* proud of you."

"He *was* tasered, though," said the Spanish woman.

"He brought a taser with him to the meeting," Michael told her. "Along with a number of people from the local rugby club." He saw the man in the turtleneck smile thinly as he made another note. "Presumably he was planning to have another go at snatching me."

"While at the same time *you* were planning to snatch *him*," the woman in the business suit said.

"All right," Michael said wearily. "We're as untrustworthy and reprehensible as each other, I agree."

"You can't just tie people to chairs and threaten them," she told him. "It's against the law."

"He was going to do it to me," he said.

"But he *didn't*, did he," she said, pointing her pen at him. "He never actually did *anything*. All you saw was a group of people getting out of their cars outside a bar."

Michael sighed.

"Did you at least get the information you wanted?" Claes asked.

"That's my business."

"No, it's not," said Theo.

Michael considered not replying – this was not after all, a court of law – but in all honesty, where would that get him? "He said he has a source who told him I was coming to Amsterdam and that I had information about some kind of change in the Essence."

"And do you?" said Claes.

"Of course not. Two weeks ago I'd never even heard of the Essence."

"Nothing at all?" Claes prompted. "Something you might have seen or heard? Something that might not have seemed important at the time?"

"I've had a lot of time to think about this, and there's nothing."

Some murmurs, around the table.

"So why would Brossard's source tell him you knew something?" Claes asked.

"I *don't know*." Michael looked around the room. "I don't know *anything*. It could be a case of mistaken identity, there could be something malicious behind it. I don't know."

"You think Brossard's source could work for your employers?" Theo asked.

"I don't see how anyone else could know my travel details. Even I didn't know until the day I left. And I'm genuinely tired of telling this story over and over again."

"Hopefully, this will be the last time," Claes told him.

Michael wished he could believe that. There was a little bottle of water and a glass on the table in front of him. He twisted the top off the bottle and filled the glass and took a sip.

"But you did threaten Brossard," the woman in the business suit said.

"Yes," he said. "I did." He put the glass down on the table and said, "I wanted to know why he was pursuing me. I wanted to know why I couldn't go home. I wanted to know what was going on. And there didn't seem to be any other way of *fucking* finding out."

There was another silence in the room, this one vaguely embarrassed. Finally, Theo cleared his throat and said, "Shall we move on to your second encounter with Colonel Stilwell?"

"Fine," said Michael.

"Whose idea was it?"

"I don't know. I didn't know anything about it until it happened."

"Nothing at all?"

Michael shook his head. "Jo suggested we take a trip to look at the Event site in Zandvoort and I said yes." He shrugged. "It wasn't as if I had anything else to do."

"And Wim and Anton went with you," said the man in the turtleneck.

"I meant to ask this before," a small, neat woman wearing a flowery blouse piped up, "but why isn't Anton here?"

"He didn't want to come," someone said.

"*I* didn't want to come," Michael said, feeling a little aggrieved.

Theo rapped on the table again. "Anton was a minor player in all this," he said. "He was only there because he's the only one of us who has used the camera before. Jo and Wim have already told us they cooked up the scheme between them; I don't think Anton could have contributed anything to this meeting."

"I don't see what this has to do with anything," the man in the grey shirt said. "The problem here is with Franc Brossard, not Stilwell."

"It speaks to intent," said a plump man with an enormous walrus moustache. He nodded at Theo. "They've been rampaging around the Netherlands, kidnapping and torturing people and causing international incidents. Who knows what else they're capable of?"

"I hope you're not including me in that statement, Jiri," Theo said, his voice pitched somewhere around the sound of a calving iceberg.

"You financed this insane caper in Zandvoort," Jiri pointed out.

"*Financed* is probably too strong a word," Theo told him.

"You gave them the money to rent the camera."

"I did," said Theo with a touch of weariness in his voice. "And I offered to stand down from this panel, and I recall no one took me up on the offer." It was weird to watch; in business and in his dealings with Intelligence, nobody would have dared talk back to Theo van Hoebeek. Things were obviously different among the essenceheads.

Michael said, "I can't help you very much, anyway. Like I said, I didn't know what was going to happen; I thought it was just a day out."

"Were Stilwell and his associate armed?" asked the Spanish woman while Theo and Jiri continued to have a staring contest.

"Oh yes."

"And they threatened you?"

"There was certainly an implied threat."

"Well then," she said, looking around the table. "It was self defence. I don't know why we're arguing about it."

"We're arguing about it because the Dutch deliberately set out to entrap Stilwell," said Jiri.

"Well, I'm not going to criticise them for *that*," she told him. "He's an awful man; it's about time somebody did something about him."

"But you'll criticise them for abducting Franc."

"That's different," she said. "Franc's one of us."

"Franc hasn't been one of us since he inherited his father's money," someone else said. "Not really."

Claes said, "Where was Thijs while you were having your little adventures?"

"His daughter was ill," Michael said, and instantly hoped nobody would notice that *was*.

"Yes." Claes looked sad. "So I understand. But she's feeling better now, no?"

"She has a brain tumour," Michael said, sticking to the fiction that Anneke was still sick.

Claes nodded thoughtfully. "Quite," he said. "Quite. But it does rather sound as though, in his absence, the Amsterdam essenceheads went rogue. No offence."

"None taken," Theo said stonily.

"I can't answer that," Michael said. "As far as I know, this is how you always do things."

"It's not," said the Spanish woman.

"Oh come on," said Maxi, "this is *absolutely* how we do things. We argue *all the time*. Let's not kid ourselves that we're paragons of virtue."

"I can't recall an occasion where one group kidnapped a member of another group and tortured them," the Spanish woman pointed out.

"Milan, '84," Maxi said.

The Spanish woman pulled a face. "That was politics."

Theo raised a hand. "Mister Brookes is right, it's not a fair question for an outsider; he's only ever seen us under stress." He looked at his watch. "Any more questions?" He said it in a tone of voice which suggested he hoped there were not.

"What happened to Stilwell?" Michael asked.

"He and his associate were arrested and are currently contesting deportation," Claes said. "The rest of his people were quietly urged to go home. They left two days ago."

That was something, at least. "What happens now?"

"We'll discuss what we've heard," Theo said, "and hopefully we'll arrive at a position." He gave the others around the table a stern look. "Then we'll put it to a vote. But not now. I think we've all had enough for one day." There were nods of agreement. Theo looked at Michael down the length of the table. "I just want to say, on behalf of us all, that I'm sorry this has happened to you. It probably won't be any consolation, but we're prepared to give you any support you need, for as long as you need it."

Weirdly, Michael found this genuinely rather touching. "Thank you," he said. He got up to go.

Maxi got up too, and came down the table and gave him a vigorous hug. "You *beautiful* man," she said.

"Maxi," Theo said wearily.

"Oh, come on," she said, without letting Michael go. "How many of us *wouldn't* taser Franc if we got the chance? I wish *I* had." She held him at arms' length and looked at him. "Seriously," she said. "If you need anything, just ask. Come and stay with us in Bremen for a while, you'll always be welcome."

"Thank you," he said, and he meant it. "I may take you up on that."

She nodded. "You see that you do." She gave him a last hug and let him go. "Go on," she told him. "You look as if you could use a drink."

He could, but when he looked into the bar he saw Thijs sitting at one table and Jo and Wim at another and he hesitated a moment before moving on and going into the dining room. It was still the early part of the dinner period, and the room was almost full, but the waitress managed to find him a table for one over in a corner by the window, and he sat and looked out on a howling gloom. Squalls of rain pattered across the window, and even through the double-glazing he could hear the sound of the wind. As he watched, the clouds lit up for a moment with a blink of lightning, followed a few seconds later by a long, leisurely rumble of thunder.

He ordered duck fillet with potato and carrot puree and Savoy cabbage, and he sat eating and watching the lightning far out over the sea. Afterward, he had a coffee and a glass of brandy – why not? Theo was paying for it all – and thought for a while. Then he got up, thanked the waitress as he went by, and went out to the front desk.

Theo's room was up on the fifth floor. There was no guard posted outside, but when Michael knocked on the door it was answered by Claes.

They looked at each other for a few moments, then Claes said, "You shouldn't be here."

"Oh, let him in," Theo's voice said from inside the room. "If you think I'm so easily swayed we might as well give up right now."

Claes stared Michael in the eye just long enough to let him know that he was letting him in unwillingly, then he stepped aside.

The room was, of course, enormous. It seemed to take up one entire corner of the building and two of its walls were glass; one looked out over the sea, where lightning was flashing along the horizon, and one looked along the coast to where he could just make out, through the rain and haze, the lights of Kołobrzeg in the distance. There was a big sofa facing a wall-mounted television, and three large comfy-looking armchairs, and doors which Michael presumed led to the bathroom and bedrooms. On a small dining table sat the remains of dinner for two. At the far end, there was a seating area with a low table and four chairs. The table was covered with documents and folders, and Theo was sitting in one of the chairs, jacket off, sleeves rolled up, waistcoat undone and tie loosened.

"Come in," he said. "I was half expecting you." He looked at Claes. "We may as well leave it for today."

Claes looked at the documents on the table. "We still have to clear up the Ehrenreich papers."

"We can't courier them out tonight anyway," Theo said. "Nothing's going to be flying out of Szczecin in this." He nodded at the window. "We'll be lucky if we can find anyone mad enough to even drive them to the airport. Tomorrow will be soon enough. I'll call Ehrenreich later and explain the delay."

Claes hesitated a moment, then went over and started tidying the documents away into folders.

"Call Berne and ask Antoni to set up a video call with the trustees in the morning," Theo told him. "Ten o'clock. And I mean *all* the trustees; I don't propose to say what I have to say twice."

"You don't want me to stay?" Claes asked with a glance at Michael.

Theo shook his head. "I think I can cope. You get some rest."

"You might –"

"I might," Theo interrupted gently but firmly. "And if I do, I'll let you know. Now you go and rest."

Claes straightened up, the folders held against his chest. "Very well," he said. "I'll wish you both a good night, then." And he turned and walked to the door.

When he'd gone, Theo pointed at the chair opposite and said, "Please, sit down. Would you like a drink?"

"Yes," said Michael. "Please."

Theo got up and opened a cupboard, which turned out to be a drinks cabinet almost as well-stocked as a pub. He selected a bottle and poured whisky into two cut-glass tumblers and carried them back to the table. "We live in a world where I can send a document to the other side of the Earth in a fraction of a second with the press of a button," he said, setting one of the glasses down in front of Michael and resuming his seat. "Unfortunately, we also live in a world where the possession of actual physical documents, duly signed and witnessed and stamped, is important. So paper continues to move around the world." He tried his drink. "And we're subject to the whims of the weather, just as we always were."

"Why's he here?" Michael asked.

"Claes? He's here because he's my personal assistant. And very good at it he is, too."

"I'm surprised the Danes let him go, if what I've heard about him is true."

"Oh, it's true. Given the right resources, he's quite capable of bringing your economy to its knees. If you weren't already doing such a splendid job of it yourselves." Theo smiled and took another drink. "He asked to work with me, apparently, and, because he *is* a genius, if a rather strange and dangerous one, the Danes agreed to his request."

"What about your Service? I presume they agreed too."

"I wasn't party to those discussions; I imagine there's some quid pro quo somewhere along the line, and his access to my intelligence work is strictly limited. He's on placement with me for a year, and after that he goes back to Copenhagen, or wherever he decides he wants to be next."

Michael took a sip of whisky, and discovered it was a malt of some considerable age and provenance. He said, "Theo, what's going on?"

Theo looked grave. Behind him, lightning illuminated the raging surface of the sea for a moment. "It all seems to have become something of a mess," he said.

"No shit."

Theo took a drink and thought about it. "About six weeks ago your Service contacted my Service and proposed an exercise, a *roleplay*, they called it. They said one of their employees had been ill and they wanted to ease him back into work, see how he coped with a simple scenario."

Michael stared.

"They wanted us to make believe that some of our economic data had been leaked; they'd send the employee over to Amsterdam, we'd give him the details, and he'd return to London." Theo looked at the window. "I thought it was a cruel thing to do to someone. I didn't want anything to do with it, but my Service insisted I would give the scenario credibility." He shook his head at the memory.

Michael remembered him not speaking at the meeting in Amsterdam-Zuid, not even acknowledging that anyone else was there. "So that whole thing was a… a *joke?*"

"A test. At least, that was how it was described to me."

Michael looked around the suite, completely unable to think of anything to say.

"Instead," Theo went on, "you seem to have discovered a *real* leak, an essencehead within your own organisation passing on information to Franc Brossard."

Michael shook his head helplessly.

"Of course," Theo mused, "that could have been the intention all along, to use you to flush out this *Kelvin*. Which would mean that your employers have some knowledge of the essenceheads."

Not so long ago, this conversation would have driven him into the Acute wing. Instead, like a drowning man, he found a piece of debris and clambered aboard. "When did you know it was me who was coming?"

Theo thought about it. "We didn't know your details until a couple of days before you arrived."

Michael shook his head. "Brossard knew before that. A long time before that. He had my name and my flight number and the address of my hotel. He had *Jo's* name."

"Yes," Theo said. "Yes, that's interesting, isn't it? The fact that Kelvin knew Jo's name suggests that he has access to your employers' file on you and knows she's an essencehead. But why tell Brossard about her?"

Well, here was the answer to the question of whether this situation would ever get less complicated, and the answer was 'no'. Michael shook his head again, unable to compute the sheer number of permutations of who knew what and when and why they did this or that or the other. He put his hands to his face.

"I'm truly sorry this has happened to you," he heard Theo say. "I was opposed to this ridiculous *roleplay* right from the start, and I should have told you about it that morning in Zuid."

"It wouldn't have changed anything." In fact, it might have done; back then, it might have caused a relapse, and then none of this would ever have happened. It was a demonstration of how far he'd come that he was simply utterly baffled, rather than crashing about the suite shouting and breaking things before becoming catatonic. He took his hands away from his face and picked up his glass and took a big drink.

"Another?" Theo asked.

Michael nodded. "Thank you."

Theo took the glasses over to the drinks cabinet and topped them up. "Wim told us you'd discovered a connection between Neville Hallam and the Kołobrzeg Event," he said, bringing the glasses back and handing one to Michael.

"It was hardly a discovery."

Theo settled back into his chair and took a sip of his drink. "It's something none of us ever suspected," he said. "So we owe you a debt of thanks." He raised his glass in a toast.

The essenceheads owed him considerably more than that, after what he'd been through, Michael thought, but he raised his glass too.

"I met him once," Theo mused.

Michael raised an eyebrow. "Hallam?"

Theo nodded. "My father knew him; he was one of the Resistance operatives who smuggled Hallam out of the country and back to England after he was shot down."

Of course he was. Everything was connected; it wasn't even faintly surprising any more. Michael took a drink and looked into his glass. "What was he like?"

"He looked fierce," Theo said. "He had the eyepatch and the big moustache and the prosthetic leg, and his left arm didn't work properly. But he was actually civil and courteous and rather gentle, I thought.

Wistful. Driven, though." He nodded to himself. "Definitely driven. My father helped him buy his flat in Alkmaar, when he came back after the War."

"Why?"

Theo sighed. "We didn't exactly distinguish ourselves in our handling of Neville Hallam," he said. "There were some – my father among them – who advocated telling him about the Essence. But they were over-ruled, and instead we stood back and watched him thrashing about looking for his Angel. People still call him 'Mad Jack'." He shook his head. "It was very disrespectful. He was a brave man; all the bomber crews were." He looked out of the window at the flickering clouds. "He was very like Franc Brossard. They both saw something miraculous, but the difference is that Hallam died without ever knowing the truth about what happened to him."

And then the Essence had killed the people who were filming his book. Michael asked, "Did you know about the book?"

"Oh yes. My father gave him the money to publish it. I've never read it, though, so I never connected it with the footage." He gestured towards the beach, almost invisible in the howling gloom. "My father *did* read it, but he was dead by the time the footage and the script surfaced. Until you came along, no one has ever made the connection, so I suppose you could say one good thing has come out of this mess."

"A good thing for the essenceheads," Michael pointed out. "Not for me."

Theo inclined his head in agreement. "It's intriguing that it fell into your hands," he said. "Not *entirely* impossible, but so incredibly unlikely that it might as well be."

"You think someone put the book in my way."

"It must have crossed your mind."

It had, but Michael couldn't remember anyone urging him to read it, however obliquely. It had just been sitting in the rickety bookcase that residents and staff referred to as 'the library', just one book among a couple of dozen battered secondhand volumes. "Even if someone *had* arranged for me to read it, it's meaningless without the footage and the script, and nobody could have known that I'd see them."

Theo grunted, and took a swallow of whisky. "There are certain degrees of hierarchy among the essencehead community," he said. "In general, the more artifacts and supporting material you have, the higher up you're regarded to be. The French, for instance, have three artifacts, so they're near the top of the pecking order. On the other hand, we just have the tennis ball and the originals of the Amsterdam footage and the Kołobrzeg footage and the shooting script, so the Dutch are definitely the poor relations."

"Not so poor," Michael said, tilting his glass towards Theo.

"Money always makes a difference," Theo agreed. "Unlike others, we've always leaned more towards research than the acquisition of physical objects, and in that respect I like to think we punch above our weight. But the point I was going to make is that, if you were to fall into the hands of the Dutch essenceheads and they were trying to convince you of the Essence's existence, there's a sharply limited amount of supporting evidence they could show you. Sooner or later, someone would have let you see the footage and read the script."

Michael thought about it. "My therapist says the human mind evolved to look for patterns," he said. "The shapes of predators, things that could be a threat. The world's mostly meaningless, but the mind keeps on looking for patterns regardless, and when they aren't there it sort of fills in the spaces. That's how we get conspiracy theories."

"Well, it's a view," Theo mused. "And I take your point."

They sat quietly for a while, watching the lightning. The thunder was an almost-continuous low rumble. Michael said, "What will happen to Brossard?"

"We haven't decided yet," said Theo. "Once upon a time, we would have imposed some degree of sanction on him, and it would have mattered. Today?" He shook his head. "We used to have conventions, ways of doing things which helped us all get along. Now there's a generation – I suppose Brossard is something of a figurehead for them – who've realised that breaking those conventions has no consequence at all, and that means they can do whatever they want. Things are changing."

"Maybe that's the paradigm shift everyone's expecting. Not the Essence, but the essenceheads."

Theo chuckled. "That would be funny, wouldn't it? Everyone waiting for a great change, and it's us all along." He took a drink. "What will you do now?"

"I don't know."

"I meant what I said about giving you anything you need. You could stay with us. I might even be able to swing Dutch citizenship for you; I'm not without influence."

Michael looked at him. "Are you trying to *recruit* me, Theo?"

Theo guffawed, which was something to see; to Michael's knowledge, Theo van Hoebeek had never been seen to smile, let alone laugh out loud. He said, "Have you told my office where I am?"

Theo shook his head. "And they've never asked."

"They haven't?"

"The day after the *roleplay*, they sent us an enquiry about how it went, and we said it had all gone to plan, because at that time we thought it had. Since then? Nothing."

"That seems… disappointing."

"I checked discreetly, and there doesn't seem to have been any increase in activity out of your Embassy or Consulate, no requests to the Dutch police and border agencies. There could have been high-level traffic between your Service and mine of which I'm not aware, but if there was, it doesn't appear to have had any effect."

Michael didn't know what to make of this news. It seemed he had been sent to Amsterdam to take part in what amounted to a pantomime, and nobody was particularly bothered about whether he came back or not. He said, "This is a lot to take in."

"We'll talk again, after this is over," Theo told him. "We can discuss the future then."

It was quite an effort, after everything that had happened, to even acknowledge that there *was* a future, rather than an endless incomprehensible present. "When will this be over?"

"I'd like us to wind up the discussion tomorrow, and put it to the vote the following day." Theo drained his glass and put it on the table. "I should stick around to deal with any fallout, but you could fly back to Amsterdam with me the day after that."

Michael thought about that long, dreamlike drive across northern Europe, imagined the return journey taking an hour or so. He opened his mouth to say something, and the entire room lit up brightly enough for the furniture to cast shadows, followed by a crash so loud that he thought he felt the hotel shake a little.

"Good lord," Theo said with admirable understatement, "that was a bit close."

By the time he got downstairs, a dense band of hail was rattling against the windows, but the sound was almost drowned out by the level of conversation. It seemed that everyone in the hotel had spontaneously decided to come down to the ground floor, and the lobby was a mass of people. Michael worked his way around the edge of the crowd. He glanced into the restaurant and the breakfast room, and they were both full. It was standing room only in the lounge and the café.

He reached the entrance and looked out through the glass doors. Remarkably there were people standing outside having a cigarette. The bad weather had winnowed down the hotel's smokers to a hard core of three or four, sheltering under the canopy outside the doors and hunching their shoulders against the wind and rain, returning soaked to the skin, and here now were the final two utter badasses, almost bent double against the wind and the rain and the hail, the peak of smoker evolution. Michael leaned close to the doors and tried to peer out into the darkness beyond.

"Sir?" It was one of the reception staff, neat and calm in her grey uniform. "We're asking guests to stay away from the windows," she told him quietly. "Just in case."

There was another massive flash outside, and Michael caught an eyeblink of a six-foot tree branch wheeling through the air past the hotel and out of sight. "Yes," he said, and moved back into the lobby. He looked out across the sea of heads, searching for a familiar face. It seemed that half the people here had their phones out, either staring at the screens or filming what was happening in the lobby, but here and there he saw others with devices that were not phones, things that ranged from slick black phone-sized objects to lumpy agglomerations of components that looked as if they had been haphazardly soldered together on somebody's kitchen table. One person seemed to have an antique Geiger counter slung over his shoulder, one hand holding the Mueller tube over his head.

"I've been looking for you," Jo said, fighting her way through the crowd to his side. "Are you okay?"

"Yes," he said, looking about him. "I was talking with Theo."

She said, "What –" and the light changed.

It wasn't like the footage he'd seen; this time the colour drained entirely out of the world and everything was black and white and everyone in the lobby fell silent except Jo, who said, "Jesus *Christ*."

And then the colour returned and a huge *"Ooh!"* went up from the crowd and all of a sudden fully two thirds of the people on the ground floor of the hotel surged towards the windows, elbowing each other out of the way and holding up various meters and detectors and antennas and cameras and speaking excitedly into phones and digital recorders. Now it was easy to tell the essenceheads from the ordinary guests; the ordinary guests were the ones who were backing away into the middle of the hotel. There were a lot fewer of them than Michael had realised.

The air pressure in the lobby changed suddenly as the smokers dragged the door open and came back inside, admitting a wave of cold air and a smell of electricity. Before the door closed again, a tall figure in a long black coat emerged from the crowd and slipped outside.

Michael walked back to the doors, Jo in his wake, and they stood and watched the tall figure, illuminated by the lights of the hotel, battling against the wind, step by step, towards the promenade.

"Is that *Brossard?*" Jo said.

A sudden gust of wind flapped the figure's coat open and then stripped it off him entirely, throwing it up and away into the night, and as the wind bowled him off his feet Michael got a good look at his face, and yes, it was Brossard, mouth open and eyes screwed up until they were almost closed, scrambling about on the short stretch of road parallel to the hotel until he managed to regain his feet, at which point the wind knocked him over again.

"He's going to get himself killed," Jo said.

Tiny violin, Michael thought.

The essenceheads had noticed Brossard by now, and some of them were filming him through the windows. He'd given up trying to stand and was now moving on hands and knees towards the beach, head down, clothes plastered to his body by the rain and the wind. Another wave of hail rattled down, and he paused until it had passed before crawling painfully on.

Oh, for fuck's sake.

Michael stepped forward and pushed at the door, but it wouldn't open. He had to lean his shoulder against the glass and put his whole weight into it before it moved, agonisingly slowly.

"What the *fuck* are you doing?" Jo yelled. "Michael, no!" And then he was outside in the howling wind and rain and the door banged shut and he couldn't hear her any more. He couldn't hear anything but the wind and the thunder banging overhead.

He was drenched through to the skin in moments. It was almost impossible to stay upright. After a few seconds trying to get his balance, he found that it was possible, by crouching over with his shoulders hunched up, to shuffle sideways like a crab, one forearm protecting his eyes. He caught sight of Jo's face, pressed to the glass of the door. She was still shouting.

The rain tasted brackish and it was full of sand and grit, and the air was full of flying bits of tree. A square metal sign with the word *Uwaga!* on it missed him by a couple of feet like an airborne guillotine blade. He was exhausted after the first half-dozen steps, and he had to pause for a second. All of a sudden, the lights of the hotel went out and he was crouched there in darkness, with only the lightning flashing in the clouds to see by.

He risked a glance towards the beach, and saw in a blink of lightning Brossard hauling himself up the steps like a prehistoric fish dragging itself up onto land for the first time. He reached the top and flung one arm out to roll himself down the other side and out of sight. Swearing under his breath, Michael wiped water out of his eyes, set his feet and started out again.

It felt like an age before he reached the promenade, and the moment he stepped out of the relative shelter of the hotel a gust of crosswind knocked him over and bowled him along for a couple of yards before he managed to stop himself. A few hundred yards along the seafront, a bolt of lightning sizzled and a tree burst into flame. He got to his knees and crawled to the steps, got up them one by one, and toppled onto the beach.

If anything, the noise here was even worse. The Baltic was *roaring*, an endless boiling surface of white spray attempting to climb up on the land. Michael lay where he was on the sand, trying to get his breath back. He turned his head to one side and saw Brossard kneeling on the beach a few yards away, sitting back on his heels and looking up at the sky. *Going to die*, he thought. *Both going to die.* He rolled over onto his hands and knees and started out again.

When he reached Brossard it became evident that the Frenchman wasn't just looking into the sky. He was screaming, "Show me! Show me!" at the clouds over and over again, at the top of his voice.

Michael grabbed his arm. "We have to go back inside!" he yelled over the sound of the wind and the rain and the sea.

"Show me!" Brossard shouted at the flickering clouds. "Come on! Show me!"

"Brossard!" Michael screamed. "We're going to die here!"

"Show me!" Brossard shouted.

And as if in answer, an eye-hurtingly bright thread of lightning touched down on the beach and danced for a moment over the sand. Then another. Then another. It was if the lightning was walking from side to side, looking for something.

Should be dead, Michael thought. *Wet sand, lightning. Should be dead.* He tugged Brossard over on his side and dug his feet into the sand and tried to drag him back towards the seafront, but the Frenchman was more or less dead weight and he couldn't get enough purchase. He gave up and lay where he was and tried to make himself an inch tall. The lightning took another walk back and forth, and then there was an enormous displacement of air, it felt as if the whole world had been moved sideways a little. Michael raised his head slightly and looked in that direction. "Oh, for God's sake," he muttered wearily.

Something *colossal* was on the beach with them.

This wasn't a blind spot outlined by a dancing curl of light. It was a formless *presence,* larger than an office building, impossible to see properly, an enormous surging murmuration made of wind and rain and hail and sand and debris looming far up into the sky, becoming *part* of the sky. All Michael could do was sprawl helplessly in the sand, waiting for his life to flash before his eyes. If nothing else, he might get the answers to some questions.

"Show me!" Brossard yelled weakly.

The presence leaned down from a height of thousands of feet and it *looked* at them. Brossard started to shriek.

And then it was gone.

Gradually, the lightning withdrew out to sea, a rumbling and flashing in the clouds, and the wind began to drop. Michael lay where he was, blinking water out of his eyes. *Not dead, then.* Beside him, Brossard was intermittently screaming and sobbing.

Finally, Michael managed to get himself little by little to his feet, and found to his weary surprise that he was actually able to stand. He looked along the beach, where that colossal presence had been, and he rubbed his face. Then he leaned down and got hold of Brossard's hand and started to drag him towards the hotel.

Brossard either wouldn't or couldn't walk under his own steam, so Michael towed him back to the steps and over onto the promenade. From there, it was only a thousand light years to the entrance of the hotel. He paused about halfway there to catch his breath. There was still a severe storm going on, but he thought the rain had begun to ease a little, and the lightning was no longer flashing almost continuously. Along the seafront, the tree still burned fitfully. He noted, in a faraway part of his mind, that nobody had come out of the hotel to help him.

The lights had come back on by the time he reached the entrance, and someone at least held the door open for him as he plodded inside dragging Brossard behind him.

In the lobby, the crowd had withdrawn from around the doors, leaving a big clear semicircle. He saw Thijs and Claes standing side by side, and Jo a little way along the line of people, and Piet and Arno's faces a few rows back, and he stood and looked at them all, and then they started to clap. The clapping spread, until everyone in the lobby was doing it. For a moment, it was as if he was a member of a theatre's audience being applauded by the cast of a play.

He dropped Brossard and waded across the wet floor towards Claes, who was beaming and holding out a hand, and Michael punched him in the face as hard as he could and kept going through the crowd until he reached the lifts. He slapped at the call buttons, but of course nothing happened because the power had gone out and the lifts had shut down automatically and nobody had bothered to reset them. Typical. He sighed, and his legs gave way.

Sixteen

He woke the next morning barely able to move, which was a problem because he really needed the toilet. He considered this problem for a little while, then he painfully dragged himself out of bed and shuffled into the bathroom.

After he'd used the loo, he looked at himself in the bathroom mirror. Someone, he couldn't remember who, had got him upstairs last night and put him to bed, and they'd put a pair of pyjamas on him that he definitely hadn't brought from the Netherlands. He opened the jacket and saw that his torso was covered in bruises. His palms and knees were grazed, and his face looked as if it had been lightly sandblasted.

He stood under the shower for ten minutes with the temperature dialled up as far as it would go, and he felt vaguely better when he'd finished. Back in the bedroom, he discovered that during the night someone had taken all his clothes away, laundered them, and brought them back neatly folded. He thought he had a confused memory of people in the room, one of them standing by the bed and taking his blood pressure, but it might have been a dream; it was impossible to know what was real any more.

It was late by the time he finally made it downstairs, but breakfast was still being served. There seemed to be a lot more staff on duty in the breakfast room, though; two of them were standing at the entrance, apparently giving hard looks to anyone who was leaving.

He made himself some toast, and then he got a tray and a plate and walked along the buffet counters and piled it up with a bit of everything, because, sod it, sometimes you just had to have a big breakfast. When he got to the end, he found a waitress guarding the cutlery station, and when he tried to take a knife and fork she stopped him.

"I'm sorry, sir," she said, "items have been going missing this morning, we're trying to make sure guests only take what they need."

Michael looked around the breakfast room, which was about half full. None of the empty tables was set with cutlery, and he couldn't see a single salt and pepper shaker anywhere. The essenceheads, looking for artifacts, had been industriously walking off with items to examine later.

"It's a strange old world," he told her.

"It certainly is," she said. "Housekeeping say we're losing bedsheets and pillows too. We caught someone trying to go out the back with an armchair. Management are talking about calling the police." She handed him a knife and fork and teaspoon wrapped in a napkin. "Please leave these on your table when you've finished. And have a nice day."

He carried his tray over to one of the empty tables and sat and looked about him. The waitress was already speaking sternly to another guest, who was unashamedly taking a double handful of condiment sachets from his pockets and returning them to their container. It would be so easy to explain all this to the clearly baffled hotel staff. All he had to do was walk over to the waitress and say, *"Excuse me, people are taking all these things because they think they have magic powers."* Simple. He shook his head and started to eat.

As he ate, he was half-aware of other diners arriving or leaving, but after a while everything seemed a little quiet, and when he looked up he saw that none of the tables around him were occupied. Everyone seemed to have arranged themselves around the edges of the room, leaving him in the middle of a sort of exclusion zone of empty tables. He also saw that Claes was walking across the breakfast room towards him, holding a mug of coffee and a teaspoon.

"Good morning," he said with a smile when he reached the table. "I do hope you're not going to hit me today." There was a disappointingly minor mark on his face.

He pulled out a chair and sat down opposite Michael. "So," he said cheerfully. "We're quite the hero this morning. And to be honest, that *was* quite a brave thing you did last night."

Michael went back to his breakfast.

"Franc's not seriously hurt, by the way," Claes told him. "Just a bit bashed about and babbling. He's in hospital, under sedation. The doctors think he'll be able to go home in a couple of days." He tore the tops off a couple of sugar sachets and dumped their contents into his mug and stirred them. "How are you feeling?"

Michael didn't say anything.

Claes finished stirring and looked around for somewhere to put his teaspoon. When he couldn't find anywhere, he put the spoon in his mouth and sucked it clean and laid it on the table beside his mug, from where it was removed almost immediately by a waitress. He watched her go back to the breakfast counters and shook his head. "Essenceheads," he said. "Sometimes they're the most embarrassing people in the world. But you'll have noticed that."

Michael put a forkfull of bacon and scrambled egg in his mouth and chewed slowly.

"Anyway," said Claes, "last night was a splendid demonstration of the power of faith, don't you think?"

Michael looked at him. "This whole thing has been a setup," he said.

Claes seemed to think about it. Then he broke into a huge grin and jokingly half-raised his hands. "Guilty as charged. Well done." He lowered his hands. "Actually, it was a little more complicated than that; Franc really did want to abduct you and interrogate you under drugs. He just didn't realise he was always going to fail. Although, to be fair, the Dutch were so hopeless that he almost got you; I had to make a couple of quick phone calls to tip them off about what was happening."

Michael went back to his food.

Claes tried his coffee and licked his lips. "Of course," he said, "*I'd* like to know what you know about the Essence, too, but it seemed to me that your presence in Amsterdam opened up an opportunity for a little experiment. All I needed to do was nudge things a little so that the essenceheads would wind up having to hold a conference. Do you think Franc liked what he saw last night? Did *you?*"

Michael kept eating.

"The Essence is a matter of faith for Franc. Real old-fashioned Faith; he believes he saw God on the Paris Métro, and he's been trying to see Him again ever since," Claes went on. "Thijs takes a more secular view. Although I suspect that belief's been shaken a little after what happened to his daughter, no?" He tipped his head to one side, waiting for a reaction, but Michael didn't look up. "Anyway, if one could get enough essenceheads, people who really believe in the Essence, together in one place – particularly in a place where a previous Event had occurred – would the Essence notice? Would it *respond?*" He smiled at Michael, who seemed not to be listening.

Claes put his mug down, but he kept his hand on the handle in case the waitress swooped in to take it away. "The problem with the Essence – one of the problems – is that it's impossible to know where it will manifest, which makes it impossible to study. For centuries the essenceheads have been happy to come in after the fact, sometimes weeks or months after, but that's like studying the scene of a car crash after all the wreckage has been cleared away, and it's just not good enough."

Michael tore the corner off a sachet of tomato ketchup and squeezed it onto his bacon.

"There are efforts to work out ways to predict Events," Claes went on, "but they've been stumbling along almost as long as we've known about the Essence, and nobody's any closer to a solution." He leaned forward a little. "If we could *attract* it, somehow, if we could *make* it manifest, that would be different. Imagine what we could learn if we could do that. We'd be closer to learning what it is, perhaps closer to learning how we can make use of it."

Michael looked calmly at him, then went back to his breakfast. Claes was the person he'd seen in town with Thijs and Brossard the other day. Discussing the *experiment*.

"It's early days yet, of course," said Claes. "We'll have to repeat the experiment several times to see if the Essence really does respond to faith. We'll have to find out if there's a critical mass of essenceheads, and how many that is. But really, this has been a very promising start. We've got *masses* of data."

Michael carried on ignoring him.

"You're angry," Claes said. "And I understand that; nobody likes to be manipulated. But it seemed ridiculous not to take the opportunity. It's for the greater good. Really."

"Who's Kelvin?" Michael said without looking up.

Claes beamed at finally getting a response. "Kelvin isn't a who," he said. "He's more of a network, a collective of interested parties who've grown tired of collecting artifacts and writing academic papers and actually want to get something *done*. The median age of essenceheads is 61, you know, and a lot of them are much older. All the seniors, the ones who adjudicate disputes and assess research, are *old*, Michael. They did good work in the past, but they're tired and out of ideas. It's time a younger generation had a voice."

"Kelvin told Brossard I was coming to Amsterdam."

Claes inclined his head. "Forgive me if I don't tell you who our source is. My secret."

"Did your *source* tell you what I'm supposed to know about the Essence?"

"No." Claes looked regretful. "No, we were never able to discover that. Are you sure you don't remember?"

Michael cut a piece of sausage and put it in his mouth.

"Anyway." Claes put his hands flat on the table on either side of his mug. "That's probably irrelevant now; we have more important things to think about. The *most* important thing is, what did you see out there last night?"

Michael swallowed the mouthful of sausage, leaned forward, and brought his fork down on the back of Claes's hand. Claes squealed and tried to pull away, but the fork had been driven all the way through his hand and into the tabletop underneath. All of a sudden, all conversation in the breakfast room stopped.

Without letting go of the handle of the fork, Michael got up and walked around the table. Claes's eyes were bugging out, and he was making gulping noises. Michael bent down until his mouth was beside Claes's ear.

"My secret," he said quietly. And he walked out.

Outside, the world seemed to have been washed and then inadequately tumble-dried. Everything was damp and oddly clean, and the air smelled fresh. A considerable amount of the beach seemed to have made a break for freedom and lay on the promenade in little drifts that were almost ankle-deep in places. A little way along, one of the kiosks had been blown over on its back and was resting on some bushes. The one beside it was gone entirely; all that remained was a square concrete base, from which protruded some pipes supporting a little metal sink, and a section of metal worktop that looked as if someone had tried to fold it in half. The tree he'd seen burning last night was just a carbonised statue now, and a bit further along the promenade a little truck with an industrial woodchipper hitched to the back was parked. Beside it, a little group of men wearing hardhats and hi-vis jackets and climbing harnesses and holding chainsaws stood around discussing how best to tackle another tree that canted dangerously out over the seafront.

The little sand berm that had run along the edge of the promenade here was more or less entirely gone, just a few clumps of grass and concrete dragon's teeth the size of microwaves remaining. The breakwaters that had been half-buried not so long ago were now nearly shoulder-high, the sand between them driven up the beach and piled against the seawall. He walked down onto the beach and stood there with his hands in his pockets, thinking about that enormous formless *presence* leaning down and looking at him and Brossard. His memory of last night was a confused howl of wind and rain and lightning, but he didn't remember feeling particularly threatened by it. He thought, actually, that it had been more or less indifferent to him. Had it really been the Essence? Had it just been another artifact, conjured for a few moments out of the night and the weather? Or, in the end, had it only been a tornado? He suspected the distinction would keep the essenceheads arguing for years.

It was still gusty, but there were great patches of pale blue between the clouds. The sea remained lively, but at least it wasn't roaring any more; he hoped he'd never hear that sound again. There were a lot of people on the beach, walking slowly along, their eyes on their feet. Poles, looking for amber cast up by the storm, and essenceheads picking up bits of sand fused into glass by the lightning, hoping that they would confer the power of flight or let them talk to animals or something.

However Claes liked to spin it, last night's near-catastrophe wasn't an experiment; it was a coup, Claes and his friends overturning the ossified rule of seniors like Theo. They'd achieved what nobody in history had ever managed, they'd *caused* an Event, and now they would be in a position to steer the essenceheads in whatever direction took their fancy. Older essenceheads and anyone else who didn't like the changes would be quietly sidelined. Things would be different now. Michael didn't think Archie would survive very long once Claes got word of him.

"So," Jo said, coming up to stand beside him, "do you believe in the Essence now?"

Michael didn't say anything.

"I didn't know," she said. "None of us did. Thijs and Brossard cooked the whole thing up between them. Theo's *incandescent* with them."

She still didn't know about Claes. Michael turned and looked at the hotel. Some of the windows had been cracked by flying debris; one, on the second floor, had been shattered altogether, and a net curtain was flapping in and out of the hole. The person the old man was really incandescent about, he thought, was himself, for agreeing to let Claes into the fold in the first place. If last night had been a genuine catastrophe – or if nothing had happened at all – Claes would have quietly melted into the background and let Thijs and Brossard take the blame while he waited for another opportunity to take over the essenceheads. As it was, he had a credible claim to have caused an actual miracle. Wasn't that how things went these days? Move fast, break things, and by the time anyone realises what's happening it's impossible to go back. He remembered a saying he'd heard somewhere, *it's easier to ask for forgiveness than it is to ask for permission*. People like Claes had no morality, no self-awareness, just an all-consuming need to get their own way, and you couldn't fight them without being exactly like them, which was how the assholes won every time.

Michael looked at Jo. "I'd like to go home," he said.

Seventeen

It turned out to be more complicated than he'd thought. The timing was going to be tricky, and he wasn't sure he could make that work, but he didn't see that he had any choice.

The conference met one last time and considered the evidence it had heard, and it put a number of proposals to a vote, but nobody's heart was really in it. Thijs had already left, and Wim refused to vote because he said it was meaningless now.

"The fuckers won," he told Michael in the hotel bar the evening of the vote. "Franc's going round saying the other night was all his idea. He's a fucking hero."

"It won't last," Michael said.

"You could drop that guy into a pigsty," Wim said sourly, "and he'd come up with a gold bar in his mouth."

Michael thought Brossard had become irrelevant; however wondrous and life-changing his first encounter with the Essence had been, the second had been terrifying, and it was going to take a long time for him to recover from it. More concerning was Claes, who had gone off to hospital to have his hand looked at, and never come back. A discreet inquiry with Housekeeping revealed that his room had been vacated and his luggage taken away the afternoon after the Event. He didn't like having Claes out of his sight.

He said, "I don't know what was out there, but it wasn't what Brossard saw in Paris; it wasn't the miracle he was looking for."

Wim nodded. "Serves him fucking well right."

In the aftermath of the Event, Michael had found himself an object of mild awe. The ordinary rank and file essenceheads gave him a wide berth, afraid to ask him what he'd seen out on the beach, and when a senior asked he refused to tell them. "Whatever it was, it knew we were there," he said, "And you were right; it doesn't care."

Wim nodded and thought about that for a while. "Well," he said finally, and he drained his glass and waggled it in the direction of the barman. "Another one?"

The essenceheads themselves were drifting off to their homes, having stripped the hotel, and most of the other hotels in the area, of pretty much everything that might have been an artifact. A lot of road signs and other minor street furniture had also mysteriously gone missing. It was as if Kołobrzeg had been struck by a plague of particularly weird locusts. Years from now, in homes all over Europe, families would still be eating meals off hotel china with hotel cutlery, and sleeping with their heads on hotel pillows.

The day after the vote, Michael had dinner in Theo's suite and they managed to put an appreciable dent in that bottle of malt whisky, and the morning after that Jo and Piet and Arno drove back to the Netherlands with Wim.

"Are you going to be okay?" she asked, handing him his phone and battery. He'd almost forgotten that he'd ever had a phone of his own.

"I'm going to be fine," he said.

"Good." She gave him a hug and went out to the car.

Later, he had dinner, and there was a sense that the hotel was returning to normal without ever realising just how abnormal things had been. Certainly the staff seemed relieved not to have to guard the cutlery any more.

Afterward, he went out and stood on the beach for the last time. The weather had improved, but evenings were chilly and there weren't a lot of people about. The Baltic was flat-calm, and the setting sun turned it to a great brass mirror. It felt remarkably peaceful out here now, as if the Event had somehow exorcised the beach. There was none of the sense of foreboding he'd felt when he'd realised that this was the spot where Matthias Weber and Hannelore Huber and the rest of the East German film crew had been erased from existence.

He put his hands in his pockets and looked along the beach towards the lighthouse. Was there a line that connected Neville John Hallam, *The Heart of the Maze*, the 1965 Event, and what had happened here a few nights ago? Or was it all coincidence? It was easy to join the dots and see the misty distant outlines of conspiracy – the brain always looks for patterns. It was, perhaps, harder, and scarier, to acknowledge that everything was random and chaotic and nothing had any meaning, that you could do your very best to put your finger on the scales of life and in the end it didn't change anything. Maybe that was really why the essenceheads and the other conspiracists did what they did, why Mad Jack had pursued an Angel and Brossard had searched for his miracle. Not to prove that there was a pattern underlying the world, but to prove that there was a point in being here at all.

The next morning, a chauffeur-driven Mercedes was waiting outside the hotel to collect him and Theo, and they drove to the airport at Goleniów, where one of Theo's business jets was waiting. Half an hour after that he was relaxing in the leather and walnut interior of the jet watching the great forests around the airport falling away below him. Szczecin and its lagoon came into view as the aircraft climbed out, and just before it tipped its wings and turned to the southwest he caught a glimpse of the sea, and he smiled.

"What's so funny?" Theo asked in the seat across the aisle.

"I was just thinking about the carbon footprint of this fiasco," Michael told him. "Essenceheads travelling from all over Europe, private jets. It's hardly environmentally friendly."

Theo grunted. "I've been meaning to get rid of one of the jets. Maybe both of them. My grandchildren say I'm a monster for using them." He shrugged. "Maybe they're right."

"It's a good thing you didn't do that yet."

"To be honest, I hardly use them any more; I don't travel a lot these days." He thought about it. "Actually, I only ever seem to travel to Switzerland for banking meetings, and I could do most of them remotely. It's not as if Swiss bankers are any more interesting in person." He stretched his legs. "It is *very* convenient, though."

"I thought a physical presence was important."

"Ach, that's the paper." Theo waved a hand. "The paper's always more important."

Actually, the jet was better than convenient; it was positively decadent. When they'd reached cruising altitude a stewardess served coffee and sandwiches on bone china, and one of the pilots came out of the flight deck for a brief chat. It was nice to have rich friends.

"I had to smooth some feathers," Theo told him. "After your little outburst in the breakfast room the other day. The hotel wanted to have you arrested."

"I'm sorry," Michael said.

Theo nodded. "It might be wise if you didn't go there again."

That wasn't high on his to-do list, right now. He asked, "What happened to Claes?"

"His placement with me has been terminated. I presume he's back in Copenhagen, plotting how to make more mischief."

"What will you do?"

"I've called a small meeting." Theo glanced at him. "Don't look like that; we can be quite agile, when we want to be. Claes is young, and the tragedy of the young is that they always underestimate their elders. We'll deal with him."

Michael wasn't sure of that; it couldn't hurt to do some nudging of his own. He looked out of the window, but there was a thick layer of cloud below them and he couldn't see out-of-town shopping malls or anything else.

The jet landed at Schiphol and spent a long time negotiating various taxiways until it arrived at a little private air terminal, where there was a car already waiting. Theo came down the steps onto the concrete with him.

"I could get used to travelling like that," Michael told him.

"It can be addictive, I agree," Theo said. "I wish you'd let me hire someone to go with you."

"I won't be on my own," said Michael.

"Hm," Theo said. "You know, I've had to pull a lot of strings with the Marechausee and the train company's security."

"I know," Michael said. "Thank you."

"I received a rather bemused text from my Service earlier, wondering what I was up to."

"What did you tell them?"

Theo shrugged. "Something vague about sending a courier to London under diplomatic cover."

Michael thought about that. Far away across Schiphol's colossal flat expanse of concrete and grass, a big transcontinental jet was coming in to land. He said, "Do you think they'd check with London to confirm that?"

"Probably not; we've done something similar in the past. And even if they do, it'll be too late."

Michael nodded, and they started to walk towards the car. "What if you don't get what you want?" Theo asked.

"I'll think of something else," Michael said. Reaching the car, he stopped and they shook hands. "Thank you."

Theo nodded. "Good luck."

Once the car had left the airport, the driver turned onto the A4, looping around the city centre to avoid roadworks and early afternoon traffic, and it only took about forty minutes to reach Amsterdam Centraal. Getting out of the car in front of the station, the first thing Michael saw was Arno, standing outside with his hands in his pockets and looking out at the crowds of passers-by as if he was waiting for someone. He ignored Michael as he went past.

Inside, the concourse was busy, but he spotted Wim making a bad job of being inconspicuous as he read a magazine over by the ticket windows, and Piet sitting on a bench looking bored. He saw a couple of other faces that he thought looked familiar from the hotel at Kołobrzeg, and he assumed there were others. He found, somewhat to his surprise, that he felt deeply touched that they had all turned out to make sure he got away safely. No Thijs or Anton, though; Claes's miracle was already changing the group dynamics of the Dutch essenceheads.

He didn't have any luggage, so passing through security only took a couple of minutes. He had a moment presenting his passport at check-in when he half expected police and security officers to leap from hiding and arrest him, but nothing happened, and he walked through onto the platform and along the waiting train until he found his carriage.

The carriage was almost empty; the couple of fellow passengers seated up at the other end were engrossed in a newspaper and a book respectively, and didn't pay any attention as he found his seat and sat down. A couple of people walked through the carriage on their way to the next one, but they didn't seem to notice him. He checked his watch and twiddled his thumbs. A recorded message came over the public address informing passengers that this was indeed the Eurostar departure to London St Pancras, just in case someone had mistaken it for the local train to Den Helder. Michael checked his watch again.

Eventually – and it seemed to take a very long time, even though it wasn't more than quarter of an hour – the doors closed and the train began to pull slowly out of the station. Michael watched the platform slide away outside, and he took his phone out of his pocket, replaced the battery, switched it on, and put it on the table in front of him. It spent a few seconds establishing a connection to the local cell network, then it started receiving texts and listing missed calls.

The first missed call, from Martine's number, had been made an hour or so after he had been spirited out of the bar, on the day everything had changed. There were several more, in quick succession, then a series of texts. Then there was a pause, then more calls and texts around the time he should have been boarding his flight home, all of them variations on a theme of *Where are you?* A gap of a few days, then more calls and texts, this time some of them from Bob. *Just checking in, old son. How's things?*

Michael looked out of the window. The train was moving slowly south through Amsterdam, and he suddenly felt a great regret, seeing the city roll past and away; he felt as if he had been more at home in the Netherlands than he ever had in London. His old life, before the hospital, seemed very far away.

There were fewer and fewer texts and missed calls as time went on, but they never quite stopped. There was a little flurry just a few days ago, when he was in Kołobrzeg, which was interesting.

The train moved through Amsterdam-Oost, then the tracks angled it round to the southwest and it began to pick up speed. The city's southern suburbs went by and the train dipped into a tunnel which carried it under the runways and buildings of Schiphol, and shortly after it emerged they were out in the countryside and the train was beginning to slow down again.

Eventually, it stopped altogether. Looking out of the window, Michael could see fields under a lowering, drizzly sky. In the distance, he saw a white van moving along a road. He checked his watch again.

After a couple of minutes, the train manager spoke over the public address and told them in four different languages that there was a signal problem ahead and they would be on their way again when it was fixed, which hopefully wouldn't be long.

A few minutes passed before the door at his end of the carriage opened and Martine stepped through. She was wearing jeans and a sweater and a green waxed jacket, and she had her phone in her hand. She sat down opposite him and put the phone on the table, and then they just looked at each other.

"So," she said finally, "as you booked your ticket with the company card and you're travelling on your own passport, I assume you want to talk. So here I am."

He sat calmly looking at her.

"Didn't it occur to you to get in touch?" she asked. "We've been going frantic trying to find you."

"Yes," he said. "I've just been looking at your texts."

"Why didn't you reply to any of them?"

Instead of answering, Michael took the back off his phone, removed the battery, and put it in his pocket.

Martine watched him and narrowed her eyes a fraction. She said, "Why didn't you at least make contact with the Embassy or the Consulate?"

"You told me not to."

"Don't be a smartarse, Mike. I told you not to contact Amsterdam Office either, and what was the first thing you did?"

"I didn't contact them; Seb contacted me." Martine snorted at the distinction, but he shook his head. "You know he did, because you told him to. You can stop pretending. I've been talking to Theo van Hoebeek; I know all about the *roleplay*."

She glanced around her. "Yeah," she said. "I was wondering where you got the money to book up an entire carriage. So, the rich bloke's your friend now, yeah?"

"How much did Seb know?"

"We told him it was an exercise, gave him a script to follow. How did he do?"

"He certainly fooled *me*." Although, with hindsight, what Seb had told him about Claes felt as if it was outside a script. Had that just been Seb embellishing his role, or was it a genuine warning? And if it was genuine, where had it come from? He said, "That was a cruel thing to do, Martine, sending me out like that for a joke."

"It wasn't a joke, it was deadly serious."

"I was barely out of hospital. I could have had a relapse."

"Yeah," she said, and she leaned forward a little, "but you didn't, did you."

He took one of his pill bottles out of his pocket and put it on the table. "Was this part of the joke?"

She looked at the bottle. "Had them tested, huh? I'm impressed. Did your rich friend arrange that too?"

He picked the bottle up and waved it at her, but it didn't rattle; he'd tipped the contents of both bottles down the toilet at the hotel the morning after the Event. "Was I supposed to keep coming back for repeat prescriptions?" he asked. "How long were you going to carry on with that?"

"As long as the shrinks thought it was useful." She shrugged.

He put the bottle back on the table. "There's a man called Claes," he said. "He was on secondment to Theo, as his personal assistant. Danish Intelligence think he works for them, but he doesn't; he's been setting up his own informal networks and he's got a source in the office. He knew about your little charade long before Theo's people did."

She nodded. "We trailed our coat for him a while ago, but we didn't have anything he wanted."

"It seems to me that he already *has* everything he wants from you."

From the look on her face, that *you* didn't pass her by. "Do you know who the source is?"

He shook his head. "It's someone with a lot of access, though."

She grunted. "No point in *having* a source, if they don't have a lot of access."

"Maybe you should have a quiet word with the Danes," he said.

"Why would I do that?"

He shrugged. "You could mention to them that Claes is freelancing. He's probably using their resources to do it; they won't like that."

"What would they do about it?"

"I don't know. Shoot him?"

"Bah." She pulled a face. "People don't do that any more. Everything's more civilised these days." She thought about it. "I might drop them a line, though. Discreetly. He could do with having his wings clipped."

He said, "How much do you know about the Essence?"

Martine raised an eyebrow.

"Don't," he said. "If one of my employees went missing in Europe for a fortnight, the first thing I'd want to know was what had happened to them. You haven't even asked."

She looked at him for a long time, then she sighed. "Okay, we know about the crazies, yes."

"Who knows? The Home Secretary?"

"Christ, no." Martine started back in shock. "Her? Are you *insane?* No. The PM gets briefed. The D-G knows, a couple of high mucky-mucks. That's it. We keep an eye on the essenceheads, just like any radical group."

The thought of the Prime Minister – particularly a couple of recent Prime Ministers – being briefed about the Essence was mind-boggling. He said, "So you know who kidnapped me."

"We know who *tried* to kidnap you. We were following you around Amsterdam and we sent a couple of people into that bar to keep an eye on you and then everything went apeshit."

"The young couple," he said. "The tourists."

She shrugged. "I don't know what they looked like. I do know they've been redeployed to do something harmless and terminally dull."

"Did you know that I was being followed by four different groups of people?" He watched her face. "You had no idea, did you."

"We knew about that arsehole Stilwell and his people, not the French; those fucking hired goons came out of nowhere. Who was the fourth group?"

"Claes," he said. "He sent someone in behind your people to make sure they didn't stop me getting away. From what I remember, he took them completely by surprise."

"Yeah, okay," she said. "It wasn't our most shining hour. Heads are still rolling and arses are still being covered. *You* didn't twig that you were being followed, though."

"I haven't had street training," he reminded her.

She sniffed. "You haven't done so badly. We're the ones who've been playing catch-up. We've been hearing weird shit from Poland. Is that where you've been?"

He said, "Where's my cat?" and he saw, for a fraction of a second, that he'd completely flatfooted her. "Where's my cat, Martine?"

"You haven't got a cat," she said.

"Yes I do," he told her. "He's a fat old tabby and he's called Walter. Where is he?"

"Michael," she said smoothly. "You've been sick, your memory's still full of gaps. You're remembering wrong."

It was the *Michael* that convinced him she was lying. "No I'm not," he said. "I've got a cat and he wasn't at home when I got back from the hospital and neither was all his food and stuff. What's happened to him?"

Looking into her eyes was like looking through a window at a computer going through possible responses at lighting speed and discarding them one by one. He supposed that was how she earned her salary. Finally she said, "What do you remember about your last day at the office? Your last working day?"

"What's that got to do with my cat?"

"Work with me, Mike. What do you remember?"

He thought about it. "I got the Tube to Tottenham Court Road," he said. "I stopped off at Bloom's for a coffee, the girl on the front desk buzzed me into the building. I went through the security gate to the lift, but the lift wasn't working." He could picture it now. "The girl from the front desk came round to see what was wrong and I said something about having to walk up the stairs." He shook his head. "Then I apparently went upstairs and started to smash up Rob's office. But I don't remember that."

Martine looked at him for a long moment, glanced down at her phone, looked at him again. "That's not how it happened, Mike."

He blinked calmly at her.

"The first thing is, you weren't buzzed into the building, because she didn't recognise you on the front door camera. There were no deliveries due, nobody on the visitor list. She says you were a complete stranger and she never touched the button to open the door, and I believe her, she's a smart kid."

He found that he had used up all the possible responses in the past two weeks. *Oh, come on. That's ridiculous. How is that possible?* He'd said these things so often recently that he would just have been repeating himself. Instead, he said, "So how did I get into the building?"

"We don't know," she said simply. "We tested the system afterwards and there was nothing wrong with it, but there you were coming up the stairs, all suited and booted with your briefcase and your university tie. You said good morning to the receptionist and you used your security card on the gate and it let you through and she switched the lift off before you reached it."

He remembered standing in front of the lift doors, pressing the button, and nothing happening. He remembered Alice/Angela getting up from her desk and coming over to him, smiling and holding something out to him. Except it wasn't Alice/Angela, it was someone else.

"You got a new receptionist," he said.

Martine tipped her head to one side and regarded him soberly. "She got transferred sideways," she said. "No black mark on her record, like

I said, she's a smart kid and she did everything right because after turning off the lift and hitting the panic button she tased you."

He thought about it, and he couldn't be sure. He'd barely got a glance at what the girl had been holding, but was it possible that he'd thought she was offering it to him when in fact she'd been *pointing* it at him?

"How are you feeling?" she asked.

"I feel fine," he told her. "Better than I've felt in quite a long time."

She smiled a thin, humourless smile. "Anyway, Security came up from the basement and they got you out of the back door and into a van and they took you out to Datchett, what used to be the London Interrogation Centre back in the bad old days." She glanced at her phone again, touched it to wake the screen, put it back to sleep. "That was eight months ago. We had no idea who you were or how you'd got into the office." She looked out at the fence beyond the window. "The Russians used to do this now and again, pull a mad stroke just to see how we'd react. They don't do that these days, I think they've lost their sense of humour. But that was our first theory."

"It's been five months," he said. "Not eight."

Martine shook her head. "You were in the *hospital* for five months; you actually turned up before Christmas."

He remembered the calendar in the hall at home, five months out of date. Remembered that sense of people having been in the house while he was away. He thought of crossing Oxford Street, that last morning; had he seen the Christmas lights strung across the road, or was he remembering that from another year?

"Where was I for the other three months?" he said. But he knew. Didn't he? There were memories there, but they were like figures moving about in a thick fog. Or was his mind just connecting the dots, filling in the gaps, looking for patterns?

"Well," she went on, "the interrogators at Datchett sweated you for a couple of weeks. And they said you were the best subject they'd ever had. You were so cooperative they thought it must be some kind of a joke. You told them the whole of your life, in nitpicking detail. They wound up with a dossier this thick." She held up her hand with her finger and thumb two inches apart, and Michael thought of Stilwell dropping that pile of paper onto the desk in the office at Eindhoven airport.

"I can't remember any of this."

"Not surprising," she said. "You were really cooperative, but you started to freak the interrogators out. You knew some of them, knew their names and where they lived and their families; not in a threatening sort of way, you just kept dropping it into conversation like you'd do if you were talking to a mate in the pub. And they'd never seen you before in their lives. So maybe they weren't as professional as they might have been and they leaned on you a little too hard and you had a bit of a conniption fit or something."

It occurred to him that the *maybe* in that final sentence was doing an awful lot of heavy lifting.

"So there we were," she said. "You were on first-name terms with us and we didn't know who you were, and you were catatonic and couldn't explain any of it, and when you did come out of it your memory was completely fucked, like your brain had done a hard reset and not quite booted up properly."

"I'm not a Russian," he said.

"There's a whole lot of things you're not, Mike," she told him. "The question is what you *are*."

"I know what I am," he told her.

She shook her head sadly. "*Do* you, though?" she said. "Do you *really*?"

And there it was, the edge of the abyss that had been there ever since he woke up in the hospital, the straggling archipelago of memories surrounded by a great empty ocean where literally anything could lurk. He heard himself say, "I had a security pass."

Martine nodded. "You did. And it's absolutely authentic, right down to all the watermarks that nobody's supposed to know about. But it's not on record as having been issued to anyone, and it was only used that one time, and we'd like to know how that's possible."

"So how did it let me through the gate?"

"That," she told him, "was one of the things we were hoping you could explain to us."

"This is another test, isn't it," he said. "Another *roleplay*. You're messing with my head to see if it brings my memory back."

She snorted. "Sure. I flew to Holland and stopped a Eurostar just to mess with your head. Can you imagine how *that's* going to sound at the next budget meeting?"

"What time is it?" he asked.

Martine woke up her phone and held it up so he could see the time on the screen. He also saw a little red dot blinking slowly on and off in the corner to indicate that the phone's voice recorder was running. "Don't worry," she told him, "they'll hold us here as long as I tell them. We've got all the time in the world."

Actually, he didn't know whether they were out of time already. At best, he only had a few more minutes. He said, "This is *insane*, Martine. I know you. You live in Guildford; your husband does something in the City and you've got two children."

She shook her head. "How can you *possibly* know that? I guard my private life very carefully."

He shrugged, "Office gossip."

She put her phone back to sleep and laid it down in front of her again. "Until a couple of weeks ago, you and I had never met," she told him. "I've watched video of your interrogations, and I visited you at Datchett, but by then you were already comatose. You can't have heard any office gossip about me, because you've never worked at the office."

"I don't believe you."

"So we've got a bit of a problem, here," she told him. "Because it gets worse. Where are you going?"

Michael had got to his feet. "I came here to tell you the department's been penetrated by bad actors," he said, taking his coat from the overhead rack. "Not to listen to this fantasy."

"You could have done that by email," she told him.

"I wanted to look you in the eye when you tried to explain what's been going on."

She sat where she was, looking calmly up at him. "Don't you want to hear the rest of it?"

"There *is* no 'rest of it'," he said.

"Oh, there is, Mike. There really is," she told him. "We weren't sitting with our thumbs up our arses while you were in the hospital. We were checking out your story. We gave it the mother and father of all vetting runs. Don't you want to know what we found?"

No. But he didn't move.

She leaned forward. "Nothing," she said. "That's what we found. Name, address, family, education, background. None of it's real. Your college at Cambridge has never heard of you. Neither has anyone in Droitwich. None of the things you told us was true." She watched his face. "Which is pretty much what you'd expect if you'd been planted on us by a foreign intelligence service."

He felt a great emptiness open up within him, like the sinkhole at Zandvoort. He thought of the sea roaring in with a noise like a train. He sat down again, coat bundled up in his lap, and Martine looked smug.

"So that was the first theory," she said. "You'd been sent with a legend that didn't really stand up to scrutiny, just to get us running around like headless chickens, but you had your collapse, and when your brain came back online you believed the legend was true." She shrugged. "It's a pretty good theory, and it's the one the lower security clearances still believe."

He took a breath and said, "My wife."

For a moment, her expression softened, but it didn't stop her saying, "There *is* no wife, Mike. There's no wife, because there's no *you*. Nobody called Christina Brookes has ever taught at the local school and there's no record of anyone with that name at your GP's. Nobody called Brookes has ever lived in that house in Finchley – the people who *do* live there have never heard of you. And that's why you don't have a cat."

He thought that if he let himself believe any of this, even for a moment, it would hurt more than he could stand. He said, "There's a photograph of us. In my study."

She nodded. "We found it when we checked the house after you went missing. It's definitely you, but we can't identify the woman; facial recognition came up blank. Here's the thing, though, it wasn't there when we dressed the place before you got out of the hospital, so somebody else must have put it there."

"*I* put it there," he said. "It's *my* house."

"It's *not*, Mike. The people who live there have been there for the past eight years. Lovely couple; he's a tax lawyer and she works for a charity."

"I was there for three days after I left the hospital," he told her, an edge of desperation in his voice. "Or do you think I made that up too?"

"No, of course not," she told him. "We set that whole thing up for you. We sent the owners off for a nice little holiday. Two-week cruise down the Rhine, they've had a lovely time. Same with the neighbours."

"I spoke to my neighbour," he said.

"Elsie?" Martine shook her head. "Elsie's family. We put her there to keep an eye on you."

"I knew her husband," he said. "I went to his funeral." But *had* he? The memory wasn't there.

She shook her head again. "Confirmed spinster, our Elsie. Never been married." She clasped her hands on the table in front of her. "The shrinks say you've been 'remembering forward', whatever that's supposed to mean. It's like you've got a little movie going on in your head all the time and you're constantly filling in background detail without realising you're doing it. You meet a person you're supposed to know, and suddenly you've added all kinds of things about them in your head. Some of it's true, and we still don't know how you do that, and some of it's not. I bet you were doing it with the house, and with Amsterdam."

"Ismail knew me," he said. "From the pizza place. He called me by name."

"There's no such person as Ismail," she said. "We were monitoring your phone and when you ordered a pizza one of the lads went to collect it and he delivered it to you."

He thought again. "I have a bank account."

"You do, and there's a lot of money in it. I mean, a *lot*, almost a quarter of a million quid. And the bank doesn't know where it came from. The best they can tell us is that it seems to have appeared out of nowhere the morning you arrived at the office. No deposit or withdrawal history, just a huge chunk of money suddenly there, and they can't explain how it happened."

"There were statements at the house," he said, becoming increasingly conscious that he was grasping at straws. "And utility bills."

Martine smiled sadly at him. "I told you, we dressed the house. We faked those up to make you feel at home," she said. "That wasn't even hard. You can keep standing these things up and I can keep knocking them down, but the truth is, all these memories aren't yours. Michael Brookes doesn't exist; he's a figment of your imagination."

The roaring in his head was getting louder. "I am not a figment of my imagination," he told her. "The Dutch knew me." And then he scowled. *Had* they known him? Really? Theo had never given any indication that they'd met before that morning in Amsterdam-Zuid. And he remembered Claes saying, "Who are *you?*"

"They didn't know you," she said. "All they knew was that you were taking part in an exercise."

"If all this is true – and it's not – why did you send me to Amsterdam?"

"Yes!" she said, sitting back and pointing at him. "Yes! Exactly! Why did we do something so utterly, *monumentally* stupid? Putting you in the hospital was a no-brainer because you needed medical supervision. But you were just sitting there like a vegetable, reading and making pots and not *remembering* anything. So we decided to set things up so you could go home, to see if that nudged your memory somehow, and that made some sense too. But why stick you on a plane and send you off into the wild blue yonder?"

He shrugged.

"The answer is, *we don't know*. We thought up a wee bit of harmless espionagey stuff to see if it got your brain working again. We babysat you the whole way – everyone on that flight to Amsterdam was ours, except for the pilots and the cabin crew. Same with the hotel. But it wasn't until you'd disappeared with the Essence crazies that we looked at each other and said, 'Why did we do that?' And you know what we came up with?" She leaned forward again and lowered her voice. "Nothing. We don't know."

"Okay," he said, standing up again. "That's enough."

The door at the end of the carriage opened and two men stepped through. They were dressed casually, and they didn't have the physical heft of Brossard's hired contractors or Stilwell's men, but they had a certain wiry physicality and they were both holding tasers. The whole world had a taser. Michael moved into the aisle and backed away.

"Don't you want to know the rest?" Martine asked, standing and following him, step by step. "Because we've barely even got started."

He kept stepping back along the carriage, and she kept coming. The two men fell in behind her.

"There was an Event in Finchley," she said. "The night before you turned up at the office."

Michael stopped. Martine stopped. The men behind her stopped. Michael said, "There's never been a documented Event in England." Which, it occurred to him, was a very *essencehead* thing to say.

"And there still hasn't," she told him. "We didn't hear about it until after you'd gone to Holland, and we put the lid on it straight away."

Michael glanced over his shoulder. He'd backed almost all the way along the carriage to the doors at the far end. The other two passengers were watching the conversation with baffled fascination.

"Couple of kids decided they'd pop into Victoria Park after it closed, for a bit of a snog," Martine went on casually. She took a step forward; Michael took a step back. "They said the streetlights sort of flickered and then it rained buttercups. Sound familiar? No, sit down, sunshine." One of the passengers had caught sight of the tasers and was getting out of his seat. "Nobody's going to get hurt. Are they, Mike?"

"No promises," Michael said. But the passenger sat down again.

"I mean, that's a hell of a coincidence, isn't it?" she went on. "An Event happening just across the road from your house, the night before you appear out of nowhere. That changes the question *completely*. Now we're not wondering *who* you are, we're wondering *what* you are." Michael stepped back and tripped the door sensor and it slid open behind him. He looked round, but there was nobody in the vestibule between the carriages. "Where do you think you're going, Mike? There isn't anywhere to go. I'm the only game in town."

"You're making all this up," Michael said, retreating another couple of steps until the door to the next carriage opened behind him.

"Oh, I wish. I really do." She stopped at looked at him. "So our next theory was that you're an innocent bystander, someone who was walking past the park when the Event happened and got caught up in the psychic backwash or whatever and wound up thinking they were someone else. Maybe you picked up the ability to make other people do what you want. Artifacts are always inanimate objects, right? But that doesn't mean it can't happen."

Martine was in for a surprise. "If I could make people do what I want, I'd be a long way from here right now," Michael told her, backing into the next carriage. But even as he said it, he wondered if that was *strictly* true. He'd wanted her to be here, and here she was, in the right place at roughly the right time, even though it would surely have been simpler to just lift him quietly as he went through passport control at St Pancras.

"It would explain why we sent you off on that ridiculous charade to Amsterdam," she said, moving forward again. "Maybe you put the old fluence on us." She held a hand up beside her face and wiggled her fingers. "These are not the droids you're looking for."

"No," he said. "That didn't happen."

She shrugged. "It's better than the other theory, which is that you didn't exist at all before the Event. Maybe you came down in a fall of buttercups." She tipped her head to one side and looked at him. "Sound familiar? Anything? No?"

"That's the most ridiculous thing I ever heard." This carriage also only had a couple of passengers; someone in the middle wearing a baseball cap and someone at the far end. Michael saw figures moving around beyond the doors to the next vestibule.

"Anyway," she said, "by that time you'd disappeared. And we looked for you really hard, we really did, but we couldn't find you. Maybe that was a bit of the old fluence again?" She waggled her fingers at him.

Michael came to a stop beside the passenger with the baseball cap. "Stop doing that."

"You see our problem, though, don't you?" Martine said. "We don't know who you are. You may be superhuman. You may not be human at *all*. We can't just let you run around Europe to your heart's content, Mike. It's not safe."

Michael glanced to his side. On the seat beside the passenger was a big denim shoulder bag and something was moving around inside it, something that had had enough of today's adventure and wanted to go home to its mum now.

"So we've got a proposal," Martine said reasonably. "Come back with us and let us try to work out what's going on. You'll be well looked-after; nobody's going to hurt you, you've got my word on that."

Michael heard the door slide open behind him. Out of the corner of his eye, he saw the passenger reach for the bag. What Martine didn't realise was that someone had known about the Event in Finchley before she had heard about it. Even before she'd sent him to Amsterdam, they'd told Claes's source that he knew something about the Essence, and Claes had told Brossard and set his little experiment in motion. There was still someone out there, pulling the strings of the people who thought they were pulling the strings.

"So what is it, Mike? Who are you? Are you a real boy who got too close to the Essence? Are you an angel? Are you a god? Are you *the* god?"

"I want my cat, Martine."

"We'll get you a cat," she told him. "As many cats as you want. All the cats you can handle. Come on, Mike. Come back with me. You can go back to the hospital; you liked it at the hospital, didn't you? We'll sort this out between us."

The passenger beside him reached out, and he felt her fingers close around his wrist.

Martine frowned. "What are you doing?"

The people behind him started to move forward. Michael looked down and watched Jo unzip the bag and put her hand inside.

He looked at Martine and smiled brightly. "Do you believe in miracles?" he asked.

About the Author

Born in Sheffield in 1960, Dave Hutchinson is the author of the Fractured Europe series of novels; *Shelter; Sanctuary; The Return Of The Incredible Exploding Man,* and *The Villages.* His novel *Europe In Winter* won the BSFA Award for best long fiction in 2016. He lives in North London.

ALSO FROM NEWCON PRESS

ANIMALS – Geoff Ryman
A powerful new novel from the multiple award-winning author of *HIM, Was* and *The Child Garden* The chilling tale of a family caught at the heart of a terrifying and transformative epidemic; an astonishing fusion of beautiful writing and pure horror as the world we know falls apart.

The History of the World – Simon Morden
To return his precious human cargo, PurLeeDah, to her home, Corbyn, a sentient ramship, must slow from near lightspeed – a process requiring thousands of years. Little does Corbyn realise that below him, on PurLeeDah's homeworld, his regular orbital passage has been noted and he has come to be worshipped as a god, inadvertently shaping the emerging culture.

The Other Frankenstein – Melissa F. Olson
Elizabeth Frankenstein's life had been carefully planned, until that future was stolen from her. Elizabeth and Heck Saville's parallel, intersecting stories encompass murder, loss, trauma and ultimately empowerment, in this stunning feminist saga that uses the classic story of *Frankenstein* as a springboard and weaves a potent tale of horror, love, and revenge.

Reality Rift – Fred Gambino
The second volume in the author's sweeping space opera trilogy, which began with the critically acclaimed *Dark Shepherd*. Breel is tired of running, of being chased to the stars for a secret she didn't even know she possessed. People have died, worlds have been overturned in its pursuit, but now she knows a little more about that secret; now she knows enough to fight back.

Blood in the Bricks – edited by Neil Williamson
Tales of the city redolent with ritual and drenched in dread. Our cities have been around for a long time, their histories built layer upon layer, their secrets long kept and buried deep. Who knows what goes on behind locked doors? These nineteen stories, from award-winning and emerging authors alike, expose the dark secrets of urban life and the chilling traditions that shaped them.

www.newconpress.co.uk

www.ingramcontent.com/pod-product-compliance
Lightning Source LLC
Chambersburg PA
CBHW021005260626
47169CB00006B/1950